Christopher George

Christopher George has worked as a teacher, lawyer and travel writer. Educated at Oxford, he now lives in Bristol with his wife and children.

Towards the Sun

CHRISTOPHER GEORGE

JOHN MURRAY

First published in Great Britain in 2008 by John Murray (Publishers)
An Hachette UK Company

First published in paperback in 2009

1

© Christopher George 2008

A CIP catalogue record for this title is available from the British Library

ISBN 978-0-7195-6907-4

Typeset in Bembo by Palimpsest Book Production Limited,
Grangemouth, Stirlingshire

Printed and bound by Clays Ltd, St Ives plc

John Murray policy is to use papers that are natural, renewable and
recyclable products and made from wood grown in sustainable forests. The
logging and manufacturing processes are expected to conform to the
environmental regulations of the country of origin.

John Murray (Publishers)
338 Euston Road
London NW1 3BH

www.johnmurray.co.uk

For my mother

I

I unhooked the ladder, set it on the floor and climbed to retrieve the tow-rope from the top shelf, upsetting a tube of tennis balls as I did so. They scattered like rabbits, hopping for cover beneath the units. I didn't pick them up. With the ladder under one arm and the rope under the other, I walked into the kitchen, stopping at the twin sinks. The garden, through the window, stood as still as a painting. A week beforehand I'd treated the lawn for moss. Not carefully enough, it seemed: napalm streaks spread out before me and ran in knots around the laden apple trees. Beyond our fence of wooden railings the untreated paddock glowed insultingly green.

Best intentions, proving futile. What point shoring up against the future? I'd have been better off trusting to fate and horseshit.

I struck out through the hall, past the row of wellington boots on their rack by the door. The smallest pairs, which Jennifer bought for the grandchildren, made me pause again. Was I looking for a reason not to go through with it? I found myself shivering in the draught. We live in a barn conversion, all flagstones and vaulted ceilings, a fortune to heat despite the wood-burning stove, but handy for London, and consequently the children, all only an hour away. I took the stepladder into the living room, scissored it open and stood it beneath another feature of the house, one of its exposed oak beams.

Between 1942 and 1944 my father dropped bombs from the air, for the obvious reasons first and foremost, but also to spite his own father, who spent the first war at sea. My grandfather knew a thing or two about ropes: I learned my knots at his knee. Perching on the ladder's penultimate rung, I tied a hangman's slipknot in one end of the rope and lowered the noose over my head. Then I tied the other end to the beam with a midshipman's hitch. The mechanics of my situation – the length of cord above me, the distance between the noose and the floor, the efficacy of my rope work – absorbed me more than the magnitude of what I was about to do in that moment, which makes me confident I wasn't really about to do it. Yet there I was, going through the motions in absolute earnestness. This is what it would be like to hang myself, I thought. I ran the rope through itself until the noose was tight around my neck. Its grip felt heartening. I climbed up on to the top step, creating three feet of slack. The stepladder – a cheap B&Q aluminium affair – wobbled reassuringly. All I had to do was topple sideways and it would skitter out from beneath my feet.

Down I'd drop and, bar some twitching, that would be that.

It was tempting. I stared at the light fittings – spotlights plugged into the plasterboard ceiling, a real fiddle they'd been to install – rocking the ladder from side to side, testing its deliciously inept powers of balance.

The letter in my pocket, which I'd received that morning, had not brought me to this threshold on its own. It was one of many threads wound into the rope above me. But after I read Mutual Friends' declaration, in words as unequivocal as bullets, that my pension, due to mature in this, its thirty-first and my sixtieth year, would furnish me with a sum roughly a third of its forecast value, the rope seemed finally strong enough to take my weight. Now I truly had more to fear in the future than I had to look forward to, more to endure than enjoy. That was why stepping from the ladder would make sense.

I looked down at the room. Though large, it seemed small from on high, too confined a space to account for our history within it. Twenty-seven family Christmases pulsed from the walls. I'd have to be careful to topple in the right direction. Go left, and the steps would fall into the plasma television which Robert gave Jennifer for her last birthday. It's enormous, and silver, and completely out of keeping with the rustic pretensions of the room, but for the past couple of years Robert has found it necessary to give presents of demonstrable worth, and although she has yet to master its controls, that television is Jennifer's pride and joy. Besides, the picture is phenomenal.

Jimmy, our middle child, is the only member of our family to have been *on* television, as far as I'm aware. He was in a show about gifted kids, featured in the section on art, or it might have been memory. Either way, they filmed him drawing Blenheim Palace and then got very excited about him having depicted the right number of windows. He still paints, but less successfully. Accuracy is no longer his thing.

Shifting my weight, I felt the ladder judder beneath me, giving a metallic chirrup. The noise was full of anticipation. It cut through the fog of my ambivalence. I believe that was the closest I came, that precise moment, to letting go.

But I was closer to death the following instant, and involuntarily, because of the phone. It — or rather they — rang. Aside from the line into my office we'd made do with one telephone, tethered neatly to itself on the hall table, for the past quarter-century. But a few years back Robert insisted we upgrade. I'm not complaining. A wireless phone is obviously more convenient. The four-phone system he bought did, however, seem like overkill. We haven't got used to it. Jennifer struggles with the tedium of returning handsets to their base stations and I have a knack, it seems, for hitting the ringer volume button instead of stand-by.

Three of the handsets, having gravitated into the living room, now burst as one into vibrant song. I flinched and the ladder wobbled. As I clutched at the rope above me and reached to steady myself with my free hand I felt a pang at not having tipped over entirely.

The danger was immediately over, but the phones, like my hammering heart, kept up their chorus. They sounded urgent, full of the present tense, each ring insisting: *answer me now*.

I thought of Pearl. Perhaps she'd heard back about

4

Felix's school situation. Then a picture of Jennifer came to mind, standing on the hard shoulder, engulfed in steam. The garage had said her Discovery's radiator would need replacing soon. Or maybe, just maybe, Mutual Friends had made a mistake. My reluctance to climb down from the ladder was undercut by a dispiriting sense of relief.

I removed the noose, descended the steps and retrieved the nearest handset.

'Yes?'

There was a second's delay, then, 'Good morning!'

'Who is this?'

'May I speak, please, with Mr Rinkman?'

'Brinkman, it's Brinkman.'

'So sorry! May I speak with Mr Brinkman this morning, please!'

I knew immediately it was a cold call. Everyone is irritated by them, I understand that, but these interruptions truly bedevil those of us who work from home. No amount of 'deregistration' (Robert, exasperated, emailed me a list of lists to join) has made a difference. I've done my share of impotent phone slamming and discovered the hard way that a barked 'fuck off', in relinquishing the moral high ground, leaves a still worse taste in my mouth. Politeness is pointless too, though, 'no thank you' being no match for the armoury of rejoinders these folk have at their fingertips. So recently I'd been fighting fire with fire by inciting the callers to waste *their* time. I'd use the new phones' hands-free facility, drop the volume, and mutter 'hmm, interesting' while doing my best to carry on with my work. Forty-seven minutes is my record. It's great when the bastards finally dry up.

Though I didn't employ this pathetic defence today, the thought of it made me laugh bitterly.

'Sir?'

'I'm Harry Brinkman,' I said.

Unsure of my laughter, the speaker wobbled before pressing on. Her pause was brief but it made her real in my mind. A person, in a cubicle somewhere – its baize walls an oppressive, snooker-table green – with dry eyes from the air conditioning and a headset-sore ear. She had a warm voice.

'Mr Brinkman, my name is Joy, and I am calling from ICBC International today. In partnership with EndZone and other accredited providers we offer a full complement of forward-planning financial lifestyle solutions. Sir, can I ask, do you envisage a better future?'

'You've asked–' I began.

'That's right, and I sense, Mr Brinkman, that your answer is "of course". I have certain other questions which will be a most valuable use of your next eight or nine minutes–'

'–at a bad time.'

'There can be no bad times to consider issues of such importance, sir. I am sure you agree. Now, what is your attitude towards risk? Are you profit orientated or would you say you seek stability?'

'I'm past all that, I–'

'Sir? Do you tend towards keeping all your eggs in one basket, or would you say your existing assets are spread too thinly?'

'I'm going to hang—'

'Please don't hang up, sir. We can diversify or consolidate as appropriate. What savings do you already—'

'Stop! *Myself*. I'm going to hang myself.'

'Do you need liquidity now or is it your wish to focus on taking care of the future?'

Even as she was my excuse to procrastinate — why else hadn't I just rung off? — this woman was goading me to do it. I was halfway up the ladder again, muttering crossly. And yet a part of me has always reluctantly admired skilled cold callers. I use the phone to generate business too, after all, and the distinction between reminding customers we're here and badgering them for new orders is often specious. Either way, I'm hopeless on the phone myself. If I as much as sense I've interrupted someone's daydream, I apologise and ring off. Yet this woman was soldiering on in my ear as I shouted over the top of her. 'I'm up a ladder now! I'm putting the noose over my head!'

'What?' she began, faltered, and pressed on, the conviction finally ebbing from her voice. 'What monthly charges would you estimate that you pay on your existing credit cards?'

'I've had enough. I'm going to end my life.'

'You don't mean that, sir.' A nervous laugh, an intake of breath. 'If we consolidate—'

'I think I do. It's you that doesn't mean what you're saying. I can tell. Your heart's not in it. I think mine is. To begin with, there's a rope around my neck, and I'm six feet up a wobbly ladder. What do you say to that?'

'Sir, we're not allowed . . . Calls are recorded, sir.'

'So? This is my life we're talking about!'

There was no click, but the caller's pause was long enough for me to suspect she had rung off. Guilt vied with disappointment in my chest. I was ashamed of burdening an innocent bystander, and disappointed to have fallen for the fool's gold – or seller's sincerity – of her voice. Squinting at the handset, I stabbed at *call end* and tossed the phone on to the couch. I swayed on the steps, looking up. The tow-rope was made of pale blue nylon. When Robert was born he came at me with the cord wrapped around his neck, thunder faced. I stayed at the head end for the other two births. The rope above me had an umbilical quality. My knee began to throb.

'Why?'

The girl's voice had a new, breathier quality on speakerphone. I stared at the sofa as if she might materialise upon it. *Why*, she'd asked me, *why?* Because of my failed pension, and my failing marriage, my failings as a parent, and the realisation that my newly dead father had failed me.

'The question isn't why, it's why not? And there's no answer to it. I . . . I . . . I simply have insufficient reason to go on.'

'You're wrong,' the girl said, repeating, 'totally wrong.'

'How in hell's name would you know?'

'I just do. Please. Calm down. Tell me your problem.'

There was something sweet in her sense of *can-do*. I was tempted to follow her orders; objecting seemed as churlish as interrupting a child's imaginary play. The flip side of that, of course, was that a child had no business interfering here and now. My resolve hardening, I found myself another rung up the ladder.

'You're not speaking, Harry.'

'I don't have to,' I snapped. 'There's no earthly need for me to explain myself to you.'

'Yes there is,' the voice said. 'I'm implemented now.'

'Impl*icated*.' I sighed. 'No, you needn't be, you're not.'

'I can hardly just go back to work now, though, can I?'

'Of course you can. Hang up and forget all about it.'

'No,' came the flat reply. 'You can cut me off if you want, but I'm not going anywhere.'

I'd have to climb back down the ladder before I could retrieve the phone and end the call, which forewarned defeat, so I stayed put instead, saying, 'I don't need your company's services. There must be a rule book to stop you harassing me like this. Put the phone down. I'm saying goodbye.'

'No,' she repeated.

'OK, suit yourself.' I jiggled the rope against the beam – soft rope, annoyingly inaudible – in a vain attempt to signal my intent.

'Mr Brinkman. Harry. You are not a selfish man.'

'Ha!' I wobbled the ladder, enjoyed the brief success of its squeaking, but she went on.

'It would be very unfair, very selfish, to kill yourself with me on the line. I would suffer trauma. Most likely I would have to quit this job.'

'Christ, woman!' I breathed out through pursed lips. 'This is hopeless!'

'That's exactly my point,' she went on quickly. 'I have

seen my share of hell and back *in person* and can report that *nothing* is hopeless. Here I am! No adversity is too great!'

The brittle defiance of her voice – heightened perhaps in its tinny, speakerphone incarnation – tightened my grip on the ladder. My shoes stood reflected in the giant plasma-screen TV. I bought a pair of slippers when I turned fifty, intended partly as a joke, which Jennifer didn't get. She immediately swapped them for new trainers. And she's replaced my trainers every year with another set of regulation size tens, each pair more colourful than the last. I think she thinks this keeps me looking young. Schizophrenic, more like, but I've never had the heart to object. So here I stood now, staring at the authentic shoes of a would-be suicide: two lurid fish suspended in an aquarium.

'Only resist!' the little voice began again.

'I'm sorry.'

'Only resist!'

'No, I mean, I apologise. I shouldn't be involving you, speaking to you in this way.'

'Only resist!' she repeated.

'Why do you keep saying that?'

'Because the act of resistance . . .' Her voice had the intensity of a candle held up against the darkness now . . . 'matters more than anything it achieves.'

'Who said that?' I played along.

'Me.'

'Of course you did.'

'I did. Not that it matters. All that *matters* is taking a stand. To beat despondency you must pit yourself against its causes. What is it that's giving you blackness in your thoughts?'

Listening to the girl's aphorisms I could stand, but I wasn't about to tell her specifics about myself. 'It's kind of you to ask,' I began, but got no farther as another, harsher voice, speaking words I could not understand, began squeaking angrily from the handset.

'Mr Brinkman!' the girl's voice again, over the cacophony, 'Mr Brinkman! You're still there?'

'I'm here!'

'Only resist!' she pleaded over the din. 'Only . . . resist!'

A new noise now rose up to compete with the censorious row on the phone: the TV screen reflected a bicycle crunching up our drive. It was a relief to find I'd already begun to free the rope from the beam. I jumped down from the ladder and picked up the handset. I wanted to apologise again. But the phone, though I pressed it to my ear to check, was dead.

2

While Fira sorted out her bicycle I coiled up the tow-rope and returned it and the ladder to the utility room. I wanted to change out of my trainers, too, but she was already in the kitchen gathering herself to start work by the time I made it to the shoe rack. Swapping them in front of her would have risked drawing attention to them. Instead I filled the kettle and set out two mugs, reminding myself not to make the mistake of automatically adding milk to her coffee.

Fira has cleaned our house for three months now. She's a Chechen refugee. I'm not sure where Jennifer got her from, but within a fortnight of the last cleaning girl leaving, there Fira was. She's thirty-two, which is the same age as Robert, my eldest son. Perhaps it's because I'm his father, but he appears much younger than her to me. When I look at him I still see an earnest boy, echoes of my own bewilderment in his face. Fira's expression, in giving so little away, is much more knowing, though what she's been through in her thirty-two years I can only guess at. I'm aware of her age, and of where she comes from, because Jennifer has told me, not because we've discussed such matters ourselves.

Working from home means I'm alone on the premises with this Chechen refugee woman for six hours a week. She wipes bristles I've missed from the basin in our en suite, hand-polishes the cutlery I put in my mouth, runs my boxer shorts through the washing machine. I've no idea what conclusions she's drawn from observing me at such close quarters, but the opportunity for insight flows both ways: you get to know a person having them in your house. Fira always hangs her quilted, knee-length parka on the peg nearest the door, for example, and that coat is always in place a good ten minutes before she's officially supposed to start work. It's normally there ten minutes after she's due to leave, too. She dusts the shelf on which my National Geographic collection sits every time she visits, whether it needs it or not. Once I saw her leafing through a copy while she was on her break. She never uses her mobile phone when she's at work, which marks her out from the last two cleaners Jennifer took on, as do her hands, which are always bare of rings and nail varnish. Between tasks she often spends a minute staring out of the window at the garden. When she does that there's a stillness about her so deep it defies interruption. There's been a problem with the immigration authorities, I know that. I've even written a reference to whomeverit-may-concern in support of her character, but because Jennifer asked me to, and without consulting Fira herself. Just as the cleaner and I ignore the insight my house – and mess – give her into me, we don't acknowledge that I know any more about her than that she prefers black coffee.

My hands were shivering as I stirred Fira's mug. She's a watchful woman, attentive to detail, right down to skirting-board dust. Taking the mug from me, she finished the stirring and ran the spoon under the tap.

'I saw a dead deer by the road on my way here,' she said, looking at the sink.

That she'd begun a conversation was as surprising as what she'd chosen to say. 'Really?' was all that I could come up with in reply.

'The deer upset me.'

'I see. I'm sorry.'

'Yes. I know that, Mr Brinkman.' She looked at me without blinking, 'I know that because you are a sympathetic man.'

I stood stupidly before her.

'And this,' she pointed at the ceiling with the teaspoon, 'is a lovely place to come, particularly after seeing something like the dead deer. It is a warm place, even when you do not turn the heating up. I am lucky to come here. And you—' She trailed off, lips parted, searching for the right way to go on. It didn't come. She handed me the teaspoon, picked up her coffee and retreated, saying, 'Today I will begin with ironing, in the utilities room.'

This speech — never mind my stint up the ladder — left me agitated. I took a step after Fira, then stopped (gathering up the spilled tennis balls — the best I could come up with — was a ludicrous pretext for following her) and instead snatched a tea towel from the rack. Chores often exert a calming, restorative influence, but not today. My pulse was still clattering in my chest as

I went to return the spoon to the cutlery drawer, which sits above the one Jennifer uses for her correspondence. I don't look in that drawer as a rule: lasting intimacy depends upon such privacies, in my opinion. But when I pulled at the handle of the cutlery drawer that morning both it and the one beneath it slid towards me as one. Flustered, I yanked the two drawers apart. A sheaf of bright blue cards shot through the sudden overbite and landed at my feet.

The cards were invitations to a surprise sixtieth birthday party – for me.

This party was not entirely breaking news. Jennifer made the invitations on my printer. Lateral thinking isn't her strong suit: cerulean being my perceived favourite colour (*his father's son, a sky thing!*), you'd imagine she might have bought some blue card. I'd fought hard not to figure out the cause of my cyan ink drought, and I'd lost. Yet sight of the invites made the party an unignorable fact now.

Jennifer has always made her own greeting cards. Though the results don't necessarily do justice to her efforts, I find her persistence with this creative endeavour endearing. These particular invitations had a military-code-style typeface and instructions to 'memorise and destroy'. She'd block-booked the Homing Pigeon, Dave and Alison's pub in St Clare. I winced, seeing this: they had the place remodelled in the minimalist style last year and took on a Korean chef, justifying a gastropub price hike. I'd unearthed a drawer-jamming number of invitations. It crossed my mind to weed out a few, but I didn't. Instead I replaced the stack of cards neatly.

What would this party cost?

I shut the drawer again, whispering, '*Only resist.*'

Fira was setting up the ironing board now. It squeaked and shivered on the flagstones, much like the ladder had done. Dead deer? Who knows where the sight of me swinging from a rope would have ranked among my cleaner's past experiences. As I stepped past the open door I caught a glimpse of her arm, bare to the shoulder, as pale as the white plastic iron she was reaching for.

Jennifer had lovely skin, too, when we were younger; her inner forearms were the colour of pared apples. No amount of fluorescent distraction in the trainer department can disguise the mottled fact of our older selves now. As I made my way out to the office – Fira's industrious presence in the house always spurs me on to demonstrative work – I thought of the sag of flesh under my wife's upper arm, which judders now when she waves. I always hoped I'd grow to love her more as we aged, that there would be solidarity in our shared frailties, but somehow that's not proven the case. There was a vindictive quality to the smile reflected in my sleeping computer screen. Feeling guilty, I nudged the mouse and reached for the phone.

'Yes. Hello?'

Despite the background shop-noise Jennifer's voice rang with flutelike clarity. That at least has not changed since we met.

'It's me.'

'What's the matter?'

'Nothing. I just–'

'Well, I'm rather tied up here.' The shop-babble dove underwater for a second as – presumably – she pushed the mobile into her palm or chest. It surfaced early. '. . . it up next Wednesday. Why call? I'll be back later.'

'I was just checking the Discovery made it. Its radiator needs looking at.'

'Oh, for goodness sake! Stop fussing. You're–'

'Just keep an eye on the temperature gauge, will you,' I explained.

'Of course.'

The phone cut out. Before I put it down I had an impulse to check whether the call centre number had registered in the memory. Unsurprisingly, it had not. That this stillborn lead disappointed me more than my unsatisfactory conversation with Jennifer was the more noteworthy fact. On a piece of paper I wrote down *ICBC International, Joy*, and circled the words twice.

I don't remember much of my wedding day. It was too generic. The headlight-white dress, rings squeezing themselves on to swollen fingers, even the halting platitudes of the speeches (mine included), it has all somehow cancelled itself out in retrospect. Nothing went wrong, I can tell you that. The day was too well planned. Ticking all the right boxes seemed to be what the occasion was about. Result: a neatly filled-in form for the file marked *wedding day* in my mind.

No, when I think what it was like to commit myself to Jennifer thirty-five years ago, I remember the day I proposed. I knew I wanted to marry her, but hadn't supposed I would ask when I did. We were shaking a woollen rug free of grass and burrs after an afternoon's picnic on the South Downs. The warm yellow light suddenly cut an extra dimension out of Jennifer. Before I knew it the flapping of the blanket became a beating sensation in my chest and the shadows it cast across the ground and Jennifer's bare legs and concentrating face were a semaphore message of *now's the moment* and there I was, down on one knee, asking. It being late summer, the ground was hard.

I waited. Despite bra-burning, the late sixties were full of flighty, girlish girls, like Jennifer at the time. This meant I truly could not be sure what she'd say. A van with a birdsong-obliterating exhaust fought its way up the road to the car park, and Jennifer's eyes grew bright with unfallen tears. The tang of diesel reached us over the hedgerow. I waited some more. The anticipation in that moment was at once the most painful and pleasurable sensation I'd experienced in my twenty-five years.

I know it sounds odd, but there was a similar elated doubtfulness in my breast as I set off for the swimming pool that lunchtime, after my morning up the ladder. The call-centre girl's plea had struck a chord. Her theory about resistance mattering more than its effect appealed to me. In fact, set within the deadline of my surprise party, *only resist* constituted a plan. I'd imposed upon her, the least I could do was follow her advice until the big day. If *resisting* made a difference by then, I'd be able to walk into the party with my chin up. And if it didn't I could always stick my head into the noose again.

★ ★ ★

I drove into town. Back when we first moved here the simplicity of that sentence was reflected in what it meant. Not now. Now the road, as it approaches the outskirts, clots into mini-roundabouts, one-way systems and cross-hatched junctions, which conspire to hamper a car's progress. And road signs! In the past decade signposts have punctured the town's tarmac with the relentlessness of wild bamboo. The good old speed limit barely gets a look-in today, not now it has to compete with the one-way arrows, speed-camera threats and exhortations to watch out for wandering heritage centres and historic ducks. There'd be no time to look at the road at all if you were to try to follow this narrative, so nobody does, of course, which is not to say that the signs don't have an effect. They do. They ensure that you arrive at your destination feeling distracted at best, and at worst harassed.

I barely noticed the signs today, however. I was too intent on reaching the army surplus store I've always known stood opposite the bank but had never before had call to use. Defying the wardens – my experience up the ladder overshadowed the threat of a ticket – I parked on the kerb, right outside. Then, with the assistant's help, I chose a pair of blue overalls, desert boots, a canvas tool bag, and a baseball cap with an adjustable strap at the back, and paid in cash at the till.

One size fits all.

Next, I filled the tool bag with a short-handled sledge-hammer, cold chisel and work gloves, all bought new from the town's ubiquitous B&Q. Overcautious perhaps, but if a quick exit became necessary I didn't want to leave my own tools – or fingerprints – at the scene.

Doing your homework, keeping your kit in order, arriving fully prepared. My father, Freddie, taught me the importance of all that. He led by example, right to the end. Over the past few years I'd noticed his smaller possessions – books, trinkets from abroad, pictures even – gradually disappearing from around his house. When I asked about it at Christmas he wheezed something about clutter. But a month ago, after he died – at eighty-five, from a brutal combination of emphysema and Alzheimer's – and it fell to me to dispose of his assets, I found seventeen numbered packing crates in the garage, into which he'd already sorted the bulk of his earthly goods. There was an index with the will: family members correlated with box numbers. My brother Ray got the history books and slide-rules; the Wisden cricket almanacs and the old man's collection of darts came to me. Ray died eight years ago himself: cancer. Still, on his own terms, my father met his maker battle-ready.

Almost, at least. He hadn't indexed everything. His will made no mention of the journal I found in his bureau, the pages of which contained a handwritten account of his war years. Fussiness is a peculiar feature of Alzheimer's. Even as the illness tucks into a person-ality it leaves small islands of self on the side of its plate. Or, put another way, the true core of a man will see off the disease's worst attempts at befuddlement. Dad's urge to confess being as irresistible as my urge to read his private thoughts once I'd found them, he must have left his notebooks for me to find on purpose, wanting me to uncover his lie, believing I alone could forgive it after he was gone.

I doubt he suspected doing so would cost me my own will to go on.

Among other things the journal tells how, when he could, Freddie used to swim in the mornings during the war. A hard-facts man, he recorded a lap-count at the bottom of each page. It looks strange there alongside the log he kept of his flying exploits – bombing sorties undertaken, targets over-flown, payloads dropped – but I suppose the water was as real to him as the sky he tore up later in the day. Swimming is like flying in a way. You're out of your element, suspended. He used to swim in the reservoir before breakfast, no mean feat considering how little rest those guys had to survive on. I imagine him face down in the water's cement-grey surface, arms out, eyes shut, gripped by the cold, undeniably alive. Or perhaps he kept his eyes open and stared into the murky depths to blank out his fear of what was to come. Either's possible: the journal doesn't say.

Though it did my back no favours, I struggled into my new overalls in the Audi's front seat, tucked discreetly between SUVs in the car park. So disguised, I strode through the leisure centre's lurid foyer. Not for me, today, the irritating hurdles – a receipt to be taken on to the poolside, a locker requiring specific change, a scuba-scabbard-sized ankle-strap for the ill-fitting key – that now stand between the simple pleasure of a man

21

and his morning swim. No, with the kitbag slung authentically across my shoulder, my cap pulled low, and my breath heavy in my chest, I stumped through the changing room and straight towards the target.

At a recent dinner party I overheard two women my age complaining that advancing years had made them invisible. Where once they turned heads, no one looks twice now.

Though we don't bang on about it as much, the same is true for men, of course. In my prime I was noticeable: six foot, square shouldered, with a full head of sandy hair. Oak-backed beneath the seaside weight of children, a bursting cooler bag in each hand, I covered beach-lengths with a sprung stride. Such vigour is magnetic even as it takes itself for granted. I never noticed how fast barmaids served me until I found myself overtaken in the line.

Still, faded grace has its advantages. At sixty I'd make a young law lord and positively juvenile pope. Not yet *old* then, but wily enough to take advantage of the fact that someone my age is generally looked upon as benign, even – on a good day – as a figure of possible authority. Whatever crookedness is ascribed to us greybeards, we're considered unlikely *vandals*.

What's the word that's always paired with vandalism? *Wanton*. Dictionary definition: 'lacking proper restraint or motive'. Since my actions in the pool were well intentioned, I don't consider what I did fell within that category. Kids who smash the slats in public benches, or spray their initials on other people's garage doors, they're the card-carrying vandals. I'm sure I could convince a jury I was acting in the public interest. At least I'd mount a spirited defence.

My cause target lay in the heart of the leisure centre, the Victorian bath bit, and specifically the men's poolside shower room. Originally, swimmers entered these showers up a flight of four narrow, steep, tiled steps. A year ago, however, the council, driven by the latest anti-discrimination legislation, ordered that the steps be replaced with a ramp. Fine in principle: I've no objection to making the place wheelchair friendly, or to the new hydraulic lift by which the disabled are lowered into our municipal chlorine soup. Except that the entrance to the shower room is shoulder-brushingly cramped, too narrow by far to admit a wheelchair.

Which in itself would not have stirred me to act. I'm as numb to civic waste of money as the next man. It's just that this particular lip-service to the disadvantaged threatened to increase their number. The ramp was tiled – the ancient baths are part of a listed building, after all – and had, because of the architecture it modified, to be short and steep, too. Since it linked a shower room to a swimming pool, the slope was invariably wet as well.

A short steep slope of wet tiles is bound to be slippery, and this one was no exception. The first time I fell I landed on my backside. It almost didn't hurt and I was too embarrassed to make an issue of the incident. Somebody else must have been less circumspect, though, for within a week a garish yellow handrail appeared. But gripping this on my tentative way up the slope a month later only made matters worse. I ripped a shoulder muscle going over the second time, and it annoyed me, enough to make me ask the girl at reception if there were plans to reinstate the steps, this being the nearest, somehow, I could come to an outright complaint.

A silver nail bobbed like a lifebuoy on the sea of her tongue as she asked me to repeat myself.

'*You what?*'

Though I went on to explain again exactly what I meant to the girl – and her manager – neither could do anything to help. Sixty years of Freddie's *shut up and put up* dictum stood between me and the next step, which was to complain in writing to the company contracted to run the leisure centre.

I learned to crab sideways up the slope, hand-over-handing my way safely along the rail.

But I swim often and witnessed other people losing their footing on that ramp a number of times, and the perversity of the thing so transfixed me that eventually I broke the habit of a lifetime and picked up my pen. Actalife plc wrote back. A short letter, but long enough to quote the legislation they claimed tied their hands.

I'd tried, I'd failed; so be it.

And yet, and yet. Freddie was dead and his putting-up and shutting-up had turned out to be a sham, and here I was bent double in newly creased overalls, fumbling to pull a sledgehammer from my tool bag, my heart now pounding in my chest.

I angled my chisel into the gap between two tiles, raised the hammer, brought it down with the first of many satisfying *cracks*.

★   ★   ★

I enjoy tools. I always have. An engineer at heart, it's a disappointment to me that making things with tools is unimportant in selling, which has become my line of work. As a boy practical stuff was my domain. My brother got cleverness, I took dependability and sport. I wasn't supposed capable of appreciating fine things myself. I must have been told this so often that by the time I'd reached adulthood it would never have occurred to me to think otherwise. Then one day I was standing before a picture of a horse by George Stubbs in the National Gallery with Jimmy, who was there to look at it for his schoolwork, and found I had tears running down my cheeks. That horse, the trepidation in its rolling eye! Happily I made it to the Gents without Jimmy realising anything was afoot.

The idea was that when I hit retirement I'd get back into making things, perhaps take a course or two. Woodwork first. *Dovetail, bevel, mortise-and-tenon*: just the sound of the vocabulary appeals. I imagine there'd be real joy in learning how to use a chisel with the precision required to make those words come true in wood.

Shattering the tiles and concrete of that particular ramp required little skill and brought no joy. I knew Actalife would replace them within a month. But the caller had been on to something: as I bent to the challenge of chipping away at the pointlessness, sparks of empowering satisfaction flew. The job took only fifteen minutes. Nobody thought to challenge me as I worked.

3

Having made a start on my own behalf, I turned to the more substantive issue of helping Robert, my storm-faced firstborn, next. There's a direct line from the heroism of Freddie's generation, through my own stoicism, to the materialism embodied by some members – Robert, for instance – of the next. It now seemed clearer than ever to me that I was to blame for having egged him on towards his suffocating success.

Even when the children were small I thought it right that they should help out with chores around the house. Robert being the eldest, I started preaching this importance-of-work stuff at him earliest of all. He was six when we first moved to the Tithe Barn. There wasn't much of a garden here to speak of back then; my first project was to clear the raggedy back field and make one. Jennifer, tied up with the two younger children, wasn't able to help, but I soon put Robert to good use, sifting through the earth I'd dug over, in search of stones.

I'm not sure what I think about that initiative now. I doubt that on its own it would have done any harm. But Robert threw himself into the task with the vigour of unconditional love, and I began to feel guilty, exploitative almost. Since a proper garden pail filled with stones would have been too heavy for a small boy to carry, he was using his beach bucket. The soil here is full of clay; he was soon clog footed, yet he staggered back and forth across that paddock all afternoon, his face a deeper red than his boots. Such hard work, I decided, deserved rewarding, and it's here that I think I went wrong. I offered him ten pence a load. He came to me each time the container was full and I made a show of scoring a new line on to my spade-shaft, which spurred him to work harder and longer still. I made forty-five marks before I stopped him, on the pretence I'd run out of handle. And I gave him a five-pound note in exchange for the last bucket: a huge sum back then, but he deserved it, right down to the fifty-pence tip. He hovered before me, his mouth working, hopping from foot to foot, too pleased to speak. My throat is knuckling at the memory. Picking him up would have ruined the moment, but I wanted so much to hold him just then, to eclipse his pride in the bigger shadow of my own.

'I'll empty it,' he stammered finally, staring at the bucket.

'No, let me. Time for your bath.'

An incisor needled at his lower lip.

'In you go now, and thanks again.'

'But Dad . . .'

'Now!'

He prised off his muddy trainers at the back door slowly, as if before a prison gate. I sensed then that something was amiss but could not bring myself to confront whatever it was, refused to let it spoil the moment. Instead, I left the bucket where it was, picked up the spade and pitted myself against another stretch of unbroken clay. I dug like something depended upon it for an hour, hoping against hope.

He'd wedged a small plastic football into the bottom half of his pail. It stuck there, afraid to admit itself, when I did eventually tip out the stones. Part of me couldn't resist laughing, of course; the other part bowed beneath the weight of an unsolicited secret. I never confronted Robert with my discovery of the truth.

Nowadays Robert works for a City law firm called Madison & Vere. He's an associate there, but well up that ladder, a rung or two ahead of his peers in the partnership race. I called his office to arrange to see him. His secretary's voice slowed down perceptibly when I said who I was; it's a cut-and-thrust industry and she must imagine me to be very old. Just that morning I had discovered, watching breakfast television, that I am younger than the actor Harrison Ford, but I wasn't tempted to mention this fact. Robert, his secretary said, was 'tied to the stake', and couldn't therefore speak. A possibly incorrect image of Ford in *Raiders of the Lost Ark* came to mind. It seemed fitting today that I make an appointment to see my son through his secretary. I encouraged her to suggest one of the restaurants Robert visits with clients, then triumphed with an Internet search that gave me directions, a preview of the menu and even the restaurant's banal 'mission statement': *to become a multifaceted culinary-commercial success.*

I was there early. Robert came through the door looking smart but harried. He handed his overcoat to the waiter without saying thank you. Authority sits increasingly comfortably on his shoulders these days. The coat-rack the waiter headed for was made from antlers and wooden swords, which summed up the restaurant's post-chrome-and-glass decor. Faux old order; a Japanese gentlemen's club with its sushi-wrapped tongue in its cheek.

'How's Marie?' I asked as he sat down. 'And little Flo?'

'Fine, Dad, by all accounts. But what's up with you? What's with this midweek cloak-and-dagger stuff?'

For a moment this hint at something clandestine made me suspect he knew about my protest at the swimming pool, but he was referring, of course, to my having summoned him to lunch.

'Nothing, I'm fine too. I'm well, in fact.'

He scrutinised me sceptically, as if, were that the case, I should not have lured him from his desk. I let him look, taking in the detail of his face. He still has his ruddy childhood complexion, but it has subtly altered to appear less healthy, pressured, as if the circuitry of blood vessels beneath his skin is shorting out in protest, signalling his inner distress. The rims of his lower eyelids also looked red.

'That's good,' he continued, glancing at his menu to avoid my eye. 'Because I saw the Mutual Friends announcement and, you know, put two and two together. Is it bad? I was meaning to call.'

Not suspecting he knew the detail of my finances,

29

it hadn't occurred to me that he would have worked out that misfortune from the news. I imagined him pausing as he read the paper to think of me. Tenderness towards him redoubling its gravitational pull, I reached out to pat the back of his hand.

'No, no. No problems there. It's a blow, but I have . . . a back-up plan.'

His hand slid out from beneath mine to realign his cutlery, wineglasses and side plate. This fiddling undermined his expression, which was one of professional – paternal almost – concern.

'You're sure?'

I wasn't sure at all but was not about to admit it.

'I mean,' he continued, 'even you'd have to concede there's something galling about the directors, Woodward and the other one, waltzing off with their bonuses.'

Though this was news to me I kept my response to a worldly nod.

He went on in a tone of overt sympathy whose undercurrent – as it often is – was condescension. 'If this is about asking me to look over the paperwork, then of course I will, Dad. I wouldn't want you to miss an opportunity to appeal.'

Robert's mobile phone rang then. He rolled his eyes at me but answered it anyway, which cut this strand of conversation mercifully short. I feigned interest in the menu as he barked at – evidently – one of his juniors. This version of my son is unappealing. Not just because it is overbearing, but because it is false. He may have been convincing whoever it was on the other end of the phone with the act, but he wasn't fooling me. When you've seen a child truly passionate – as he was about pterodactyls, Luke Skywalker, windsurfing and, once he'd met Marie, learning French – you can tell when it's put on. I looked up to check. Sure enough, the earnest little 'V' above the bridge of his nose had deepened, as it did when he dutifully built those model aircraft my father used to buy him, or dressed for judo, or – more recently – talked about Chelsea FC.

This pretence made me ask, 'Has Marie mentioned heading south again?' when he put down his phone.

'No, no. That's under control.'

'But it's still your plan?'

'What is?'

'The water-sports academy. Southern France?'

Robert raised an eyebrow. 'Er, Dad, plans change. You know how things have moved on.'

I did. I was responsible for the metamorphosis. I'd bundled up Freddie's 'knuckle down' edict with the rest of his genes, and I'd passed them on to Robert, loading him up with conventionalism, sinking his water-sports academy dream before he'd had a chance to float it.

Robert met Marie at an international windsurfing event when they were both seventeen. He was always the sort of boy to hang on to his first love; miraculously she was that sort of girl, too. (Whenever I consider this piece of luck I picture it as the decoration Jennifer had made for their wedding cake: two little figures gripping the same wishbone-shaped windsurfer boom, either side of an iced sail.) Neither of them, it turned out, had what it takes to make it professionally, but the day he finally conceded this and, on my advice, applied for university, Robert was adamant that he would find a way to work back among the dagger-boards and battened sails he loved. Marie's parents, nearing retirement now, run a water-sports school on the Mediterranean coast near Perpignan. As late as when Marie was pregnant with Florence, just five years ago, Robert talked of their plans to reinvigorate the business, and of the advantages to be had from bringing up his family in France. Cheap cheese and so on. I smiled and nodded and suspected he would never bring himself to abandon everything I'd encouraged him to work so hard for here, and since then my suspicions have, to my recent dismay, proven true.

'But, son . . .' I said now, and tailed off.

He raised his eyebrow again, expectantly this time, then hailed a waiter and checked his watch. It's a diving model, good to a hundred fathoms: we gave them both one as wedding gifts. The watch spurred me on.

'When did you last get home to see Flo before bedtime?'

'What?'

'Or take a whole weekend off?'

'Sashimi selection for two,' he told the waiter, then nodded at me saying, 'if that's OK with you?'

'And when was the last time you did something you truly enjoy?' I persisted. 'Something you're passionate about.'

'Plus two sparkling waters.' Robert closed his menu deliberately, as if it were a church service programme, and handed mine to the waiter with it. I had crossed a line by talking to him this directly; in ignoring me he was giving me the chance to step back.

'You're living in your future now, son, it hurts me to see—'

'*Your future's now*,' he said in a grave, voiceover voice. 'What's with this Sunday supplement stuff?'

I felt my confidence snag on his blitheness. The restaurant had been a bad choice; his allegiance – midweek, midday – was to it, or the version of himself it confirmed, not the child I was appealing to, not to me.

'How's Mum, anyway? Does she know about the pension?'

'No—'

'Not looked up from the tee to take notice yet, then?'

'The future—'

He bent forward, close enough for me to make out the worst of the broken capillaries in his puffy cheeks, and said, 'The future is exactly what I'm working to secure, Dad. I mean, look at . . .' He sat back, shrugged. 'Oh, never mind.'

A small gesture, the rise and fall of his shoulders. Yet it opened up a distance between us, conferring leverage, with Robert farther from the fulcrum than me. The shrug said he'd suspected all along my efforts hadn't been enough. What I'd needed was a job like his. An ache in the small of my back telegraphed pain down my leg. I don't, of course, imagine myself immune from the criticism of my children, but here, now, Robert's unspoken allegation was hard to take. There was truth in it, but – a platter of immaculately parcelled sushi arrived at our table – the truth was wrapped in a lie.

Robert tucked in. Children can do this to their parents: wound lightly and move on. It's not a conscious meanness, just the bones of our original relationship – gods don't bleed – showing through its mature skin. I wasn't unduly bothered, either by the slight, or by Robert's having brushed off my poor stab at advice. Thirty-two years of one sort of encouragement weren't about to be undone over lunch. I had time, and if time didn't work I had the ace up my sleeve – in Freddie's terms, the big bomb to drop – as a last resort.

We ate in silence. I like the newness of sushi. Something familiar about our waitress was pleasing, too. But the throbbing down the back of my leg would not go away and nor would an undercurrent of annoyance, the cause of which – it's good brain food, raw fish – became clearer as I ate on. I was disappointed because I hadn't managed to convey to Robert the novelty of my situation. Shattering those stupid tiles had been a liberating experience. I wanted to share it with him, explain how anything was possible now.

But where do you begin? The cloth of rebellion is marked out for children to cut, not parents. As in one of those optical tricks where the space between two faces turns out, when you've stared at it for long enough, to be a wineglass or a plummeting eagle, I suddenly felt how Robert had fixed me in place with his expectations, as well as the other way around. I sat there watching him tidy up his plate, wipe his mouth, refold his napkin, methodical as ever, searching for a way to show him how I was trying to break free. The swimming-pool tiles would baffle him, worry him, even. I hadn't yet done anything else. As I struggled in vain for a convincing way to *pitch* myself to my son the waitress stretched across me to collect a plate. Her bare arm was inches from my nose, very pale, strong and feminine at the same time. I could almost feel its heat.

'I'm supporting Fira's application to stay in the country,' I said.

'Eh?' said Robert.

'Fira. Our cleaner. She's got visa problems. I'm going to sort them out.'

Robert's brow lowered (the same expression he used to put on when it was his move at chess). 'Mum mentioned she'd not last long.'

'Mum got me to write a reference, yes, but just to show form. I'm going to do more.'

'I don't know anything about immigration law, Dad—'

My leg throbbed. 'I'm not asking for your help, son. I'll find out what's necessary and do it myself.'

'Right.' Robert blew out through loose lips, signalling relief and – I felt – a crushing lack of interest. 'Good-oh,' he said.

Then his mobile phone went off again. This brought the meal to a close, since he carried out the formalities of signalling for the bill, paying it and bidding me an apologetic goodbye without breaking from his conversation. I left him in the kitsch Japanese portico that frames the restaurant's Tudor doorway. He had his eyes screwed tight shut and a finger wedged into his free ear: an affected *I'm concentrating* expression redeemed only, for me, because he is my son and his silly countenance so clearly echoed the *I'm not looking* face of our *Doctor Who*-watching days.

4

I've always wanted a dog. Man and boy, a dog is just something I've always felt in my heart I should have. But boy and man there's always been a compelling reason for me not to have one.

Freddie refused to buy me a dog as a child, point blank. And not because he didn't like them. Far from it. He loved dogs. Where he came from – 1920s rural England – they were pretty much de rigueur. Until his cataloguing-for-death exercise claimed it, a framed photograph had always stood on the hall table showing Dad beneath the wing of a parked, looming Lancaster bomber, his crew gathered around him, a Jack Russell – *his* Jack Russell – held nonchalantly under one arm. Fitch, that dog was called. It was smiling in the photograph, as was Dad, as in fact were they all. The photograph was evidence that a dog should be part of things.

For obvious reasons Fitch couldn't ride in the plane. He was ground crew: specialist role, impatient waiting. Unless restrained he would rush to greet Freddie before he was even out of the cockpit. Wartime airfields were busy places; personnel stood in short supply; dog-sitting was low on the list of military priorities. There was an accident, inevitably. By all accounts Fitch's death hit Freddie hard. After the war he used our nomadic air force lifestyle and the rabid UK quarantine rules as the official excuse to deny us a dog, but I always knew Fitch's empty boots were to blame.

Childhood trauma was Jennifer's excuse. When she was aged five – so the story went – a tethered collie's teeth met through the instep of her left foot. The scar faded fast, as – when I brought the subject up one Christmas – had her elder sister's memory of the incident. Pity won out over resentment back then. I understood: fear of the dark will spawn its own ghost, given time. But I noticed how when we encountered a dog – out walking, say, or picking up one of the children from a friend's – Jennifer did not shy away. True cynophobes give dogs a wide berth. An old jogging partner of mine would turn back down the towpath rather than pass one close by. Yet in the Pyrenean campsite we stayed at with the children in '84 I saw her scratching the mountain guide's German Shepherd behind the ears. Her line after that changed: it's the mess a dog would cause which means she won't have one in the house.

As I've never had a dog, it's no surprise that I've coped fine without one. But it's also no contradiction to say that I've never quite got used to there not being a dog around. Out walking through the woods, I've felt the absence of a dog ferreting through the undergrowth up ahead. The nook beneath the window in my office would be a perfect hunting ground for dream rabbits. Amputees talk of phantom limbs; I'm not putting my dog thing on a par with their loss, of course, but when

I've considered their suffering the sympathy I've felt was dog shaped.

The obvious thought had come to me after my conversation with the call-centre girl: Fira cleans our house, not Jennifer now. Added to which, fifty-nine years of forbearance for the benefit of other people was long enough. If I'd stepped from the ladder, I would have died having lived a dogless life. Freddie's revelation, which prompted me to tie the rope to the beam, would have deprived me of the dog consolation he refused me as a child. Only resist: I would enter my surprise party with a dog at my side. I'd made enquiries at the rescue centre. Returning home from my lunch with Robert, I drove straight to my appointment at the dog home on the other side of town.

Early on in his journal Freddie describes what his flying comrades referred to as 'the chop look'. Faced as they were with the nightly Russian roulette of wartime operations – in all some 55,500 Bomber Command personnel never made it home – a belief grew among airmen that those marked for death on a given raid wore 'the chop look', that their expression on the day in question bore a premonition of their fate. It's unclear from the journal whether hard-facts-Freddie had any trouble accepting so unscientific a notion at first, but by late 1943 at any rate it seems superstition had won out. The entry for 4 December that year reads 'NG146DX B-Billy lost tonight. Flight Sergeant Fulton navigating. Chop look at breakfast: eyes rounder and whiter than my fried eggs.' On 12 January 1944 Freddie describes a thrashing he received at snooker in the mess from one Flight Lieutenant Swann – a friend he'd known since pilot training – whose 'fingers were bitten raw, right down to the chop look quicks'. Swann's Lancaster ditched in the North Sea that night, having limped some four hundred flak-raddled miles from Munich on two of its four Rolls-Royce Merlin engines. Fog and a broken altimeter finally did for them, Freddie supposes. All on board perished.

But can you really read a person's destiny in their face? From experience I'd have to guess not. The morning I put my head in the noose I'd spent the customary five minutes in front of our bathroom mirror, whittling my face out of shaving foam, and I can't say I'd noticed anything different. The same bent nose (rugby) and jutting chin, contradicted by the same creased eyes. Then again, I didn't go through with topping myself, so who am I to say for sure? My take on the chop look is that it was a statistical certainty: with so many young men destined to die each night it would be hard not to read foreknowledge into the memory of their shaking hands and unfocused eyes.

Dog-home dogs have the doomed-look market cornered. As I made my way down the line of kennels it became clear to me that, bouncy puppies aside, the competition is all about who can appear most forlorn. I was determined not to be swayed by good acting. The dog I'd always imagined owning looked, unsurprisingly perhaps, very much like Fitch, but I wasn't put off by the fact that there were no terriers-to-go that day.

I caught myself pausing before a pair of border collies, then realised why and moved on: spiting Jennifer was not my aim. All the while the resettlement officer, a girl of about eighteen whose elfin looks were heightened by her drainpipe jeans, was reminding me about breed-specific characteristics, and reciting stuff about 'the responsibilities those characteristics confer upon a prospective owner', and I was nodding and making what I hoped were the right noises about working from home and the size of my garden and the routine walking I already do each day, until I found I'd pulled up short and was asking an unplanned question.

'Which dog is down to die first?'

'Pardon me?'

'You don't keep them for ever, do you?'

'Not indefinitely, no.'

'Well, who's been here longest? Who's next to go?'

'There's no schedule as such, sir. We don't rehouse dogs with serious behavioural disorders. Traumatised dogs, with hitherto developed aggression problems. We put them out of their misery straight away. But older dogs, too. They tend to be harder to accommodate. We have to . . .'

War wounded, I was thinking. Boy veterans, downed aircrew. The girl continued talking. She picked up the pace, too, shepherding me along the row of wire doors, a specific kennel evidently in mind. We stopped before it. The girl stepped to one side – theatrically, there was something quite Paul Daniels about her – and said, 'If you want to grant someone a reprieve then perhaps Spongebob's the dog for you.'

★   ★   ★

I sell valves. It's strange how that statement has come to be true, but I'm so used to it now that the oddness, like that of my broken nose, strikes me only once in a while. When I see myself in profile say, or fill out the occupation slot on an official form.

After university – a 2:2, mechanical engineering, Sheffield – I took a job with Stennen Parkes, the Reading-based aeronautical designers, on the marketing side. Fifteen years later my card said Sales Director, and a week after that the company was the subject of a hostile takeover bid. Redundancies and restructurings followed. This was the recession of '82, turbulent times. Miraculously, I bobbed up on the other side of the rapids as the head of a new revenue stream called S.P. Components Ltd, in charge of the old company's pump manufacturing plant. We were based on an industrial estate outside Staines. For ten years the screech of metal-work drilled through my office walls. By the time the recession of '92 hit I'd grown to appreciate that noise as a symphony. Though I didn't play an instrument myself I was the conductor and I admired my performers: disbanding the orchestra – costs – saddened me deeply. I felt I'd failed my workforce. Yet Skinny Pete, the foreman, driving me home after our last day (I'd had to leave the company Granada on the forecourt), pointed out the obvious as we turned on to the dual carriageway. 'I knew the writing was on the wall when they did that,' he said, nodding at the place where the old 'Industrial Estate' sign used to stand, now replaced by a sponsored 'Enterprise and Initiative Park' hoarding in a cornflower-blue font.

Despite voluntary liquidation I was sure the old customer pool had not dried up. People still need water here, air there, petrol everywhere, and a pump is a pump is a pump. I was also aware that we'd lost least money on industrial valve components. The world can't get enough of these, it seems. Since we had been most comprehensively outperformed by our Far Eastern competitors, my choice of manufacturing subcontractors was obvious. Enterprise and initiative. A modest mark-up in exchange for an English-speaking frontman and here I am, all these years on, having survived, more or less, and sure of one thing at least, that when the dogs-home literature required me to state what I did for a living my answer to that question should stare down the pomp and circumstance of company director, entrepreneur or even self-employed salesperson. *I sell valves*, I wrote. Skinny Pete, incidentally, was a very fat man. He retrained as a gourmet chef.

'Spongebob' was an absurd name for a dog. The rescue girl knew as much. She sped across the words, trying to avoid them, but I heard her all right and had to check my curiosity, not wanting to offend girl or dog. She'd been through this before.

'Named after a cartoon character, apparently. The woman's children picked it. He's five. He lived in a flat on a council estate in Peckham, which means despite his size he's used to small spaces. And kids. Four of them, in a two-bedroom flat . . .'

She went on but I focused on the dog, Spongebob. He was curled asleep at the far end of his pen, his leonine back to the door. Or at least he was pretending to sleep; I'm pretty sure I saw an eye flick open and shut. There was something unconcerned about him. Stoical, not morose. He looked as if he could cope with anything, including not escaping the dog home. Such valiant delusion was immediately attractive.

'What sort is he?' I asked.

'He's a mongrel,' the girl said, in a voice that told me I'd dropped in her estimation.

'Of course.' I tried to regain some ground. 'But do we know what his, er, lineage, is?'

'No,' she said flatly. 'His previous owners hadn't a clue. There's definitely some Rotweiller in there, or Doberman, in the black-and-tan colouring, and I'd say some Lab, or Ridgeback, maybe some husky, even, in those light eyes. He's a healthy, strong dog, aren't you, Spongebob?'

Humouring her, the dog beat its tail once. At least he had short hair; Jennifer would thank me for that. I was thinking I could get round the 'Spongebob' problem. I wouldn't have picked it, but plain 'Bob' wasn't a bad name for a dog. Still, I could tell from the girl's fidgeting beside me that there was another factor for me to consider, so I asked, 'Name aside, what's Bob's issue?'

'Spongebob', she iterated carefully, 'is tricky around bicycles. He was hit in the park by a BMX. Broke a back leg. This was six months ago. The leg's all mended, but he's still nervous near bikes. Absolutely wouldn't hurt a living thing, but show him a bike – even a parked, stationary bike – and unless you've got hold of him he'll go for its wheels. Maybe in time–'

I don't cycle and neither does Jennifer. You couldn't avoid bikes in the city but where we live it wouldn't be a problem. Or at least it'd be a problem we'd have enough space to work around. Bikes aside, the dog was evidently phlegmatic. It intrigued me to think that he'd put up with life on an inner city estate. Thumping music, broken lifts, feral kids. I'd often wondered what it would be like to know – properly – somebody who came from such a place. Here was Spongebob. The girl could see I was interested. She'd moved into selling mode: all dog-home dogs, evidently, are served up vaccinated to the eyeballs. I cut her pet-insurance proposal short.

'Come on, Bob,' I whispered. The dog didn't move. 'You'll do.'

5

A week having passed since my last ride on the sit-on mower, I should have attended to the lawn when I returned home from the rescue centre, but I decided to put the job off that afternoon. Long grass, coupled with the scorch marks from the moss treatment, would provide useful cover for Bob as he settled in. Making the most of Jennifer's absence – golf – I instead spent the time showing the dog around his new home, starting with the house, then the garden, and finally the office. Bar some cursory sniffing, he appeared unfazed by this tour, seeming reluctant to move on only when standing in the space behind my desk. The office was once a working garage, complete with a deep engine pit. Carpet tiles obscure the trapdoor to what is now an empty wine cellar, but Bob, with the unfathomable sensitivity of his kind, must've grasped that he was standing above a void. I lifted the hatch and gave him time to peer into the brick hole.

The phone rang as I stood looking down at Bob's inquisitive, pricked ears. The short delay and Indian accent caught my attention, and my pulse quickened when the speaker said she was calling on behalf of ICBC

International, but in vain; I knew this voice did not belong to the same cold caller.

'I've already spoken with one of your colleagues,' I began.

'I know, sir. That conversation is what I'm calling about.'

'I'm not interested in your company's services. She'll tell you as much. But–'

'Again, we appreciate that, sir–'

'But it's lucky you called. I want to speak to the girl again.'

'I'm calling to head that enquiry off, sir.'

'To do what?'

'As you're aware, Mr Brinkman, ICBC operates under a strict code of conduct which, regrettably, our representative breached. We take our obligations under the code very seriously.' Like her subordinates, this woman was reading a pre-prepared speech, I could tell. 'Mindful that you might wish to raise a complaint, I'm hoping to reassure you that the woman in question will be disciplined appropriately. You'll be pleased to hear that the process is already–'

'Hold on–'

'Please hear me out, sir. I understand that you are vexed. You'll be glad to hear that the process is already *in train.*'

'Vexed? No!' I laughed. 'I don't think you do understand.'

'The woman's indiscretion–'

'There was nothing indiscreet about her!' I laughed again. 'I as good as threatened her with my suicide and she was decent enough to take me seriously. I want to thank her.'

'ICBC does not deserve your thanks, sir. Not yet. I don't wish to prejudge the disciplinary process, but in all likelihood when it's complete you'll have reason—'

'You've jumped to the wrong conclusion. I don't want anyone disciplined.'

'We respect your point of view, sir. But as with the products we are proud to offer our customers, ICBC is a step ahead in this regard. The disciplinary—'

'But I don't want to complain! I just want you to tell me how I can speak with her again!'

'That won't be necessary, Mr Brinkman,' the voice replied slowly. 'We have the situation in hand. Thank you for your time today.'

The speaker cut me off before I could protest further. I cracked the phone back into its holder with more force than I'd intended; the dog flinched, turned from the trapdoor and regarded me quizzically.

A few years ago, when Jimmy was at art school, he went through a phase of trying to 'improve' me with books he'd found enlightening. One such book contained the writings of Albert Camus. Hard-going stuff: I gave up early on, but not before coming across a line in which the former goalkeeper (Jimmy thought the man's sporting prowess might appeal to me) had described a cat as 'the visible soul of a home'. I'm not a cat person; the idea seemed pretentious when I read it. But now, as I stood looking down into the dog's reproachful eyes, it struck me that if a cat could be said to embody soul, a dog clearly gave its owner's conscience an extra dimension.

'Sorry, Bob,' I murmured, as I shut the trapdoor.

The dog, ignoring me pointedly, retreated into a corner of the room, turned in a circle and lay down.

I sat too, enjoying, as ever, the pleasing reciprocity of the air-sprung swivel seat Robert bought me (he was right, it has helped my back) until a thought, flitting quick as a bat's wing, darkened my mood: what did Fitch's untimely dash on to the runway reveal about Freddie's true inner state?

War, it seems, cuts hideousness with propriety. That's the way Freddie's journal recounts the early days, at any rate. He includes more detail about dinners in the officers' mess, promotions and parades, than he does about the terror of flying over enemy territory, comrades lost, or the target cities he helped lay to waste. Which makes sense, of course. If the canvas before you is too horrible to look at, better to concentrate on the picture's gilt-edged frame instead.

The dog's breathing had slowed. I opened the office door and looked out on the garden. Autumnal wind stirred the yellowing willow leaves. Bugger the lawn for now. Freddie indexed his possessions in preparation for death. I have not faced anything like the hellfire he endured, yet I inherited his preoccupation with niceties all the same. Result: the heart of my life has been wasting away for decades, while I have spent my days maintaining its surround.

★　★　★

Jennifer arrived home as I sat on the office step, her Discovery sweeping over the gravel with the force of a breaker hitting a pebble beach. An old model, it dates from the decade when three children (but no dog) served as its excuse. We should have traded it in for a newer, smaller, more economical car years ago, but Jennifer wouldn't hear of it then and I have given up suggesting as much now. The truck lurched to a stop, a door flung itself open and my wife hopped down with the sprightly optimism of a pilot returning to base. It occurred to me, as I rose to greet her, that I still hadn't told her about Mutual Friends' letter. The Discovery ticking hotly behind her, we hugged, me thinking: she's holding out for a new one from the pension money, I suspect.

There was smoke in her hair.

'Good game?' I asked.

'*Round*,' she emphasised. 'Yes, not bad. Ropy off the tee but I made up for it on the greens.'

'I have something to tell you,' I said, standing back.

'Me too. Pearl's coming to dinner, with Felix, tonight. She's on her way.'

'Righto. I—'

'We need more wood. The shopping's in the boot. And I could do with a hand making up beds.'

'Of course. I—'

'Well?' She was smiling broadly, her eyes wet and black and excited in the late afternoon light. 'Spit it out.'

'Promise me you'll keep calm until I've explained,' I said, stepping aside.

She laughed. 'For heaven's sake! What is it?'

I whistled, then called, 'Out you come, Bob.'

The office doorway stood empty. Sensing Jennifer stiffening beside me, I strode forward, repeating the dog's name.

'You haven't,' Jennifer said behind me.

Bob was where I'd left him, and didn't move though I now called from just feet away. Not until I muttered, 'Spongebob, then. Here, boy. Spongebob,' did he beat his tail, lift his head, rise and slink after me on to the drive.

Bomber Command, as Freddie's journal makes clear, experimented with many different tactics during the war. They flew by day, by night, as lone planes, small squadrons and, eventually, in great 'thousand bomber' raids. The idea was to find the best way for crews to achieve the strategists' deadly ends without coming to their own. Drawing on nature's precedent, they pitted the safety in numbers of baby turtles crowd-surging to the sea against the solitary wolf's element of surprise. The reptilian approach prevailed: it turned out a higher percentage of planes came back if they flew in vast swarms. But Freddie feared participating in those raids most. *A real chore*, he called them. However sensible the statistical argument, he hated relying upon it, couldn't stand the thought that his survival depended not upon his skill and cunning, but on the hope that the enemy's searchlights, swamped with targets, would mark out somebody else's plane for destruction, instead of his.

Of course, true terror lay in the opposite scenario,

the threat of a searchlight homing in on *him*. And panic stood a step beyond that, in the chance that after one beam had fingered him, more would latch on, and more, 'coning' the plane in a tepee of blinding rods, well nigh impossible to evade en masse, leaving Freddie and his crew pinpointed for the guns and night fighters to condemn at will. Though the same fate could befall a lone aircraft over the target, *it might not*; with planes blanketing the sky, nothing was more certain than that the blanket would end up full of holes. As Freddie puts it: 'I'd sooner rely upon surprise every time. I'm here to drop bombs on the ground, not explode in the sky!'

Jennifer looked surprised. She took a step backwards as Bob arrived at my side and said, through tight lips, 'Where did that come from?'

'He came from the dog home.'

'But whose is it?'

'Ours.'

'Ours? What on earth are you talking about? I don't want a dog.'

'Mine, then.'

'But,' she spread her feet on the gravel, the better to oppose me – I imagined her toes curling in her shoes – and repeated herself slowly, 'I do not want a dog. You know that.'

'And you know that I do, that I always have.'

'Harry.'

Faced with this tone from my wife I'd ordinarily have begun talking, persuading, nailing together the planks of an argument, to board up her anger if nothing else, with carefully struck words. I'd already thought of some things to say, about how Bob was only with me on trial (partly true – the rescue home girl had said I mustn't hesitate to contact her 'in the unlikely event of his failure to thrive'), about how she would not have to feed, exercise or clean up after him, and about how the dog bars I'd sourced would not, in any case, fit her giant car. As it was I just shrugged.

'You're serious.'

'Yes.'

Her eyes narrowed. Then it was my turn to feel surprise, as the narrowing turned into a slow blink of understanding. Jennifer nodded, as much to herself as to me, and asked, 'Does Freddie's . . . passing . . . figure in this?'

'Dad? How?'

'It's just that you've been so withdrawn since the funeral.' Keeping one eye on the dog, she approached and gently gripped my elbow. 'Understandably, of course.'

Now was the moment to explain the letter, but that way lay insurmountable difficulties, so I patted the back of one of Jennifer's own elbows and conceded, 'I don't know. Perhaps.'

'What's it called?' she asked, glancing down.

I gave her the dog's truncated name.

'Bob. I see. Well, if he can help you move forward . . .'

She trailed off. The therapy-speak, absorbed not from a couch but the babble-saturated women's magazines she reads, annoyed me, not just in itself, but because it somehow stood in the way of me thanking her genuinely for her flash of understanding, for granting me this gift.

The best I could manage was to clasp her upper arm again and smile.

Squeezed within its fuzz of fleece-sleeve the arm brought to mind an overripe peach.

Ten years ago I didn't think much about simple chores such as bringing in the firewood. I just did them. More recently, though, anything involving physical exertion has become something of a test. Each basket of logs I lug in from the woodshed, for example, I heap high, proving myself capable, still, of carrying a proper load. Result: there's more iron in my arms now than there has been for a decade, and my sore leg is at its worst.

I fetched the logs in modest armloads today, at a leisurely pace, and didn't rush with the shopping, either. Pearl's hybrid pulled through the gate while I was still outside fishing golf clubs from the Discovery's capacious boot. Grateful for Jennifer's apparent kindness over Bob, I'd decided to clean them for her. It had been a wet and muddy week. Yet as Pearl's headlights turned across the twilit gravel they illuminated a set of sparkling club-heads.

'They're not yours, are they?' Pearl, unbuckling Felix, called over the roof of her car.

'These? No.'

'Just that you're looking at them as if you've finally given in!'

'God, no, don't worry. No such thing as golf for me.'

'Neither is there such a thing as "God"!' Pearl told Felix, setting him on the ground.

'No golf. No God,' Felix repeated obediently. Without

meeting my eye, he squatted down on the drive and began to pile up a tower of little stones. 'G is also for gravel,' he said.

Like little Flo, Robert's daughter, my grandson Felix has, just by being before me, an ability to render me speechless with love. I do not exaggerate. The sight of him prompts a surge of benevolence so unconditional it's incapacitating. A sense of responsibility towards my own children tempered the full strength of such feelings as I may have had when they were young, I think. Responsibility for them, and influence over them, and, in a dark corner of my heart, the unspoken knowledge that, should they come to harm, I was still young enough to rear another, substitute child if need be. My grandchildren, by contrast, are supposed to be beyond my control, and not my fault, and yet, ultimately, they are the only footprint I will leave behind. Knowing as much terrifies me. I feel it as an idolatrous appreciation of the perfect glaze of their milk teeth, the brilliant tangle of their hair, the luminous miracle of their skin.

I made myself squat down opposite the boy. My left knee creaked.

He didn't look up, acknowledged my presence by saying, 'Pizza,' instead.

'She's planning on mushroom-and-squash risotto. But if it's pizza you want, there's some in the freezer, I think.'

'No. A leaning tower.' He squinted at me finally from beneath an uneven fringe, prodded at his pile of stones and announced, 'Timber!' as they toppled over.

'They're doing Europe at nursery this week,' Pearl explained.

As far as I could, I gave my children the best start in life. I encouraged, I cajoled, above all I tried to pass on the self-discipline Freddie instilled in me. If the bar of my expectations stood high, I made sure the kids had a fair run at it, and that they took off from solid ground. Their needs ranked ahead of mine. Selling enough valves to put the three of them through good schools kept me at work late, and wide awake until the small hours, more times than I'm able to forget.

Robert, dutiful, flourished. In his own haywire way, Jimmy also made the most of his head start. Pearl, however, was always determined to cut her own path. Which is not to say that her rebellion was anarchic. Far from it. With her the self-control also stuck. But from birth she applied her zeal as she saw alone saw fit. A colicky infant, she refused both breast and bottle: we had to coax her through the first four months of life with a medical pipette. Her mother has a cordon bleu certificate and makes her own gourmet sausages: Pearl's vegetarianism hasn't wavered since she was six. At twelve we offered to buy her a pony. Why else have a paddock, and a daughter, if not to complete that triumvirate? She turned us down, added Freddie's birthday money to her savings and bought herself a BMX instead. The day she turned sixteen she joined the Communist Party and pronounced me a self-serving capitalist.

Were we terrain, and Pearl a river, my daughter would have found a way of flowing uphill. So I learned to play flat ground.

Gently, cautiously, obliquely, I tried to tip her in worthwhile directions, like a drop of mercury through a maze: we've all seen those old executive toys. I had less and less success. As soon as she left school, and home (the same week), and passed beyond the sphere of my immediate influence, I was forced to concede that my only hope of winning her back was to lie down entirely, and wait.

When she decided against university in favour of volunteer work for Friends of the Earth, I held my tongue. When she moved in with Rees, her rat-tailed Plaid Cymru boyfriend, I drove up to Dalston to help decant her belongings into his flat. When, three months later, he abandoned her for a tree-planting job in Haverfordwest, I drove up again, refilled the estate, and siphoned her back.

My even-handedness has, in its way, begun to work.

Pearl revealed to me first (a fact Jennifer would have been so hurt by that I concealed it) that she was pregnant with the Welsh boy's child. I managed to choke back the words 'you needn't keep it' long before they could come out of my mouth. (Huffing at the television news fifteen years ago, I gave away that I am pro-choice: result, Pearl has since been vocally pro-life. Never mind how this sits with her atheism, which, since distrust is as far as I have got with God, must have sprung up in opposition to Jennifer's enthusiasm for helping out with the flowers in the village church.) I held back from suggesting I'd pay for Pearl to have the baby privately, knowing she'd stamp the offer into the ground, and was further rewarded: she let me help out with a deposit on a new place. It's in East London still, but in an area that describes itself as up and coming, which at least means the street is clear of boarded windows. There's a boxroom for the baby, which Jennifer and I equipped as well.

Though it has cost me many white hairs, I have kept up my restraint beyond Felix's arrival, until now. But in recent months keeping quiet has meant having to pull some of those white hairs out. The fact is, Pearl's self-sufficiency (she's insisting on calling the deposit a 'loan', and chipping away at it with microscopic repayments) will mean Felix going without, and I can't bear the thought of that. Also, I sense that Pearl, at the ripe age of twenty-seven, is softening in her militant opposition to all things *us*. My forbearance, the mountain of her single motherhood and the minor success of the 'loan' have opened up a space in which, until the advent of the association's letter, I'd begun, secretly, to have hope. Because the fact is, although I know that Felix is Pearl's business, not mine, when I think of him the distance I should maintain telescopes shut. No, I simply can't see him sacrificed for anyone's principles, not even hers. I owe it to the boy. He's fatherless, and has Jennifer's long fingers, and the perfect circuit of his veins pumps my blood.

Blood which, when I'd finished with the luggage and followed the pair into the kitchen, Jennifer appeared about to spill. Bent in half at the waist (village hall yoga keeps her enviably supple) she was hugging the boy, with both arms around his back and a twelve-inch knife, gripped in one red hand, perilously close to his neck. The blade caught the light as she joggled him up and down. Yet not three weeks ago she'd said letting Felix climb six feet up the willow tree was irresponsible! Wisely, the child stayed frozen until released, then melted into the designated 'grandchildren's corner' by the Rayburn, took off his satchel (plain canvas, no 'Bob the Builder' branding for him) and filleted its wooden contents on to the tiles.

'So, Penny Chichester is now an Adcock,' Jennifer, turning back to her chopping board, informed Pearl.

'Great.' Pearl swiped a celery stick. A calculated move: Jennifer, a tyrannous cook, deems any such liberty trespass.

The knife speeded up.

'Yes. It was a wonderful wedding. Dad and I were invited. I helped with the pew ends.'

'Wonderful,' echoed Pearl.

'The salmon was a bit dry but that aside it was a lovely, lovely day.'

'I'm pleased.'

'William is her new husband. Evidently he already has a detached house in a new close on the far side of town.'

'On the estate,' Pearl suggested.

The Vietnamese instructor on Jennifer's Taste the Orient cookery course was so moved by her prowess that he presented her with his knife. Not having used the Kenwood Chef since, she's fiendishly quick with a blade now: the mushrooms, complicit, were fanning themselves apart at a frightening rate. 'It's a very quiet road they live on,' she said. 'A cul-de-sac.'

'Who wants wine?' I asked, stabbing at the bottle top with clumsy hands.

'A dead end for Mrs Adcock,' said Pearl.

'It's cold,' I offered.

'Plenty of space outside for the children to run around in. No traffic.'

'They popped one out before wedlock too, did they?'

'Pearl. No. But in the future.'

'Here,' I said, thrusting a full glass at Jennifer. She nodded at me to put it to one side. Happily, Pearl concentrated on hers and this subtle shift of attention – Pearl focusing on her wine, Jennifer on slaying vegetables, me on Felix's quiet little shoulders – interrupted the conversation for long enough to me to start another one.

'Schools?' I asked. 'What's the latest?'

Schools, you see, are, or were, my great hope. The one thing Pearl – who has, for the past two years, juggled part-time study for a degree in anthropology with single motherhood and her Friends of the Earth job (I admit I was wrong: she's done well) – and I tacitly agree about is the importance of setting Felix off with a fair wind. She never entirely condemned the sacrifice I made for her education; in recent years I've almost read gratitude in the way she has fallen back upon her exam results. Before I received the news that

Mutual Friends had unilaterally collapsed my retirement fund I was working up to making Pearl an offer: I would apply the old salve – *cash* – as a pre-emptive remedy for the wound the local authority would otherwise inflict on the boy's schooling. Little fair wind there: more fetid air! A few resistant enclaves excepted, the borough Pearl insists on living in – with its *vibrancy* and *liveliness* and *verisimilitude* (no one place is any realer than another, in my opinion) – is blighted by sink schools, underfunded and overflowing with the sorts of delinquents Spongebob grew up alongside. This would not necessarily be a problem. Though she hated her name enough to swear, at thirteen, that she would apply to change it by deed poll as soon as the law allowed, *Pearl Brinkman* would sit on an application form as well as any other middle-class place-contesting parent's. But the few good schools she'd want to put Felix down for are, it turns out, *faith* schools: Church of England, Roman Catholic and Jewish, and although Pearl would consider it a victory to plant an atheistic viper in the bosom of such a place (she survived the religious undertow of her own schooling, after all), it seems that although faith schools are statutorily encouraged to accept all comers, the truth is that they . . . don't.

Bugger level playing fields! It turns out you have to prove allegiance to the local god before they'll even consider you for their squad.

Pearl didn't reply immediately. She lifted her wineglass with a brittle jerk. Her face, distorted by the crystal balloon in front of it, looked pale and suddenly small.

Against the yellow liquid her pursed lips were greenish blue. And then, with the glass a chalice again, gripped two-handed in front of her chest, she glanced at me furtively, and seeing I was still waiting for her answer said, finally, 'No news.'

I saw then.

Somehow, she'd intuited what I'd hoped to be able to promise.

As much as I was hanging on to the possibility that she might have news which would make my stillborn offer unnecessary, she'd been expecting me to make that offer plain.

And I couldn't!

Jennifer, chopping more slowly, said, 'The school in the village gets terrific reports.'

'Bully for it.' Pearl fortified herself with another gulp of wine.

'That security light I installed,' I said. 'Is it still playing up?'

'Small classes, a uniform, well-behaved children,' Jennifer continued.

'I made an appointment to visit the hot school, St Silas's, the one at the end of my street. It was pretty stuffy, in fact. The head had dead-fish eyes, no spark. And inside, the place didn't look up to much.'

'The sensor should be aimed squarely at the front steps.'

'She gave me a leaflet explaining the entrance policy. Unbelievable! They don't even try to hide the truth. Line one: *The school welcomes everyone!* Great, I thought.'

'Polly Aston's son works in London too. He commutes.'

'Bollocks, I say!'

'Pearl!'

'They're *lying*, though. The leaflet goes straight on: *Preference will be given to children who have been baptised into the church and attend weekly services, as verified in writing by the Rev. Frayn.*'

'It's angled too high if the light is still coming on when people walk past on the pavement.'

Jennifer again: 'The village school has access to a wonderful sports field.'

'But I can adjust it. It's easy to adjust.'

'*Preference*, my arse! Apartheid! That's what it amounts to. State sponsored, in the name of *faith*. They're bussing kids across towns: brown ones that way, white ones this. Unbefuckinglievable!'

Jennifer brought her knife down hard enough to stick it into her chopping board, and glared from Pearl to Felix and back again. The boy was busy parking cars (Robert and Jimmy's 1970s Matchbox originals, we did well to keep them) in a neat row with their hoods, boots and doors all open. They looked like metal bumblebees, stretching their wings. He didn't stir.

'I know,' Pearl conceded. 'I know. But really—'

I interrupted her. 'A letter from the vicar, you say.'

'Yeah. Certification that you're certifiable. He's better off out of there anyway. If only the local alternatives weren't . . . worse.'

Here she paused again and gave me a searching look. Gravity redoubled its pull. I braced myself so as not to let my shoulders slump, yet felt my empty hands hang open, each fingertip heavy with impotence. She took another slug of wine. So did I, thinking *only resist*. Between now and my birthday, pension payout or not, I'd find a way to fix this mess. Ever pale, Pearl's brow, cheeks, neck had a ghostly translucence then, a defencelessness that made me want to weep. I've always worried that she doesn't supplement what she misses – vitamins and whatnot – through not eating red meat.

'The porch light's fine, Dad,' she said. 'Blinding, in fact.'

After he'd had his supper I took Felix out to the office. Bob wasn't very forthcoming, but it didn't matter. When I introduced them . . . the boy's face!

6

I like dark chocolate, the blacker the better. Inevitably, I've curbed my taste for it, with Jennifer's help. She keeps a stash of Belgian Gold for cooking with. Tangy as aniseed, bitter as coffee, addictive stuff. It must be fifteen years since, raiding the tin, I found she'd taped a picture of Vegas-fat Elvis inside the lid. The morning after Pearl's visit I topped the Discovery's radiator up with the watering can and waved Jennifer off to her bridge. Then I detoured to my office via the larder's top shelf.

We celebrated Freddie's eighty-fifth birthday four months before he died. It had occurred to me again in the night: another quarter-century, genes prevailing, still lay ahead! Elvis was predisposed to chubbiness. I have my father's physique, and Dad wore his belt on the same notch his entire adult life, despite a daily dose of fried eggs. Reading his journal makes the beginnings of that addiction clear. Pretty much every raid began, and often ended, with the panacea of a fry-up in the officers' mess. Unsurprisingly, furred arteries didn't show up on the radar of the aircrews' perceived risks. I wonder how many of Freddie's survivor-comrades hit fifty before partnering their left arms in the waltz of death?

He never remarried after my mother died, never — to my knowledge at least — had so much as a 'special friend'. Freddie would have regarded moving on in such a way as an act of betrayal, to her memory, but also to Raymond and me. Our birthday visits to Mum's plaque, bearing a bouquet cut from the garden — *her* garden, which he tended, or tried to tend, until he died — was all the spelling out the sentiment needed: war heroes' vows last beyond the grave. I never questioned it, Dad was just built that way. Yet if I'd come upon a secret stash of love letters in his desk, instead of that last entry in his wartime journal, I'd have been less taken aback, less deflated.

I found Mutual Friends' website. The pictures there divided neatly into two camps. Half showed beautiful older people engaged in outdoor pursuits: sailing, standing arm in arm on hilltops, strolling in New-England-fall-style woods and so on. The remainder featured handsome executives peering intently at laptop computers, standing at odd angles in front of skyscrapers, and striding through airports. I ate my chocolate thinking, Give me a manufacturer's website any day: *we sell valves, like these ones, here, and these, here.* Everybody associated with the association had, it seemed, a luxurious head of hair.

I was looking for a way of making a complaint. There was a procedure, but needless to say it was buried behind corporate good news. Apparently Mutual Friends had reduced their overheads by successfully outsourcing their call centre work to India. Ha! Everybody's at it. I cut my way through swathes of slogans — *let us listen to your needs* — and statistical boasts — *first quarter fund perform-ance exceeds expected peak!* — to get to the complaint form I needed, but when I unearthed it I discovered it wasn't a form I could fill in there and then. I had to order it and wait for the postman. Ho-hum. They'd never reply before my birthday anyway, and when they did it wouldn't be in my favour. Lawyers — of Robert's calibre — would have double-checked the loophole (terminal bonus slashable, guaranteed minimum annuity rate void) before driving my savings through its minimising eye. No matter that this chicanery rendered the association's forecasts — filed, neatly, for thirty-one years, in a folder now spread upon my corduroy knees — redundant. And never mind that as a result, before I made it a third of the way from where I sat to Freddie's eighty-five-year target, the money, and house, would be long gone. I couldn't let it matter. I ordered the form anyway — if the call-centre girl was right, the act of resistance mattered more than its effect — and offered my dog the last square of chocolate, saying, 'Don't worry, I've funds enough to outlast you, Bob.'

A doomed explorer, I was cutting a path back through Mutual Friends' website when a lost tribe surprised me. Clever lighting could not hide the fact that this lot, the senior management, were a race apart from the models they'd deployed to advertise their products. Weaker chins, forced grins, and poor hair to a man. One name stood out from the list: Anthony Woodward, FRCA. Hadn't Robert mentioned something about a newsworthy bonus for him? The accompanying head-shot certainly looked satisfied with its lot. When the printer finished whirring I pinned the result on to my corkboard, next to a drawing by Felix which Pearl had labelled 'Tithe Barn'. There are no windows in the depicted house: the boy evidently does not share his Uncle Jimmy's gift.

I was planning on visiting Jimmy that afternoon. As I sat considering how best to help him tackle his problem, a familiar hushing noise, similar to the one the hosepipe makes when I drag it up the drive, reached me through the office's open door. Even as I realised, with horror, what it was, the dog shot out into the light. His bark is shatteringly loud. It sounded as if somebody was smacking the timber facing of the office with a scaffold pole. I lurched outside after him, wood-enly slow, hollering, 'Bob! Stop! Bob!'

Too late. Fira lay on her side with her fallen bicycle between her legs. Bob, the ridge along his spine pulsing electrically with each bark, stood yammering viciously into her face. The bike's back wheel was still spinning.

'Bob! Stop! Bob! Stop, I say! Spongebob! Please, Spongebob, STOP!'

He'd backed off a pace by the time I reached him, but was still scream-barking at the cleaner, murder yellow in his eyes. Though I feared he might bite me, I grabbed hold of his collar – taking a handful of fur with it – and hauled. For a second he opposed me. His muscle-bound shoulders bunched. One proper lunge, I sensed, and the dog would have me over with ease. But he let me drag him back. Twisted sideways so as to keep an eye on the fallen bike, he allowed me to pull him towards the office and in through its door.

'All right, Spongebob,' I hushed him. 'It's OK. Lie down.'

My pulse was thudding in my ears as I helped Fira up. She'd grazed her arm. Chippings of gravel stuck to it. I brushed them away, my heart lurching harder at the sight of broken skin, pinpricks of orange-red blood in the deeper dents.

'Jesus, I'm sorry. I'm really, really—'

'It attacked the wheel.' She was bending towards her bike, pointing with her free hand at the front tyre, which was flat.

'I'll mend it,' I said lamely.

'What animal is that, anyway?'

'He's mine. I'm sorry. I'm—'

She shrugged. 'The wheel only. He did not bite me.'

Though she'd righted the bicycle with one hand, I was still somehow holding her other wrist. She looked at this point of contact and smiled. 'I am OK. You are the man who is shaking. We will go inside.'

Jennifer has kept a bottle of witch hazel in the bathroom cabinet since the children were small. The same bottle, in all likelihood. While Fira washed her arm at the kitchen sink I bounded upstairs to retrieve the antiseptic. It occurred to me, as I rummaged among the toothpaste stores (laid in to see out a nuclear winter) and Nurofen 'caplets' (what's wrong with 'pills'?), that Fira could probably have located the bottle more quickly than me: in her thoroughness she's no doubt wiped down the cupboard's darkest recesses. But she didn't seem to know what to do with the ointment when I presented it to her, so I tore off and soaked a wad of cotton wool and pressed it to the graze and blinked with her as she winced. It wasn't a bad cut. I think she understood: a plea for forgiveness lay behind my attentiveness.

'This dog is here from now onwards?' she asked.

I nodded.

'Your wife. She likes dogs?'

'Not exactly.'

She smiled at me – I was sure of it – a glint in her eye.

Then Fira recapped the witch hazel, wiped the outside of the bottle, the countertop, the taps, gathering herself to start her chores.

'What do you call him?'

For some reason I pronounced the dog's full name.

She did not comment. 'We must work him to over-come his anger at bicycling,' she said.

I drove the back way to the bike shop in town, through St Clare. The village is designated *historic* now by sign-planters who, in their wisdom, have also chosen to *thank you for driving considerately* before you even hit the first *calming measure*. I dropped the Audi a gear, floored the accelerator and swerved into the middle of the road to straddle the speed hump: no amount of pre-emptive gratitude was about to slow me down in my hunt for new bike parts.

Bob had put four holes in Fira's front tyre. Like the back one, it was bald anyway. There was also a tear in the saddle, though I think 'historic' might more usefully have been applied to that defect than the village through which I sped. A child at Halfords sold me new tyres and inner tubes, a pump, a helmet, some chain oil and, to go with the soft new seat, a pair of plush grips to replace the tape on Fira's handlebars. By the time she came to leave I'd transformed her bicycle. She looked it over without speaking, then suggested I 'familiarise the dog' by showing him the old tyres. Understated, sensible, Slavonic gratitude! I had to insist before she would accept the helmet.

Since discovering Freddie's war diary I'd been rereading its pages with an addict's self-destructiveness. There was intoxicating bravery here, despite the lie it foreshadowed. The journal starts with an account of his training. It was brief. He spent the summer of 1941 opening the batting for his school's first eleven (they had a good season), reported to the recruiting depot in August (on the morning of his eighteenth birthday), and flew his first mission over enemy territory the following spring, before – he calculates – the groundsmen at his alma mater would have begun rolling the new pitch. An air of unreality hangs over my father's description of his preparation for war. It skims past such peripherals as his first solo flight, the computational headache of learning to navigate, and disorientating night flying, and dwells instead on incidents such as the time he and another 'sprog' broke up some of the furniture in their icy lodgings to use as firewood. Discovered, they spent three harrowing days fearing the consequences. 'Wilfully damaging barracks' was a serious offence, and mention was made of Colchester Military Prison. Imagine Freddie's relief when the wing commander, turning a kindly blind eye, waved him on to operational duties instead. Such expeditiousness ensured Dad was raining bombs out of a star-filled Munich sky with just 120 hours' flying experience in his logbook, a bare nineteen of them racked up at night. Perhaps Freddie's pathological preparedness later in life was a reaction to this baptism by enemy fire. The journal makes no link. He mentions prematch nerves, not fear, and goes on to say, 'It felt marvellous to be doing my duty – giving it back to the Hun – at long last.'

Tracer fire, Freddie also recalls of that first trip, arcs upwards in elegant curves, 'like pee swayed from side to side'.

Later that day I stood in the Kite, a pub in Acton opposite Jimmy's lodgings. Most men my age pee less forcefully than when they were young: happily I still manage a vigorous stream. The Kite has an old-school urinal. I found myself zeroing in on cigarette butts in the porcelain trough, sweeping them towards the plughole, itself guarded by a dome of wire which brought to mind a Lancaster's gun turrets.

Jimmy doesn't have a phone. He prefers to call us (every Sunday evening, at 7.30 sharp) from the public box at the end of his street. This being the case I had no choice but to surprise him with my visit. His night-watchman stints aside, like me, during the day, he works where he lives. I often think of him stretching canvases and washing his brushes in the brick-backed city while

I market my pump components a green belt and half a world away.

I hadn't envisaged that he might not be in, but he wasn't, so I'd retreated to the Kite to wait. It's a working-man's pub, full of cement-dusted boots, football shirts and hard swearing. For all their false *grit* the TV soaps Jennifer's mother was addicted to remain unrealistic in their inability to reflect the true, casual violence of such conversation. I took off my quilted anorak at the door and, folding it over my arm, walked slowly to the Gents. It's not that the place made me feel frail, just unusually conscious that I didn't want to draw attention to myself by, say, missing my footing (the swirling carpet seemed designed to obscure the steps). The landlady wore a lot of jewellery and a top that revealed her doughy midriff. Most of her clientele had shaven heads.

It upset me when Jimmy cut off all his hair. Losing my own, I found consolation in his blond shock. It grew that way when he was small, giving him a sudden ungovernable look. Still, I'm used to his shorn appearance now. I left my pint half full on seeing the back of Jimmy's head float past the window en route to his studio-digs.

'Wait up, son!'

'Dad. Dad! Come in. Give me your . . . This is great! But milk, milk—'

'It's OK, I'm not thirsty. Let me look at you.'

He stopped on the landing, his face darkening. 'You're *here*. There's nothing wrong, is there?'

'Not at all, no.'

'Great. Good.' Immediate, trusting relief. 'But milk, tea. Sit down! I'll be back in a minute.'

With this he raced back down the stairs. Despite his invitation there was nowhere immediately available to sit. I considered moving some of the heaped newspapers, magazines, books and jottings from one of the kitchen chairs, but thought better of it: stringent order often lurks in Jimmy's chaos. Standing, then, I looked about me, at the unmade single bed pushed up against the near wall, at the galley kitchen buried in dirty crockery, at the paperback towers squint against exposed brick walls (Felix's pebble Pizza flashed through my mind), and at the rafters hung with clothes and un-expected model aircraft and strings of what looked like conkers, or dried fruit. Down towards the vaulted work-space end stood tabletops cluttered with oil paint tubes and jars of up-thrust brushes and palette knives and rolls of underlay and canvas and strips of pine and tins of glue and resin. And, propped against the enormous far wall on milk crates, there were four door-sized grey canvases cut with faint lines showing . . . nothing, or at least nothing that I could be sure of. I sighed, breathed in. There was a pleasing smell of turpentine. The kitchen I could help with. I emptied the sink of coffee cups and was washing up when he returned.

'Leave that, leave that. Come and look at this.'

He threw the milk carton on to the bed, reached beneath it, withdrew a tin chest brimming with loose-leaf papers, rummaged through them and came up with a bundle which he thrust at me. There being no tea towel, I dried my hands on my trouser legs. The drawings were close-ups of military airplanes. Among them I recognised a sketch of a Lancaster's distinctive twin-finned tail. The boy's prescience has always been uncanny. My first thought was that Jimmy had somehow got hold of a copy of Dad's journal, too: fear of which prospect made it hard for me to speak. Thankfully, he filled in his own gap.

'Funeral really got to me. Started me thinking about how Grandad took us to the Air Force Museum at Hendon. I dug these out. I'm going to paint something from them, to honour him, I think.'

I glanced towards the far end of the loft. 'Will we be able to . . . tell what's in these new paintings when they're finished?'

'Dad!' He clapped his hands together and winked. Until he was thirteen both his eyes were green. Then a playground fight turned one of them brown. He swore he'd been hurt in a games accident, but Freddie's hand–eye coordination came to him through me (Robert and Pearl missed out) and I didn't need his form teacher to tell me that a fist was the culprit, not a cricket ball he'd missed. Children abhor difference. Most adults do too, come to think of it. Jimmy has never knowingly been guilty of conspiring to fit in. I'm ashamed to admit that part of me sympathised with whoever had had the urge to knock the strange corners off him back then, but by far the larger part had to hold myself back from turning up at the school gates and walloping seven kinds of hell from the first bully-shaped kid to come through them. He'd winked his green eye. Now was time to make amends.

74

'Your show,' I said.

'Which one?'

'You know the one. The big one.'

'Battleships?'

'Yes.'

'What about it?'

'That journalist.' This was new ground. Family lore maintained that the review I was referring to had never existed.

'Oh, that!'

'His name,' I fought out. 'The paper he writes for. Who? Which one was it?'

'Battleships,' repeated Jimmy. 'It's a while since I thought about them.'

'Yes, well.'

He took the drawings from me, flicked through them, handed one back – showing what looked like the underside of a wing in close-up – and flung the rest on to the bed. 'Rivets,' he said. 'Bare metal. Inside and out. Not a soft surface anywhere.'

I could probably have retrieved the article from the Internet; in turning to Jimmy for the details I was seeking his consent before confronting the man. Yet as my son skittered sideways (snatching the drawing from me, jumping to root in a cupboard for tea-bags, bounding back to the bed to retrieve the milk) I decided I did not need his permission at all. Freddie's journal applauds a 'press on' attitude which holds fast at least: as Jimmy handed me my tea (with the tea-bag, keel up, still partly submerged) I resolved to take steps on his behalf come what may.

'Son, that man poleaxed your career.'

Jimmy sipped from his cup; then, with that familiar slow blink of his, brought his attention to bear. 'Look around you. New work. I'm still here.'

'Yes, but not in Dover Street. The gallery dropped you because of what he wrote.'

'Ah, no. Can't blame him for that. They could have weathered the storm.'

'That's too even-handed a view.'

He laughed. 'Earth to Dad. Come in. This doesn't sound like you!'

'He lied about your paintings, ridiculed you with misquotations. Not a thought for the consequences. In any other profession . . .' I began, then pulled up short, sensing that what I was about to say wasn't true.

'In the art business any attention is better than none, Dad.'

My knee had begun to ache. I must have glanced around for somewhere to sit down. Jimmy picked up the nearest chair and summarily tipped its contents – bills and books – on to the bed. One of the paperbacks flopped broken-winged to the floor. I sat down gratefully on the chair and looked at my feet.

'Jimmy, these airplane pictures. Will there be a new exhibition?'

'I'll show them, of course.'

I looked up hopefully. 'You'll approach Peterson again?'

He laughed. 'Oh no. Here. For friends and family, like the last lot. Only this time I'll tidy the place, too, I promise.'

I looked back down. The fallen book was *The Rebel* by Albert Camus. I picked it up and stared at its cover, astonished.

Jimmy said, 'You know there's litttle point me going near a commercial gallery again. And anyway, I don't need to. The security-guard money keeps me in bread and materials.'

I looked at the hands clasped in his lap. They were flecked with grey paint.

'He can't unwrite his nonsense,' Jimmy said.

'I know that.' I shook my head.

Jimmy picked a pencil from the floor and took Camus from my hand. Though the least predictable of my children, and the least comfortable with physical affection, he's the most intuitive, and the one I most often ache to hug. He began writing inside the book's cover, reciting as he did: 'Bill H. Marshall. H for Harold. Freelance critic, wrote mostly for *Frieze* magazine, though the article you read was in the *Financial Times*, and now he mostly does fluffy op-ed stuff for the *Independent on Sunday*. His card showed a mobile number – 0798 1518206 – and the following address . . .'

I still wonder whether, with his gift for recall, art is the best career path for Jimmy to have chosen to tread.

7

'What is it that *you* do, exactly, Mr Brinkman?'
'That's not relevant.'

'Oh, but it is. What do you do?'

'I run a business selling machine components. Valves, pumps and the like.'

'Right, then, machines. And would you think it appropriate for *me* to advise *you* on, say, the proper way to market a combine harvester?'

'I don't sell that kind of thing.'

'You're missing my point.'

'No, no. I'm not.'

He was bigger than I had anticipated, and built like a prop forward, not my mental picture of an art critic at all. I had been hoping that surprising the man on his doorstep would put him on the back foot, but to his credit he appeared to be taking the confrontation in his stride.

'Your son's . . . paintings . . . held no appeal for me. I said so in print. That is my job.'

'Your article was headed "Faux Naïve Fakes by a Blue Peter Freak".'

'The sub's choice, not mine, but I stand by it.'

'You attacked Jimmy, not his work.'

'He was *copying* the style and subject matter of Alfred Wallis. Pointless detail, distorted perspectives, deliberately clumsy execution. The similarity was too great to overlook. Incidentally, I'm no fan of the originals, either.'

'But Jimmy's work *was* original. I looked into this Wallis character after you ran your piece. He painted fishing boats, not battleships.'

Bill H. Marshall huffed. 'I'm afraid,' he said, 'I don't have time to debate this now. You have my address, why not put your views in correspondence?'

'I'm right, though, aren't I? It wasn't the paintings. You took against Jimmy because of what he said about winning a Blue Peter badge.'

'Only because the statement was puerile, indicative of a gimmicky, facetious attitude reflected in his art.'

'But you're wrong. He meant it. That's what got him started. It was seeing his Houses of Parliament drawings on television that made him want to paint.'

'Listen, Mr Brinkman. I'm sorry if your son was affected by what I wrote. But sooner or later he's going to have to accept that a facility for accurately reproducing the number of portholes, anchors, gun turrets and whatnot on a battleship, in paint, amounts to nothing in the world of fine art.'

'But neither should that talent disqualify a painter from serious consideration. He was doing well. A prize in his final-year show, gallery representation, that Swiss collector buying his last year's work. You wrote an unfair appraisal. At such a crucial, fragile moment in his career. You accused him of *plagiarism*. It wasn't true, but it stuck.'

'Well, I'm sorry. Even—'

'*Influence*, you should have said. Or *allusion*. *Homage*, even. I know the vocabulary! I've thought about it long enough!'

'Even if—'

'But "Emerging Artist I Don't Much Care for Paints Pictures Which Echo the Work of an Established Great I Don't Much Like Either" isn't as big a story, is it?'

Bill H. Marshall took a step back into his hallway. He was wearing a cycling clip around one ankle. It undermined him, emphasising as it did the extraordinary size of his feet. My blood was up after my visit to Jimmy: I'd immediately plugged the address he'd written beneath Albert Camus's roguish head-shot into the Audi's satellite navigation system. It's a fabulous tool, the sat-nav! Bill H. Marshall also lived in West London, it turned out, though Chelsea is farther from Acton Central than the six or seven crow-flown miles between the two boroughs would suggest. The houses here weren't painted so much as iced; the wrought-iron railings around the square had the wet shine of narwhal spikes. During the war many of those old railings were ripped out for use by the armament industry – in guns, tanks, aircraft and the like. Now, I couldn't help noticing, a parking attendant was xylophoning her hand across the gleaming metalwork as she advanced along the edge of the square. My pulse was fizzing.

'I'm not about to retract what I wrote,' the journalist explained.

'No.'

'Then what is it that you want?'

'Give me a chance,' I said, 'and I'll explain.'

On descending the newspaperman's front steps I plugged 'Tithe Barn' into the sat-nav and readied myself to follow its laconic instructions. I'd only turned my back for five minutes, yet something about the windscreen had altered for the worse. Not bird shit (though I had parked beneath overhanging branches) but, inevitably, a parking ticket. I undid my seat belt, peeled the plastic envelope from the glass, stuck it to the nearest railing and set off on my automated route home.

Under way, I decided to call Robert. The car has a hands-free phone. My eldest son's office had a Robert-free desk that afternoon too, so I spoke to his secretary again. Her talking-slowly-to-an-old-person voice informed me jarringly (I couldn't locate the speaker volume fast enough) that since the rest of Robert's day was 'client-corralled' I should not wait up for him to return my call. Maybe her imagined version of my life – the dream that one day she too will nap through the day and go to bed early – keeps her going. Why disappoint? I left a log-fire-and-teacakes pause before saying 'Thank you, dear,' and ringing off.

Confronting the cultural commentator had a liberating effect. No parking ticket could undo my elation; in fact its insignificance helped. How the man would respond to my suggestion was anybody's guess, but having done something about Jimmy's situation buoyed my spirits. I sat in peristalsis-slow traffic for an hour and a half, enjoying the cocoon of surround-sound, climate control and sophisticated dashboard lights, and answered cheerfully when Jennifer called.

'Where are you?' were her first words.

'Hello, love. I'm in the car.'

'Doing what?'

'I popped up to see Jimmy.'

'Jimmy? On a Tuesday? Why on earth?'

Laughing, I axed my search for an excuse. 'Do I need a reason? He's my son.'

'Well. What an odd thing to say!'

'How about you, Jennifer? What have *you* been up to this fine autumn afternoon, anyway?'

'Golf,' she emphasised. It was as if I could hear her lips pursing. The defensive tightness in her voice persisted as she went on. 'You know that. Why are you acting so strange?'

'Happy, not strange! You called, I'm pleased. What was it you wanted to say?'

'Oh, yes.' The fine blonde hairs on her upper lip would be settling back down now, as she regained safe ground. 'Our milk. Have you been feeding it to your dog?'

'No.'

'Well, we've run out again, or we're about to, anyway. There's enough for my tea but we'll need more for breakfast. Pick some up on your way home, will you?'

The dog line was a poor attempt to deflect attention from the fact that she'd forgotten to run this errand herself. She passes near the shop on the way to the golf club. I let it pass. 'Of course, love.' I said 'No problem, none at all.'

★　　★　　★

The supermarket – more properly hypermarket, since that word exists – was built twelve years ago in a new development on the near side of town. As competition dictates, the shop is extraordinarily well stocked with fresh and exotic produce: kumquats to swordfish fillets, it's all on those labyrinthine shelves. Despite this obvious advance, Pearl berated us for buying our supplies there from the start, saying that doing so made us complicit in the murder of local shopkeepers. I had little sympathy with her view: the mini-markets, grocers and butchers she was referring to were dowdy, overpriced places with restrictive opening hours, and using them, for us, meant driving right into town. But more recently certain things about the hypermarket have started to annoy me.

I noticed them afresh today.

For a start, where once I swept uninterrupted into the car park, I now had to slow down to negotiate a ticket barrier, despite the fact that, as ever, most of the thousand or so spaces surrounding the shop stood empty. And once inside, slogging past the deli counter en route to the dairy sector, I was reminded of something I heard recently on Radio 4 about how the milk fridges in these shops are always placed at the point farthest away from the entrance, to tempt you to buy a slab of Argentine beef or crate of Häagen Dazs to go with your cup of tea. To defend my good mood I forced a smile at the cynicism of this ploy as I selected my pint of milk, and I kept the smile in place for the trek back through the aisles to one of only two attended registers in the row of thirty checkout tills. Even when, pausing before a bank of stationery, I considered that the only reason we need to pick up our own milk these days is because the post office in St Clare (and its attendant paper and milk rounds) shut down last Christmas, I doused my annoyance and made a mental note to enjoy the experience of telling Pearl she'd been right all along.

'Just that?' The checkout girl enquired in a glossy accent.

'Yes, thank you.'

'A pint of milk.'

'Yes.'

'You parked outside, though, am I right?' She cocked her head, perching on her stool with the poise of a ballerina. Clearly a drama student of some sort, perhaps researching a role.

'I did.'

'But you realise there's a three-pound fee for parking if you spend less than ten pounds in the shop.'

'I . . . no. I didn't.' (Less risk of senility here than an honest 'I forgot'.)

'Want to reconsider?'

Part of me did not. But paying £3.53 for a pint of milk would be madness, not resistance. Added to which, the girl's bearing was so self-assured, so actorly in fact, that I had an absurd fear we were perhaps being filmed. Summoning all my nonchalance, I managed to laugh and say, 'Good point, hold on a second,' before turning back into the shop.

I retreated to the baby food aisle to take stock. Muzak, which had washed over me unnoticed until now, pulsed disingenuously from above. I was determined not to

84

buy anything I didn't need. Fizzy water, I thought, we'd always get through that. Jennifer fell to the addiction first, but I'm as hooked as she is now. The beverages aisle (what's wrong with 'drinks'?) lay back up by the dairy sector. Once there again I discovered, happily, a special offer on the 'own brand' (a contradiction, surely?) we favour. Nineteen pence per two-litre bottle. A swift calculation sent me, grin still fixed, back to the shop's entrance in search of a trolley.

'Sir?'

A security boy in a maroon polyester suit barred my way.

'Trolley. I'm just fetching—'

'And have you paid for that produce in arrears?'

'In arrears? I don't understand.'

'Have you purchased the milk prior to exiting?'

'Not yet. I will, though. I just need a trolley.'

'For a pint of milk, sir?' The boy obviously had his eye on a job with the force. 'If you don't mind my saying, that doesn't quite add up.'

'You hold it!' I suggested, thrusting the milk into his stomach. He avoided it with a matador's swerve.

'I'm afraid I can't. Not while I'm on duty.'

A row of trolleys glinted at me outside in the sodium glow. Very slowly I said, 'Right, then, I'll just put it down here, at your feet, until I've got a trolley.'

As the boy struggled for a way of ordering me to pick the milk up and return it to the other end of the shop, one of his hands gave him away by reaching up to finger the acne on his forehead. I winked at him and stepped outside.

The trolleys were jammed together. I tugged hard, but the nearest one wouldn't separate from the pack. Looking more closely at the problem, I saw that this was a deliberate ploy. Before the shop would trust me with a trolley I had first to free it from its chain-linked brethren with a (returnable) one-pound coin. I turned out my pockets: a wallet full of credit cards, but no change. Ring-road hum blurred the tinny forecourt speakers. We were a mile from the nearest housing estate and three from the town centre: anyone determined enough to steal a shopping trolley deserved one, in my opinion. I would have driven home there and then (Freddie: 'abandon aircraft . . . we're going down') but for the new parking fee. Instead I turned out the Audi's glove compartment and map pockets and came up with a pound in loose silver. The third shopper I accosted exchanged this bounty for a single coin. With priestly serenity I unshackled a trolley and, after picking up my pint of milk at the door, set off for the water again.

Was serenity resistance? I paused beside a cliff of cat biscuits and decided not. Protest, however pointless, was the point. I loaded my trolley with a hundred litres of sparkling hill-water, then waited in line for my turn with the platinum checkout girl. Only as she finished scanning the bottles of water (unblinkingly composed from one through fifty) did I realise that the answer was staring me in the face. There, alongside the Thomas the Tank Engine lollipops and romantic paperbacks and bottles of knockdown wine – aimed at toddlers, divorcees and alcoholics respectively – stood a rack of batteries, light-bulbs and whatnot: bait cast for unsuspecting dads.

The girl smiled. 'Ten pounds four pence.'

'And this, please.' I grinned back, handing her a packet of superglue from the rack.

'Of course. Thirteen pounds three.'

The smile she gave me as I left proved my risked compliment worthwhile. 'Hang in there,' I chanced. 'You'll make it big, mark my words!'

I crabbed my fizzy water bottles across the sloping tarmac field and loaded them into the Audi's boot. The milk I put on the passenger seat. From the footwell beneath it I retrieved the cap I'd worn during my swimming-pool maintenance escapade. I worked the superglue tube free of its pointless packaging and broke open the spout. Then, with the cap's peak pulled down low, I rattled back to the forecourt and stabbed my cart into the open mouth of a chain of thirty or so empty ones in the designated bay there. The muzak egged me on. I inserted the trolley's security key into the lock of the one sheathing it and retrieved my pound coin. And after that, working methodically, I aimed a squirt of glue into the trolley's lock, and the lock of the next one, and the lock of each and every trolley in the line.

The genius of superglue! Cyanoacrylate's power of instant bonding. Midwifes, apparently, have been known to use the stuff instead of sutures. My criticism of its packaging was perhaps harsh: even with the extra card-board there is not enough space to spell out the possible uses, sabotage included, for this highly effective stuff.

Once again, nobody thought to accost me as I worked.

8

I walked the dog when I got home. Since launching himself at Fira that morning he'd done his time, curled on a travel rug I'd laid out for him on the office floor. Travel rugs, like thermos flasks, toolboxes and flashlights, will last a lifetime if you look after them. As the dog stretched and yawned (what a mouth!) I realised the tartan blanket he'd slept on was the same one I'd flapped in the sun before proposing to Jennifer, all those years ago.

Dusk conceded defeat to night as we walked, stars emphasising the fact, needling as they did through fast-moving clouds. My favourite route starts out over the paddock gate and follows a footpath up to the village, then returns on the other side of the road, cutting along a path that hugs the mile-long hawthorn hedge bordering Johnson's field. Never mind the dark, I could savour this loop blindfold if need be. Spongebob, a black shape sniffing in and out of the hedgerow, appeared to be enjoying it as well. Spongebob, I thought. As with any name, it becomes its owner in time. I had called him that to myself, momentarily numb to the daftness of the word. Experimenting, I confirmed a suspicion: the dog ignored plain Bob but raised his head when properly addressed. Why part him from Peckham entirely? The flip side of duty is conformity, fear of standing out. Vanity — what other reason did I have for wanting to rebrand my dog? — was worth resisting, too.

I dried the dog's feet in the utility room using the towel Jennifer keeps there to wipe down her golf clubs. It was clean. So would Jennifer be shortly; pipes ticking and gurgling above my head confirmed she was running another of her marathon baths. My nose twitched. Impossible to smell from that distance, I know, but Pavlovian instinct told me she'd have the scented candles and oils out again, fumigating the bathroom, landing and — if the door wasn't shut — our bedroom as well. 'Soap, Spongebob,' I told the dog. 'That's what I miss. Imperial Leather preferably, in bars.'

Camus poked from a pocket as I hung my coat on the hook. I decided to take him and Spongebob into the den. Why not? I felt closer to Jimmy than I had done in years that evening, and he evidently enjoyed the Frenchman's writings. It being a Tuesday, I knew Jennifer would commandeer the lounge later for an evening with her celebrity chefs. I admire the spirit with which she watches those programmes (collaboratively: she could give those boys a tip or two, given the chance) but jerky camerawork or not they send me to sleep. Having settled the dog down I found myself pouring two glasses of Lindeman's

Reserve. One for me, one for Spongebob, or at least to soften Jennifer's attitude towards him, here in the house. The bathroom door eased open when I knocked and immediately I regretted performing such a kindness with ulterior intent. Never mind the aromatherapeutic fog, or what it was supposed to conceal, the sight of Jennifer, candlelit, encased in bubbles but for her protruding knees, shoulders and face, thawed me.

'I thought you might—'

'Oh, thank you, thanks.'

I lowered the glass to the floor. From this angle it appeared that Jennifer was set in protective polystyrene cladding. I still hold my wife as she sleeps, from time to time. The duvet, ceiling and roof over us are like those bubbles: inadequate protection from the rushing night above.

I've mentioned Jimmy's uncanny prescience before. Half an hour after starting on Camus I had turned back to the cover photograph and was staring at it, searching for a spark of recognition in the philosopher–goalkeeper's soulful eyes. Perhaps the pleasurable wholeness of a dog at my feet had quietened my cynicism. That, or the wine. Either way, chunks of *The Rebel*'s introduction read like a manifesto, aimed at me, Harry Brinkman, in this, *my* time.

An awakening of conscience, no matter how confused it may be, develops from any act of rebellion and is represented by the sudden realization that something exists with which the rebel can identify himself — even if only for a moment.

Something or some things; he was on the right track.

Up to now this identification was never fully realized. Previous to his insurrection, the slave accepted all the demands made upon him. He even very often took orders, without reacting against them, which were considerably more offensive to him than the one at which he baulked.

Orders. Freddie, my inheritance. This was the stuff.

He was patient and though, perhaps, he protested inwardly, he was obviously more careful of his own immediate interests — in that he kept quiet — than aware of his own rights. But with loss of patience — with impatience — begins a reaction which can extend to everything that he accepted up to this moment, and which is almost always retroactive.

The spirit of scholarship had me up and looking in the Collins dictionary for a definition of *retroactive*. It meant what I thought. Redressing past imbalances. Encouraged, I took another slug of wine and read on.

Immediately the slave refuses to obey the humiliating orders of his master, he rejects the condition of slavery.

Better and better.

Having previously been willing to compromise the slave adopts an attitude of All or Nothing.

And better and . . .

Better to die on one's feet than live on one's knees.

And . . .

I came to, smelling sausages. 'Three G Special', I think: grouse, Gruyère, Grand Marnier. That these are my favourite variety was either a mighty coincidence or evidence of reciprocated kindness. Jennifer put the tray down beside me and returned to the kitchen the long way – around the back of the sofa – so as to avoid disturbing Spongebob. This also appeared considerate, until I recalled how she dealt with the unwanted appearance of the Gutersons at Agua Azul in 1984, by ignoring them entirely, insisting we forge on with our family holiday as if these near-neighbours were not there.

We ate separately. I couldn't tell whether the decision was mine or Jennifer's. Bringing me a tray in the den raised the assumption we'd be eating there, but she didn't come back. Then again, neither did I follow her through to the lounge. Might she think I was pointedly siding with Spongebob? Not wanting to implicate him in this way, when her cutlery stopped tinkling I retrieved Jennifer's spent tray.

'Coffee?'

She shifted in her chair.

'No, no,' I said. 'Stay put. I'll wash up.'

Nodding her thanks, she craned farther sideways, intent on keeping Gordon Ramsay in view.

Spongebob, his claws clicking pleasingly on the flagstones, trotted through to the kitchen with me. He'd not accompanied me into the lounge: might he instinctively have been keeping out of Jennifer's way? I knelt down with an uneaten end of sausage and fed it to the dog. Gentle when taking it from my hand, he then dropped the scrap to the floor, snapped it up a second time, and choked it back wolfishly.

I washed up. Returning our cutlery to its tray, I was tempted to check who'd replied to Jennifer's party invitations. She'd definitely be keeping a list. Recognising this urge – to head off the unexpected – as a trait of Freddie's, I resisted it. He hated surprises. The announcement that he'd won the tennis club raffle back in '76 made him flinch and bite his lip, as if – come to think of it – he feared he might forget himself in the moment and let something slip. I did not open Jennifer's drawer. At least some of the shock I'd feel on entering the party – *you're* here, and *you!* – would be real, never mind what it would cost me to feign (and pay for) the rest.

In extreme times money loses its significance. Consider Freddie, on the day of his first live operation. He blithely lost four months' wages to Pilot Officer Lou Weaver playing a game of whist. *Better luck next time, eh!* his journal notes. This and the reference to 'pre-match nerves' are the only indications of Freddie's scrambled state. My entire life I never knew the man to gamble his money, but that day on the frozen Fens, having seen his crew listed on the ops board, waiting in the shabby officers' mess (on a seat made from a plank lain across two bomb-fin cases) to find out the target, and no doubt wondering whether he would make it back in one piece, money understandably lost its meaning.

That first raid was one of the worst. Briefed to attack the heavily defended dockyard at Emden, Freddie spent three dark hours droning through patchy cloud over the North Sea, only to have it break up entirely over the target, revealing a curtain of search-lights, tracer hosing heavenward, the thunderous flash of heavy flak above and below. With four HE 500-pound bombs aboard, his Hampden – call-sign L-Lion – had a ceiling of 12,000 feet and couldn't manage more than 140 knots: for all Freddie's gallant weaving they flew into this barrage the hard way: slow and low. He remembers sliding the cockpit window back: if hit, he wanted be able to bale out quickly. Then he closed it again, in part because of the knifing cold but also, he says, because the sheet of plexiglas felt like protection against the flak. A heavy shell made immediate nonsense of this idea, holing the cockpit as it burst above L-Lion's nose. Shrapnel took a chunk out of Freddie's left eyebrow (it never grew back). The next explosion slammed the plane sideways 'like a child's toy stubbed across the nursery floor'. In disbelief – that he wasn't more badly hurt, and that his controls were still responsive – Freddie fought the Hampden back on to the straight and level and made it to the aiming point without further incident, then dived and turned out to sea. Aside from stating that the flight back was 'fearfully cold,' the rest of his entry for that trip describes only how his bomb aimer – F/S 'Rabbit' Sharples, a twenty-year-old electrician from Deptford, with a passion for cycling and a fiancée named Edith – crabbed forward from his position and insisted on opening the medical kit to attend to Freddie's face. Elastoplast of the 1940s lost its adhesiveness at low temperature, apparently, but Rabbit would not be put off. He buried the strips in his armpit until they were warm enough to stick.

The journal does not report whether L-Lion's payload hit the docks or not, but the pattern of Freddie's war was established. For proceeding to the target injured and bringing his crew home safely he was immediately honoured with a Distinguished Flying Cross, *gong*, in the parlance, or DFC. He mentions this, of course, but dwells longer on how, at an impromptu officers versus NCOs spring sports day held the following week (how many of them would see high summer?), he smashed his personal best for the javelin with a throw of 129½ feet.

The next time Fira came to clean she parked her bicycle at the end of the drive, beneath the shedding horse-chestnut tree. I heard her footsteps outside and looked up through the office window just as she glanced through it. We exchanged an awkward wave.

I'd been doing some thinking about Fira, and about

what I might do to help her with her asylum case. The Internet lacks sat-nav's conclusiveness: after trawling the immigration advice sites I understood there were instruments to fly by but not how to read them, not how to land Fira on English soil. As Robert had suspected, she needed a lawyer to pilot her through the haze. Lawyers are expensive. I'd just lost two-thirds of my pension, had no idea how I was going to see myself through my remaining days. And my wife, spurred on by love and guilt, was arranging an expensive party I did not want, accelerating us over the cliff.

Though I'd played by the rules the game had changed. Following directions led nowhere safe.

Looked at from Camus's point of view, this uncertainty was liberating.

Stuff prudence now.

Fira takes a fifteen-minute coffee break at eleven o'clock, on the dot. At five to the hour Spongebob and I slunk inside to boil the kettle. When she appeared in the kitchen, her bare arms glowing and a sheen across her forehead – it can be physical work, cleaning – the ground beans were billowing in the cafetière.

'Oh, hello.' I looked from the pot to her and back again. 'I've made some good stuff. Would you like a cup?'

Her eyes were as liquid black as the coffee. She turned them on the dog, dropped down to his level and said, 'Yes.'

'Listen, Fira.'

'How are you, Spun Bob?' the girl asked.

'I've been meaning to say. That letter, the character

reference. Did it do any good? Are the immigration authorities' (this phrase tasted censorious on my tongue) 'still giving you a hard time?'

'Have you attacked anything else?' She lifted the dog's muzzle firmly and looked him in the eyes. He blinked: nervous or bashful, I couldn't tell.

'Spongebob,' I explained. 'With a G.'

'No. It did not do any good.'

'What's the situation, exactly?'

'He has yellow teeth.'

More pompous still: 'With the Home Office?'

She shrugged. Her long fingers dug into Spongebob's sleek neck.

'It matters to us, Fira,' I heard myself saying. 'We're very happy with your work here.'

She pushed her hair from her face. Faint blue veins watermarked the luminous back of her wrist. With her hair held like that the sweep of her brow was visible, a gentle yet provocative widow's peak.

'And I like to work here.' She turned back to Spongebob, gripped his muzzle again and shook his head from side to side. 'Grrr!' she said.

At a loss, I heard myself babble, 'You're very confident with him, all things considered.'

Spongebob's jaw flopped open as she let it go and his tongue dropped happily out of the side of his mouth. With her middle knuckle Fira rubbed the top of the dog's square head, then tapped him once between the eyes. Quite hard. His smile didn't change but he blinked again.

'You don't scare me,' she told the dog, then returned

her gaze to me. 'My daddy trained bears for Chechen State Circus.'

'Gosh. Really?'

'No,' she replied flatly. 'He was university lecturer at the State University. But he did have a dog.'

I laughed. 'Of course.' She was looking at me so evenly I felt transparent. To avoid her reading my deeper thoughts I said the first thing that came into my mind: 'What was his subject?' then qualified myself with, 'Your father's, I mean, obviously.'

Still looking through me: 'Pedagogics.'

'I see, OK.' Any moment now I'd be asking her what that meant. A diversion necessary, I focused on the cafetière, pushing down on its handle with way too much force. A loop of pressurised coffee spat from the V in the cafetière's glass rim. *Widow's peak* and *hosing tracer,* I thought, as the scalding wetness hit my foot. I gave an involuntary hop. We both looked down, at a black island melting into the orange-and-lime Goretex of my trainer top.

'Quick,' she said, motioning for me to take the ridiculous shoe off.

'No, no. It's fine. These old—'

'Now!' She snapped her fingers, a forthright, clear sound that somehow summed her up.

In the time it took me to prise the trainer off and hand it to her she'd wiped the spill from the floor and countertop. Now she ran the shoe under the tap, her mesmerising wrists and fingers turning and dabbing with a cloth. My foot pulsed inside its damp sock. Fearing she might tell me to strip that off next — my feet are ugly, lumpen things – I poured the coffee and retreated to the fridge for milk.

'My appeal is for December thirteenth,' she said, as I handed her a mug. 'The Advice Centre says your letter is no use since this is an illegal job. If the appeal fails they will deport me to Chechnya. Your shoe,' she said, nodding at the trainer, 'will not stain.'

Jennifer took Fira on. I wasn't sure of the details, hadn't asked. No matter how determinedly I'd turned this blind eye, news that I was breaking the law would ordinarily have made me spit my drink out. Muscle memory made me pause today, mug to my lips, then I realised why and took a leisurely swig.

'This Advice Centre. Do they sort out representation for you at hearings?'

'I think so. A boy first, then a woman who was late. Last time there was another man, who could not say my name.'

'Right.' I put my shoe back on and flexed my toes inside it, galvanised. 'Short staffed, overworked, I get the picture. What we need is a proper lawyer, devoted to your case.' My chest felt rugby deep again; I went for the line. 'With your permission, Fira, I'd like to organise that for you. An expert, to help you stand your ground.'

She set her mug down slowly and said, 'No.'

'Please, please,' I began, in the wrong tone, fingers spread to fend off her gratitude, then realised she'd refused the offer, gripped air and let a third, more imploring 'Please' slip from my lips. Struggling to sound more offhand, I continued, 'No strings. I'll pay.'

In this light her eyes were North Sea grey. They narrowed in the pause that followed.

'Not out of your earnings,' I went on. 'With my own money. While we're at it, I'll have the chap look into your employment status. See if we can pull you above board. Numbers aren't Jennifer's thing. I wouldn't be surprised if she's pegged you to less than the minimum wage.'

Her eyes were fierce slits now, and her mouth had hardened, too. Had I offended her? No. Her lips hadn't set in disapproval; she was biting the bottom one to keep it from giving way. I couldn't look at her in this moment, focused instead on the top of my coffee cup, a well I'd have liked to fall into. A moment passed, in which she collected herself and I said nothing loudly. Eventually she asked, 'Why would you do this?'

'The truth is,' I began to gabble, 'I've had a bit of luck. Financially speaking, things have changed for me now. And, I mean, it's not as if I'm not already lucky, in a good position, so to speak. We're already very fortunate here.' I raised my hands. She glanced sceptically at the stencilled border that runs around the top of the kitchen wall. I went on hurriedly. 'I can't think of a better use for the money. Your situation puts ours in perspective.'

'You don't know my situation.'

'Yes, well. You're right, of course. But I suppose I think I can guess.'

'Can you?'

'You're at the mercy of banal forces beyond your control.'

Suspicion darkened her brow. 'What is this "banal"?'

I looked out of the window for help. It always surprises me how far into autumn the lawn keeps growing here. The moss-killer stains were still visible, but they appeared to be melting into the leaf-strewn grass, like espresso swirl in the froth of a cappuccino. Jennifer steams milk for coffee when we have guests she particularly wants to impress. I put my cup down next to the girl's.

'Fira. Helping you now is just something I'd like to do. For my own, selfish sake, OK. Let me, please?'

She folded one arm across her chest. The work-glow had faded; save for the graze on her arm, visible as she raised a hand to her mouth, her skin was milk-pale again. She appeared to be reaching for difficult words. The shrug of indifference that accompanied them was valiant but transparent; she sounded awkward speaking through her fingertips.

'If you like,' she said.

9

Rugby first did for my knee. I played wing-forward, or flanker, as it's called today, to club level. The position affords the worst of both worlds injury-wise: you're expected to take a close-quarter pummelling at the breakdown, then chop and be chopped in open play. Nineteen stone of Irish prop forward snapped the cruciate ligaments in my left leg back in February '79. My foot was planted in the mud at the time, while three trunk-wrapping arms held me firmly in place. The Irishman worked for a firm of shipping brokers. He torpedoed my knee from the side: it sounded like a whip cracking as the strings gave way. I made it back on to the pitch ten months later but was never the same player again.

Yet there was a try-scorer's spring in my step as I returned to the office after my chat with Fira. Touching the ball down is an unbelievable feeling. No matter how tired you are, the act of crossing the line melts the aches away. Some players, backs particularly, can't wipe the grin from their faces. To keep my journeyman's façade up, the instant I turned around from scoring I would study my teammates' expressions. Were they relaxed, relieved or resolute? There's no better time to check the barometer of a team's morale than the moment after a score.

I'd been persevering with Camus. You need a clear head – I do, at least – to follow the man's reasoning, so I'd confined myself to reading a page or two before work each day. Rebellion, he says, is ultimately a selfless act:

> The appearance of 'All or Nothing' demonstrates that rebellion, contrary to present opinion and despite the fact that it springs from everything that is most individualistic in a man, undermines the very concept of the individual . . .
>
> If he prefers to risk death to a denial of the rights that he defends, it is because he considers the latter are more important than he is. He acts, therefore, in the name of certain values which are still indeterminate but which he feels are common to himself and all men . . .
>
> Why rebel if there is nothing worth preserving in oneself? The slave asserts himself for the sake of everyone in the world when he comes to the conclusion that a command has infringed on something inside him that does not belong to him alone, but which he has in common with other men – even the man who insults and oppresses him.

I knew in my heart I would never finish the book, but was delighted to recognise Camus's point nevertheless. It struck me he could have reinforced it by mentioning team spirit, specifically the work of the rugby pack. All that crushing and straining and gauging, just to pop the ball up for someone else to run in. Never mind the offensives I'd launched for Fira and the children, my attacks on the swimming-pool ramp and shopping trolleys were public spirited, too. Jimmy often annotates the books he reads; with an HB pencil I wrote two words in the margin next to this passage. They were *rolling* and *maul*.

The phone rang as I shut the book.

'Mr Rinkman?'

'Brinkman.' I remembered who'd last made this mistake as I corrected it. 'With a B.'

The speaker took a breath. 'That's not what we have down here.'

'ICBC International, right?'

'Yes, sir. That's correct.'

Camus and Fira had put wings on my heels. 'Great,' I said quickly. 'I'm pleased you called. I want to discuss taking up one of your plans–'

The speaker cut across me. 'I'll transfer you through to Sales in a moment, sir. For now you're talking with Compliance.'

'Fine. If I could speak to the girl who called originally when we're finished,' I went on, 'I'd be grateful. Joy someone–'

'That's not going to be possible Mr Brinkman. Now, I am pleased to be able to tell you that this is a courtesy call.'

There was a pause. Either there was interference on the line or the caller was asthmatic: the receiver swelled and emptied like a seashell cupped to the ear.

'Great. As I say, what I need is to speak with–'

'Yes. I am likewise pleased to tell you that we have concluded our investigation into the representative who called you originally and that she has been disciplined accordingly.'

'What does that mean?'

'In compliance with code guidelines we have relieved her of her interface role.'

'You dismissed her?'

'This was not the woman's first infringement. As such we have fulfilled our obligation to terminate her contract, yes.'

I needed a surname. Outside, the wind flayed the last leaves from the willow tree. It wasn't interference, or asthma, but this official was a mouth-breather, definitely; the swell and hush of the sea filled my right ear. Seashore. 'Miss *Shaw*?' I heard myself say. 'Fired, because of me?'

'Shaw?'

'Joy Shaw's the girl's name, right?'

'No. This case concerns Mrs Joy Ghosh.'

'Joy Ghosh,' I repeated. 'Thanks.'

'But—'

'How do I get in touch with her?'

'But . . . I'm . . . I'm afraid' — the woman's breathing crashed louder in my ear — 'I'm not at liberty to divulge contact details. The code—'

'You fire someone on my account but refuse to put me in touch with them?'

'The code stipulates—'

'Bugger your code, woman! It's supposed to protect me, not get in my way!'

The breathing stopped with a click. I put the phone

down and immediately began trawling the Internet for the company's *portal*. What a nonsense word. As infuriatingly pointless as their refusal to put me in touch with the woman wronged on my behalf. They *fired* her! Against my wishes! Following rules written for my benefit, because she'd spoken up to save me from myself! Only resist! At least I had her name. There was a head office address here. My blood still up, I wrote Joy Ghosh a letter, with instructions for the personnel department to forward it to her home. Would it get there? I'm not a religious man but when I dropped the letter into the postbox I did so with a prayer.

There was a funeral going on in St Silas's. I parked in a residents' bay outside, next to the empty hearse. Pearl normally gives us a ticket to put on the dashboard when we visit; wanting to surprise her with the outcome of my meeting, I hadn't told her I'd be in the area today. Parking Solutions is the name the local wheel-clamping firm goes by. What a job that must be. Freezing in winter, cold-shouldered the entire year. Parking enforcers are practised at looking tough and inscrutable, but I doubt they feel the cold any less keenly than the rest of us do.

Nobody had clamped the hearse. My Audi is charcoal grey. Perhaps they'd think I was in the funeral party, too. Flowers in the boot would have helped: a motorbike made of white carnations was fixed with wire to the hearse's roof. 'Beloved Son' chrysanthemums completed the story, lying on silver rails where the coffin must have stood. I had Freddie cremated. *Dresden*, I thought, as he slid from view. No flowers: he was a war hero, not a horticulturalist. I sent a hundred pounds to the poppy fund instead.

I took a seat at the back of the church. Making sense of death, that's what religion is for. When it comes to ushering people through life's stages – christenings, weddings and funerals – the church has the market cornered. The state's attempts at marking such occasions wind up more civic than ceremonial, conjuring lino and skylights rather than ivy and tolling bells. Militant atheism like Pearl's has a leisure-centre shabbiness as well. Arrogance pokes through the curled carpet tiles of its reasonableness. Somebody was sobbing in the front pew as the speaker tried to stitch sense into the death of a son who had driven his motorcycle into a wall. The bike had symbolised Carl's free spirit, she explained, sounding unconvinced herself. I looked up from my downcast stare (deference in church has stayed with me since school) and was surprised to see that the speaker was the vicar. Reverend Frayn, a woman! Clearly, she hadn't known the boy in the casket personally. As such her 'inspiration to us all' rang hollow.

A school secretary had told me I'd be able to speak to the vicar here now; perhaps the funeral was running late. That aspect of being a priest has always struck me as contrived, the way they have to duck from joy to grief and back again in a morning's work. Unlike my new baseball cap, solemnity isn't a one-size-fits-all commodity. Men (and women) of God cannot convincingly jump-cut between such extremes.

Presumably I'd have to wait while the vicar helped

deal with the physical aspect of poor Carl's death. If St Silas's ever had a cemetery, it has long since been returfed with asphalt no-parking bays. Some cultures – I forget which, no doubt the Discovery Channel will remind me again soon – bury corpses standing up, which, if you must inter the dead, seems the obvious, space-efficient way of doing so. We sprinkled Freddie's ashes into the Thames at Wallingford. Not quite a burning gat on the Ganges, but it's a stretch of river he was fond of, full of Home Counties bird life plumped up with Waitrose picnic bread. Confusing the urn with a thermos flask, six glossy ducks swam expectant figures of eight among Freddie's ashes before they had a chance to sink.

The Reverend Frayn's eyes pointed in different directions. Not wildly so, but enough to be noticeable, enough to make me question which pupil I should focus upon when, funeral over (practicalities subcontracted, her involvement ended with the service), I introduced myself at the church door. I chose the left eye first but immediately jockeyed to the right, then thought that one seemed to be looking over my shoulder so toggled back to the left. She blinked. A long, calming blink intended, I was sure of it, to help put me at my ease. Disabled people must forever be having to accommodate other people's limitations in such ways.

'Do please call me Margaret.'

'Margaret.'

'They phoned to say a prospective parent might be popping by today. What's the name of your child?'

She pronounced *child* with an exaggerated reverence.

Lambs, mangers, stars crowded to mind. 'Oh no,' I explained. 'Felix isn't my son. Pearl is my daughter, you see. He's her son, not mine.'

Both the vicar's eyes sought the ceiling in choreographed puzzlement. 'So you're . . . the boy's . . .'

'Grandfather. That's right. He's just four. A very bright boy, loving and, well, very bright.'

'Wonderful!' she replied, with another blink. 'It's great you're taking such an interest in his education.'

I was struggling for a response to this platitude when she suggested we might talk somewhere less draughty. She ushered me through the church to a cluttered antechamber. Two dark green leather armchairs crouched unnaturally close to one another in the centre of this room, as if intent on keeping within the circumference of the threadbare rug beneath them. A child's desk burdened with ancient computer equipment stood to one side, opposite a chrome-and-black dining table piled high with boxed Tesco Cabernet Sauvignon. An image of the vicar struggling to free a shopping trolley flashed before me. There wasn't a window to look through: yellowed paint had flaked from the one wall not lined with box files. The vicar drew a blue velvet curtain across the door and repeated something about conserving heat. High above us, a strip light droned. Reverend Frayn did not take her robe off but sat down, cocked her head inquisitively, removed her shoes and began to massage her stockinged feet.

'So. Yes. My daughter, Pearl, lives at the end of this street. She wants to send her son to St Silas's.'

'Great! It is a wonderful school. But,' she shook her

head sadly, 'very oversubscribed.' Over the vicar's shoulder the computer screensaver scrolled: *And he is before all things, and by him all things consist. (Colossians 1.17).* She left off kneading her toes for a moment and spread her fingers wide. 'I very much look forward to welcoming her here in any case.'

'That's the thing.' Perhaps because of the vicar's eyes, rolling my own – *kids, what can you do!* – seemed a self-conscious act. 'I'm afraid Pearl's not really a church-goer.'

The vicar clasped her hands on her lap. 'Ours is a faith school. The ethos is Christian. Church of England, Voluntary Assisted. She understands what that means?'

'Of course. Yes. She's not opposed to exposing Felix to religious teaching, ethics, discipline and whatnot, not at all. It's just that she's not sure she wants to sign up to it herself.'

'Ah.' Now the woman's default compassion was edged with pity. 'It's a partnership, though; school, church and parents all working together for the children's benefit. Christ isn't something one party can opt out of, I'm afraid!'

The screensaver: *My little children, let us not love in word, neither in tongue; but in deed and in truth. (1 John 3.18).*

'The school encourages all comers to apply, though. That's what the website says. Doesn't it?'

Reverend Frayn slow-blinked at me again and murmured, 'Of course. Do ensure Pearl reads the entrance criteria in full, though. Maintaining the school's Christian ethos is our overriding duty, always.'

Duty, breathed with the reverence reserved for *child* earlier, was an ill-chosen word. Freddie's journal is awash with the stuff; I grew up in the belief that hard work and prudence would be rewarded in the end. Save up and you shall be saved! Tell that to my Mutual Friend. No, duty has not served me well. The vicar had intended to mark her contradiction with piety, but only succeeded in illuminating the heart of the lie.

'Listen, this is Felix's local school. His local *state* school. Pearl wants him educated here.'

'There are plenty of non-religious schools in the borough.'

'This isn't just *a* school, it's the best school around.'

'Exactly. St Silas's is an excellent school because of its ethos.' The vicar slowed down for emphasis, eyes closed. 'Our parents, you see, are committed Christians.'

'Committed to getting their kids a good education, I'll give them that. All of them come to church here every Sunday, do they?'

'Not all of them, no. Not all the time.'

'Is it mostly when they're trying to secure a school place that they show up to polish the organ?'

She laughed. Not, as I would have expected, *I can take a joke* laughter, but a moment of genuine release, as if lifting a veil, acknowledging that we were both playing a part. I found myself laughing with her. Together we flew straight through my sleight (tracer, wide and high).

With neither eye aimed directly at me the vicar said, 'Parents can support the church in many different ways, Mr Brinkman.'

Something about this sentence was hard to grasp. I saw a parachute bloom against the stars. Airmen had a code. Although not everyone kept to it, honour dictated that when a flyer bailed out he ceased to be a target. No matter that seconds beforehand he'd been as intent on destroying your home town as you were on folding his plane into a ball of flames, the moment he jumped he was reborn. Only cowards shot up parachutists. Umbilically suspended, they were immune; a change of rules as baffling as Christmas football in no man's land or, dare I say it, legalised theft from a pension fund paid into for thirty years.

'But hold on,' I said. 'Those other schools, the non-religious ones, they're open to children of religious parents too, aren't they?'

'As far as I know faith is not one of their entrance criteria.'

Screensaver: *If thou canst, believe. All things are possible to him that believeth. (Mark 9.23).*

'Which means children of non-churchgoing parents are discriminated against in half the borough's schools. State schools. Funded by taxes we all pay.'

'Discrimination is a strong word.'

'Which word would you use?'

The vicar made a spire of her fingers and pushed at her plump lower lip. Skewed eye aside, she wasn't an unattractive woman; now she'd warmed up her skin had a crisp glow reminiscent of Felix's. 'Choice,' she murmured. 'Parental choice.'

'But not the child's.'

'Parents are responsible for their children,' she said simply.

'We're talking about apartheid! That's what it is. Christians in one school. Muslims in another. Brown kids on this bus, white ones on that.' I spoke Pearl's words loudly, but as if into the wind. The vicar just beamed at me, apparently enjoying the debate.

'If you feel so strongly, shouldn't you want a *non*-faith school for Felix?'

'Of course we should, in theory. But you can't hang a child by your own principles. This is his education we're talking about. The truth is that the other schools around here are for the immigrants. English as a third language, that sort of thing.' I paused; in opposing the system's unfairness I'd somehow admitted a prejudice of my own. As Reverend Frayn pressed the steeple of her fingers into her lips again, the screensaver-strip-light intoned: *And the Lord added to the Church daily such as should be saved. (Acts 2.47).* Clawing back to the high ground I said, 'This religious discrimination hurts immigrants most of all. It prevents true integration. Without a concerned Christian grandfather they're ghettoised into failing schools; they haven't a hope.'

'Christians come from all walks of life,' the vicar said. 'And for those who open their hearts there is *always* hope.'

Our chairs were too close together for me to stretch my aching leg. She'd rehearsed these arguments to eternity: my words just slid to the floor like raindrops off a feathered back. I thought of webbed feet stirring Freddie's ashes and said, 'Rigged, that's what it is,' more to myself than her.

'The school's entrance procedure is the law of the

land, Mr Brinkman. I also believe it to be God's will. Even if I wanted to make an exception, my hands are tied.'

'But . . . but . . . !' The woman's chop-logic raked over me, a studded boot. To stop myself committing a retaliatory foul I stared at the boxed wine. Obviously it was for communion. Blood of Christ, transfused in bulk. My first half-century saw Church influence drain away. That was God's final, benign gift: the reins. Yet here was the backlash of the last ten years! Vicars like this one, gatekeepers again, granted the keys to schools throughout the land. Only resist! 'But,' I said more calmly, 'as you say, for those with open hearts, there's always a way. What would Pearl have to do to make Felix eligible for the school?'

Though I may have imagined it, both the Reverend Frayn's eyes seemed to converge upon mine for the first time. 'She'd have to have him christened and attend church,' the vicar said softly, adding: '*regularly*.' Then she reached for her toes and began to knead them again. Over her shoulder, the screensaver: *And Jesus said unto him, Go thy way; thy faith hath made thee whole. (Mark 10.52)*.

'Does it have to be her?' I asked eventually.

'I'm sorry?'

'I'm a committed Christian,' I said. Then, truthfully, 'I was even confirmed. I'll bring Felix to church. I'll have the boy baptised.'

She smiled at me sympathetically. 'The child's home life must reflect Christian teaching, not just the time he spends with a grandparent.'

Since it had come to this, I lied outright: 'But he *does* live with me. Pearl works shifts. I'm retired. I'm up here looking after the boy the whole week.'

'I see.'

'So, would it work?'

She smiled. 'I'll make enquiries. But I doubt it. I certainly can't promise anything.'

Here she paused. Once again her eyes, omnisciently askew, drifted over my shoulder and fixed on separate patches of flaking wall. When she went on her voice was a notch quieter, her implicit meaning more plain.

'Despite appearances – and our premises – we are a modern, pragmatic church. As I say, there are many things a man of your apparent means can do to help us in our wider mission.' Here she looked up – to heaven, or the buzzing strip light at least – and hugged herself as if against the cold. 'Things which may well ease Felix's eligibility impasse, even make it likely an application to the school on his behalf might succeed.'

Unwilling to disappoint me, the Parking Solutions people had wheel-clamped my car. I called the *hotline* number beneath the *do not attempt to move it* wording. As ever, the chap who answered gallantly refused to speak to me until I'd given him my name, rank and number – or credit card details.

'Wait with your vehicle until the crew attends to remove the clamp,' he stipulated.

'When will that be?'

'Some time between now and four.'

'Four hours? Give them this number, can you? I'll

find a pub. I don't want to risk arrest for loitering in the street.'

'They don't use phones.'

I laughed.

His silence said, 'No, seriously.'

Some of the vicar's equanimity must have rubbed off. 'OK,' I said. 'I'll pop back at four. They'll have sorted it by then at the latest, yes?'

The man sighed, patiently. 'That won't work.'

'I don't follow.'

'They might reclamp the vehicle again before then.'

'Hold on. You're saying you'll put the clamp back on again if I'm not here when the car is released?'

'Not immediately.'

'When, then?'

'Depends when they're next in the area.'

'But they could drive a hundred yards, do a U-turn, and rob me again on their way back down the street?'

The man sighed again. He had a rich palette of sighs: this one was patient still, but faintly amused, too. 'Yes, they could clamp you twice, theoretically.'

'I have to wait with my car in the cold for the next four hours, full stop, that's what you're saying?'

'Get in it, I would. You never know, they may be along well before then.'

I looked up above the church door. Its Norman arch surround bristled with tiny wire spikes, a defence against the Devil's pigeons and their threshold-besmirching shit. If the vicar came down those steps and saw me she might think I was stalking her. Even if she noticed the clamp, there'd be the obstacle of her *bad luck* pity to

116

hurdle next time we met. I didn't want to run into Pearl, either; not until I'd worked through the implications of what the vicar had said. There wasn't a pub within sight of the car, but up past the postbox a row of local shops (*vibrant community!*) crouched in the November drizzle. Who trusts family-run electrical suppliers in this era of Dixons and Comet? I bought Spongebob a fake-bone slipper in the pet emporium next door and spent half an hour choosing a reflective cycling vest for Fira in the bike shop next to that. Given this gloom she'd need one. The last shop in the row was a hardware store. You can never have too much moss-killer. Twenty minutes of fake browsing later I found myself staring at a pack of roofing nails. Big flat heads, dagger points. The Parking Solutions van drifted past the shopfront so serenely I had no choice but to add them to my basket. Deliberately not catching a person's eye may be a good clamper tactic in general, but it worked against the Solutions employee that day. I dropped a handful of spikes behind his front offside wheel before introducing myself, and managed to sprinkle a few more under the van's rear wheels while he crouched behind the wing of my car. He was a black man with a shaven head, beautifully round, shiny as an olive. I made sure to thank him with a *no hard feelings* smile as I sped from the scene.

10

Throughout my married life Saturday evenings have carried the promise of sex. One of the advantages of the Tithe Barn (I noticed it when we first looked around the place) is that the master bedroom is separated from the others by a gallery with a door at each end. When the children were young and inclined to come searching for us these doors – with their radar hinges and Morse code squeaks – served as an excellent early-warning system. Only Jimmy ever disturbed us in the act, which isn't bad given three kids and thirty-odd conjugal years. I heeled the duvet up as fast as I could but he was already in the room, six, serious, with a vital presentation to give. 'Fruit bats,' he explained, placing his self-illustrated handout on the pillow. 'Their wings have an edge called serrated.'

'Brilliant!' I panted. 'Like a . . . like a . . . maple leaf.'

Jennifer slipped out from under me, her wetness quickly cool against my leg. 'Or golf umbrella,' she suggested.

Nowadays, of course, we could leave the doors wide open if we wanted, but the truth is, occasional Saturdays aside, over the past eighteen months they've remained purposelessly closed. Which is a shame. Our time in bed, like the Tithe Barn's joists, both bound and supported our togetherness.

Jennifer is good between the sheets. Cooking aside, sex is perhaps her strongest suit. Of the two of us, she has always led the way, set the agenda, been – whatever it really means – the more *liberated*. Which has meant that in our long marriage I've pretty much never succumbed to the temptation of unfaithfulness. Twice only, separated by eight years, and both times in the same circumstances, when away from home, travelling in the pump-and-valve business. The truth is that both encounters were a letdown. Illicit frisson aside, neither woman had Jennifer's commitment. Her attacking rhythm, hissed demands and complete present-tenseness; the way her eyes turn to slits in the moment or, afterwards, her curled contentment.

We're not twenty-five any more. I've mentioned the sag above Jennifer's elbows; my blurred reflection is duller now, framed by the leaf-veins around her eyes. But set against our peers we're not in bad shape. Jennifer nibbles at what she cooks, jogs lightly up our oak staircase, and the distinctive, amber sheen of her brown hair is still there. She's rightly proud of that miracle. Last December I remarked how, in the right light, her hair knocks fifteen years off her and a week later, while warming the Discovery, I saw the word *fifteen!* materialise in its fogging windscreen. Yet I know my sixtieth worries her more than me. Three years from now she'll face the same hurdle. We don't speak enough about what matters. Even as she has withdrawn I've not managed to explain how, although the feel of her in my arms has evolved with time, holding her is an unchanging privilege.

The day after I'd presented Parking Solutions with a problem of their own to solve, it struck me I should use the episode as a way of revealing my pension problem to Jennifer. As a 4x4 driver, her wheel-clamp wrath obviously eclipses mine. She also finds the faith I've placed in playing by the rules exasperating. So here was a twofold opportunity to get my wife back on my side, before confessing that our team had been relegated and would shortly be evicted from its ground for good.

I was returning from my Saturday afternoon swim. (Although Actalife plc hadn't rebuilt the ramp, they'd closed the poolside changing room. We men had to use a school's facility – all waist-high pegs and miniature urinals – instead.) Perhaps Jennifer would cope with the news better than I imagined. There was exercise-fizz in my blood, Saturday-hope in my thighs. If the wheel-clamp anecdote went well, I might even move on to the shopping trolleys. St Clare's go-slow chevrons strobed past. *Thank you for driving considerately.* Once again I accelerated and swerved into the middle of the road to avoid the calming measures, and was still absent-mindedly straddling the white lines as I entered the first post-village bend. A shape loomed sudden and large: the Discovery bearing down. Thank heavens for traction control! I stamped on the brakes and yanked the wheel left and all four tyres bit smartly; in a shutter-snap I was safely past. My heart, quick before, now beat faster still, hail-harsh in my chest. Jennifer's tail-light coals faded to dots and died. I brought my car carefully to a halt in the gateway of a ploughed field. A minute passed, perhaps ten. Two seagulls, luminous against the black furrows, swaggered left and right in the five-barred gloom.

I knew who I'd seen in the car with her.

But could I be sure that the glimpse I'd caught – of two faces flashing past, two rear-viewed heads silhouetted against the inky sky – had been real and not a trick of the light?

Yes, because I already suspected Jennifer was seeing somebody else. In much the same way as I suspected that the brickwork under the eaves on the Tithe Barn's gabled end wall needed repointing. The sort of suspicion that knows it is true but hopes it can unthink itself, given time. Who knew, perhaps, when next I looked, the crumbling mortar would have magically solidified again? For the time being there were no consequences to deal with: our house was watertight yet. Wasn't it?

Tears slid between my fingers and clung to my knuckles. I wiped the back of my hand on my cords and asked the seagulls: 'What the hell am I crying for?' Freddie's journal came to mind. I sobbed: a strange tumbling sound that I felt deep in my shoulder blades. Robert and Pearl and Jimmy and little Flo and Felix – oh, Felix! And vicars and critics and lawyers and pension funds and godforsaken mini-roundabouts. Freddie. And dogs, dogs in dogs' homes, the chop-look slack in their eyes, and now Jennifer. A self-pitiful current threatened to drag me down. I gripped the Audi's leather steering wheel. *Nothing is hopeless.* In my selfishness I'd cost that poor girl her job. *I have seen hell and back.* Me? Ha! Hell with a herbaceous border! Hell isn't hassle, or hardship, or heartbreak even. Hell is fear. I'd only ever glimpsed its shadow on an (exposed-stone) wall. F for fear. F for Freddie. And Fira, Fira, Fira!

Crying was a new experience. Though his journal reveals otherwise, I grew up thinking that Freddie – like Camus, I imagine – had no recourse to waterworks. The last time I cried I must still have been too young to form a reliable memory of the event. My face was soon surprisingly wet. You'd have thought my supply of tears might have dried up over the years through underuse; the idea of all that salt water standing ready to flow struck me as both marvellous and strange. For once, the glove-boxed tissues Jennifer equips us with came in handy. I wiped my face. Resistance? Pah! I'd have been doing us all a favour if I'd steered *into* the Range Rover, met it head on. Come to think of it, why didn't I find myself a nice wall to accelerate into now, and have done with the charade? A guilty shudder fell through me. I blew my nose. Then, very deliberately, I reversed the car back out into the lane and drove home.

But I didn't wait in the house for my wife's return. Spongebob provided a good excuse to take a walk. I changed into my boots, climbed the paddock fence and set off with him for the village again, in the dark.

We've done that route a number of times now, so when, as we neared the village, Spongebob's steady panting dissolved in a scattering of paws, I was not worried about him losing his way. I carried on up to the St Clare stile, expecting the dog to rejoin me on the path. But after five minutes he hadn't, so I retraced my steps, calling out his name and whistling by turns. Only then did I fully appreciate the Baltic wind that had sprung up. It whipped my calls to insignificance and, as I stood waiting, cut through my anorak (why hadn't I worn a proper coat?), pressing a cold ache into every bone. My teeth started to rattle. Gun-turret chatter. I thought of Freddie in his holed cockpit, clamped to the controls. Why didn't I just carry on, or go home? Because family lore has it that if we're split up we return to the point where we saw one another last, and wait. It worked for Jimmy in Versailles and it would prove Spongebob a Brinkman as well. High above me the moon rushed to stay in place among smoke-quick clouds. I clutched my sides and jogged woodenly on the spot, the pain in my knee my only source of heat.

And it did work: eventually the damned dog came back. He stemmed my tirade by dropping a dead rabbit on the path and turning round and round, exploding breath and treading, in his excitement, on the corpse. Lobster-clawed, I picked the rabbit up. Its faint warmth only emphasised the cold.

'There's a pub among those lights up there,' I told the dog. 'With a log fire, and Timothy Taylor's on tap. I need to thaw out. Don't think of this as a reward.'

But the Homing Pigeon had flown the coop, so to speak. As well as refurbishing the old pub, Dave and Alison had renamed it (in lower case) *the dove ascending*.

Gone were the alcoves, beams and horse brasses; in fact they seemed to have torn out the whole upstairs floor. In place of these conventionalities stood a much bigger, cement-rendered space, whose only concessions to decor were some spotlights, high-tensile cables and fist-sized bolts. I liked the new look, or at least it suited my mood. They'd filled in the inglenook and covered the chimney breast with a towering blank wall. Out of respect for the brushed steel underfoot, I took my wellingtons off at the sheet-metal door and was delighted to feel, as I walked to the tungsten-lit bar, that the whole floor was heated. Spongebob I remembered too late; he'd already followed me inside, leaving a trail of muddy paw-prints. The pub was empty save for a couple my age adrift at the far end of the room. It was early yet. I liked optimistic Dave and his visionary girlfriend Alison. Here he was now, in a black turtleneck, ready to take my order.

'Do Koreans cook game?' I asked, laying the dead rabbit on the bar.

Beaming, he gestured at the new beer taps (the old pump handles were gone) and replied, 'Not sure, but I can ask.'

The bitter was off (for good, it seemed) so I ordered a pint of Belgian lager, which turned out to be a litre, and a whiskey chaser, and asked, 'How's business?', indicating the distant ceiling. 'Place looks marvellous.'

Dave tapped his bulbous nose. 'We're quietly confident. Kim's impressed some foodie reviewers at least.'

I nodded approval.

'The credit's Alison's of course. She's already eyeing

two other village pubs to work the same magic on. "Rurapolitan Revolution", the *Sunday Telegraph* called it. The photographer they sent made us wear black tie and pose with pitchforks.'

I widened my eyes.

'Party bookings are rocketing.' He reached to tap his nose again, then flinchingly converted the gesture into a vigorous stab at the corner of his eye. That turtleneck looked a little tight, running as it did into the udder-bulge of his double chin. I thought about admitting to having discovered the sixtieth invitations, but held back long enough for him to recover his footing. Expertly, he asked after each of the children in turn, even mentioning little Felix by name. This facility (I must be one of many acquaintances) is Dave's chief skill. It alone makes him an excellent host. I seldom think about the man unless he's in front of me, and don't imagine he dwells on me in my absence either, but when we're together his apparent interest in all things Brinkman is beguiling. Once we'd exhausted my family (and I'd managed to dredge up a question about the quad bike he bought his (glaringly unnamed) son) he set off with the rabbit in search of his chef. Spongebob growled until I shushed him, perhaps unhappy to see his hard work disappear.

It was powerful beer. I took Robert to Belgium once, to help with a history project on Napoleon's final campaign. That was also a bitter day. We both froze, trying to conjure infantry movements and hoof-pounding cavalry from a drizzle-soaked mound in the plain. A litre of this beer could warm anyone up. But it would also cloud your judgement, as Napoleon's was uncharacteristically compromised on the battlefield in June 1815. Robert and I took the car ferry and slogged to the flatlands from Calais. Now there's the Channel Tunnel, of course. Much faster, but surely a terrorist target in waiting. Freddie admired the Chunnel. Not that he ever went in it; he just loved the idea of the French setting off from the Gare du Nord in Paris bound for England, and a station named after their worst defeat.

'Waterloo!' I said, when my eldest son picked up.

'Dad? Hold on.' I overheard muffled instructions ending in, '. . . what a try-on, muppets!' and then, to me again, 'Bit tied up here, but—'

'Sorry, son.'

'No, no. Go on. What can I do for you?'

'What was the name of the Prussian general who caught Napoleon out at Waterloo?'

'Come again?'

'Boscher, was it, or Britcher?'

'What? Where are you, Dad? There's an echo of some sort.'

'Heaven. *The dove ascending* at least, in little letters. It's a big empty space now, but slowly filling up.'

'Are you OK? Hold on.' (Muffled again: 'Tell him to stay put, I'll fit him in.') 'What's all this about?'

'You're at work, son. You should be with your family, with little Flo.'

Slowly: 'Not this again, Dad. I'm busy here. Ecstatically so.'

'But it's Saturday evening.'

'Correct. You've not lost your touch with the calendar, then.'

'You were mad about history once, Robert. Bonaparte and all that. Now you can't even call to mind his nemesis.'

He laughed. 'As you well know it is hotly contested whether or not the late arrival of the Prussian force altered the outcome of the battle of Waterloo. Having weighed the evidence for GCSE I recall concluding that the Duke of Wellington had worn Napoleon out long before the Prussians arrived.'

'That was Napoleon's problem, wasn't it? He bit off more than he could chew. Somebody should have saved the man from himself.'

'Mind if we chat about this when I'm next back at the Tithe Barn? I've got to–'

'Sevastopol, son.'

The phone pulsed silence, cut with the faint fed-back echo of glasses tinkling on the metal bar-top.

I went on. 'An age ago for you, I'm sure, but to me it feels like just yesterday you were all crumply mouthed in my little office, agonizing about blowing the whistle, telling your boss, Mr Lovett, wasn't it, the full story.'

'Why on earth would you mention that now?' He laughed again, but gamely now, without mirth.

'Either you ease off the suicidal hours or I'll make them pointless for you, Robert. Understand? For your own good. How much would your odds in the partner-ship race lengthen if I let on that you'd lied on the job to protect a mate?'

'Mate? I can barely remember the bloke's name.

Anyway, he's long gone. As is the Sevastopol deal, and the client, and . . . and . . . and: you've got to be kidding! I'm going to spell this out once more, Dad. Please listen carefully. *My job makes me happy!* You mean well, but you're not seeing things from my point of view.'

'It's not the done thing, intervening, I know, but in time you'll thank me for this,' I explained, though my last words were drowned out by a party of pub-goers whose laughing arrival bounced like Tube-noise from the walls of the modernist-medieval hall. I pressed the phone hard to my ear.

'The pension,' he was saying. 'That must be it. We should organise for somebody to take a look and see if anything can be done.'

'This isn't about me. Rebellion, Robert. Camus says it's a stand we take on each other's behalf.'

Misconstruing my tone (the noise my end hadn't died down much), Robert laughed. 'Still listening to "Thought for the Day", then?'

I could visualise his smile. Though written on his newly puffy face, it would be the same look of relief he had as a boy when he thought he'd squirmed past charges of bullying made by Jimmy or Pearl. 'You stand yourself a drink there on me,' Robert said. 'I've got to get on.'

'I'm not kidding about this.'

'Of course you're not.'

'Head me off, then. Come and talk.'

A ringing phone nagged in his background. 'Soon. In any case, it's not long until your–' Mistake looming, he cut himself short. 'I have to answer that one, Dad.

The Prussian general's name was Blücher, with an umlaut on the U. You take care now.'

The noisy group had arrived at the bar. One of them trod on Spongebob's tail. He flinched, but I heard no yelp or growl. There was something familiar about the man now apologising to my dog. It's a small village: I worried that I should have known his name. Fear of a failing memory is part of growing old; in fact what I forget most is how bad I was with names and faces as far back as school. This fellow wore his jeans a size too small, in defiance of his paunch. He looked uncomfortable, bending down to assuage Spongebob. The roll of fat on the back of his head (he had no neck to speak of) bristled with what was left of his hair. Cropped, it undulated as he moved, like iron filings drawn by a magnet inside his skull. 'Lovely mutt,' the man told me, heaving up straight. I ordered the same again and retreated to a silver table in what passed for a corner of the room.

No, names and faces have never been my strength. But without a doubt the man riding shotgun in Jennifer's Discovery had been the golf pro from her club, Ryder Evans. Though I'd only met him once, the memory – *Evans as in Chris, Ryder as in Cup* – had stuck. Presumably he used this aide-memoire when introducing himself to his students. We were both holding plates of cold meat and glasses of Jacob's Creek at the time, so didn't shake hands. His eyes held mine only for a second before drifting (shyly, I thought) away, which gave me the chance to have a good look at the man whose golfing prowess and patience as a teacher I'd heard so much about. He had a freckly Celtic complexion and a sportsman's jaw; when he took a bite of drumstick (a manoeuvre made awkward by his wineglass) I noticed that the shock of ginger hair his mnemonic alluded to was echoed on the backs of his forearms, hands and knuckles. *Orang-utan*, I thought. Pearl once volunteered to spend a summer protecting those lovely creatures from Malaysian loggers, but the project never came off.

'How's Jennifer's game progressing, then?' I asked the pro.

He bounced on the balls of his feet as he finished his mouthful. 'You know, honestly', (did he think I'd doubt him?) 'she's the most improved lady player this club has got.'

'She raves about the lessons. Tells me you've unblocked her swing.'

'Ah, well, there has to be talent there in the first place,' he corrected me kindly, 'to unlock.'

Jennifer joined us then. She'd taken it upon herself to solve the evening's wineglass-and-buffet-plate awkwardness by fetching some of those glass-holding clips from the club kitchen, and had brought us one each. Gripping the edge of my plate firmly, she stabbed a clip on to its rim. As I secured my wine I noticed something. Instead of performing the same functional kindness for Ryder Evans, Jennifer took his drink from him, gave him his clip and steered his hand as he fitted it to the plate himself. Her fingers lingered even after the holder was in place, sliding from the wire-sprung back of his hand across his wrist.

★　★　★

'Something the matter with the beer?' Dave asked, sitting down with a tooth-splitting, metal-on-metal scrape.

'Sorry? No!' I drained the glass.

'What's up, then? Can't have you drinking alone with that look on your face. You'll scare the clients!'

Pubs serve customers; *clients* are for lawyers and prostitutes. There was nothing wrong with the beer, but it had shrivelled my capacity for small talk. I turned my gaze on Dave's blithe, chubby face.

'I was thinking about my father, Freddie.'

The smile melted expertly into a nod of sympathy.

'He was a bomber pilot during the war. By the time of his nineteenth birthday he'd come close to completing his first tour. That's thirty missions over enemy territory. An average of five per cent of planes sent on any given raid didn't come back. So by operation twenty you were on borrowed time.'

Ever equable, Dave kept nodding, but the whites of his eyes appeared larger – and bluer, in the strange lighting – than before.

'Nineteen,' I repeated. 'He hadn't yet learned how to drive a car. The journal mentions this more than once, how embarrassed he was about it, and the scheming he did to make sure none of his crew found out.'

I sipped my chaser and took in Dave's polite surprise.

'Eventually he asked the station adjutant, John Chapel, to teach him on the quiet. Chapel was top of the station darts ladder. He was also a "penguin". That's what they called the ex-aircrew who were too old for wartime flying.'

'Penguins,' Dave repeated, shifting on his stool.

'Four days after Chapel had expedited my father a service driving licence, Freddie was sipping coffee in the control tower, watching planes take off for a raid, when a Hampden lost an engine after take-off – at just three hundred feet – and crashed two miles from the runway. Four thousand pounds of explosives; all that fuel! The flight commander ordered Freddie to super-vise the collection of bodies in the station van. Coffins, that was Freddie's first land-borne cargo. What they couldn't find to fill them with he had his men replace with sand.'

Dave's double chin wobbled as he shook his head in horror. His eyes were still wide; partly in sympathy, also intent on escape. Yet he had taken a seat with me. That fact, and the beer, gave me a right to speak my mind. Better he hear how in September 1942 Freddie was 'offered the chance' to retrain on Lancasters, the air force's new flagship heavy bomber, than I embarrass him with the tale of my wife's affair. *Affair*: as distinct from a one-night stand as the marathon is from a sprint. By completing a tour Freddie had earned himself a non-combat role. But perhaps Dave knew about Jennifer. Perhaps everyone did. I pressed on regardless, telling Dave of Freddie's instant decision. Heroes accept such offers, even when a second tour is the cost of the priv-ilege. Never mind that he later confided to his journal that the real price of the station commander's hand-shake was tears pressed into a straw-filled mattress.

'I cry quite often,' said Dave. 'When Carl was born, when they told us he was deaf in one ear. Even when the builders relaying the drive hit the stupid sewage main.'

It was my turn to offer sympathy.

'But I'd have flown my plane or rowed my boat or taken my place in the mud of the Somme.'

'That was the First World War.'

'No matter, my point is those were extraordinary times. They brought extraordinary qualities out of people. But the people were like us. No better, no worse. The same.'

The truth in this simplification was annoying.

'Freddie was back over Germany in a Lancaster in under three weeks,' I told Dave. 'In command of a new crew of seven men, with just eighteen hours' flight experience in an entirely new plane, six of those gained in one night flight. His bomb aimer didn't know how to work the new switches. Their conversion course hadn't included practice bombing, you see. Before the live op Freddie didn't even have a chance to do a practice run!'

'We hadn't designed a pub interior before this one,' Dave countered. 'You make mistakes, but learn as you go along.'

Now he was joking, but the sliver of truth was still there. Its perversity resonated: within every surge of bitterness I felt towards Ryder Evans there were eddies of goodwill. He was making Jennifer happy. Relief pulsed alongside grief. The interior of *the dove ascending* was like a little aircraft hangar; perhaps that's why I found it appealing. Freddie made it through his second tour, of course, though along the way he lost a rear gunner to German fighters and was forced to ditch in the English Channel (he ran out of fuel, a holed tank was to blame). He put the Lancaster down on the water (landing along, not against, the line of the waves) at 0446, just before dawn. Everyone made it into the lifeboat before the plane sank. Then the sun came up on what Freddie describes as 'a glorious summer's day'. They were picked up by teatime and back at the base eating more eggs and bacon before midnight. 'What a do!' the journal reports, the only hint of incipient panic being his admission that 'a night in the drink would have been quite another thing'.

Dave had gone to the food hatch while I was staring into my drink. In spelling out my father's heroism I had been guilty of perpetuating his fraud, but I wasn't about to tell Dave the new truth. He'd no doubt shrug that off as understandable in the circumstances too. Beaming like a schoolboy, the publican now set a shallow bowl before me, heaped with slick green leaves, noodles and glistening shredded meat. 'What you need is a good feed, Harry. On the house, which isn't as generous as it sounds, since we used your ingredients. Bloody marvellous, that Tony Kim!'

'Rabbit?'

'What else!'

Freddie's dead tail gunner was a twenty-two-year-old farm labourer from New South Wales by the name of Warren Downing. Australians know a thing or two about rabbits. During the spring of 1943, with the airfield overrun by them, he taught my father how to set snares and prepare meat. The night Downing died his guns had jammed as he tried to bring them to bear on a German Me 109E fighter. Trapped in his seat, the gunner did not die immediately, but – in Freddie's words – 'set

134

up a screaming which, had I not cut the intercom, God forgive me, would have proven more than I could take'.

'Kim said he hadn't in fact cooked a rabbit before,' Dave, still mesmerised by the bowl, confided. 'Adapted this from an old cat recipe of his mum's. Too bloody resourceful if you ask me!'

I thought about keeping Spongebob on the leash for the return journey, but didn't. Perhaps concerned by the less-than-certain course of his master's feet, the dog repaid my trust by staying close to heel. Jennifer was taking a late, long soak when we arrived home. Emerging from the bathroom fug, she glowingly ignored my absence at dinner; a doubly unusual leniency since, judging by the mess in the kitchen bin, perishable soufflé had been on the menu. I didn't mention our near-miss on the bend outside St Clare and neither did she.

11

Mutual Friends' complaint form arrived with my morning post. *Our future is yours as yours is ours*, read a message franked on to the envelope. Such megalomaniacal bravura raised a smile, but the audacity of the envelope's contents had me laughing hard enough to bounce the air-spring in my swivel seat. Mindful of the cost of postage perhaps, the envelope-stuffer had seen fit to fold the complaint form I'd requested into a sheath of promotional flyers for a sample of the association's other products: tax-clever savings schemes, share brokerage services, gas and electricity supply, car breakdown cover, even pet insurance.

Oh, Spongebob!

But that wasn't all. The auto-signed covering letter cheerily informed me that team players in the customer satisfaction division were *looking forward* to receiving my complaint. That's right, the prospect of receiving it made them happy. It wasn't a real complaint at all, you see, rather *an opportunity to improve their services*. I hadn't even begun to fill the form out yet, and already the strength of the gale I'd be hurling it into was making itself felt. Such a vortex of self-certainty brought the Reverend

Frayn to mind. Her saintly detachment in the face of specific criticism, that sympathetic nodding, those upturned palms: *I hear you, really, I feel for you, deeply: but thus it is, what can we do?* Now I was hearing a corporate echo of the same sentiment. There was even a pre-paid postcard among all the bumph, inviting me to report my satisfaction with the complaint process to date. Had I received my form punctually? Was it easy to fill out? Did it meet my specific needs?

I stepped out into the garden with this lot in my hands. The year's first frost had come early, giving the now straggly grass a crimping brittleness; my footprints were dark and flat and destructive as I walked towards the weeping willow tree. 'Mother of God!' I whispered to the fallen silver leaves. 'Where's the *give me my money* section, the *we are sorry* line, the *your thirty years returned* box to tick?'

Turning to face the Tithe Barn, I gazed up at the gabled end. It's a big expanse of wall: *the dove ascending*'s interior came to mind. But instead of grey render this surface is herringboned brickwork, and although the top of the wall was two and a half storeys above me, as I walked towards it I could see that the condition of that façade had worsened. The patch of blistered bricks had grown. Their exposed innards were, in places, the pinky white of an undercooked chicken breast. From between the layers (courses, the professionals call them) the frost and rain and wind and time had gouged cater-pillars of worn cement. Too much sand in the mix up there, perhaps. Whatever, like acne kneaded across the security boy's forehead, my pointing issue had spread.

I reached the foot of the wall. The washed gravel path, bordered with wavy-edged tiles (which Jimmy chose fifteen years ago, and helped me set, end in, twelve for every one of the sixty-seven metres of pathway the garden boasts, over a disc-slippery bank holiday weekend) was flecked with rare to well-done scraps of brick-meat.

I adopted a wicket-keeper's crouch.

Flakes of rust, these brick bits looked like, close up.

Manifestly a problem, yes, yet between forefinger and thumb the evidence crumbled to dusty nothingness.

I'd already received a letter from the mortgage company, giving notice that the time had come for me to pay off the remainder of my debt. My (now dead) financial adviser (who'd himself put forty years into a company long since bought out, floated and liquidated) and I had worked it all out on the kitchen table behind that wall. Pension to mature this month, final mortgage instalment due the next; lump sum payable under the former to account for the latter, leaving an income more than sufficient to cover such necessities as sausage skins, aromatherapy oils, dog biscuits (in an ideal world) and, of course, the odd bigger-ticket item like, say, help with a grandchild's school fees, the down payment on a new truck for the wife, or repairing a wall of blown bricks.

The frost needled through my trainer toes. I tossed the association's nonsense – complaint form included – into the wheelie bin on my way back to my office. I'd have to find another path of resistance if I wanted it to lead anywhere in time for my party. The situation wasn't really comparable, of course, but as Dave had suggested, we deal with what is put in front of us, and against the backdrop of my life so far this pension crisis had, well, weakened the fabric separating life from death. At what point did Freddie, battling homeward in his shot-up 'crate', understand his fatal fuel shortage and realise that no matter what he did he wouldn't be able to coax the Lancaster across the Channel, let alone back to base? How long did he press on for before deciding to ditch? Every mile closer to friendly soil made a difference, didn't it? Well, so did every night spent within the walls of a castle which, through the strange osmotic passage of time, now wept my blood in its rusty tears.

Rounding the house I saw Fira struggling with Spongebob in the driveway. Three explosive paces – and a jarred knee – later, I stopped short: the tussle between girl and dog was clearly in jest. They were playing tug of war with a bicycle tyre. First Fira bucked backwards, yanking Spongebob across the gravel, then he shook his end of the tyre, unbalanced her, and regained the lost ground. Neither of them let go as I approached.

'He's strong,' Fira panted, 'but stupid. With stiff legs, like a table. By showing him a centimetre' – she feinted towards Spongebob, then heaved backwards again – 'I can unlock them and steal a metre. Grrr!'

Spongebob, chippings of stone between his claws, growled with as little intent.

Fira's neck glowed blossom pink. She took up the slack, her tummy taut above her jeans, and lurched away with quick stabbing steps, so that I almost feared for my dog's teeth. His growl became a gargle. She shook and twisted and braced herself against his weight; his ears flattened themselves, his shoulders hunched, his hindquarters dropped to within an inch of the drive. Then, with comical suddenness, Spongebob lurched backwards as Fira let the tyre go.

'Just rubber tyre, dog,' she said. 'Nothing to scare, you see.' With this she turned her gaze levelly on me.

'You're here bright and early,' was all I could muster.

Fira conceded that she was with a nod of her head. 'I wanted to thank you for my appointment with Mr Bannerman, before cleaning,' she said. 'But you were gone so I am helping Spongedog instead.'

'Spongebob, with a B,' I said, continuing excitedly: 'You saw the lawyer? Was he helpful? What did he say?'

'That he will present me, at my appeal hearing.'

'*Re*present. He thinks you have a good case, then?'

Fira shrugged her shoulders. 'You have paid this man. I am grateful.'

'That's fabulous, Fira.' I beamed at her. 'I'm delighted.'

Fira shrugged again, but smiled back at me. 'He is a lawyer. This means he is hard to see into, I think. He is not like you, Mr Brinkman. I am pleased with you for arranging help, but what will happen I do not know. Mr Bannerman smiles with his mouth only.' The ice in her gaze had melted to a mobile shyness. 'Unlike you, too. And he has thin grey lips which are also different.'

My mouth did not know what to do with itself all of a sudden. I focused on Spongebob. Intuiting the hollowness of his victory over Fira, he had quickly discarded the bike tyre. Although I could not bring myself to look at her I sensed that Fira was still smiling at me, and felt myself colouring up. Yes, despite the cold, my ears were glowing. Scrum ears, raw with human contact. In vain I tried to look thoughtful, keeping my traitorous mouth pursed. It was no use. I sensed Fira moving towards me. She took my hand and I had to look back down at her. 'Again,' she began, her lips the pale, bluish pink of little Flo's thumbnails, and warm on my cheek. 'Again, thank you for your trying to help,' she said.

I'd become my own puppeteer, controlling myself remotely. With a ghastly woodenness I drew back from Fira and said, 'Please, just Harry, not Mr Brinkman.' I pointed at my office. 'Must get on.' Then, trying not to hobble, I ushered Spongebob inside and drew the door shut behind me with a regrettably defensive click.

I sat before my desk, swivelling on the frictionless axle of my office chair. Spongebob was revolving too, nose to tail. Eventually he dropped on to his preferred carpet tiles – above the old engine pit – but I, unable to stop fidgeting, stood up stiffly and limped the length of the room. Stepping past the dog, I saw he was watching me out of the corner of his eye with a surreptitiousness that reminded me of my own feigned indifference – intent on the crossword, retreating to the kitchen for unnecessary coffee – towards Robert when, after that first windsurfing course, he was trying to summon the courage to call Marie.

'What?' I asked Spongebob out loud, then sat down again, riffled through my organiser, and tapped out Bannerman's number. Dog and bone, phone.

The lawyer was on another call. I told his secretary

I'd hang on. My work has furnished me with plenty of experience of time on hold: I've learned to enjoy the suspended feeling it creates. It's impossible to concentrate properly on anything other than the waiting, yet no amount of focusing on that can make a moment's difference to how long it lasts. My eyes skated over the emails in my in-box, which included – among the raft of Viagra and Cialis advertisements – an enquiry from a German shower manufacturer called Wasserreich, asking me to quote for the supply of specialist washers for their new range of high-pressure pumps. My sphere of perceived usefulness was shrinking, it seemed, from engineering to pumps, from pump components to valves, from valves to silicone rings. Still, I'd sourced washers from a Chinese supplier in the past, so topped and tailed the email to make the enquiry mine and, glancing from the rain-spotted window to my computer screen again, forwarded it to Henry Tan (Tony Kim, Henry Tan, it's daunting the way they're prepared to Westernise their names in the pursuit of our business!) at Stone River Light Industrial Co. Ltd, Wuyi City, Zhejang. Beyond the water-marked pane the sky, winter-grey, was the exact same colour as Fira's eyes.

Bannerman finally came to the phone. He lost little time in pronouncing Fira's case *a proper challenge.* I've noticed this about lawyers, Robert included. They are excited by the prospect of technical difficulty, regardless of the implications for their client. When we bought the Tithe Barn the right of way at the bottom of the paddock was *problematic* enough to make our conveyancing solicitor rub his hands with glee.

'She's lucky you brought her case to us,' Bannerman swaggered. 'Real muddle. This is not the sort of appeal that would have worked itself out on its own.'

'Muddle?'

'Her story has all the well-founded fear of persecution we could need, I'm confident of that, but the problem will be garnering sufficient evidence to prove it. The file shows a woeful lack of focus on that to date. Also, she was a fool not to claim asylum immediately. Her delay in reporting to Croydon will be a headache. Still–' He paused, as if what was about to come was obvious.

'Still what?'

'This only serves to make the case interesting. I've a very bright assistant, Sandeep Raja, working with me. He's first rate.'

'But you're in charge? My son specifically recommended you.'

'We do hundreds of these, Mr Brinkman. Your girl has been through enough. She is in good hands now.'

'She's not my . . .' I trailed off. 'I'm pleased if you're optimistic.'

'Yes, well, good. The extra work will need to be factored into our fee estimate.'

The worrying implications of Bannerman's parting statement mattered less than the resonant jargon he'd used: *well-founded fear of persecution*. It struck me again that I didn't know what Fira was afraid of. Aside from understanding that her father had lost his university professorship, I had no clue what she had been through at all. The lawyer knew more about her than me now.

I paced my office floor again. It wasn't my place to pry. The detail of a person's past aren't always necessary, or even helpful, as a means of appreciating who they are now. Or are they? I tried to convince myself that Fira's calm presence was all that mattered, but it didn't wash. I wanted knowledge, every last shred of it: though my altruism had been honest it had propelled me to cross a line.

As with the chop-look, I prefer to make sense of co-incidence with probability and reason, rather than invoking God or fate. Still, what happened next was uncanny enough to give me a sudden view of myself through the wrong end of a telescope: insignificant, prey to conspiring forces I could not hope to understand. I've mentioned before that my office was originally a garage. The old engine pit, for obvious reasons, was sunk centrally into its floor. Spongebob's favoured resting place – the carpet-tiled trapdoor now covering the brick-lined cellar – is therefore bang in the middle of my workspace. In the aftermath of my conversation with Bannerman, still pacing from the plant pots on the windowsill to my huge, gunmetal filing cabinet and back again, I forgot to mind out for my dog, and trod on his tail. Or rather, I half trod on it. My heel landed safely on the carpet, but as my weight rocked forward I felt the slender whip of bone – or is it cartilage? – begin to roll (unevenly, jerkily, like a flat-sided pencil) beneath the ball of my foot. Thank heavens for Zola Budd and the sensitive-soled trainers she inspired! Even before Spongebob had time to react my right knee gave, crumpling to absorb my full weight, which would otherwise have pressed down on his tail. Since my left foot was still in midair this manoeuvre came at a cost. I stumbled, reached out to steady myself on the back of my chair, felt it rotate away from me with a miraculous – in engineering terms – lack of resistance, and pitched headlong into the filing cabinet. It sits on wheels, but the wheels were locked. I bounced sideways off it and swept a coffee cup from my desk as I fell, kneed the printer from its plastic perch, and brought a forearm up to halt my slamming progress into the wall. Spongebob, yipping, sprang instantly to all fours. I sensed him there as I stared at the head-shot pinned to the corkboard not three inches from my left eye.

The man looked different yoked into his regulation shirt, suit and tie. And placing faces isn't my forte. I might well have missed the connection, had not the sickening flexing of my dog's tail beneath my foot been uppermost in my mind as I stared at his dot-matrix smile. As it was, I was certain that the photograph I'd printed out – of Anthony Woodward, one of Mutual Friends' executive directors – showed the face of the man who, at the bar in *the dove ascending* just days beforehand, had also trodden on my poor dog's tail.

I took down the picture and shushed Spongebob. He quietened immediately, evidently more startled by my fall than his own discomfort. I've read that in domesticating dogs we've pinned them into puppyhood. Floppy ears and pug noses signal stunted dependency. The more wolfish a pet dog looks, so the theory goes, the closer he is to his 'natural' adult state. At the dog home they'd suggested a measure of husky in Spongebob's likely lineage. Well, sled dogs are hardy: never mind a pinched tail, they'll happily kip in a blizzard. True to his fore-fathers, Spongebob blinked his eyes at me now and flopped straight back down in the middle of the floor.

Did Anthony Woodward live near by? There was always a chance that he'd come to *the dove ascending* as a visitor, but I doubted it. The photograph alone did not account for the familiarity of the man's face in the pub. I'd seen him somewhere in the flesh before then, I was sure of it, and anyway, the coincidence of Spongebob's tail suggested – no, *promised* – that our paths were already more thoroughly entwined.

Catching myself falling prey to this hogwash I said, 'Get a grip,' out loud.

Then I set about the practical tasks of reshelving my printer, mopping the coffee dregs from my mouse mat and retrieving the mug from behind the wastepaper basket, before returning to my computer screen with my reason restored. All companies must file annual returns at Companies House; to safeguard the public against rogue directors those annual returns must include details of directors' home addresses; and in the interests of corporate transparency annual returns for every company in the land are available to you and me, downloadable for a mere £1 from the World Wide Web.

Woodward, the form declared baldly, lived at West End Farm, in the nearby village of Waverly Edge.

I did not have to look up the address to confirm exactly where that was – not five miles over the escarp-ment, on the other side of St Clare – but since Robert showed me the Google Earth site I've enjoyed using it to pinpoint, in carto-photographic detail, the pictorial location of places (Felix's nursery school, holiday spots we've frequented in Cornwall and Greece, Newlands Corner on the South Downs where I proposed to Jennifer) that mean something to me, and Anthony Woodward's address was immediately important enough to require the same treatment. Like sat-nav, Google Earth is a miraculous tool! There, in a shudder of pixels, was an aerial view of the man's house, just outside Waverly Edge, at the head of its own long straight drive, squat and square and standing – it appeared – in front of a kidney-shaped swimming pool. I panned out. In jerky hops the screen refocused on a copse, the B-road linking Waverly to St Clare and, in a last ripple, the area north of St Clare itself, which meant that the two clumps of pixels at the bottom and top of the screen, though minuscule, were Woodward's West End Farm and our own Tithe Barn.

I bookmarked the page and limped outside again.

An abstract enemy was a convenient feature of life in Bomber Command. Freddie describes the experience of raining incendiaries on civilians from thirty thousand feet as 'lighting up the town', 'a firework display' and 'putting on a fearsome show'. In much the same way as the corporate façade of electronic platitudes and pre-franked questionnaires distanced Mutual Friends from the likes of me, such glib phrases combined with the dead air between the plane's metal belly and the flames below to separate airmen from the horror they wrought. Words kept things simple back then. Making it to the target against the odds meant understated *bravery*, *decency* and *heroism*. Turning back without good reason implied unspeakable *cowardice*, *cheating* and, so bad it was referred to by an acronym alone, *LMF*. Men with this last label were a race apart for my father. He mentions the term just once in the journal, pitying Matt McEwan, a nineteen-year-old Scot who'd won his wings on the same course as Freddie, only to be shot down over the target on his sixth raid. He bailed out, landed safely, but was immediately captured by maddened civilians from the burning target town. Face to face with his enemy, Freddie explains, McEwan feared a lynching, but he was conveyed safely to a local policeman's house, from which, with the man's New Testament stowed in his flying jacket, he escaped that same night. He made it over the French border and into the hands of the Resistance, who took six months to help him home. Such a 'scrape' usually bought the right to non-operational duties, but McEwan, whose fiancée had married a member of the ground crew in his absence, preferred to fly on. Except that he couldn't: an overheating engine afforded the excuse to turn back on his first raid, an intermittent problem with the altimeter on the second. After the third questionably aborted mission he was grounded and awoke to the sound of kindly penguin Chapel (still unbeaten at darts) chalking the initials LMF upon his door. *Lack of Moral Fibre*. His dereliction of duty had nothing to do with the Bible, Freddie reports McEwan saying before he left the base, or the fear of being shot down again: 'but the thought of people sleeping below, warm-blooded people, some of whom would not wake up to see what I had done'.

I'd walked to the end of the garden where the apple trees stand. These old trees were here the autumn we arrived, choked in brambles but heavy with fruit. A ready-made orchard. Windfalls with a rind of frost now lay at my feet in the unkempt silvery grass. Abandoned eggs in badly made nests, they looked like, or a tundra pocked with unexploded bombs. As a rule I gather the windfalls for Jennifer to make into her fiery chutney. It's a great antidote to a winter head-cold, that stuff, Madras strength, not for the faint hearted. She hadn't mentioned my failure to retrieve the fallen apples this year, or the fact that I'd not harvested the tree for use in pies and crumbles either.

I picked up an apple. The fuzz of white frost melted immediately beneath my touch, showing fingerprints first, then moons of russet and green. A flat dent on one side revealed a bruise, but although it was imperfect this was *my* apple, mine to pick up or leave to rot as I chose. With the bruise in my hand I bit into the clean side, felt the crunch of my teeth puncturing the skin, heard the hiss and tasted the fizz.

Ryder Evans. The Reverend Frayn. Mr Lovett. Bill H. Marshall.

And now *Anthony Woodward*, with his fat neck and iron-filing hair.

Duty, for poor Matt McEwan, meant bombing innocents. When he couldn't do it they labelled him a coward. My own responsibilities have always been so humdrum: work, save, play the game. Yet to have shirked in any way, or even complained, would, I always felt, have given Freddie the excuse to chalk LMF upon my door. If only I'd known all along that he'd already conceded the ground I was fighting to hold. Only resist! I took another bite of cooking apple. Some things we know the effect of without understanding how they work. Think of those monkeys that gorge themselves on fallen, fermenting fruit to get high: we've all seen the footage. The apple's sharp taste was as bracing as learning who I had to oppose.

12

Single motherhood is no joke. Pearl, having made it a point of principle to cope, does well juggling Felix and her job. *Juggling* is fashionable now. Not just the metaphorical kind; there's a shop in town that survives on a stock of kites and circus paraphernalia alone. Hoops, balls, knives, skittles, they sell the lot, even those sticks you dip in meths and set on fire. For me the spectacle of a juggler is as much about precariousness as control. Deep down I expect, hope even, that the balls will come tumbling down. Felix is a watchful boy. Secretly I've wondered whether, shuttled between nursery, childminders, babysitters and his twinkle-toed mum, he *feels* juggled; he certainly looks as if he's keeping an eye out for signs of imminent collapse.

From time to time Jennifer steps in to help Pearl out. I could tell from my daughter's polite enquiry – *how's business?* – that she hadn't telephoned to chat with me, and guessed, before she asked if her mum was around the following day, that this was a call for back-up.

'What's going on with the little man?'

'He's good, he's good. Still into all things nautical.

Gave himself a fright in the bath tonight testing to see whether he was amphibious.'

'He'd appreciate a trip to the aquarium tomorrow, then?'

'The pond in the park would do. Nursery's on half-term. Is Grandma free?'

'*Grandad* is.'

'Ha ha. Could you put her on?'

'No, I'm serious. I'll take Felix tomorrow. Then, when you get home, we can have a chat. There's something I want to talk about face to face.'

A mention of Jennifer's scheduled golf lesson clinched the deal. Though surprised, Jennifer herself skipped lightly into the kitchen when I told her I'd offered to help out, and spent half an hour assembling the grand-mother of all picnics: a touching act, it seemed to me, of penance. The strange thing was the undercurrent of pleasure it gave me to see her so relieved.

I left early the following morning. Too early: I'd assured Jennifer that Pearl's schedule meant I absolutely had to beat the rush hour, but in truth I just wanted to set off. Turning left in St Clare instead of right, I figured out why. This lane, glittering with headlit frost, wound up over the escarpment and on to the ring road the long way, out past Waverly Edge. I'd have crept along anyway in those conditions (the beautiful dashboard computer had outside air temperature at minus two) but purring through the copse and on towards West End Farm, the car so quiet, I slowed to an absolute crawl: it felt appropriate to move with an air of stealth.

Needless to say, Woodward's house was anachronistically named. The place no longer showed signs of agricultural intent.

I drifted to a stop opposite the gated driveway. Behind Spongebob, in my rear-view mirror, tail-lit puffs of exhaust blurred to nothingness. Though they hadn't been discernible from the aerial photograph, two rows of poplars stood either side of the man's driveway. His drive was longer than mine, and they were beautifully tended trees – I think the term is *pollarded*. It was like looking down a gun barrel, staring up the colonnade towards the house of my Mutual Friend! There was even a notch immediately in front of the house, a gunsight, no, a flagpole, set in a circular flower bed. What sort of standard did Anthony Woodward fly? While I strained to see, a light went on upstairs. Top executives have a gruelling schedule, or, to put it another way, the right to rob pensioners does not come cheap. He was probably shaving. An electric-razor man, almost certainly. I put the car into gear and, straddling the humps – *thank you for driving carefully!* – continued on my way.

My offer of a trip to the aquarium fell on pre-paved ground. 'A zoo for fish is' – evidently – 'as horrible for them as it is for the animals too.' Delivering this in his grown-up voice, Felix even sounded a bit like Pearl. I was tempted to press on (he'd have loved it: apparently these days there's even a petting pool where you can stroke the manta rays) but I didn't want to queer the pitch on my first stint at the crease, so opted, as Pearl had suggested, to visit the carcinogenic ducks in the local park instead. Spongebob approved. I had to keep him on the leash en route, but once we were inside the railings – and past the *no bicycles* sign – the risk of letting him go seemed a fair one to take.

Ducks be buggered, my dog transfixed little Felix! He and Spongebob chased one another round that scrubby little park until *my* leg began to ache. When I say the park was little, I mean it. I would put money on it being smaller than Woodward's pad. To a passer-by observing us through the railings we three, together with the handful of other mummified park-goers, must have looked like inmates in our own zoo cage. There was even an enclosed area set aside with monkey bars, slides and swings for more stimulating play. I relieved a red-cheeked Felix of his bobble hat (oh, the sweet heat of the boy's forehead) and suggested we might try that apparatus next.

Hopping from one foot to the other, he appeared keen.

But the gates to the play park were locked. I rattled the chain and checked my watch. According to the sign the play area should have opened half an hour ago. Turning to explain matters to my grandson I saw two things. First, that according to Felix's out-thrust, wobbling lower lip (exactly like his Uncle Robert's at that age: there's no accounting for genetics) he already understood the problem. And second, with immediate relief, that in the distance up the path a woman dressed in park-keeper-green weatherproofs was ambling towards us. She was swinging a bunch of keys. I shared this good news with the boy, but my relief was already coloured by the first hint of annoyance. Why was the attendant dawdling when she was already half an hour late? I resisted the impulse to say anything – or even check my watch – when eventually she arrived and undid the padlock. Instead I put Spongebob on his lead and took hold of Felix's hand. She removed the chain. Yet as I led the pair forward the woman calmly shut the gate in my face.

'Excuse me?'

'Frost,' she said.

'What?'

'Frost,' she repeated, staring me straight in the eye. The woman had skin the colour of Jennifer's home-made puff pastry, before she puts it in to bake. She'd already rethreaded the chain.

'Grandad?' said Felix.

Realising I was squeezing his hand hard, I pumped it once to reassure him and let go.

'I don't have to open when there's frost,' the woman said conclusively, and refastened the lock.

'What do you mean? There's the same amount of frost out here as there is in there. Which is not very much! It's just about thawed.'

'In your opinion,' she said.

'I'll take responsibility either way,' I explained as kindly as I could, but failed to stop myself continuing, 'On this reckoning children in Stockholm would have to stay indoors half the year!'

'Take that up with the council,' she countered. 'Who's losing their job if I let him in here' – she nodded dismissively at Felix – 'and he breaks his neck?'

'How about if I start my complaint to the council by saying you turned up for work half an hour late? What if I say they've given you a job, a very simple job, that requires you to turn up on time, open a gate and sit in a cubbyhole drinking tea and watching children play, but that you're unprepared, incapable even, of doing it? Frost! There isn't any bloody frost. Even if there was, even if it was a bloody ice rink in there, there still wouldn't be any need to shut the one play area these kids have, because ice in there means ice out here, meaning everywhere's as bloody safe!'

Imitating my accent the woman said, '*Cubbyhole,*' with a smirk, then turned her back and ambled off.

'Grandad?' said Felix.

I knew my arguments were undoing me. This woman, though at fault, was not to blame for the council's idiotic decree. But the confrontation had my heart pumping: there was no way on earth I could let her walk away.

'What's a cubbing hole?' Felix asked.

'There's no frost,' I told the boy. My voice rising to bridge the gap between us and the retreating attendant, I went on, 'And even if there was, it shouldn't be a problem. That woman is a very silly play-park attendant. Lazy. There's no frost, but she won't let us in. Keeping an eye on children is her job, but she doesn't want to do it today.'

The boy was pulling at my hand now. In a pitiful attempt to distract me he said, 'Penguins like ice. Steam is when water boils away.'

'Quite so. But there's no ice, or steam, today.' I picked Felix up. He looked heavy in his bulky coat, but modern

156

fabrics are ingenious, full of air. Puff pastry. Both boy and coat breathed out as I pressed him to my chest. The cold had made his nose run. I wiped it between my fingers and, speaking more quietly, asked, 'Now, would you still like a go on those swings?'

He blinked uncertainly but nodded.

'Right, then!'

Perhaps it was adrenalin which made him feel so light in my arms – that or my years of lugging a heaped wood-basket about. Though tipped with spikes, the railings were only shoulder high. I lifted Felix above my head, so quickly he squealed with delight. I hung him out over the fence, and let him slide through my grip, armpits to hands, until he was dangling just inches above the ground on the other side. He sat down when I let go. I looped Spongebob's lead through the railings, put a foot in the V where the diagonal bisected one of the uprights, and climbed straight over the gate. If I'd slipped . . . it does not bear thinking about. I'm not sure when I last took such a risk, but I can tell you two things: first, my anger quickstepped to laughter the second I hit the playground tarmac, and second, that modern trainers offer a marvellous combination of grip and air-cushioning.

Felix picked himself up as I stretched my sore hamstring and regained my breath. I was trembling. Beyond the sandpit the attendant emerged from her cupboard, stared at me over crossed arms, then shook her head and went back inside.

Playgrounds have come a long way. Midway from the fence to the swings I realised that my trainers weren't entirely responsible for the bounce underfoot; the surface beneath them was also full of spring. Very safe, like the roundabout we passed; no grinding gap between platform and concrete here, some whizz of a designer had worked out how to set the thing flush with the ground instead. And they'd reduced the risk of injury-by-swing, too; the seat harness I lowered Felix into was ergonomic perfection, if suspended by disappointingly short chains, making it more of a 'prod' than a swing. It's all well and good, safety. Felix's grin (lit for my benefit, I'm sure) quickly faded: risk and fun are inextricably linked.

I cajoled the boy down the slide a couple of times and attempted to interest him in the climbing frame, but the metal was so cold it stuck to his hands, and besides, an intuitive fellow, the oddness of our being alone in the play area was working on him. That and my own growing sense of unease. I'd challenged the woman's authority, insulted her even; the little chap knew as well as me that she wasn't the type to turn a blind eye.

'Is it time for lunch soon now?' Felix prompted.

'Of course. Grandma's made us a giant picnic.'

'At home inside the house please.'

'Come on, then.'

We walked back to the gates. They were still locked, of course. The attendant, leaning in her doorway, was looking our way. Without the elixir of rage, delivering Felix (and myself) safely over the fence again seemed an altogether more difficult proposal. Some great sportsmen, McEnroe for one, use anger to play their best. I hadn't thought that was the case for me.

Spongebob stood up and wagged his tail. His head was at waist height. It wasn't just a deficit of adrenalin I had to overcome, I saw: landscape gardeners had chosen to sink the playground into the park, meaning we were a step lower on this side of the fence. Resignedly, I turned to ask the attendant for permission to leave.

'I am a little bit cold,' said Felix.

'Me too. Wait here a sec.'

I made it halfway to the woman's hut (she'd retreated inside again) before spotting the police car nosing along the park perimeter. My heart sinking, I called out, 'We've finished here, would you mind opening the—' but she shut her door before I got to 'gate'. The police car, inevitably, turned towards the playground. It looked comically big as it drifted along the path. I knocked on the attendant's 'private' sign, saying, 'Come on, just open the damn gate, will you,' but she'd magically exited from the back of the hut and popped out from behind it now, holding a broom across her chest, like a stave. 'Oh, for God's sake!' I said. An engine cutting out near by left a hole in the city-noise.

'That's a police car,' Felix reported.

I turned back to my grandson, saying, 'So it is, you're right.'

'But parks are for people called pedestrians.'

'True—'

'Why are its lights on?'

'Good question.' I smiled at the advancing officer. 'Maybe the policeman will tell us.'

The police do a tough job. The younger they've got, the harder that job has seemed, to me. So the little officer on the other side of the gate started out with my respect. Though he was young, and short (I'm sure there used to be a height limit, for sensible reasons), the policeman's seen-it-all-before face was convincing. Sunken eyed, he looked tired and bored, rightly annoyed at having been called here to deal with such a non-event.

'Hi–' I began.

'This is the man.' The attendant cut me off. Broom still braced, she sidestepped around me to deal with the lock.

'What are you doing in there?' the officer asked.

'Trying to leave.' I shot the attendant a look.

'In the first place, though. It's shut today.'

'Yes, but–'

'It's shut, locked, closed to the public.'

'I know that.'

'But you're inside. Cheryl here reported that you abused her racially in front of this child, then terrified him to make your point, which was what? That it's OK to trespass? What?'

'But she's white? Racial–'

'I'm Irish. *Lazy. Stupid.* That's what you said, in front of a child.'

'This is ridiculous.'

'Did you dangle the boy over these railings?' the officer asked. He had a bulldog's neck. A young, short, weightlifting policeman. Perhaps he was annoyed by the height of the fence: no matter how strong or authoritative he made himself he would never be able to convey Felix safely over it, from either side.

'Dangle? No. I lifted . . . because . . .'

'The kid was screaming,' the attendant told the officer. 'Then he dropped him on his back.'

'What? Felix!' In turning to the boy for help I nudged him over a new edge.

'I'm cold,' he sobbed.

I started towards him but the policeman stepped between us and asked me point blank: 'What is your relationship to this child?'

'I—'

'The apparatus is iced up. No wonder the boy is terrified. He forced him on to the scramble-frame and down that slide.'

Felix's crying acquired a new, audible dimension.

'*There's no ice!*' I hissed.

'That boy comes here often,' the attendant went on. 'With his mother. I've never seen this man before.'

I moved to sidestep the officer. He feinted my way and put up his hand. 'Hold on, hold on. I want to clarify this situation first.'

'Clarify? He's my bloody grandson! Now . . . do you mind!' Again I moved towards Felix, and this time, since the boy was all but wailing, I did so with more commitment. The policeman was scrum-half sized: at wing-forward it was my job to brush such obstacles aside. Of course, I see now that it was a mistake to treat the officer with such a lack of physical respect; more interestingly I knew as much then, even as I made my play. In my defence I can only say, as I've said before, that the grandparental bond is a primal one. The policeman and I didn't actually collide (he moved too quickly for that) but neither did I make it past him to Felix. No, the next thing I knew the young officer was marching me – stumbling, unbalanced by his fierce grip on my upper arm – towards the squad car, beckoning for his colleague to fetch Felix, saying, 'Let's sort this out in the car, shall we. Get inside.'

A strange calm descended as the rear door clumped shut. Spongebob's barking was muffled for one thing, but more than that the policeman – I saw – was right: we'd sort this muddle out now. Also beyond bewilderment, Felix had already stopped crying by the time the second officer – a woman, it turned out – placed him on the passenger seat.

'It's all right, chap,' I told him. 'You'll soon warm up in here.'

Inaudible words passed between the park attendant and the bodybuilding officer before the latter returned to the car and climbed inside. The point in arguing having been blunted, I drank in the woman's malevolent grin while the young policeman took down Pearl's telephone number, and I kept on staring at her through the side window while he called my daughter to check that I was indeed *in loco parentis* (Latin, eh, properly solemn stuff) for Felix that day. The fright the officer gave Pearl was regrettable, but quickly over, and since I could do nothing to prevent it, or forestall its repercussions, I allowed myself instead to marvel at the technological wizardry crammed into the cockpit of the car, which put even the Audi's in the shade. A far cry from the tinny Fiestas they used to have. The young officer lectured me sternly about trespass and racism and respect for the law, but as the park attendant retreated and my focus shifted to my dog I knew that whatever the implications, it had still been worth resisting her, because she had been in the wrong and I had been in the right. Reassured that the car wasn't about to move, Spongebob stopped barking and expressed an interest in the rear end of a passing dog not a quarter his size. The dog was bald and shaking uncontrollably. Never mind a caution, the officer went on, he could have arrested me on any one of a number of counts. I reached past the headrest to gave Felix's puffy little shoulder a squeeze and the edge faded from the man's voice. Proper crime was crackling over the radio: this being the inner city he could only devote so much time to a non-job. I thanked both officers, apologised, and was working around to suggesting that Grandad's mistake would at least provide Felix with a better sense of right and wrong (to say nothing of an exciting stint up front in a police car) when the hairless dog Spongebob was sniffing shivered forward, pulled by a woman on the other end of its lead. The Reverend Frayn looked younger – and more attractive, curvy even – without her robe. For a second, two, three, I hoped against hope, but she was less than six feet away when she passed the car and, without doubt, as she looked through the window, she stared straight at me. Perhaps her boss eye worked better in natural light. Either way, as I had recognised the vicar, so her double-barrelled blink now acknowledged me.

13

It's hard to be appreciative and censorious in the same breath. Pearl's work trip had run on late, so she was due home after Felix's bedtime, meaning she would be doubly grateful that I had taken care of him that day. I hoped this might help her forgive me for the policeman's call. And I was grateful on my own account, too, since the delay meant my time looking after Felix ended with an improved ratio of normality to strangeness. Perhaps I needn't have worried on that count. Four-year-olds (even clever ones, like Felix) are present-tense creatures. (Very old people – their memories a blizzard – are the same.) Jennifer had given me some coloured bath foam for our grandson. By story-time his vampire-pool of crimson bubbles was the day's key event.

There's nothing quite like reading to a rapt child at bedtime. The focused stillness, the bath-glow through pyjamas, the way they don't want it to end. Felix chose a long book about a family of goats. Unlike many children's stories, this one did not end with the disingenuous device of everyone going to sleep. With no Pearl to chivvy us along, I looped back to the beginning and read until Felix dozed off on my lap. Jennifer's lotions do not compare to the smell of my grandson's freshly towelled hair.

Pearl had bought me a thank-you bottle of red wine. I opened it there and then: anything to work some colour back under the girl's skin. Beneath the kitchen's harsh spotlight (just the one, it's a tiny room) her eyes, lips and nose appeared magnified in the translucent sliver of her face. Shadows lifted her cheekbones and dug deep into the dent where her brow met the bridge of her nose. She looked pinched. Still young, but withering on the city vine. You'd think Friends of the Earth might be based closer to nature. She was watching me over the rim of her glass – with enough glowering consternation to prompt apologies.

'Stop! Forget it!' she interrupted. 'You're not the first person the police have harassed and you won't be the last!'

'It wasn't harassment.'

'Save it, Dad. At least it was an old white male this time, instead of some young black kid, humiliated for what? Jumping a playground fence? Perhaps now you'll think twice before voting those idiots extra powers.'

Never mind gratitude, it was – of course – foolish of me to have worried about Pearl's criticism. Camus (I'd not yet given up) distinguishes between many types of rebel. '*The rebel slave*' – he says – '*affirms that there is something in him which will not tolerate the manner in which his master treats him*' – whereas – '*the metaphysical rebel declares that he is frustrated by the whole universe.*' I think that makes Pearl a metaphysical rebel. She has thin eyebrows, shaped like the leading edge of a gull's wing.

They've always looked like that, a genetic forewarning of her inquisitorial attitude, perhaps, or maybe she grew up to fulfil what they promised, who knows? The barber trims my eyebrows now. Not every time I visit – he says the rugged look suits me – but about once every six months. Did it really matter if Pearl saw a specious abuse of power in my park scrape? I lowered my brow; the tension relaxed from hers. At least she thought I'd been prey to an injustice and not unjustified myself.

'Felix's school thing,' I said, in time.

Pearl put her glass on the work surface, slopping some wine, and busied herself with a cloth in silence.

'I had a chat with the vicar.'

'You did what?'

'Reverend Frayn. She's a woman.'

'Is she now?' Pearl wrung the cloth out over the sink. 'Women priests, there's a phenomenon. Can you imagine wanting so badly to join a club that had subjugated your kind since the beginning of time?'

That wasn't the point. Still, with a shake of my head I agreed, saying, 'I talked to her. About Felix's school place, at St Silas's. I hope you don't mind. She's the bouncer on the door whether we like it or not and, you know, well, I have the time. I thought I'd find out what we had to do to get Felix a place.'

Pearl still had hold of the cloth. Her knuckles blanched as she twisted it in both hands. 'Did you eat with Felix?' she asked. 'I'm starving. All they offered us today was sausages on sticks and cubes of processed cheese. There's broccoli soup in the freezer behind you. Pass it here and I'll . . .'

I gave her the soup. It was in a Tupperware container, exactly the same sort as Jennifer uses. Tupperware is virtually indestructible. You can hole it, melt it, reduce it to uselessness, but you'll never get rid of it entirely. In that way it's similar to parental influence. I'm not saying Pearl had copied her mum's choice of food storage solutions; for all I knew we'd given her a set of the stuff for Christmas one year. No, but the way she was deflecting attention from something she didn't want to talk about, deploying food as a diversion, there was more than an echo of Jennifer there. I watched her set the container down. The sight of the thing conjured a tenderness in me towards my wife, even as it filled me with exasperation.

'You know,' I went on, 'the situation isn't as bleak as all that. There's a way through it, I think. Room to wriggle, so to speak.'

'Wriggle-room.' Pearl echoed my forced light-heartedness. 'I bet. The bowls are on the drying rack.'

'I think Felix stands a fair chance of a place. All we have to do is jump through a few hoops.'

'Salt. Pepper,' said Pearl.

'Nobody actually has to *believe* anything. By going along with the charade we'll be mocking the system, in a way.'

'Spoons.'

'Once he's in, you can criticise the entrance policy all you like. Felix, in a sense, will be our Trojan horse.'

Pearl had lifted the soup to pour it out, but now put the container back down. 'What hoops?'

'We just have to take him along to church a bit. Wave at the vicar, make our presence felt.'

'Right.' She thrust her hands into the front pockets of her jeans and balled her fists against the denim, rocking impatiently from her heels to her toes and back again. '*Just* go to church. That's it?'

'Yes. And, of course, well, we have to let them stick Felix's head in the font, too. But only the once.'

'Baptise him, you mean?'

'You were baptised,' I murmured. 'It didn't do you any harm, did it?'

Pearl jerked her hands out of her pockets and turned back to the soup, pouring it out with elaborate care. Why did it feel as if I was in league with the vicar, defending the absurd system? There being nowhere to sit in the kitchen, we went into the lounge. Felix and I had left the little table there in aircraft-carrier mode, strewn with an eBay haul of miniature fighter planes. Pearl tolerated this influx of military hardware because it was a present from Uncle Jimmy, but even then, only just: there was venom in the way she swept the display from ship's deck to carpet. A tidal wave. Barefoot, she then trod on a sharp piece of wreckage.

'Fuck! Fucking fuck!' she said. 'It's all fucked.'

I gathered up the fallen planes, saying, 'I don't envy you; it's hard to be tidy when there's not much space.'

'I'm not having him baptised,' she countered. 'Or taking him to church, even once. Sorry, but I'm not. Understand?'

I understood the pointlessness in confronting Pearl directly. A familiar, infuriated love rose up in me at that moment, the sort of frustrated admiration that would, until recently, have made me back down. Yet resistance meant I could no longer keep quiet. 'Of course,' I said. 'But what if I took him? The vicar didn't categorically say that that wouldn't work.'

'No! That's so not the issue, Dad. The issue is that nobody's getting Felix stamped by a witch doctor! And neither are we going to bulk out the church's bums-on-pews statistics. If the school won't let him in as he is he won't go there and that's that. Come to think of it, I wouldn't send him there even if they would have him!'

'Where *will* he go, then?'

'That's my problem, Dad. Is the soup hot enough?'

I'd been thinking some more about my finances. With enough money I could have swept this problem away, much as Pearl had dispatched Felix's air force. *Here's a cheque for the school fees.* Let her turn down help like that! I'd already spent money we didn't have on a lawyer for Fira. What double standard was stopping me coughing up for Felix, too? Because the few grand Bannerman would charge did not compare with what Felix's school fees would set me back. I'd have to flog the Tithe Barn now to commit to that. Yet if selling up was not a matter of *if*, but *when*, why not do it early and free up some cash? Because I still hadn't told Jennifer about my pension, and even if I did she would never agree to such a sacrifice. Not when Pearl could have solved the problem herself by moving in next door to Penny Adcock, or taking Felix to church.

'Mum still makes pew-ends,' I said.

Pearl snorted into her soup cup.

Freddie used to do something similar: breathe a pre-verbal *I have won* through flared nostrils.

Tupperware again.

It always surprised me how well Pearl and Freddie got on. They would have disagreed on just about everything, had either aired their opinions. But Freddie never mentioned his support for hunting and capital punishment in Pearl's presence, and Pearl never challenged her grandfather to justify his existence, the way she did Jennifer and me.

It wasn't just the buffer of a skipped generation, or Freddie's soft spot for the first little girl in his family. No, Pearl and Freddie had something deeper in common: moral certitude. It was as unthinkable for Pearl to pretend she believed in God as it would have been for Freddie to pretend that he did not. They both stuck to their codes. I'd tried all my life to conduct myself with Freddie's rectitude. Now that he was dead it seemed I'd failed to live up to a sham.

I thought about Freddie as I watched Pearl eat her soup. Discovering his fallibility in the journal had helped push me up the ladder, but more because of what it said about me than him. Of course he was flawed. That wasn't what had depressed me. Confronting my naivety was to blame for that. Resistance now meant not making the same mistake with Pearl. Certitude, pah! She'd change her mind about Felix and the school once I found a way of getting him in.

Back in the car I selected 'Tithe Barn' from the sat-nav's list of pre-programmed destinations. Since the screen invited me to say whether I wanted to go *via* anywhere, I put down Waverly Edge. An obvious *point of interest*. Part of the beauty of an automated navigation system is that it frees you up to look at your surroundings. *Vibrant communities* benefit from vendors that stay open late. I glided past a kebab shop, an upholsterer's, a bookmaker's, two pubs, a barber's with an old-fashioned pole, a shop selling porcelain figurines, brooms and fairy lights, another bookmaker's, a newsagent's (*6 Stella for £5!*), a grocer's whose awning kept the icy drizzle off trays of exotic vegetables, an Indian restaurant, a third bookmaker's and a fish-and-chip shop thronged with teenagers – some black, some white, some Asian – forking up steaming chips. Though the council does what it can to keep the various immigrant groups segregated – by schooling the children separately and enforcing observation of Diwali, St Patrick's Day, Passover and the like – the integrating power of English chips is impossible to resist. Last year they rebranded the Christmas holiday Winterval. It made a sort of sense when Pearl explained the reasoning, but such projects seem to have reduced the budget for mundanities like street-sweepers and binmen: polystyrene cups, flyers and chip papers whirled in the Audi's wake.

Following instructions, I drifted out to the city fringes, through the vale of self-storage units, revolving billboards and flyover bridges. I knew the way, of course, but it was a treat not to have to think. It was like being at the cinema as compared with reading a book. Freddie loved Westerns, but he never grasped what the sat-nav computer was about. By the time I showed it to him his own hard drive was failing. Alzheimer's, in attacking short-term memory, gradually erodes your sense of the here and now. Like most sufferers Freddie tried to cover his disorientation with feigned understanding. He nodded a lot when I told him what the computer did, said 'hmm' and 'quite so' in the right pauses, but I knew he hadn't taken in the system's import when he finally declared it 'most entertaining'.

Or maybe he considered the gizmo an affront. After all, at the start of the war he'd had to navigate the hard way. They had four means of finding their way through the sky back then. First was simple map-reading – tricky on a clear day, let alone over cloud or at night. Second came the optimistically named 'dead-reckoning' – plotting your position using a stopwatch, the plane's heading and its speed – calculations easily compromised by crosswinds. Next (it seems laughable now) were celestial readings taken with a sextant – manageable on the ground but fraught with difficulty in a plane at speed. And lastly came radio direction finding – which worked only in range of a transmitting beacon and had the unfortunate side effect of broadcasting your position to the enemy. Radar wasn't widely available until later on. Even when it was, interpreting its crude picture was hard: not everyone could distinguish land from sea. Planes got lost. Ensuring yours wasn't one of them pitted the pilot and navigator into a constant struggle with their instruments for the duration of each flight. Freddie's navigator, Len Rushworth, had been a maths teacher before the war. There was a big space between his two front teeth. He would whistle through this gap when concentrating. It pleased Freddie to think of Len whistling for ten, eleven hours at a stretch. Together, through luck and judgement, they became very good at getting to and from the target in one piece. So good, in fact, that Freddie and his crew were encouraged to join the Pathfinder service at the end of his second tour. Pathfinders were an elite group within Bomber Command. They found the targets and marked them with flares ahead of the arrival of the main force, meaning they flew above the guns – in circles, often – without the security of numbers. A third and fourth tour beckoned. Instead of extra pay or promotion, pilots who 'took up the invitation' were given a small golden eagle to pin on their left breast pocket. 'Duty is a harsh mistress,' Freddie records in the journal, also admitting that he was finding it hard to sleep. A number of entries end with the postscript: '*night-sweats*'. Maybe the idea of a soothing voice telling you the way to the shops and back wasn't so much incomprehensible to him as a luxury so unjustifiable as to be absurd.

I stopped outside West End Farm, silenced the engine and turned off the headlights. Spongebob needed to stretch his legs so I encouraged him to make use of Anthony Woodward's grass verge. If I'd been a smoking man, now would have been the time to light a cheroot, but I'm not, so I warmed my hands by blowing into them as if to make the noise of an owl hooting. Nobody likes an audience when they're about their business. I looked past my squatting dog and up the tree-lined drive to the square-fronted house. It seemed a lovely place, big yet cosy, bathed in its security-lit glow. A fox trotted out of the darkness and stopped on the drive. If Spongebob had been looking that way I'm sure he'd have given chase, but he was concentrating on other matters. The fox sat down and scratched its ear with a hind leg, then it looked at me, stretched and took off. The car ticked, Spongebob huffed. Waverly Edge is closer to town than St Clare. The distant drone brought aircraft engines to mind, but it was of course the sound of the ring road.

14

I received a postcard from India. It made me think about corporations. One body, greater than the sum of its parts. But less, too, because although a corporation harnesses the will and work of many people, it has no use for each individual's conscience. In fact the whole point of a company is to limit liability, to protect the members, directors and employees from adverse consequences of their collective action. *Reap rewards, not repercussions* is the work-song the incorporated sing. The standard image is of an anthill or beehive, full of worker-drones, which isn't fair, of course, for although the corporation may have no use for its employees' inner lives, it cannot edit them out entirely. The postcard I received was from the tele-caller Joy Ghosh. Somebody in ICBC's personnel department, somebody with a heart, had forwarded my letter to their fired ex-colleague at home.

The postcard read:

Dear Mr Harry Brinkman,
I was sincerely delighted to receive your letter which must mean you are making steps towards progress of your own. Please promise to keep your ladder for its

intended uses in future! Reaching things, et cetera.
As for your kind apology, do not worry. It wasn't
your fault that cost me but a failure in the minds of
my superiors and above. They have lost their most
profitable operator for July through September which
shows further paucity in imagination. As for me, I
have dug myself out from worse holes than this. Only
resist!

Your friend, with my very best wishes, Joy Ghosh,
Mrs

I say postcard, but it came in an envelope, a rectangle
of off-white vellum headed with the sender's contact
details in an ornate font. I imagine there's a stack of
similar cards on a leather desk in West End Farm; it's
only a matter of time before Robert has some printed
up, too. The message lifted my spirits at first, but I soon
saw through its breezy front. Joy didn't deny that the
episode had *cost* her, cast her into a *hole*. Now she had
to *dig herself* out of it. Ha! Digging would only make
things worse. Whatever she claimed, I still owed it to
her to help her out.

Jennifer was loading her golf clubs into the
Discovery's boot. She waved at me through the office
window, a bright smile in place, too keen to please.
Penance and subterfuge are closely related: she'd lately
started saving the leftovers for Spongebob's dinner,
too. I waited for the 4x4 to rumble off the end of
the drive before picking up the phone. It rang and
rang. The address at the top of the card read *Apt 198.5*
Channut Wadri Bldg, Simba St, Calcutta 4440. Did 198.5

mean Joy lived in half an apartment? The phone was still ringing. In an empty flat, surely. I was about to put the handset down when a man's voice spoke gruffly.

'Who is this?'

'Oh. My name's Harry Brinkman. I'm calling to speak with Joy Ghosh, if she's available, please.'

'Why?'

'I, well, if you don't mind I'll explain to—'

'Explain what?'

'ICBC International,' I blurted.

'Go away!' the man growled.

'Hang on, I—'

'No!'

I was so taken aback I couldn't immediately reply. The conversation, sudden as a dogfight, was about to end. I'd placed the call but this fellow, having come out of the sun at me, was bringing his guns to bear. I wove wildly:

'I . . . I'm the one. I cost her job! At the call centre. ICBC International.'

'Leave her alone!' the man shouted, and hung up.

I stood back from my desk, turned round, sat down again and picked up the phone. But I couldn't redial the number. I was trembling. In cold-calling terms I'd not performed well, not well at all. 'What am I trying to sell?' I asked aloud. I couldn't get her her job back. Did I want to apologise again, then? Penance and subterfuge! I'd already done so in writing; saying 'sorry' out loud wouldn't make her feel any better. *Forgiveness* is what I wanted, warm honey poured into my ear. The man's rebuttal made a sort of sense. In cutting me off he'd also cut me to the quick. Certainty filled the wound like clotting blood. I'd ruined Joy's life and I must make proper amends.

I didn't know how.

I stared out of the window at the sky. It was newsprint grey and unmoving. The flag up Anthony Woodward's pole would be hanging in heavy folds. An email blipped for attention on my screen. It was from Henry Tan, my Chinese pump-component-manufacturing friend. Washers: silicone rings: tiny synthetic 'O's! The unfairness of Joy Ghosh's dismissal threatened to undermine her advice. Since she'd talked me down from my ladder I'd covered half the distance to my party, and yet – petty sabotage excepted – I hadn't achieved anything concrete. What, really, was the point of resisting in vain?

Henry, always thorough, had shown his workings. I doubled a few of his figures, added a handling fee and forwarded the quote on. That was quite enough work for one day. Bannerman wanted payment on account for 'disbursements' – expenses in anybody else's language. I put my chequebook in my pocket and led Spongebob out to the car.

The lawyers' offices weren't quite the marble-and-steel edifice of Madison & Vere, but Robert had said Bannerman's was a respectable outfit and it looked like one. The girl at the front desk wore flight attendant make-up and peeped at me around a vase of arum lilies (Jennifer's favourites), which emphasised her tropical-parrot look. She asked whether I had made an appointment. I told her I had not. I would have gone on to explain that I didn't need to see the lawyer in person but her incredulous stare (what fool doesn't make an appointment?) prompted retaliatory rudeness: I pulled my chequebook out and said, 'I've come to hand over my first pound of flesh.' You don't see mauve eyeliner often. Bannerman, the girl backtracked, was in court that morning but, if I had a *billing enquiry*, the assistant on my case would be only too keen to help. She showed me into a room to wait. As I followed her I couldn't help noticing that she was stockier from the waist down than her top half intimated, and was evidently trying to do something about it: she'd forgotten to change out of the trainers I guessed she wore for hiking to work.

Sandeep Raja was soon reversing into the meeting room. Hot with haste, he smelled of rich cologne. He was also very young, twitchingly nervous, and weighted down with folders, which he immediately set about stacking on the middle of the table. Lawyers like documents. I bought Robert a lovely attaché case when he first started work but he changed it for one of those suitcase-sized leather holdalls the profession prefers.

'How can I help?' Raja asked, once he was satisfied with the display.

'Mr Bannerman said you'd need some money up front, for court fees and pub lunches.'

He nodded at me earnestly. 'Yes. It's all evidenced. I prepared the estimate myself. It's all in here. I can find it again. Just, you know, give me a mo—'

The boy's hairline, with his face crunched in concern, was extraordinarily low. It more or less joined up with his eyebrows. I'd clearly caught him off guard, unprepared for he knew not what. It took me three attempts to convince him I was just there to drop off a cheque. He began offering me coffee, fizzy water, sandwiches, anything to show his gratitude. I accepted. Off he shot. Scatty people don't inspire confidence, but – I thought of Jimmy – disorganisation can be a sign of deeper intelligence.

Raja was gone a long while. Last time I went to the dentist I found myself studying ancient history about Janet Jackson's pop-out breasts: any reading will fill the vacuum waiting creates. It's little wonder, then, that I was tempted to start on Fira's case notes in the boy's absence. I knew full well that he should not have left me alone with the files (strictly speaking Fira is his client, not me) but protocol, too, was worth resisting.

Here's what I found out.

Before she fled Chechnya, Fira lived with her father and two older brothers, their wives and children, in a house in the capital, Grozny. She had been training to become a vet at her father's old university. I thought of her confidence with Spongebob and winced: this woman now spent her days cleaning my house. On the second of January last year the family gathered to celebrate her father's eighty-fifth birthday. That was exactly Freddie's age when he died. It turned out there were further similarities between the two men. Before setting out on his academic career Fira's father fought during the war. He was a decorated Red Army soldier, another hero! As uncanny, her mother, like mine, died when she was in her teens. Fira's eldest brother (inspired by his father, perhaps) was a teacher, the other worked as a surveyor for an oil company. None of the family, Fira included, was politically active, let alone involved with the separatist movement. Like most Chechens they were more interested in peace than independence. So, the notes said, she had no real understanding of why, on the night of her father's party, shortly after the family had taken their seats at the dinner table, Russian soldiers kicked down the front door, dragged the men out into the street and beat them up. No understanding, that is, beyond 'in Chechnya, soldiers sometimes come'.

Fira tried to intervene, so she was beaten, too. My fingers were already digging at the coarse hair behind my left ear before I thought of the thin patch she has there. The soldiers drove away with her brothers in a military truck. Fira and her father they left for dead, correctly in the latter's case, though Fira, of course, survived to bury him, casting the first dirt left-handed since her right arm was broken in two places, which mattered less than the fact that neither brother had made it home for the funeral. Nor could Fira discover their whereabouts in the weeks that followed. Her persistence spurred the soldiers to visit the house again, but the new front door held just long enough for her to flee. Within a fortnight she'd acquired a fake passport and made it over the border to Georgia, where she bought a plane ticket for London. Fearing the forged ID would count against her, she did not claim asylum until she'd been in England for twenty-four days.

Raja arrived back with refreshments. He'd worked up a new lather retrieving them: an equestrian sweat augmented his cologne. Robert's firm has an in-house catering team. Raja would have to learn to compete on other grounds. By protecting his client's confidences, perhaps, or keeping their billing information more readily to hand. I liked this boy, though. There was something more than courteous about the way he poured my coffee, genuinely keen I should enjoy it, properly concerned when he saw I was shaking, quick with a glass of restorative fizzy water. He focused on the lunch, giving me time to compose myself, and kindly overlooked Fira's open folder, which was still spread on my lap.

'How's the case going?' I asked when he sat down with his plate piled high.

'Case. This one? It's fine. Quite interesting, actually, the Bosnia part at least.'

'Chechnya, you mean.'

'Yes, of course. The history. I studied history at college, before law.'

Detail was probably his thing. And sandwiches. In seagull snatches he was gulping them down.

'You're optimistic that we'll win?'

'Excuse me.' He took a swig of water. 'Win. Yes. Seb, Mr Bannerman, he has a good record. I'm learning a lot. About this sort of thing, in particular.'

I shut the file and put it back on the table. Then I wrote out a cheque for the amount Bannerman had suggested. The junior lawyer's ineptitude had to be a smokescreen. Perhaps Raja had wanted me to read about Fira's case. His insistence that I at least dent the lunch, and his nervy laughter when I wrapped up a round of sandwiches in a napkin for Spongebob (I explained what I was doing), cemented my opinion that he had a kind heart.

I thought about kindness after I left Bannerman & Co.'s offices. It is concern for other people's happiness, I suppose. Pearl's campaigns are global but she puts herself out for strangers (trees even), rebelling on the slaves' behalf as well as her own. There's no way Jimmy makes those weekly phone calls to Jennifer and me for his own benefit now. No, and his pictures are gifts without strings, not pleas for approval, which perhaps explains why he's never whinged about the way Bill H. Marshall stymied his career. I fed Spongebob the sandwiches and climbed into the car. In her way Jennifer is still kind too. She hardly eats the sausages she so laboriously stuffs and isn't throwing this party for the sake of good form alone. What about Robert? It would be too easy to dismiss his lavish presents as empty gestures, but they're not: when he gave us the plasma-screen TV he printed out simplified instructions on a card for Jennifer, so keen was he that she should learn to use the new remote control, and it was those instructions, not the price tag on the side of the box, which made my Adam's apple rise in my throat as I cleared away the wrapping paper. The card would have taken him five minutes of bill-able time to make, about £50 in the world of Madison

& Vere. How long before Robert would have his secretary take care of such niceties?

Last weekend he and Marie invited us to lunch. That's not quite right. They invited us for lunch three Sundays ago, postponed the night beforehand and rearranged for this Sunday just last Friday. Fine by me, and – surprisingly – by Jennifer too: she despairs of Jimmy's disorganisation but makes allowances for the pressing schedule of her elder, more successful son.

I wore my trainers. Lately I've felt more comfortable in them than my other shoes.

Robert and Marie live in Belsize Park, which is a bind to get to, being on the other side of London. They have a large flat, or *maisonette*, a ridiculous word redeemed only when it comes out of Marie's mouth. Big, but their windsurfers are still stored in my garage. The place set them back roughly what the Tithe Barn is worth, and for that they get an upstairs neighbour who twice in three years has flooded their front room. Last time it happened I suggested it might be a sign from above that they should get out on the water more often, but Robert didn't take the joke well, itself a telling sign that he should spend more time doing something he's passionate about. I didn't have a chance to bring this subject up with him again on Sunday. Before lunch I was too busy carving the beef (little Flo: '*boeuf*') while Robert took a conference call from Japan; it would not have been appropriate to harangue him in front of his wife and child during the meal; and immediately after we'd eaten a car turned up to spirit him to the airport.

'I'll take you,' I offered, as he gathered his luggage.

'Don't be silly.' He patted my shoulder. 'The client pays. Stay and chat to the girls.'

I followed him out into the hall. Expensive ornaments – artefacts, almost – have started springing up around the place recently. Here was a finely painted Chinese vase, stabbed full of umbrellas, in the hall. It looked top heavy and unwisely close to the front door, particularly with a small child in the house. Perhaps there was a weight in the bottom.

'Freddie wrote a journal,' I said.

'Oh yes?' Robert stock-took his pockets for wallet, keys, phone.

'It's illuminating. Your grandad wasn't what he seemed to be. Or he tried to be something that didn't exist. I can't quite make sense of it.'

'Get a copy made and I'll see if I can help you out.'

'He was chasing something unreal. A destructive force.'

Robert unsnapped the front door's lock, saying, 'He was fighting a war.'

'Exactly. There isn't a war now, but you're slogging after phantoms too. You're suffering for something that isn't worth having.'

'I will be if I miss the plane.'

'Robert.'

'Dad.' He patted me on the shoulder again. I wanted to put him in a half-nelson. Windsurfing gave him strong arms once but I have a log basket now. 'Seriously,' he continued. 'I'll be late. Let's go out for a drink when I get back.' He nodded at a black Mercedes purring flush with the kerb. 'Some time soon.'

I watched the limo's brake lights stutter away. The

street wasn't designed with cars – let alone one that size – in mind. I tested the Ming umbrella stand's centre of gravity. Six months, at most, before little Flo had it over. When I'd calmed down I went back inside.

Jennifer and Marie were drinking coffee. Little Flo was playing with a plastic zoo.

'You can't put the lions in with the flamingos,' I explained.

'*Pourquoi non?*'

'Because lions are scared of pink.'

She has a chirrupy laugh: it almost sounds as if she's hiccupping.

'How many lions are there, anyway?' I asked.

'*Un, deux,*' she explained.

'What about this one?'

'*C'est un tigre.*'

'No it's not! Tigers have stripes!' The lion in question had a mane. Flo speaks French with her mum and English with her dad. The male: another species. I looked up from the model, a 'Daddy lion' spiel on my lips, and saw she was shaking with suppressed laughter at her joke.

'Lion lion lion!' she chirruped.

Flo has her mother's brown eyes and olive skin, which, it being November, had a greenish tinge. She suffered bad chickenpox six months ago. Up close the scar above her right eyebrow looked like a raindrop dent in the sand. I slapped my own forehead, laughed with her and reunited the lions, saying, 'A family of lions is called a pride.'

Marie was extolling the virtues of her new three-piece

suite, which Jennifer approved of. They would be having the room redecorated to go with the apricot Nubuck, my daughter-in-law explained. I joined the circle, suggesting leather would withstand scuffs and spills, and Marie said, 'Robert is nearly there, you know.'

'But he's only just set off.'

'You know what I mean. He's hearing some good noises.'

'Fabulous,' said Jennifer.

'He's putting everything into it. I am very proud.' Marie beamed at us in turn, stopping on me. Her smile is beautiful, but since Flo was born there have been evergreen bags under her eyes. Attachment theory is the culprit: Flo's not one for sleeping alone. As I've said, it's tough being a single mum.

'How are your parents?' I asked.

'They are fine.'

'Have they packed up the centre yet?'

More quietly: 'No.'

'They're still hoping to pass it on as a going concern, then?'

'They have scaled back. It's more competitive down there now, for such a business, you know.'

I supposed so.

'There's one other lawyer challenging Robert for the partnership place,' Marie went on. 'She is a popular woman with big clients. Iceland, for example, and Dyno-Rod. But Robert has stronger key-partner support, he says.'

Jennifer: 'Will you redecorate through into the kitchen, or stop at the partition?'

'All the way through.'

'Does Flo miss Robert when he's away?' I asked.

'It's strange. But no. It's like she understands — intuits, is it? — that he must go. We don't make a fuss. That way, when he is free, he just slots right in.'

'I think that's wise,' Jennifer concurred. 'Right through, a clean sweep.'

'Wouldn't it be sensible to wait until after the next flood?' I winked.

'Harry!' Jennifer slapped my hand. 'This old fool's just jealous, you know!'

Marie's smile swivelled Jennifer's way. 'Have you done something new with your hair?' she asked. 'Or lost some weight? There is a new radiance in your face. Definitely. Of the two of us I am looking like the older one!'

It was kind of Marie to have paid Jennifer such a compliment. My wife deserved it, and glowed lovelier still with the blush it raised in her cheeks. While I'd been reading about Russian soldiers beating Fira, Jennifer had been having another golf lesson with Ryder Evans, who lives next to the eighteenth hole in a flat provided by the club. Sex also lifts blood into the face. I doubt the golf club runs to a maisonette. When I climax a pink glow flares across my chest. It has become more noticeable as the dark hairs there have turned to silver, although recently, of course, I've not had a chance to check. The idea of Jennifer and Ryder Evans was upsetting, but paled when set next to the contents of Fira's file. One revelation stung, the other made me sick the stomach. Imagine how cleaning houses must feel if you wanted to be a vet.

Spongebob blinked at me in the rear-view mirror. I smiled back at him and said, 'I don't feel like going home just yet.'

Instead I drove away from Bannerman's office with the sat-nav switched off, following my car's nose. It's surprisingly pleasurable, and unusual, to inch around central London purposelessly, at one with the prevailing traffic jam. I sat in Baker Street for fifteen minutes, perfectly happy, resisting my resistance to resistance, so to speak. The Sherlock Holmes museum pays for a teenager to dress up in a period police outfit and stand outside number 221B. The boy on duty that day was very tall, but unenthusiastic. He kept looking at his watch. They needed a drama student. Someone like the hypermarket checkout girl, I thought; she'd have been much more convincing.

In thickening dusk I devolved to West London. Narwhal spikes came to mind. I decided to check on Bill H. Marshall. Fixing upon a destination threatened my traffic-zen at once, of course, but I didn't rush. There was no answer when I knocked on the critic's glossy door. Looking up the straight-faced house I saw steam pouring from a vent at the top of the wall. I sell valves, for shower pumps sometimes. I walked off around the square. A newsagent's stood where the square joined the main road. I bought a can of leaded Coke (we only have the diet stuff at home) and a lottery ticket (my first in ten years). It's not just lesbian table football my pound would help fund, I thought, and then I thought harder: even if it did, did I care?

The critic's bathroom light was still on. And the gate

into the square's centrepiece garden was ajar, I noticed, as I headed back to my car. No doubt Spongebob would also like to stretch his legs. He sniffed about among the shrubs while I sat in the gloom on a bench opposite Bill H. Marshall's house and drank my Coke. Not so long ago cans of pop had ring-pulls that came off on your finger. A billion aluminium sycamore leaves fluttered to the ground. Whoever designed the modern opening deserved a Nobel Prize. The fan window above the critic's front door flashed cheerily to life.

'Stay here,' I told Spongebob, and jogged out of the communal garden.

'You again,' the man said, answering his front door.

'I have a venue in mind,' I began. 'A gallery of sorts. What's the word? A *space.*'

'Good for you.'

'So I thought I'd drop by and ask you again.'

'What about writing? They print an email address at the foot of my column. You could have saved yourself a trip.'

Beneath the chandelier in the hallway the big man's forehead was pink; the tops of his ears shone. Definitely, he'd been showering. I saw that his right ear was scarred; the piping around its rim, crushed of all detail, was a cauliflower mass. Rugby.

'Come on,' I said. 'You told me you'd consider it. Just take a look at his new show, won't you? It's your job, after all.'

'I can't go to every show, can I?' He was smiling at me as he said this. 'Your boy has had his fifteen minutes of fame.'

'Yes, but!' I looked about me. 'You made a mistake. A refereeing mistake. It's a confusing place, the scrum. Loose-head, right? Even the best referees haven't a clue what goes on in the front row. You must have been done for your opposite number's crimes once or twice, yes? Or for nobody's crime at all? They get it wrong sometimes. Fine art is like rugby. It's as simple as that!'

'Exactly the same,' he said, fingering his ear. 'Astonishing that I haven't seen it before.'

'Look, there's no need to take the—'

Bill H. Marshall raised his hands, fingers spread wide. 'Relax. I'll come.'

'You will?'

'Yes, but this is all grist to the mill, right? The new column goes beyond reviewing. Between you and me, the inches are sometimes hard to fill. If I come I'm going to write all this up, too, yes? To extend your — ingenious — analogy, there're no rules on this pitch.'

'Write what you like about me. I don't give a damn. Just take Jimmy's new work seriously.'

He laughed at me silently.

The front row is a treacherous place.

The sport's authorities have tried to stamp out the more dangerous stuff that goes on there, but to little effect. The last team I played for had a particularly strong loose-head prop — Keith, an Australian who drove a JCB — and a psychotically powerful Rastafarian hooker called Giles. Together they could (and often did) inflict the ultimate front-row insult: lifting the opposition's tight-head and hooker clear of the turf as the ball was put into the scrum, darkly referred to as giving 'flying lessons'. Shoulders popped, windpipes were crushed. Yet injuring your opponent wasn't the point, the point was to intimidate him into ineffectiveness. Give a flying lesson early on in a match and you'd ensure psychological supremacy – and turnover ball – thereafter.

Bill H. Marshall must have been every bit as strong as Keith in his heyday.

Do critics sit in the front row at the theatre? I wondered.

Now that I paid it attention, the thickened bridge of his nose suggested it had been reset. I considered having mine sorted out once, but there seemed little point while I was still playing, and by the time I stopped I was used to it. At Keith's leaving party his nose was a terrible mess. He'd appointed himself flying instructor to a Welsh labourer at the start of his last match, and received a stupefying headbutt as he went down for the second scrum in part payment for the lesson.

If the critic had intended to cow Jimmy by his review he'd failed. My son was painting yet.

Bill H. Marshall signalled that our chat was over by reaching for his coat. It was bright yellow, which mattered, though I didn't know why. He checked his watch and bent down to fiddle with his trouser leg. I told the top of his head the date of Jimmy's show, said I'd email the details, and thanked him, through gritted teeth, for agreeing to come. His infuriating smile was still in place when he stood up. I said 'goodbye' and turned to descend his chequered steps.

A word fluttered out of reach as I skirted the narwhal railings. There was Spongebob, weaving through the flower bed on the other side of them, nose to the black earth, sleuthing for scents. A surprising number of squirrels make central London their home. A door slammed behind me; Spongebob raised his head. The word was a long one, two together in fact, joined by a hyphen.

Bicycle-clip.

I turned to shout 'Stop!' but the critic's yellow jacket was already strobing past the parked cars. I shouted it anyway, hoping against hope that one of them at least would take note. No such luck. I started running. The critic's bike moved swiftly, especially considering the bulk it carried, but Spongebob was faster, a streak along the inside of the railings, a blur towards the open gate. His car-crash bark shattered the calm.

'Bill!' I yelled. 'Bill, look out!'

Rugby, particularly for forwards, axiomatically for the front row, is all about meeting pressure with equal and opposite force. I darted between two parked SUVs just in time to see Spongebob leap at the critic's front wheel. Bill H. Marshall steered straight into him. The collision threw both dog and man off balance, but the critic managed to keep from falling. He slewed to a stop and jumped off his bike. Spongebob was crabbing sideways, his nose low between his front legs. The critic ran back towards him and kicked him in the side of the head. Unfortunately the blow brought my hardy dog to his senses. Spongebob had hold of the man's calf when I arrived, and he clung on despite the punches, the gouging, the tearing at his ears.

'Here, stop, leave! My! Oh!' I threw myself on top of Spongebob, cheek to bony skull. A classic wing-forward tackle. His growling was a desperate low rumble in my chest. We broke from the critic. Spongebob allowed my weight to press him into the tarmac. Our hearts thumped together.

'Holy shit!' Bill H. Marshall was inspecting his torn trouser leg (the cycle-clip was now at half-mast around his sock). 'You're braver than me!'

'Easy,' I whispered. 'I have you.'

'Mind it doesn't get a hold of you, too!'

Spongebob's growl rolled like an oil drum down a metalled hill.

'Where's the fucking owner? It came from the garden. Dogs aren't allowed in there!'

'I don't know,' I began disloyally. 'I didn't know . . . that the garden was out of bounds. To dogs. He's scared of bikes. It's my fault. I wasn't thinking.'

'This is your dog?' The big man, standing above us, put his hands on his hips.

I said nothing. Still smothering Spongebob, I worked my fingers through his leather collar, stroked his neck and brow with the other hand. It came away wet.

'Christ! I've seen it all.' The critic shook his head. 'An attack dog. What the fuck is coming next?'

'Your leg,' I said.

To his credit the big man still had his front-row attitude to a ruckus. He looked at the blood dribbling down his shin with interest, shrugged, and dropped his trouser leg. Then he collected his bike. Remounting it he said, 'Probably best for its health if I never set eyes on that animal again.'

Spongebob tensed beneath me as he cycled away.

There's a lot of pointless bravado in the cauldron of the scrum. I've seen players get set to go down with flaps of forehead hanging loose.

'Easy!' I whispered. Spongebob's growl dissolved to a whine as the bike left the square. His right ear was ripped at the root; there was blood all over my hand. I thought of Fira, her arm raised in self-defence, Chechen army boots. She'd be angry about this. It would set Spongebob's familiarisation therapy back weeks.

I was shaking.

Weeping, in fact.

'Easy, boy.' I lifted my dog up as I got to my feet. 'Easy, Spongebob.'

15

Talking Pages pinpointed an emergency veterinary clinic in Shepherd's Bush; the sat-nav delivered us to its door. As in casualty there was a queue, which Spongebob endured stoically, ignoring the other patients entirely, content to sit with his bloodied head in my lap. The young vet who did eventually see us whistled 'You Ain't Nothing But A Hound Dog' as she conducted her examination. I thought of the gap-toothed navigator, Len Rushworth, and of Freddie's return trip from his first raid. Perhaps the cold air rushing through the holed cockpit perspex dulled the pain of his slashed eyebrow. Modern anaesthetic is, of course, miraculous stuff. Spongebob didn't so much as flinch when the vet, whose sewing wasn't as sure as her whistling, stuck the hooked needle in.

It was late when the she finished patching up my dog. I carried him – floppy, warm, dozy – out to the Audi, and laid him in the street-lit back. Before I drove off I had to unpeel another parking ticket from the windscreen. The vet's bill had been £290, not including VAT. The worse your luck gets, the less you feel it, sometimes. What did another £60 matter in the scheme of things?

I phoned Jennifer before setting off. Her anger (why hadn't I checked in earlier?) was tinged with a gleeful note, which rang loudest when she told me she'd put my helping of toad-in-the-hole in the dog's bowl. She was pleased to have a reason to be cross with me, it seemed. I didn't tell her about Spongebob's injury. The sympathy she'd offer would be less genuine than her exasperation. Instead I asked whether there was anything she wanted me to pick up on my way home. 'No,' she said, softening. 'All I need is a bath now, then bed. Please don't wake me. I've had an exhausting day.'

With Spongebob snoring gently behind me I made my way past Brook Green towards Hammersmith. Instead of scooting south beneath the flyover, however, I ran up on to the elevated A4 and headed out west. Jimmy does his nightwatchman job on a light-industrial estate in Gunnersbury, out this way. I plugged the street name into the computer and followed its instructions, my reluctance to go home overtaken by an urge to see my younger son.

I called in at a takeaway en route. I was famished and Jimmy often forgets to eat.

But he wasn't in the forecourt security cabin when I arrived. Though I blipped the horn nobody came out of any of the shut-eyed warehouses either. The chicken jalfrezi on the seat beside me was pulsing heat; I could also smell the nan bread's buttery warmth. Even if Jimmy wasn't on duty there was no point in letting good food go to waste. I was searching for a plastic fork in the bag when a tap on the window made me jump.

'What's going on with the dead dog in the back of your car, Dad?'

Jimmy flicked his torch-beam from the car's rear to the food in my lap and back again.

'I was in the area,' I told him. 'I thought I'd bring you a bite to eat.'

The dashboard lights illuminated his broad smile. 'Five minutes and all you'd have been offering me is a lick of the container lids.'

We took the food into the Portakabin. Though I'd dropped Jimmy off for work once or twice, I'd never been inside before. We sat on plastic chairs before a Formica table pocked with cigarette burns. A decade's topless models posed on the walls. Jimmy smiled cheerfully again after I'd taken in these surroundings and ran a what-can-you-do hand across his shorn head. I shrugged too. While we ate I explained where I'd got Spongebob from, and why, and how he'd come to be hurt; it was pure Jimmy to be more concerned about my dog's injuries than their implications for his career. He looked at me quizzically when I asked what he thought.

'If the vet says his ear will mend, that's good, of course.'

'Not about the dog.'

He looked at the empty curry boxes. '*That* was great. I didn't know how hungry I was until I started eating.'

'Come on, son. Will you do it?'

'Do what?'

'The exhibition. Marshall may still show up.'

'You think? I'll bet he promised you that just to get

rid of you, never mind his run-in afterwards with poor old Spongebob.'

It struck me that Jimmy was the first person I'd told my dog's name to without thinking, and that he'd used it without comment.

'Maybe,' I said. 'And yet—'

'I couldn't care less whether he comes or not, Dad.'

'No. Of course. But for me, then. It's my birthday party, after all.'

'Your birthday is only a couple of weeks away. I'm into the paintings, but they're not finished yet. And they're huge, bigger than anything I've done before. I'm not sure they'll sit well next to the needlepoint and watercolours in the village pub.'

I explained *the dove ascending*'s metamorphosis.

He laughed, said, 'I'll do my best,' and fell silent. His eyes disappeared into shadow as he looked down at his raw-boned hands. Jimmy has always been hopeless with secrets. We had to keep everybody's Christmas presents from him when he was a child; he just couldn't stop himself from explaining what lay beneath the wrapping paper before it was time to rip it off. Even when we didn't tell him, he had a knack for guessing correctly and coming out with the truth, more and more reluctantly the older he got, but he'd come out with it all the same. I sensed a revelation in the air, was too slow to head it off, and still don't know how he intuited what he disclosed next.

'You do realise,' he said, 'that Mum is throwing you a party because she's having an affair?'

The calendar page immediately behind Jimmy's head

showed Miss August 1999. The poses are timeless, but it's amazing how fast hairstyles change.

'I know she's spending time with somebody, yes. But I don't believe she's throwing the party out of guilt alone, or to conceal the fact from me.'

'Right.' Jimmy narrowed his eyes. One brown, one green, both muddied with scepticism.

'Your mother thinks she's doing the right thing.'

'And you're OK with her seeing somebody else?'

'I wouldn't say that, quite. She's happier, though. And if that's the case then, somehow, I don't feel entirely sad.'

'Oh,' he said, his gaze clearing. 'Oh. Right. In which case, I'll give it a real go. I'm having difficulty pulling off the gun turrets. Window panes, the number of them . . . accuracy is hard to resist. But when they're done I'll only have two tail sections and a bomb bay left to paint.'

As I've mentioned, Jimmy didn't think much of hugs as a child; there was a time when I didn't dare touch him at all. Now, though, it felt right to say, 'Good,' and reach out and put my hand on his shoulder. He did not flinch. He looked me in the face and nodded. Then he picked up his torch, said that he had to make another round of the premises, and suggested that I head for home. Premises, promises. A detour via Anthony Woodward's West End Farm aside, I did as I was told.

Fira arrived for work the next morning. It was raining. Proper, November rain, icy spears slanting from a turbid sky. I'd put a clean towel in the tumble dryer at ten to the hour. It was as warm as new bread when Fira passed the kitchen window, hunched inside her bike helmet, at nine o'clock sharp. She took off her sodden puffa coat and dropped it straight into the sink. I hovered, hoping to hand her the towel, while she unpacked a dry pair of jeans from her rucksack and hung them over a chair. *Waterproofs*, I thought. It seemed she was about to peel off her wet trousers in front of me. Alarmed, I thrust the towel at her (she took it without offering unnecessary thanks) and retreated to my office straight away, so missing my opportunity to make our early morning coffee.

The post on my mat that morning was representative.

In view of the prevailing drought our local water company (I'd like to source mine from Scotland, please) were proud to announce they would shortly be charging us by the litre. I thought of Jennifer's capacious bathtub, winced, and wrote back, praising their initiative, but hoping they'd understand my decision to sink a well: I sell pumps, after all.

Would the driver of Range Rover Discovery J267 RPH, clocked exiting St Clare at forty-seven miles per hour on 27 October, please raise their hand? Before I could stop myself I'd ordered the photographic evidence, as much to put the police to the trouble of sending it as for the perverse pleasure to be had from a shot of Jennifer with any passenger she might have been carrying.

The last batch of chemical feeder metering pump

sleeves I'd processed had, apparently, been bored by my Polish manufacturer two millimetres wider than the specifications (too narrow and I could have had them remilled), meaning they were useless and en route back to Warsaw again, at my expense.

At least the shower people wanted samples of Henry Tan's silicone rings, despite my silly quotation. Their hard-copy letter was a signal of intent, though not one that tempted me to waste ink and time on a real letter of my own to China; I added the words 'exciting opportunity' to my copy-typed email, pasted in Henry's address, and hit send.

Having cut the above with time spent soothing Spongebob (he seemed cast low, perhaps troubled by his ear now the anaesthetic had worn off) and watching the rain lance at the skeletal hawthorn hedge, I made it to 10.43 before ducking back inside to reboil the kettle.

Fira had already stopped work to do the same.

Surprised, I hovered as she washed out the cafetière, which was clean before she started. Her hands seemed jittery under the taps. Feeling – absurdly – as if I was putting her off the task, I square-danced around her (for a farmhouse kitchen the room seemed suddenly small) and retreated to the far cupboard for mugs, then put them down next to the two which, in the meantime, she'd dried and set out. Acknowledging this silliness defeated me; not mentioning it felt as unnatural as ignoring a lightning strike. Fira spilled coffee grounds as she tried to spoon them into the cafetière. I fetched a cloth. Something had definitely reduced her capable, precise fingers to a state of twitchiness. Perhaps she'd broken an ornament in another room. Mortified to think she'd think I cared, I reached to wipe the dusting of coffee from the countertop, as if cleaning up that spill would mend whatever it was she'd smashed, or at least restore her faith in me. At the same moment Fira put her fingers on the work surface, right next to the spill. I looked at the hand, its apple-white wrist, the arm bare to her shoulder. Did she want to wipe the countertop herself? I let go of the cloth. But instead of picking it up, Fira's fingers brushed over mine. At first I thought – wilfully stupidly – that she'd touched me without meaning to, but there was nothing uncertain about this movement, and when she repeated it I knew it had been no mistake.

I breathed out and I breathed in, cautiously, as if air was new to me and I had to test it before taking in a whole lungful.

I looked from Fira's hand to her face, saw the patch of thin hair behind her small, pink ear, and that she was focusing on her fingers, which were now closing over mine. Her hand's slenderness, set against the weathered wood of my own, felt right and looked wrong. She had stepped into the wedge of space between me and the countertop. Her thigh was touching mine.

I heard myself think 'What are you doing?' and realised, as she stopped moving, that I'd asked out loud.

She said, 'You have sausages instead of fingers.'

My hand was burning beneath hers, and her thigh was moving against mine again, and the sweet pale oval of her face was tilting up into my own, and she was still sliding towards me; any further and her hipbone would press into the stiffness of my zip.

I felt her breath against my lips as she went on.

'But you are a good man, with the best wishes, and your kindness to me with this lawyer is nothing, not really, not compared with the rest of you, your generous heart. I want to return this generosity, I must, I have to . . .'

(I knew what she was trying to say before she managed it, felt myself pulling away from her as the words came out of her mouth.)

'. . . to thank you—'

'Thank me?' Both my hands had found my pockets. I'd taken a step back, was taking another, and another. 'No, Fira. You don't have to thank me. *Thank* me. Christ, no!'

She started to follow me but thought better of it and turned away. Later I was reassured by the fact that she did not apologise; later still, I was appalled by the fact that I had not apologised myself.

Fira made the coffee.

I watched in helpless silence.

My mind was an empty hangar. I could think of nothing, absolutely nothing, to say. All around us abandoned aircraft flamed to the kitchen floor. Silence, more silence, hours of expectant runway and blank, vacant sky. I had to put a speck on the horizon. Something, anything, for hope's sake alone.

'Spongebob attacked another bicycle,' I heard myself say. 'He had to have his ear sewn back on, by a vet.'

'Poor dog,' murmured Fira, so quietly I had to carry on.

'Yes, he's OK, and I'm sure the ear will heal, given time, but the stitches look rough to me. The woman who put them in wasn't very skilful. So do you think, perhaps, that you could take a look at them?' Then, by way of explanation: 'I know you're not a cleaner, Fira. I know you're really training to be a vet.'

She flinched at these last words, rendering her subsequent stillness unnatural.

'You are unhappy with my work in the house?'

'Of course not. You know—'

'Then I should carry on with it.' She handed me my cup of coffee and, leaving her own untouched, walked out of the kitchen.

'Fira,' I said, to her retreating back. 'Fira, please.'

I returned to my office through the strafing rain. My shirt hung heavily from my shoulders after I shut the door and I dripped on the carpet tiles as I stood behind my chair.

What had I done?

There being no answer to that question, I shunted Spongebob off the cellar trapdoor, lifted it up and climbed down the little steps into the old engine pit. A garage mechanic had once stood in this hole to mend cars, but irreparable emptiness loomed above me now. I closed the hatch to shut it out.

Total darkness.

My palms slid over the brickwork. I sat down on the cement floor. I put my head in my hands. The damp dust smelled of regret.

Regret at having failed to convince Fira I wanted nothing in return for my help.

Regret at having been blind to the signs in the run-up to her advance.

Regret at having so clumsily rebuffed her.

Regret at having humiliated her by letting on that I knew about her past.

Regret at having trespassed there in the first place.

But most of all, gathering like pain in the aftermath of a cut, and with the force of the truth dispelling excuses, regret that I'd not reached out for Fira, held her, kissed her, *taken her when I had the chance*.

Time passed. Spongebob, who had begun to pace to and fro as I sat in the darkness beneath him, now began to whine. I growled back. His ear had made me mention Fira's damned veterinary studies, which meant that part of this mess was his fault. Having someone to blame is a beguiling luxury: here I was, a man of nearly sixty, howling at a mongrel in the dark. It occurred to me, once again, that I should just give up, stay put in that hole, expire there, make it my grave. Resistance had not restored my moral compass. That compass was calibrated by a war hero, whose true north I could no longer trust, yet without him I was losing my bearings. Satellite navigation is no use when you're squatting in a hole. I lay on my back, eyes open, staring at the damp hollowness, falling into black sea.

Heroes are not impervious to fear. They simply cope with it better than the rest of us. By 13 June 1944

Freddie's heroism was at its vertiginous height. He had a long way to fall.

The day did not start well. Instead of 'S-Sugar', the Mark II Lancaster in which Freddie and his crew had flown their last twenty-six operations, they arrived at dispersal to find 'P-Peter', a nearly new Lancaster Mark III, waiting for them. It wasn't simply superstitious attachment to their old 'crate' which made them suspicious of the replacement, though Freddie underlined 'why on the thirteenth of all dates?' in his journal, or the fact that he and the crew knew every reassuring rattle and whine in S-Sugar's repertoire; the newer Lancasters were fitted with Rolls-Royce Merlins, which were less powerful than the four Bristol Hercules engines that powered the older planes.

The target that night was the Opel works at Russelsheim, in western Germany, said to be 'spitting out V_I flying bombs like baby rabbits'. An experienced Pathfinder by now, Freddie took on the deputy master bomber role, making him jointly responsible for guiding the other ninety Lancasters to the aiming point. A groan went round the briefing room when the group captain told the crews that they would be flying a dreaded 'straight-in straight-back' route: this meant coming home through the swarm of German night fighters they'd have stirred into action on the way to the target.

As ever, Freddie had salted away his Benzedrine 'wakey-wakey' capsule into his school washbag ('falling asleep on the job isn't my fear') long before he climbed into the left-hand cockpit seat. Once there, he began his pre-flight checks with engineer Tom Spears, a twenty-two-year-old optician from Brighton. Gap-toothed Len Rushworth, whistling a big-band tune, tossed his charts on to the navigator's table behind the open cockpit, checked his pockets for his torch, rulers and coloured pencils, and pinned back the black-cloth curtain he'd later draw against the glare of searchlights and flak-bursts. The three gunners climbed into their turrets. Among them was mid-upper gunner Bryne Falkirk. Born in Perth, he had completed seventy-two hours of dual and solo training on Tiger Moths before learning that, at five foot four, he would be too short to reach the rudder pedals in a bomber. This wasn't true; in fact there was a backlog of trainee pilots at the time, and Bryne was considered an ideal fit for a gun turret. Freddie taxied to the holding point. Seventy feet of fuselage shuddered as the engines ran up to speed. At 9.27 p.m. flight control gave P-Peter permission to taxi to the runway and shortly afterwards, as the rear gunner reported 'tail up', Freddie pressed his St Christopher to his as yet hairless chest.

The trip out went smoothly enough. Following Len Rushworth's instructions, Freddie aimed P-Peter straight across the Dutch coastline, arrowing towards Russelsheim. Up they climbed, to 20,000 feet. As the temperature in their turrets dropped to thirty below, the gunners switched on their electrically heated flying suits. Bryne Falkirk announced that he was having to knead frozen condensation from his oxygen mask. Freddie, unimpressed, told him to shut up and keep his eyes peeled: 'happy valley' – or the heavily defended Ruhr – was passing below. Just then, knitting-needle searchlights pinpointed a Lancaster half a mile off P-Peter's starboard wing. Freddie watched it jump suddenly with flames and spiral to the ground, but his journal offers no comment on the fate of the crew. Instead he reserves his concern for the moment when, approaching Russelsheim, a radio transmission from the master bomber was chopped short mid-sentence, and stayed cut out. 'This was a blow. A strange coldness gripped me. I informed Len and the crew that it was up to us now to direct the show.'

Freddie descended to just below the patchy stratus. Len Rushworth had done his job well; the crew had no trouble picking out the moonlit factory. Freddie instructed the main body of Lancasters to delay their arrival over the target by five minutes. He started his run. P-Peter dropped four target markers, then circled in light flak to check their accuracy. Satisfied, Freddie put the plane into a steep climb above the clouds and released the main force, instructing them to aim directly at his illuminations. Before long these first flares were engulfed in dust; Freddie descended again through worse flak and tracer, and relit the target with his remaining six markers. Once the rest of the force had pulverised the site, Freddie made his last run over the Opel works, dropping four thousand-pound high-explosive bombs – fused for delayed action, to hamper search-and-rescue attempts – and climbed again to tag on to the end of the bomber stream.

He had flown unflinchingly, yet at a cost; as soon as

he turned for home the strange, cold feeling worsened. 'It was a wholly new fear,' the journal states, 'tinged with panic. I felt it as a horrible mask of ice, clogging my mouth, my throat, my chest.' In the distance he saw another Lancaster dropping like a comet through the night sky, and heard Len Rushworth, still hidden behind his curtain, give him instructions for the 'straight-back' route home.

Freddie ignored him.

'I don't know why. I simply decided we'd return to base another way.'

Freddie was the skipper, entitled to the final say, and he ordered his navigator to plot a new route. But Len stopped whistling and demanded that Freddie put the plane on the correct heading. For the ex-maths teacher the war was about wringing survival from exactitude. Freddie, changing the subject, gave orders to throw out 'window' – metallic strips to confuse the enemy radar: the plane would be more vulnerable to it now, separated from the pack – and veered farther west. He then made matters worse by doing something all navigators hated, weaving unnecessarily ('I can't explain it, keeping straight and level was simply impossible'), making it difficult for Len to keep track of the plane's position, let alone guide it home.

The journal does not describe how they made it to northern France, but I imagine Len Rushworth, furious in his curtained cubicle, struggling to keep up as Freddie wove his lone course for England. With the moonlit Channel in sight, and the news awaiting them at base that sixteen of the ninety Lancasters had not returned, he might have felt justified in having acted on his hunch. But just as he was about to order 'coffee-up' Bryne Falkirk spotted a Ju88 night fighter above and behind the Lancaster, in the same quarter as the moon. Night fighters worked in pairs. Before the mid-upper gunner could complete his warning the sky was perforated by streaking green tracer. Some of it slammed into P-Peter's airframe. Freddie dived to port, hollering at his gunners to return fire. Bryne Falkirk already had. As the Lancaster levelled out, both the mid-upper and rear gunners saw the Ju88 roll on to its back and fall away, trailing flames and smoke.

There was no time to feel relief. The second Junkers was already closing in on the Lancaster from astern. Rear gunner Michael Harris spotted it first, but his guns jammed. He shrieked into the intercom and Bryne Falkirk opened up again with his Browning .303s. The Junkers returned fire. It raked P-Peter with heavy-calibre shells from tail to nose. Freddie's hands leapt and shuddered on the controls. But Bryne, swivelling in his turret, had also struck his mark: the fighter tore past Freddie's cockpit streaking white flame. While my father struggled to regain control, Bryne's matter-of-fact Australian voice confirmed that he'd 'hit the number two', that it was 'going down' and, eventually, that it had 'popped'.

P-Peter's rudder pedals were spongy and its control column felt 'like a spoon stirring porridge'. Somebody was shouting something unintelligible over the intercom. Freddie opened his mouth to shut them up, but Bryne's guns were already roaring again, and he realised a third attack was in progress. My father stamped and flung and heaved the plane into a vicious corkscrew to starboard. Pouring tracer, the bomber plummeted. When it reached seventy degrees of bank, Freddie, who had lost sight of the night fighter, tried to level the wings.

Nothing happened.

Part of the Lancaster's starboard aileron had been shot away.

Freddie ordered 'stand by to abandon aircraft' and said (to himself as much as the crew) that he would attempt to pull the stricken bomber through a half-roll. His ears filled with engine-scream and shouting voices, cannon fire and intercom whine. The wings revolved through the vertical and kept going. With the Lancaster upside down at 10,000 feet, Freddie pulled back on the stick. Its latticed nose dipped slowly towards the sea. Freddie throttled back all four engines to idle.

And he, and his crew, waited.

The third Junkers, missing its tailplane, followed P-Peter down.

At 5,000 feet Freddie pulled the Lancaster past the vertical. The sea, sheet metal in the moonlight, swung up to meet them. Freddie's forearms, shoulders and calves burned as he heaved back on the stick: popping rivets didn't matter now, they'd be no worse off if he ripped off the wings, which he didn't, P-Peter's new airframe proving a match for the strain. At 1,800 feet, cold tears mingling with his sweat, my father had the Lancaster level again, if pointed back towards France. Behind them, the third Junkers exploded as it hit the sea. Freddie began to tell his crew that he would try a gentle turn to starboard, but was silenced by Bryne Falkirk again, this time hollering: 'Mid-upper to skipper, the starboard inner engine's hit. We're on fire.'

Freddie looked at his engineer, Tom Spears, who was poring over the instruments, and shaking his head.

'That's not what it says,' Tom said.

Part groan, part shout, Bryne: 'Get up here and look, mate! It's got fucking great flames shooting out of it.'

As Tom Spears feathered the starboard inner engine's propeller, the port outer stopped of its own accord. To make matters worse, Len Rushworth was growling accusatorily in Freddie's headphones, something about fuel streaming from the wing. P–Peter was losing height in the turn. But a Lancaster could fly on two engines – at least, S–Sugar, with its Rolls–Royce Merlins, could – and Freddie's doomed hope was that they might make it home yet. Len was still jabbering over the intercom, but less coherently: 'Wrong route, safety of the pack, skipper's fault,' but if what he was saying had any importance at all, it evaporated as the second starboard engine cut out.

Freddie bellowed over Len. 'Abandon aircraft! Bale out, bale out!'

Nose gunner Mark Oldfield had evidently been waiting for the order; the words had hardly left Freddie's mouth before he was tightening his parachute straps, twisting the escape hatch latch and, with barely a glance back at the flight deck, dropping into the black air.

Night roared into the cockpit.

Spears followed Oldfield out of the hatch.

Len Rushworth appeared at Freddie's side. His face was contorted: 'not in fear', the journal notes 'but rage'.

He was mouthing something at Freddie, something Freddie couldn't hear.

The Lancaster, elephantine, wallowing, lost more height.

Freddie did not know whether his bomb aimer, second navigator or rear gunner had managed to jump, but he guessed Bryne Falkirk had not. Though a small man, the mid-upper gunner's bulky heated suit restricted his movement: it would take him more time to wriggle free of his turret. At 1,100 feet Freddie broke off his mayday call and screamed at Len to drop through the forward hatch.

My father knew this: many, many of his fellow pilots had sacrificed themselves holding stricken planes level to give their crew a chance of escape. It was a captain's duty to be last out. 'But I could barely hold P-Peter at all,' the journal implores. 'Damned crate wanted to flip on its back and die, and I didn't have it in me to do the same.'

There's a space in the journal, a line missed, and on the next one Freddie's handwriting, always precise, is tighter and smaller still.

'At 900 feet I jumped. My parachute opened. Then I was in the sea again. It was so cold. But my heart, my heart. My heart was pumping ice.'

For the second time in as many months Freddie returned to base having been 'dunked'. When pulled aboard, he was overjoyed to see the rest of his crew in the rescue launch. All of them, that is – his joy snuffed instantly to misery – except one. On my father's orders the little boat kept circling until dusk. Throughout that time Len Rushworth sat in the cabin blinking at a book of nautical charts. 'Never mind talk to me, for a whole day Len would not meet my eye,' the diary states.

Later the station commander called my father into his office. 'I'd dinged my leg jumping and the wretched stick they'd given me wouldn't stay still, no matter how hard I leaned on it. Len had already talked with the old man, who was rearranging the collection of shell casings on his desk to buy time, I was sure of it, struggling for a way to say the words. Court martial. Hearing them would have been a relief of sorts. I nearly fell over when instead he said that for taking control of so successful an op he would be recommending that the powers that be add a bar to my gong. Instrumental in his decision, he added, had been my navigator's report.'

The 13 June raid put the Opel works out of production for nearly a fortnight. Freddie did indeed receive a bar to his Distinguished Flying Cross for his courageous leadership. And Bryne Falkirk was also honoured. Credited with all three of P-Peter's confirmed kills that night, he was given the Distinguished Flying Medal, the highest decoration available to non-pilots. His award was posthumous.

My phone was ringing. I didn't try to resist it. I opened my escape hatch and climbed out of the cellar. As I reached for the handset its chirruping cut out, and nobody left a message, but that didn't matter, for although it might have been anybody on the other end, I could think only of poor Joy Ghosh. Outside, the rain had turned to sleet. The sky was the colour of wet elephants.

India again. But I saw it only in snatches, snow-blind, my eyes full of tears.

I had Joy Ghosh's address. Why not send her a cheque to help her get by until she found a new job? Two reasons. First, because I could not be sure that she would receive the money (I did not trust the man who'd answered her phone), and second, because as much as I wanted to give her my cash, I needed it more – for Bannerman's bill, never mind Felix's school fees, or my wretched birthday party.

My eyes came to rest on the photograph of Anthony Woodward pinned to my office wall. A bullfrog. Even if he wasn't entirely responsible for driving me up the ladder, and so precipitating Joy Ghosh's downfall, the lack-of-funds problem was undeniably his fault. I am a businessman. I know my pension involved an element of risk: the value of investments can go down as well as up, and so on. But Woodward lied to me about the nature of that risk. He encouraged me to give him a share of what I earned every month, and I paid up in good faith, for thirty years, on the basis of statements he sent me saying how much I could expect to get back. Then, at the eleventh hour, he tore the statements up. Sixty-three per cent of what I'd saved, he decided, was a 'bonus' that he had the right to slash. And, for having the balls to cut it, he'd given himself a handout. I stared out of the window at the leafless apple trees. He'd shaken the fruit from my branches, then declared the pickings his own private windfall. Result: my walls are crumbling, but he has a colonnade of pollarded trees and a kidney-shaped swimming pool!

I found I was grinding my teeth. In '82, when Stennen Parkes went under, the dentist gave me a special gumshield to stop me damaging my molars in my sleep. As always happens, past anxieties seemed trivial now.

The sleet was shot through with hail. It bounced from the driveway, ricocheting knee high, bringing the gravel chippings to life.

As I stood dumbly before my window, Fira walked into view.

If I'd stopped to consider what I was doing, I'd have convinced myself out of it, but I didn't pause. I stepped straight outside and took her by the arm. Bowed beneath her cycle helmet, she did not see me coming. She looked up quickly, her eyes red and wide. I steered her to the Audi and pushed her down into the passenger seat. She said nothing. I retrieved her bicycle from the end of the drive. Quick-release fittings are a marvellous advance: in the old days I needed three hands (two for spanners, one to hold the wheel) to repair the children's punctures. Now the wheels came off just like that. Even so, the heavens had pasted my shirt to my back again by the time I'd stowed the bicycle bits in the estate and climbed inside. Immediately the windows fogged up.

I rolled the car to the end of the driveway and stopped, realising I had no idea where Fira lived. I glanced at her and she flicked out a finger and pointed right. *She's been crying*, I thought. There was only one speed for this journey, very slow. Through St Clare we purred (at last, for *driving carefully*, I deserved the village's thanks), and on into town. At first the silence between us felt brittle, but as the demister cleared the Audi's windows, so the tension in the car dissolved. Fira's breathing, quick to start with, relaxed in time with mine. Modern engines are fantastically quiet.

I thought of Freddie. He should have drawn a line after the Opel works raid. Something changed that night, and he knew it. The code he'd lived his war by no longer applied. In trying to stick to it despite the shift he went on to do something he would have to lie about for the rest of his life.

Why had I rejected Fira's advance? Was it really because I thought it sprang from misplaced gratitude? No. It was because admitting I'd fallen in love with my cleaning lady, and was prepared to betray my wife for her (really betray, unlike the shallow failings of my two earlier indiscretions), went against a code I'd tried to live by. A code I'd *succeeded* in living by until recently, but a code that itself had ceased to apply.

Sparkling club-heads, and Woodward's colonnade, and a frosty play-park, and the Discovery's fuel bill, and narwhal spikes, and the Tithe Barn's flaking brickwork, and apricot Nubuck, and Ryder Evans's wire-sprung orange knuckles crowded to mind.

Fira was very good at pre-empting my need for directions, as good as the sat-nav in fact. Gone was her fidgety uncertainty with the coffee cups; her hands were precise and sure again. We came to a halt outside the old grocery in the middle of town. Its front was fly-postered now. Fira peered up through the windscreen at an unlit window. I looked up too. I'd never been in a flat above a shop before. She began warning me about the parking restrictions. I laughed and pulled two wheels up on to the kerb. I stepped out into the road and walked around the front of the car. I liked the way she waited for me to open her door, and the grace with which she swung her feet on to the pavement.

16

The hallway was narrow and strewn with junk mail. This was where Fira kept her bicycle. Its handlebars had scored a line down the left-hand wall. The place smelt ratty and felt damp, provoking my knee to phantom creakiness, which for a second made me feel uncertain, and old. I was buoyed by the sight of my orange trainers bouncing me up the carpeted stairs.

Three doors squared up on the landing, municipal in their uniform blankness. Fira dug her keys from her jeans. The bedsit she led us into made a palace of Pearl's London flat. Tiny, it somehow managed to be both bare and cluttered. One wall was fitted with a sink unit, above which hung a single kitchen cupboard. Also against that wall, next to the draining board, stood a table on which were perched a microwave oven, kettle and toaster, all in matching white plastic. Jennifer insists on chrome. The three leads from these appliances snaked in competition towards a lone plug socket embedded in the skirting board. Somebody had stuck a notice next to this, prohibiting the use of adapters (why on earth?) in a number of languages. A miniature fridge cowered between the table's legs. Two school chairs, one stacked on top of the other, floated in the awkward sliver of space between this assembly and Fira's bed, whose ugly Formica headboard was redeemed by a richly embroidered counterpane. The only non-functional item in the room, this bedspread glowed. I fixed upon it, not wanting to confront the thought of Fira cycling seven miles from this horrible cupboard to my beautiful home, or the fact that the bathroom had to be out on the landing, shared with the other bedsit, or Fira's closeness to me, which, now that she had shut the door, was suddenly as distracting as it had been in the kitchen earlier that morning.

But eventually I had to look at her, and when I did I saw that she was smiling.

'This is a very easy place to keep clean,' she said.

Now that my back wasn't pressed into a car seat, my damp shirt felt cold. I think I shivered. Fira stepped towards me, undid the buttons on my shirt, and slipped it from my shoulders. The watery grey light falling through the room's single window seemed unforgiving as I looked down at myself, the salt-and-pepper hair on my chest, the curve of my stomach above my belt. Fira pressed her cheek into my breastbone, her nose into the hollow of my throat. I kissed her hairline. Her fingers worked at my belt buckle.

I wanted to shut the curtain, and to keep it open, to close my eyes and to drink in the light.

Fira pushed my trousers down. Jennifer keeps a pot of hand cream by the kitchen sink, but there was a roughness to Fira's fingertips as they moved across my thighs, a worked grain, almost like pumice. She pulled my polka-dot boxer shorts down, too. Then she knelt down, undid my shoelaces and slipped off my socks, one by one.

I stood before her, stripped bare.

I stared down at the cream-white line of Fira's parting and traced its length with my thumb. Unfathomable: not half an hour ago this head had been encased in cycle helmet, and she'd been crying about me as she put it on.

'You have very nice legs,' she said, stroking the backs of my thighs. 'Strong.'

I'm ashamed to say that I started to tell her about the reconstructive surgery I'd had done on my left knee back in '79, but trailed off as, for a meltwater second, she took hold of me. When she stood up she kissed my stomach, my chest, my throat and lips.

'I will look at the dog's ear,' she promised.

Then she turned from me and undressed. When she undid her bra its clasp left a bluey-pink dent between her shoulder blades.

My heart was drumbeating in my head. That something as unattainable as Fira's back should now be beneath my hands made little sense. I kissed the plane of a shoulder blade, tasted salt, and thought of her standing on the pedals to climb the hill from St Clare. I ran a hand up the inside of her arm and across the curves of her chest, down her flank, into the softness of her hair. With her palm on the back of my hand she tapped her fingertips against my nails.

'I don't forgive you,' she said, turning, pulling me down on to the bed.

'For what?'

Her knees came up either side of my hips; my face was an inch from hers. She drew my head down and kissed me. Her tongue was hard in my mouth, then soft, then hard again: she owned the kiss, and finished with it, and turned her face away so that the tip of my nose was pushed into the warm shell of her ear. It smelt of shampoo.

'For thinking me so stupid.'

My gasp came back at me, hot against my lips, as she pulled me inside her.

'I didn't mean—'

There was heat, and wetness, and the astonishment of having to hold back, and the absolute newness of her, the different way she pushed up at me, and felt around me, and gripped me with cool fingers from under her thigh.

'For thinking me so stupid,' she went on, 'that I would misunderstand your help. Or try to thank you for it this way.' She drove up at me.

'I'm sorry.'

She drove up at me.

'I was unsure. I didn't dare hope.'

She drove up at me.

'I'm sixty, for God's sake.'

She drove up at me.

I tried to concentrate on the thread of the bedspread, gold and red, but it was hopeless.

She drove up at me.

'No you're not.' She stroked the back of my head. 'You're fifty-nine.'

★   ★   ★

In drawing the counterpane across us, Fira slid out from under my weight. I rolled on to my side and noticed that my chest had flared red. We lay breathing into each other's faces. My amazement, reflected back at me, was the last thing I saw before I closed my eyes.

When I next opened them the furred shadow cast by the window frame had drifted down the magnolia wall. Fira appeared to have been watching me. She winked, got up, bent over – naked, matter-of-fact – to swap the plugs, and set the kettle to boil. While it did so – slowly, the element had to be on its way out – I got dressed. I couldn't stop looking at Fira. Her nipples had been soft and pale beneath my chest; in the cold they were tipped with dark chocolate. When she turned her back to me I saw daylight between the tops of her thighs. She needed to put on some weight. The doll-size cup she handed me was only half filled, but with coffee the colour and consistency of creosote.

'Enough of your cafetières,' she said.

I sat down on the windowsill and noted, with interest, two pot-bellied skinheads loading my car on to the back of a tow-truck. The Audi's trusty alarm went off when they started up the winch.

'What happens now?' I asked Fira.

'I will get dressed.'

'I mean after that.'

'After that you can marry me now and we will run away.'

I looked at her quickly, saw she was smiling, but still protested, 'I'm already married.'

Fira snorted. 'No you're not, not really.'

There was a pause. The rain thickened outside and blew against the window. It sounded like television static. The atmosphere in the room shifted. Fira said, 'I lied about the deer.'

'The what?'

'When I arrived at your house and told you I had seen a dead deer, it was not true. What I had seen was you untying the rope from your ceiling, and I knew what you had been doing, and I had to say something, so I came up with that.'

'A dead deer?'

'Yes. Because when I was a girl I found one that had been hit by a car. I stopped my bicycle next to it and the deer came back to life. It changed its mind about dying and got up and ran away. I was very happy. And when I caught my glimpse of you untying your rope, and heard you putting your ladder in the utilities room, the memory came back.'

A spasm of dread fell through me. Please, God, *pity* would be worse than thanks. 'Utility room,' I heard myself say. 'It's just utility, without the "s".'

'What? I am telling you how surprisingly happy I was you changed your mind.'

'But surely . . .' I trailed off, muttering, '. . . even to think about it was weak.'

She slid between me and the window. 'When my father died . . . after he was killed . . .' She put her head on my chest and left it there for a minute, until I could feel warmth through my shirt-front. 'I know you have been troubled, too, with your wife and another man. Your children. With being surrounded and on your own.

I watched these things and I have seen how still you go on buying a dog and working at business and carrying wood. I am like you. After my father, and my brothers, and . . . I thought hard and I decided not to do it. So you see we are not very different.'

I bent my face to meet hers. A Chechen refugee, and a valve salesman from the Home Counties. Not very different? My nose was as blunt as hers was fine, but when they touched it felt right. Outside, over the top of Fira's head, the skinheads had finished strapping my car to the back of their pick-up. Off they went, through the rain.

Fira kissed me again before I left, but it was the way she took hold of my hand which stuck in my mind as I stood coatless on the wet pavement. A firm grip. She's not the sort to linger at a window. Without looking to check, I put my head down and set off for the car pound on foot.

Clearway plc, the local parking enforcers, appear to run a graduate recruitment scheme. Unlike his colleagues in the tow-truck, I imagine, the young man who worked behind the company's customer-services counter (chest high, harder to vault) had a Radio 4 accent, a golden ponytail and delicate, vegetarian wrists. Perhaps, I thought, as I reached for my wallet with a smile, he had been motivated to sign up for environmental reasons. He might even have been right to do so: I was in no mood to argue. (When Fira unpeeled her vest her hip bones had knuckled proud of her waistband; the skin that covered them felt like cool velvet.) This fellow had laid aside a book entitled *Practical Ethics* to deal with me, and he said, 'There you go, sir,' when he handed me the credit card chit to sign. All in all I felt like giving him a tip.

But I didn't. Confining myself to a cheery 'Keep up the good work', I waved at him (and his colleagues, eating delicious-smelling fish and chips in the back room) on my way back out into the rain.

With the heater roaring in the Audi, and the sat-nav screen glowing, and the phone winking at me from its cradle, I crawled out of the pound into a world dripping with possibilities. It may sound perverse, but I wanted to share my excitement with Jennifer. She deserved to benefit from its warmth. I had no idea what I would say, but I called the Tithe Barn anyway, and her mobile, and was disappointed when she did not answer.

I pulled over and thought for a second. Spurred on by largesse, not malice, I asked directory enquiries to put me through to the golf club. The girl who answered was only too happy to accept my booking for a starter lesson – on the driving range – with the club professional, Ryder Evans. Initiative sent sparks to my fingertips. I spent the next ten minutes organising a meeting with Robert's boss – James Lovett – on the pretext (his secretary demanded one) that I wanted to discuss an old deal of his called Project Sevastopol. Arranging a second slot with the Reverend Frayn was easier. I simply told her I'd been thinking about things I could do – what we as a family might be able to offer the Church, so to speak – to help with Felix's school application and, as

I'd guessed might happen, she invited me in to discuss the matter that very afternoon.

It's amazing how quickly the improbable can take on the concrete cast of a fact. The stuff about old dogs and tricks is all wrong: when things happen, people – all of us – adapt. A morning ago Fira was a dream; now the spot of rain on my steering wheel reminded me of the pale freckle on her collarbone, and it was the rest of the world's job to catch up.

Anthony Woodward's pad looked much the same through my new eyes. With time to kill before my audience with the vicar, I'd cut off the ring road a stop late and headed out to Waverly Edge. Now I was parked on the verge opposite his gates, which were still tall and wrought iron and electric, the only difference being that through them today I could see a speedboat on a trailer poking out of the big house's stable (now converted into a triple garage).

Though I've never had one, I'm a sailing-boat man myself.

While I sat watching, the trailer backed from the garage, pushed by a racing-green Range Rover, and smoothly circumnavigated the flagpole at the end of the drive. Reversing a trailer like that is quite a skill. In my buoyant mood I wanted to applaud it. But the 4x4 had straightened up and was crunching towards the gates, which swung inwards, revealing me, in my car and, as it happened, in the way.

I didn't rush. I let them get right up close before nudging the Audi backwards along the lane. Woodward's Range Rover was a new sports model with alloy wheels.

He was in the driving seat, talking, and his wife, a redhead, was laughing uproariously. Teenage heads bobbed behind them. He was serious about his boating: it was late November and he'd taken the Friday afternoon off so they could go away for the weekend. Devon, almost inevitably. Anthony Woodward waved thanks at me for letting him past. I waved back. It wasn't a speedboat on the trailer, but a pair of jet-skis.

I don't imagine water sports are a vicar thing. They have more opportunity for badminton, table tennis and cards on the church hall circuit. Each of these activities has something clandestine at its heart. Sleight of hand, flicking wrists. The clergy (think of confession) are second only to magicians in their ability to keep a secret.

With subterfuge in mind, I dropped into the little electrical shop opposite the church on my way to meet Reverend Frayn.

'Margaret,' she reminded me, on the pigeon-spattered steps.

'Of course.' I beamed at her, thinking to add, 'And my Christian name is Harry.'

Her squiffy eye twinkled. 'Well, I've been cooped up inside all day, Harry, but now it's finally stopped raining . . .' We both looked at the ashen sky and then back at each other. '. . . shall we walk? I missed lunch. There's a passable patisserie not far away.'

I needed relative quiet for my plan to work, yet could see no plausible way of objecting to a stroll. Best instead to delay the important conversation until we reached the café.

'Last time we saw one another was through the side window of a police car,' I announced, by way of diversion. 'Perhaps I should explain.'

'I wouldn't pry, but if it's your wish—'

'Which it certainly is. You see, the weather was a problem too, that day . . .'

I began to waffle my way through the iceless park story, more or less truthfully, since no amount of embarrassment, or rain, could dampen my spirits. The vicar's reaction was of no consequence. Instead of looking for it, or at the gutter-grey street scene we were picking our way through, I recalled the sweetness of Fira's lips, the way her fingers stroked my neck as she kissed me, and the scratchy softness of that marvellous counterpane beneath my knees, toes and forearms. Here I was, walking down an East London street at dusk, past a scrapped washing machine with grass growing out of its open door (what sort of people dump their old white goods in front of their homes for whole seasons?), with a boss-eyed vicar on one arm, nonsense coming out of my mouth, and an erection straining against my fly.

'Frost plays havoc with old roofs,' interjected Margaret Frayn.

The patisserie was within sight, so I played along, saying, 'And brickwork. It's a problem I've experienced first-hand.'

With the vicar nodding sympathetically we took seats at a window table. There were plenty to choose from: the place was empty, and valiantly French. Its chequered tablecloths looked clean but my menu (Tour Eiffel baguettes, Place de la Concorde omelettes) stuck to my fingertips. For a regular the reverend inspired slow service. My mouth began to water (sex gives you a hill-walker's appetite) as I reminded her of my concerns to secure a school place for Felix.

The vicar slow-blinked and nodded, murmuring, 'I'm sure one day he'll thank you for this marvellous show of commitment.'

'And the Church will appreciate your wisdom,' I replied. 'Your hunger to see the bigger picture, its wider mission, your vision, so to speak.' (Hearing myself, I shut up; another moment and I'd be in 'one eye on this, one on that' territory.)

'You *are* kind.' There was no denying the open beauty of her smile. 'Either way,' she went on, 'church work sharpens the appetite.'

She bit into her baguette, which wasn't fresh, so shattered, showering the griddled tabletop with flecks of crust. I thought of confetti. You're not allowed to throw it in churchyards these days; the vicar at the Adcocks' wedding reminded us of that before, during and after the ceremony.

Maintenance costs are to blame.

I flicked the switch in my pocket and repeated the phrase, 'The bigger picture.'

'Indeed, yes.'

'You mentioned there are ways a man of my means can help the Church.'

'I did.'

'Well, I've thought about it, and I'd be pleased to offer whatever assistance you'd consider appropriate.'

The vicar took another bite of baguette; more

chippings sprang to the tabletop. Though I waited until well after she'd finished her mouthful, she did not elaborate upon her contented smile, so I was forced to force the issue. 'What support, exactly, do you see me providing?'

'We must all give according to what we have.'

'Of course.' A thought flashed to mind, of Fira's stomach pressed against mine. It emboldened me. I cut to the chase: 'If I made out a cheque for fifteen hundred pounds to the St Silas's roof appeal fund, would that be enough?'

'Hmm.'

'Two thousand?'

'It's not so much the amount, as who exactly you were giving the money to, and in what form.'

'I see.'

'The maintenance committee doesn't always target our resources wisely. Funds don't necessarily reach the projects which need them most.'

'An individual would be better placed to manage the money?'

'Perhaps.'

'Someone like yourself.'

The Reverend Frayn shrugged modestly – and inaudibly.

I tried another tack. 'What reassurance would I have that my . . . offering had been enough?'

'Assurance? My letter in the short term. And a welcome pack from the school before long!'

'For which you'd expect–'

'A donation in the region of the sum you've mentioned, the latter sum. Which I will look after in person.'

'Two thousand pounds, paid direct to you,' I clarified.

'Yes.' She smiled brightly again. 'That should do it. But rather than a cheque, we'd be happier with cash. So long as that suits.'

Now it was my turn to shrug cheerfully. What I wanted to do, of course, was pull the Dictaphone from my pocket and show it to her, but I didn't, and not because I was frightened she might succeed in wresting it from me (Friar Tuck and Jonathan Edwards aside, I can't think of many athletic Christians), but because I didn't want to risk a public scene. People will do anything when they're cornered. I saw a Discovery programme once about a species of little monkeys which, encircled by baboons, kill their own young. No, far better to let her dwell on a copy of the tape, sent through the post. We finished our snack in agreeable silence. Perhaps it wasn't the vicar so much as the café's authentic Gallicism; the waitress also ignored the only other customer to arrive before we left.

Two thousand pounds! The church would barely be able to pay for scaffolding with that, let alone launch a roofer up it. Who knew what Margaret Frayn would really do with the money? Who indeed cared? My investment — of twenty quid, on a pocket recorder — would make her spending plans irrelevant. I played the recording back in the Audi's hermetic hush. Oh, technology! Never mind our conversation, the little machine had picked up every detonation of French stick.

On my way home I cut across the St Clare ring road

and fiddled around the one-way system to stop outside Fira's flat. There was a light on in her window but I did not knock. I'd come to deliver her a present. It had leapt out at me in the electrical shop where I'd bought the Dictaphone, which also sold fund-raising postcards of St Silas's. I wrote the card on my lap and stuck it straight to the packet with superglue. She'd understand the exact significance when I explained. In the meantime 'only resist' made its own sort of sense, glued as it was to a three-way plug.

17

Jennifer was in the kitchen, stuffing sausages with her famous curried filling. She uses lots of turmeric. Hundreds of bright yellow lifeboats lay beached on the granite work surfaces, but she was still going strong at the machine. And not just to amuse our granddaughter. Though Jennifer winked collaboratively at me over the top of little Flo's head (she and Marie were staying while the decorators worked on the Belsize Park maisonette, and Robert was away), I guessed her true intent. Tony Kim be damned: my wife would never throw a party – let alone one the size of my planned sixtieth – without serving up one of her own signature dishes.

I pecked her downy cheek, put the kettle on to boil, and turned to see her wipe her face with the back of her hand.

'You crank the handle and I'll feed in the gunk.'

Little Flo, mustard to the elbows: '*D'accord.*'

'I tried to call you yesterday,' I said. 'Around lunchtime, but you didn't answer.'

'Golf.'

'Your mobile, though. I tried that, too.'

My wife sighed and told the top of Flo's head, 'They're forbidden on the course. What were you calling about?'

I wanted this question. Answering it promised the reckless whoosh of cutting a bend on a normally empty road. 'The car,' I said slowly. 'It got towed.'

'Not again! Don't turn it too fast or we'll end up with chipolatas. You poor thing. Where from?'

'Town. Outside the old grocery.'

'Hmm. That is bad luck. What were you doing parked there?'

'It's where Fira lives.'

'Is that so?'

'Yes, I drove her back to her flat. It was tipping down. But you'll remember that, of course. You must have got soaked playing your game.'

'Hmm? Yes. Now, Flo, that's a long enough string. You do the snipping. And I'll lay them out like so.'

'Or perhaps you didn't get wet.'

'No. Careful, don't cut them too close.'

'Because you'd have been wearing the right kit. Your Gore-tex trousers and so on. Fira doesn't have any waterproofs.'

'I suppose not.'

'No. She has virtually nothing. I saw inside her flat. It's tiny, and empty.'

'Yes, well.'

'And while I was inside Fira's flat the parking attendants towed my car away.'

'As you've said, Harry. But what of it? You've got the thing back again now, haven't you? I'm sorry I wasn't around to help. Good girl, that'll do.'

'I have got the car back, yes. It's on the drive. I just wanted you to know.'

Little Flo came out to my office later, with a bowl of surplus sausage mix for Spongebob. Since his fight with Bill H. Marshall he had been cast low; his tail flopped listlessly when Flo put her offering down but he did not immediately rise to eat.

'He is sick,' she said.

'It's just a cut ear. He'll be better soon.'

'When I had the earache I stopped eating, too.'

'And look at you now. He says thank you.'

'*De rien.* Why do you work in a barn?'

I laughed. 'It's not a barn, it's an office. Would you like it if your daddy had his office in your garden, too?'

'We have a patio heater. And a gas barbecue. And two bird tables. There would not be room.'

'I suppose not. What do you miss most about Daddy when he's away?'

'He isn't away,' she confided. 'Because of the song. If I sing it I can make him be in my head and at work at the same time. It's like a magic spell. We are lucky because it only works for us. And so we do not need an office barn.'

Flo's eyes were bottomless just then. I could not hold her gaze, let alone bring myself to ask what the song was. When I was flat out at Stennen Parkes, 'The Bare Necessities' worked for Robert and me. I focused on his daughter's yellow forearms and said, 'You forgot to take off your rubber gloves.'

'Grandad!' she said.

★　　★　　★

237

Like lawyers, the parking meters outside Madison & Vere charge for their time in six-minute chunks. I raided Jennifer's piggy bank (for years she's been salting away my loose coins) to be sure of having enough change for the slot, but my pocket full of reclaimed silver still afforded me less than an hour's stationary grace. No matter. What I had to tell Robert's boss, Mr James Lovett, wouldn't take long.

I sat in reception, trainers crossed, watching the charcoal suits come and go. Robert's colleagues are an earnest, young lot. They looked like school prefects rather than paid professionals, the same faux-stern expressions on fresh faces. I was always on at Robert to grow up and act responsibly; here was proof he'd taken me (and himself) seriously. The secretary steered me to a lift. It was made of glass, and rose up the inner wall of a vast atrium surrounded by see-through office spaces. Robert once had a book of cross-sectioned things: aircraft carriers, termite mounds, eyes, and so on. Until Jimmy demoralised him by reproducing a slice of castle from memory, my elder boy enjoyed copying those diagrams, labelling all the parts meticulously. Perhaps working here reminded him of that. I arrived on the twelfth floor, and found myself in another reception area, identical to the one in the lobby, with leather sofas and brushed-metal coffee tables set out on a sea of peach-and-dove carpet tiles.

'Mr Brinkman? James Lovett. Shall we step this way.'

This wasn't a question but a statement, made by a man who had already turned his back on me and was striding towards another set of glass doors. I followed him. We arrived at a meeting room dominated by a lacquered boardroom table, which James Lovett sat at the head of. He shot his cuffs, revealing a big watch. Its dial winked beneath the recessed spotlights. With pink fingers the lawyer smoothed a wing of suspiciously black hair: though younger than me he was a long way out of school. Bezels and buttons, a diving watch. I thought of the one we bought Robert. Tastes connect people: no doubt this Lovett character approved of my son's ability to keep time underwater.

'I'm Robert Brinkman's father.'

'You referenced one of my old deals when you called. For what reason?'

James Lovett turned up a fresh page in his notebook. The fountain pen he uncapped was as thin as a knitting needle. It made me think of searchlights. He looked up at me as if over the rim of a pair of glasses, but he wasn't wearing any. I fought an urge to laugh.

'Do you have children, Mr Lovett?'

'Project Sevastopol. What was it you wanted to discuss?'

'Are they still at home, or grown up?'

'I'm here to talk about my former client, not my family, Mr Brinkman. What do you have to say about Project Sevastopol?'

'That sense of knowing what's best for your child, you learn to bury it, but it never goes away entirely, does it?'

Lovett recapped his pen. 'If you're not here to discuss business then I think we should wind this meeting up.'

'But I've stopped trying to deny my concerns, you

see. I know that my son is on the wrong track and I have decided to put him back on course.'

The lawyer pushed his chair back from the table and shrugged. 'I'm happy for you. Really, I am. But I'm afraid it's not my place to comment on your relationship with your son.'

'I'm talking about his job.'

'Sorry?'

'His job here, at Madison & Vere.'

'Hold on—'

'He's not happy.'

'What do you think this is, parents' day? Your son's career at our firm is manifestly a matter between him and us. Confidential. I couldn't discuss it with you even if I wanted to. Now, if you'll excuse me—'

'I thought you'd say something like that.'

'Fine. I have. Now—'

'That's why I brought up Project Sevastopol. To make you listen. Robert told me all about it. Money laundering. How you fired one of his contemporaries for trying to come clean. Robert agonised about whether he should say something himself. Now I'm doing so on his behalf.'

The lawyer rocked forward in his chair and pinched the bridge of his nose between his fingers. His hair moved in one piece as he shook his head. Perhaps it was a wig. A fraud. I'd hooked him now, he'd have to listen. But when Lovett looked up again my treacherous knee began to throb. Far from appearing concerned, his face split into a bemused grin.

'I remember the chap's name,' I added, to bolster myself. 'Lawrence Penn.'

'Ha!' Lovett's shoulders shook. 'Ha, ha, ha!'

'You sacked him!' I said.

'*Lewis* Penn as good as fired himself! And not just for breaching client confidentiality. We don't as a rule employ people so witlessly intent on the wrong end of the stick.'

'Robert broke client confidence discussing this Project Sevastopol with me.'

'If I remember rightly your son was a trainee at the time. Good for photocopying and making tea. The boys in the post room had a better understanding of the deal than him. Money laundering! Hilarious! Thank God he's wised up since then.'

'I want you to pass Robert over for partnership.'

'I'm sorry?'

'You heard me.'

'What on earth has he done to you to deserve this?'

'It's what I've done to him that needs redressing.'

'You're playing some sort of a joke here, am I right?'

'No, I'm serious.'

Under his breath: 'You're seriously out of your depth.'

'Robert doesn't want to work here,' I said simply. 'Not deep down. I think you should bear that in mind.'

'He's doing a very good impression to the contrary. Listen, Mr Brinkman. You're a lucky man. Lucky, for a start, that your son has better judgement than you. But more importantly, you're lucky that Project Sevastopol is ancient history, that it and the client we ran it for, UKI, no longer exist. Because if you were capable of the attempted blackmail it seems you're threatening here, I'd simply inform my litigation department and, never mind Chinese whispers about the clients we represent or the deals we organise for them, you'd wish you'd never heard of this law firm, let alone turned up here today with your . . . vindictive little scheme . . . to ruin your son's hard-won career.'

The lawyer appeared happy with this speech. He slapped his notebook shut, shot his cuffs again and checked his timepiece. Good to two hundred deep-sea metres. Was this conclusiveness a front? I couldn't be certain. My wristwatch is an early digital model by Casio, less robust under pressure. James Lovett stood up and turned away from me, signalling the end of our discussion. From behind, his hair looked like a helmet, onyx black. It wasn't a wig, but still had to be dyed. I imagined him in the bath, shampooing in the colouring agent, his wrists hairy in clear plastic gloves. Vanity betrays uncertainty. He'd dwell on what I'd told him later, no doubt.

We walked back to the lift, or rather I walked after James Lovett, who strode. He didn't descend with me. The glass box dropped through the building, an Adam's apple sinking in a throat. Water twinkled at me from the bottom of the atrium; a swimming pool, it turned out, beneath a glass ceiling in the lower ground floor. Robert had mentioned this pool once as evidence of the firm's commitment to its employees' well-being. Nobody was swimming in it today.

To the Royal Stables Golf Club, then, via good old Waverly Edge. The sat-nav picked us a duff route (all things are fallible) around a cone-strewn section of M25, but my frustration had more to do with James Lovett's feigned imperviousness than the bumper-to-bumper hour Spongebob and I endured. I say 'Spongebob and I', but in truth my dog was oblivious to the delay. He snored all the way to West End Farm, and was slow to rouse himself even then. I had to help him out of the back of the Audi. His Listerine eyes, blinking open, were murkier than usual. If he recognised where we were (why should he have? – what resonance could the place have for him?) he did not show it, just sniffed at Woodward's iron gatepost, hindquarters shivering, before lifting a desultory leg.

It was a windy day. Woodward's flag snapped and flopped on its pole. At full stretch it showed a yellow design on a navy-blue background, a crest, the detail of which I could not make out. Those trees are pruned close: aside from the flag's flickering nothing else on the premises stirred.

We continued on to the golf club, whose gates dwarf even those of my Mutual Friend. Though it was the first of December flowers lined the entire half-mile drive. Cyclamen they must have been: no expense spared. Runway lights – and Freddie – came to mind. I rolled the Audi to a stop in a free space near the club's entrance. Then I saw a sign which read 'Ladies' Captain' beyond the car's bonnet, so reversed to a humbler slot across the gravelled lot. Spongebob had fallen asleep again. I ran a hand across the barrel of his chest, slopped some sparkling water into his bowl (I'd kept a few litres in the rear footwell for this purpose) and set off in search of my lesson.

Golf! It's seductive. Part of the reason I haven't taken it up is because I know I'd fall for all the sport's trappings if I did. Just walking into the pro shop confirmed my suspicion of that. The paraphernalia! Quivers of beautifully made clubs. Military-grade waterproofs by the rack-full. Hats and visors to put my ratty one-size-fits-all number in the shade. And the more esoteric stuff, too. Widgetty, dent-digging forks for repairing greens. Motorised wheely-carts built to withstand re-entry from space. I spent five minutes examining a selection of exquisitely engineered telescopic poles, each tipped with a metal mesh eggcup, before working out how useful such a tool would be for retrieving golf balls from the bottom of a pond. Essential even. There's something bewitching about such necessary pointlessness. Just standing amid the ephemera made me want it, and the thought of fulfilling that want sent a warm feeling all the way to my trainer-clad toes.

The shop assistant was delighted to sort me out a set of hire clubs. She directed me to the driving range. Ryder Evans (*Evans as in Chris, Ryder as in Cup*) would join me on the range, she said. In fact he was there already, fiddling with a ball-dispensing machine. With a bucket hanging from each long arm, he swaggered towards me, and past me, and into a stall at the far end of the concourse. He hadn't recognised me, had no idea who I was! I watched him set the buckets of balls down, and straighten the mat of artificial grass in the stall, and stand and stretch and bounce on the balls of his feet, a sportsman's fluidity gracing every movement, and I felt a peculiar tenderness towards him, the warmth – almost – of kinship.

I ambled along, giving his memory every chance to reboot, but it was only as I said, 'Harry Brinkman, it's a pleasure to see you again,' and offered up my hand, that he understood who I was. I know, because he blushed the best shade of red I've seen a grown man go. There was innocence in it; clearly he'd been fore-warned of my attendance at the club do when I'd first met him, but had no idea I was turning up for a lesson today. I found myself clapping him on the shoulder, shaking it in comradeship, then gesturing pointlessly at the floodlit range. 'Dusk, so soon,' I said. 'The days have really drawn in.'

Ryder Evans agreed that they had.

'Thought I'd try my hand swinging a club or two,' I went on. 'I'm nearly sixty. Retirement beckons. About time I caught Jennifer up, if you know what I mean.'

Ryder Evans suggested that he did.

'So, where should I begin?'

Teachers of golf are known as golf professionals. It was fitting then that Ryder Evans should recover his composure so quickly, that he should deliver such a thoroughly professional golf lesson to me, the husband of his lover, in the bitter gloom of that December afternoon. And I enjoyed it, I really did. Undoubtedly Fira – the velvet knobs of her hips, the pale scoop where her bum meets her spine, her deadpan, North Sea eyes – made it easier for me to feel goodwill towards this man, but I think my afternoon in her bed had also loosened my joints, refired the synapses between sporting hand and eye. I concentrated, hard. On the ball, on the club, on what Ryder Evans was suggesting I should do to send the former into the distance with the latter. And it worked. Although I scuffed the odd ball nowhere, missed one or two entirely, hooked and sliced others left and right, the majority of the balls set in front of me melted on impact, arrowing straight down the faux fairway beneath the floodlights. The essential frivolousness of sporting accessories simply reflects sport itself. Like meditation, random focus is the point. A ball in a net, a dart in a board, a horse across a finishing line. Concentrating on the fundamentally banal task that lies at the heart of every sport is its own reward: an all-consuming, purging, release.

My wife's lover declared me a natural.

Catching himself saying 'for a man of your . . .' he managed to substitute 'experience' for 'age' and declare that he'd not, in all his years of coaching, seen such potential. Then he handed me a driver. I thought of Anthony Woodward, and my years spent lugging that log basket, and I let fly. To see such accuracy, balance, timing and raw club-head speed, in a novice such as me, was – evidently – a first for Ryder Evans's eyes. Beginner's luck, I'm sure, and hockey, which we played at school alongside rugby. It's comparatively easy to smack a ball when it's sitting still.

'Evolution,' I said, wiping my brow. 'You mentioned something about a swing's natural evolution.'

'Yes, I–'

'My wife started out as your pupil, didn't she?'

Ryder Evans bent to pick up a stray ball.

'And now she thinks very highly of you, very highly indeed.'

Ryder, straightening: 'And I her. She is a first-rate player. Dedicated, as well—'

'That's not what I'm getting at.'

'No?' The golf pro's gaze drifted over my shoulder.

'No. I'm talking about evolution. And . . . love.' Saying the word out loud was as difficult as swallowing a golf ball. 'Love evolves, too, don't you think?'

Ryder Evans rubbed his chin with a wire-sprung ginger hand.

'What my wife and I feel for each other now may not be the same thing we felt thirty years ago, but it's still love. In my case a love that has become more . . . nurturing, or protective.' I slotted the driver back into the golf bag – more forcefully than I meant to – continuing, 'It pleases me to see Jennifer happy. But I would hate to see her hurt.'

Ryder Evans's stare was fixed on the two-hundred-and-fifty-yard marker. A motile fellow, his stillness now seemed doubly unnatural. I took in the ball-dotted expanse with him. Gauzy drizzle had begun to fall. Blown by the gusting wind, it looked as if fireflies were swarming around the floodlights.

'She's throwing me a party next week. A surprise party. Perhaps you know about it.'

The golf pro narrowed his eyes.

'Either way, I'd like it if you came.'

'You're asking *me* to your birthday party? Why on earth would—'

'Because I want to invite you. Believe me, it makes perfect—'

'No, I meant to say, why would *I* want to come to that? Awkward doesn't begin to . . . besides, Jennifer . . .'

'I'll warn her. Don't worry. I'll tee the thing up.'

The sportsman's jaw dropped a fraction and he shot me a range-finding glance. *Tee the thing up.* Why had I come out with that? Caught by the strip light above us, a few curly hairs were clearly visible sprouting from Ryder Evans's ears. In the fifteen or so years before *his* sixtieth birthday a thicket of ginger would take hold there.

'Think about it, anyway.'

I described how to find *the dove ascending*, in response to which the golf pro reached for and shouldered my bag of hire clubs, a reflex so fluent and unthinking it brought to mind the way the young Pearl would scoop Pincher, her crocheted lobster, from the crack between her pillow and headboard, every morning as she got out of bed.

'I'll return these for you,' he muttered.

'Thank you,' I said. 'And please believe me, the invitation is sincere.'

I let Ryder Evans leave ahead of me. The swirling wind now blew curtains of drizzle into the golf hutches, prompting the woman two cubicles from me to pull a waterproof jacket over her orange-and-grey diamond-patterned tank top. Peach and dove, the same colours as Madison & Vere's carpet tiles. Though youngish, the woman had a cramped, crabby golfing style. She didn't pause at the top of her backswing as Ryder Evans had told me I should.

As I settled up for my lesson in the shop, a gift box of chocolate golf balls caught my eye. As a mark of respect for Jennifer I did not buy them, but chose her a 'golf-scope' (for determining yardage and club selection, apparently) in a leather case instead.

18

Something was up with Spongebob. I returned to the car to find him flat out in the back; he didn't appear to have to touched the water I'd set out for him, which suggested to me he'd been asleep all that time. More significantly, his breathing seemed laboured, a step beyond snoring; I opened the tailgate and bent low over him to hear the hiss and drag of wavelets on a shale beach.

When you've had children, the threat of illness takes on a new cast. That a being so pristine should be destined for imperfection, inevitably compromised, is hard to bear.(In my darkest moments, I've almost wanted the worst to happen, so that I could stop dreading that it would.) After the doctor first referred Jimmy to a child psychologist (to see why he was 'special' – what a word, but they used it) I lost half a stone in three weeks and had to resort to the old Stennen Parkes gumshield again, to stop myself destroying my teeth in my sleep. Spongebob was a dog, not a child, and a Peckham-hardened adolescent, not a toddler, but the fluttering in my lungs echoed the same panic: please, let this pass, please.

I drove to Fira's place, via the speed camera on the edge of St Clare (*pop – thank you for driving carefully*) and a slalom of straddled calming humps. The Audi handles superbly in the wet. Fira's light was on. I parked on the kerb beneath it, right outside the old grocery, buzzed both doorbells at once, and was still staring up at her window when she tapped me on the left shoulder and kissed my right ear. She was carrying a carton of Kentucky Fried Chicken.

'You!' she said. Unmistakably, excitement flashed in her eyes, defying the cool façade to kick in. 'You should learn where you can and cannot park.'

I explained my concern for Spongebob.

'There's no need to make him the reason. I am pleased to see you. It is better than waiting another day.'

Her glittering eyes told me she meant what she said.

'He's in here.' I kissed her forehead as I popped the tailgate. Spongebob blinked. I stroked his shoulder and chest, and was aghast to feel that his stomach was drenched – in pee, presumably, since dogs don't sweat. 'Christ!' I said. 'He's soaking wet!' Spongebob raised his head from his paws, beat his tail when he saw Fira (or perhaps when he smelt her dinner), then flopped back on his side. 'What's up with him?' I asked. 'And what should I do?'

Fira crossed her arms. In the lamplight her wrists were pale blue. She leaned into the back of the estate and stuck a finger into Spongebob's water bowl. 'Was it empty when your journey began?' she asked.

I shook my head.

'How shameful for you, with your driving, to accuse him of watering his bed.'

'But he's been so listless – floppy, sleepy – and his breathing was odd.'

'You snore too after exertion,' she said.

'I'm serious.'

'So am I. He has had a fight, and an injury, and a big painkiller, I think, which he has now worn out. He is mending himself through sleep. It is better than complaining.'

'You think so?' I asked, but the fluttering sensation was already subsiding.

She shrugged. 'I think probably, with the history of his events.' She took a piece of deep-fried something (it smelt marvellous) from her bucket and offered it to my dog, who rolled on to all fours in order to sniff, lick and – with his familiar snatching gulp – swallow it down. She set the container in the car.

I kissed the thin patch of hair behind Fira's left ear. Though her takeout supper smelt good, the apple shampoo she uses (or perhaps it's *her* smell, not from a bottle) is something else. In fact, it caused me to catch my breath. What right had I to a stake in such a moment? Just weeks beforehand I'd seen fit to lower a rope over my head. A tow-rope knotted into a noose, umbilical, pale blue. The prospect then of standing with an arm around Fira and my nose pressed into her ear had . . . well . . . there'd been no prospect of it at all. That the view past her blurred cheek and lower lip might have been of my *own* dog's head in a bucket of Kentucky Fried Chicken beggared belief. Since the late 1970s there's been no fast food at all in the Tithe Barn.

'Can I take you out for supper?' I asked. 'I know a pub—'

'No.'

I glanced at her sideways. There was fondness in her smile, but her eyes cut it with something else. Hunger, I think.

'Just park sensibly and I will buy some more portions for us to eat. Then I can show you how my light and kettle now work at once illegally.'

When I arrived home later that evening there was a hollow buzzing in my stomach, a sense of trepidation I recognised as the pre-match nervousness of excited dread. Ryder Evans would surely have spoken to Jennifer. Since Marie and Little Flo were still staying, I clumped the car's doors open and shut a few times, for no good reason other than to make sure Jennifer knew I was back, and then I let Spongebob explore the garden for five minutes – fried chicken is restorative stuff – in the hope that she might join me outside. She didn't. The cloud had cleared while I'd been with Fira, discussing God, among other topics. He hadn't proven himself to her, either, but she did believe in predestination; my stoic attitude towards my trainers had apparently led her to me. That and our shared preoccupation with ladders. I stood on the patio and stared at the bullet-riddled sky: with no moon the stars appeared to be pouring light. To my disappointment, I know nothing about astronomy. Freddie did, of course, but although we often asked him to teach us our bearings he always had an excuse not to, and the journal suggests why. His last months of war were plagued by nightmares, including one in which the map of stars leading him home had been maliciously realigned. Ignorance would keep his boys safe from that disorientation at least, I suppose.

'Lost something up there?'

I was startled to find Jimmy standing at my side.

'I'm going to buy myself a book on it,' I murmured. 'Constellations and so on. No reason not to now.'

'I've got one I can lend you if you're prepared to wait . . .' He spoofed a glance over his shoulder. ' . . . for the big night.'

'Is that why you're here?'

'Yup. Mum's pleased with the exhibition idea. It didn't take much to make her think it was her own. We're off to the Fiery Phoenix in the morning to look at the site.'

'Good, that's good.'

'Now, remember not to look surprised when I'm not surprised you're surprised to see the paintings there.'

There was no point testing the logic of his nonsense: it would add up. I smiled sideways at Jimmy. With his hair so short, and his face upturned to the darkness, his neck appeared massive, cast in stone. Both his eyes were a wet-pebble colour, too. An Olympian statue, if he hadn't been bouncing on his toes.

We went inside. The kitchen table was set with the silver service Robert and Marie gave us for our twenty-fifth. Tactful, I thought, greeting my daughter-in-law.

Jennifer had her back turned to me. She was working at the sink. Candles on the table flickered in sympathetic uncertainty with me as Jimmy shut the door. I moved towards my wife. Her hands appeared to be fighting one another underwater. Was she wringing them? No, the glance she gave me over her shoulder was humdrum, distracted, it turned out, by a bowl brimming with exotic fruit. I crossed the last tiles to her side.

'Mango,' she said. 'Durian, longan and lychees. This is a ramputan. Jamie's right, they're tasty, but a right fiddle to peel.'

Was she acting? As Jennifer spun back to the sink her face was aglow, but that had to be the spotlight reflecting up at her from the deep enamel tub, didn't it? I patted my wife's upper arm and waited for her to ask me where I'd been. She didn't. Instead she said, 'You must be hungry. We certainly are. Lucky for you I put the Yorkshire puddings in late.'

Unlike the candles, her blithe self-certainty didn't waver during the evening. She prepared our meal and served it and ate her own modest helping (I managed my larger plateful, too, all of it, somehow) and cleared the dishes with the brusque assuredness – professionalism, almost – that is her domestic trademark. Only when Marie revealed that the decorators had used the wrong paint in Belsize Park (the right colour, but vinyl matt instead of vinyl silk – Jimmy: 'No way! Does it look different, or just feel it?') did Jennifer get worked up, and even then her indignation ('Ignore Jimmy, it's unacceptable') was in part put on for Marie's benefit.

Later, I thought, in the privacy of our bedroom, she'd confront me then. But the water in the glass she placed on her bedside table shivered itself calm in a heartbeat and other than that – three folds take the counterpane to the foot of the bed, cushions (we don't use them, why have so many?) stacked neatly on the old nursing chair – there wasn't so much as a ripple in our bedtime routine. We never say goodnight before going to sleep. Jennifer rolled over and shoved her bum (bigger than Fira's, of course, but as warm, and heartbreakingly familiar) into my side, and was quickly, deeply, asleep.

Should I wake her up and tell her myself?

No, I decided, I should not.

Bannerman called the following morning. I was making coffee for Fira at the time (twelve heaped teaspoons of grounds in a half-filled cafetière today); he bounced through to the voicemail and left a lengthy message. Justifying the full six minutes, no doubt. His spiel went as follows:

'Ah, Brinkman, Seb Bannerman here. I trust you're well. Calling about your girl, of course, the fair Fira. We've taken steps, made some progress. Young Sandeep did a terrific job at the CMR, that's the case management review hearing, and we're in pretty good shape, all things considered, for the substantive appeal next week. This is a fascinating case. We're well positioned, given the circumstances. Yes. So, now, I've had Sandeep researching the current profile for Romania, the situation on the ground if you will, since that's a key factor.

My mistake, Chechnya. The position for native Chechens like young Fira returning to her country. What, exactly, are they on their way back to, and so on? That's something the tribunal must take into consideration, of course. And Sandeep's unearthed some interesting stuff. About camps. Refugee camps. Apparently there are thousands of displaced Chechens living in tented villages in a place called Karabulak. Some godforsaken border town, no doubt. This is a challenge for us. At worst, it's a material problem. The Home Office will argue these tents and whatnot afford a safe haven, a sympathetic insta-community for Fira to return to, if you will. It's all specious, of course. We'll have to persuade them of that. Apparently your girl is very convincing in person, and Sandeep is on the hunt for reasons these tents aren't suitable. He's very thorough, it's all in hand. This sort of stuff always comes up. No such thing as plain sailing. Then there's the delay between her arriving in the UK and turning herself in, which I've mentioned, but that's a bog-standard problem. We'll do our utmost, let me assure you of that . . .'

On he went, circling his real reason for calling, which was to soften me up for his interim bill, which, he explained finally, was in the post. As I listened, standing in my office, two feet planted together on one carpet tile, I had a sense of the floor beneath me receding. I felt like one of those monks, vertiginously alone on the top of his pillar of rock. Hunger, they say, focuses the mind, even as it give you the shakes. In that way it's like fear. And strong coffee. Only resist. There was less than a week to go before my party now. I put my mug down on the desk and picked up the phone. Bollocks to Bannerman's bullshit, I'd pay him double to tell me the real score.

But the lawyer was on another call. His secretary forwarded me to his junior, the trusty Sandeep, who punched the wrong button on his console (despite myself, I sympathised) so that instead of listening to 'Greensleeves' I heard him attacking his filing cabinet and muttering, 'Brinkman, Brinkman, where the . . . this, no, that's the one, fucking hell, oh,' before he cut me off entirely.

I called straight back.

'What's the matter, Sandeep, with Fira's case? What does "material problem" mean? Just tell me the—'

'Matter?'

'Yes. Mr Bannerman left me a message. He sounded concerned.'

'Oh no. Cautious, I'm sure, but not concerned. I was working on your case this morning as it happens. Somalia—'

'Chechnya, for Christ's sake! Fira's from Chechnya!'

'I know that, Mr Brinkman. Pedagogics professor, appeal next . . . Thursday, I know the case. I was about to say that I've found some helpful IAT precedents with which to tackle the Karabulak camp problem among cases concerning asylum seekers from Somalia. Very helpful, in fact. Tents everywhere, there, and nobody thinks them a viable "haven". I've booked a slot with Seb – Mr Bannerman – this afternoon, to talk him through my findings.'

Sandeep, Sandeep! Cufflinks and cologne. I knew

there had to be more to him than that, and I was right. The boy knew how to pack a parachute. I stepped from my pillar of rock and floated safely to the swivel chair.

Through the window I caught sight of Jennifer and Marie making their way outside to play with little Flo beneath the black-limbed apple tree. Trussed cylindrical in her red hat, scarf, coat and wellington boots, my granddaughter looked like a miniature postbox. Jennifer prefers to be out while 'the help' cleans her house. Yet these three had been together in the sitting room, cutting out paper snowflakes, when Fira crunched her way up the drive today. The sound of her footsteps then prompted in me a flash of uncertainty, delicious because it would so quickly be over, and disappointing because that was the case. I was right that nothing would come of her arrival. In contrast to the surprised excitement in her eyes the day before, Fira's gaze had a thousand-yard range today.

My family weren't playing beneath the apple tree, I saw with a start, but gathering frozen windfalls. Today, of all days. I immediately cajoled Spongebob into taking a turn with me in the garden (he was reluctant, sluggish again, perhaps he's not fond of the cold?), curious to see whether Jennifer intended anything by this foray among my unexploded bombshells.

I approached obliquely. Silvery grass, stiff with frost, crunched beneath my trainers. I paused by the laurel hedge while Spongebob nosed in among its lower branches unenthusiastically. Evergreens have always appealed to me, something to do with their imperturbability, perhaps, but the laurel's waxy rubber leaves looked fake today. Jennifer was bobbing up and down, filling a Waitrose carrier bag with fallen, frozen fruit. That yoga does keep her supple at the waist. The bag bulged. Straightening, she swapped it from one hand to the other and back again, as if testing the heft of a weapon. Marie wasn't helping much. She was bemoaning the fact that the Nubuck sofas would not fit through the maisonette's front door, so would have to be winched through a butchered window casement instead.

'They should have warned you about that,' Jennifer agreed.

'And now we will have to have the sash frame repainted all over again.'

'It's too bad.'

'*Cinq, six, sept, huite,*' said little Flo, her nose lowered over her harvest.

Although I was now directly in Jennifer's line of sight, she had not acknowledged me. She couldn't fail to register Spongebob, though, since he was sniffing at her free hand. He seems to like her. At least, they have an understanding, based upon leftovers. Jennifer so hates to see good food go to waste that she prefers – endearingly, I have to admit it – to spoil my dog with titbits. I stepped closer.

'Still,' Jennifer cast a knowing smile at Marie, 'Robert shouldn't be too worried about the extra expense just now at least.'

Jennifer's bag was full. Having tied its handles together she at last took note of me, swinging the thing up at me – no, for me – to take. I did so.

'Apples,' I said.

'What's left of them, at least.'

'You're picking them up.'

Jennifer said, 'Ye-es. Do I need a licence?'

At the same time little Flo said, 'Grandad, can gobstoppers make a horse choke?'

'What's that?' I kept my eyes on my wife's face. Her crimped smile seemed genuine enough.

'We're off to the retirement stables,' Jennifer explained.

'With these freezing apples. And the horses there have old teeth. They will have to suck them' – Flo's carrier bag, which she lifted now, was from John Lewis – 'like gobstoppers, I think.'

I dropped to my granddaughter's level (sparks of protestation crackled in my knee) and rummaged through the windfalls. 'Custard,' I said. 'In a flask. With apples this cold the horses will need something warm as well.'

'Ignore him,' Jennifer told Flo. 'They'll thaw out on the journey, like I said.'

I returned to my office reassured that Jennifer's foray among the windfalls meant nothing. At worst it was a smokescreen for her trip to *the dove ascending* (Jimmy, on tiptoes, winked at me as he slunk to take a seat in the back of her truck). Why, then, did I not feel relieved? Because a part of me wanted her to know I knew about Ryder Evans. I also wanted her to find out about Fira. Resistance and hardship are linked. I wanted her to know so that I might suffer, and savour, the consequences. Nevertheless, I waited for the Discovery to shudder from the drive (it doesn't like the cold either) before venturing back inside.

Pledge furniture polish. It's a confusing smell, now so evocative of Fira's presence in my house, but reminding me also of Jennifer, who's always bought the stuff.

I found Fira in the utility room, doing the laundry. A shaft of pale winter sunlight slanted through the window and across the ironing board, cutting out her puppeteer hands. She looked up at me but did not stop working. The handkerchiefs she was folding were mono-grammed with my father's initials: the rest of his clothes Jennifer took to a charity shop but the handkerchiefs ('we only bought him these last Christmas!') she'd declared too good to waste. Since I hadn't had a cold it appeared she had been using them herself.

Something about the precision with which Fira's hands moved made it hard for me to speak.

I imagined them in surgical gloves stitching up a dog's ear, then raised above her head to ward off blows, and finally I saw them again, lemon bright in the swarming light, casting bird shadows across my utility room's flagstone floor.

The confidence I'd felt after speaking to Sandeep Raja dwindled to nothing as I stood watching her work. There seemed no way to bring up the subject of her appeal without conceding that it might not succeed. And yet not mentioning it, which I hadn't since rescuing her from the rain, implied worse.

'Your son is handsome,' Fira said.

'Jimmy? You think so?'

'Yes. But he should clean his fingernails.'

'It's just paint. He's a painter.'

'Very romantic.'

'I suppose so. But they're safe hands, too. He's a security man when he's not painting. But you're right, you'd find him too messy, he's not right at all for you.'

She shot me a withering look. 'Without my help I think you would be messy as well.'

'I'm actually fairly . . .' I trailed off, a simple question – *your trip to Croydon, are you prepared?* – temporarily blotting out this silliness, but then found myself saying 'tidy' anyway.

'Tidy is easy in a big house like this. When we are married and living in my tent, then we will see.'

'Tent?'

I stepped backwards and sat down heavily on our wicker laundry basket. Beside me the washing machine whined menacingly.

'Yes, Jimmy is quite handsome, but he is too young for me.'

'What did you mean by tent, Fira?'

'Robert, he's more my age, and better for money too, I am thinking. But from his photograph it seems he will be fat soon.'

'There'll be no tents, you hear me?'

In answer she ran her hands across the tops of my shoulders and up the sides of my neck, and then she gripped both my ears and jiggled them. (Immediately – I couldn't stop myself – I thought of Bill H. Marshall and was thankful I played on the edge of the scrum.)

Now she cupped my right ear and whispered into it. 'Tent, castle, bedsit, it does not matter to me.'

'I'm serious.'

'You often say that. I like it.' She brushed my lips with the ball of her thumb, then kissed them. The watermelon smell was a taste now, spiked with coffee. 'I like it because it is true. You even have a serious way of walking. Pretending you know where you are going. It was one of the things that made me like you.'

She turned back to the ironing board. The wedge of sunlight rippled up her body as she did so, making her at once more solid and ghostlike. She folded another handkerchief and asked, 'Will you trust Mr Bannerman to arrange your divorce as well?'

The stepladder was still leaning against the shelves at the far end of the utility room, a dull silver arrow pointing to the tow-rope's lair. Look! A stain had spread across the whitewashed plaster up there. What did that mean? Nothing, of course, except that winter was winning its battle against my wall of shot brickwork, which stood guard at this end of the Tithe Barn. Pink and frostbitten and waiting to fall. Nothing more substantial stood between Fira and me and the world. I own two sledgehammers now; one has a long handle, the other is short. It wouldn't take me long to climb the ladder and knock a hole through that stain, I thought. My eyes began searching the shelves for my toolbox.

I heard myself say, 'I think I have more faith in his assistant, Sandeep Raja. He's working on your case as well.'

Fira snorted.

My toolbox was in the shed, of course. I didn't retrieve

the sledgehammer from it: even if it had been to hand I doubt I would have holed the wall.

Instead I went back out to my office and read the hard parts of Freddie's journal again. When I'd found it in his bureau, the day after he died, I had not gone all the way through it immediately, and not because I was frightened of what I might find. No, I wanted to savour the experience. He was dead, but Alzheimer's meant he'd been gone a long while. I didn't know my father during the war, of course, but those were the years in which he'd been drop-forged, in which he became what he later expected me to become. The journal, I'd hoped, would remind me of Freddie's molten essence.

Work hard, play fair, do your duty, my son.

What I'd found instead, and what I now felt compelled − like a motorist rubbernecking an accident − to reread, revealed that he'd broken the code he later instilled in me, a code which − in any case − had failed him so badly. It wasn't the lie which upset me. In a way discovering Freddie's cover-up confirmed his fallibility and justified my own, but the fact that he'd gone to his grave without coming clean filled me with regret. I'd first read the journal in bed. Now I sat poring over the pages again in my strip-lit office, as if by rereading them in a colder light I might find that the story had changed, but of course it had not.

A knock on my office door made me start. Spongebob's tail thumped the carpet tiles. I wiped my face with the palm of my hand and shut the journal and was saying 'One moment!' when Fira came in anyway.

'Oh. I'm sorry.'

'No. Yes. It doesn't matter.' I reached to put the journal away.

'I would come back later, Harry, but,' she looked at me closely, 'but there is a problem, with a leak.'

'What's that?'

'Come with me.' She steered me through the door, continuing, 'I have tried to mend it but failed.'

'Mend what?'

She led me back to into the utility room, where the washing machine had been pulled out from its slot under the work surface and now stood taut on its pipe-leash in a pool of water.

'It is not the waste pipe or water connections. I have checked. The pump, or perhaps a rubber part. This spill is still growing.'

There's a lump of concrete in the bottom of that washing machine; I had to enlist Jimmy's help when I installed it. Jennifer wouldn't have thought about trying to move the thing, let alone mend it.

'I am sorry,' Fira repeated. 'But if this is the pump then perhaps you . . .'

'Yes, yes,' I said. I skirted the puddle and bent to turn off the water at the mains beneath the sink.

'This is a bad time to disturb you,' she ventured more softly. 'But sometimes it is better to have a machine to fix instead of real problems.'

I knelt before the machine again, as if considering my next step, and said, 'I've no more real problems than the next man.'

'This is one of the nice things about you,' she went

on, 'that you say this. But you are not right. Your father has just died. I know he wrote you a book, and I know it upsets you. Also it makes you more reckless, buying a dog, parking everywhere, sleeping in my bed. I have watched this happen to you, the good and the bad.' She knelt next to me, her denim knees blotting up water. 'Spongebob and me, we will help steady you through this.'

Fira's having registered Freddie's funeral was enough of a surprise, never mind that she had noticed the journal's effect upon me. You *expect* a man of sixty to lose his father if he hasn't already; it takes a leap of sympathy to realise that having for ever to prepare only intensifies the blow with it comes.

I said, 'If we switch the machine back on with the mains off the water that's left in it will drain away and when the cycle has finished we'll be able to open the door. You know, to take the clothes out.'

Fira regarded me unblinkingly. 'If there are difficult things in your father's book perhaps you can explain them to me.'

That this was wise and kind and impossible and the sort of thing that Jennifer would never say made me swallow hard. Fira and I were still squatting in the puddle, but her knee was now resting against mine. It felt natural. I pinched the bridge of my nose and she touched my face with the ball of her thumb again, running it gently across my creased brow.

I said, 'I don't know why you feel for me, Fira, but I believe that you do.'

A shadow – bashful, shy – passed across her face. 'No,

no. It is just my cunning, to steal you.' She lifted her chin again. 'Like with this machine, which I broke to catch your attention.'

'Really?'

She rolled her eyes and said, 'Stay here, I will fetch some towels.'

19

A weekend passed by without Jennifer mentioning my encounter with her golf professional. I thought she might be waiting for Jimmy, Marie and little Flo to leave, but by Monday afternoon, when they'd all returned to London, the prospect of a frank discussion seemed, if anything, to have receded. Though I took a bottle of Wolf Blass and two glasses into the sitting room, Jennifer preferred to spend the evening in the kitchen hand-tooling canapés. Perhaps that was it, she was waiting for the party. She and Ryder Evans had decided that he should accept my invitation. It made a red-wine sort of sense. His presence at my sixtieth would speak more eloquently about the situation than Jennifer and I could. I went to bed fuzzily hopeful.

But the following morning's logic swiftly uncoupled that train of thought. Jennifer was unable to meet my eye at breakfast. She gouged us open a grapefruit each, then sliced the ball of her thumb cutting up an unnecessary third. This gave her an excuse to retreat to the bathroom. I in turn headed for my office, steeled myself with a morning's spinning on my chair, then marched back inside for lunch determined to speak plainly, only to find her forcing salad-flecked Parma ham shavings upon Spongebob. Unsuccessfully: my dog appeared too listless even to raise his chin from the kitchen floor. Something oblivious – mean even – about my wife's generosity knocked me off course.

'Give it a rest, Jennifer. He's not up to it. Can't you see that?'

'Well. If that's the thanks–'

'It's not about gratitude. He's off colour.'

'Perhaps . . .' Jennifer tipped the ham cuttings into the waste disposal. '. . . you ought to have had him passed fit by a vet . . .' She flicked the grinder on (Spongebob flinched) and off. '. . . before lumbering us with a sick animal to deal with on top of everything else.'

I knelt before Spongebob. His eyes now had the watery-yellow tinge of my breakfast grapefruit halves. 'It's just the after-effect of shock,' I said. 'Some air, that's what he needs.' I took down his lead (hung on the hook Pearl's riding tack never occupied) and bent to lift him on to all fours, whispering, without meaning to, '*Only resist.*'

'What's that?' asked Jennifer.

'I'm taking him for a walk. Will you be here when I get back, or out playing golf?'

As Spongebob had started at the noise of the waste disposal unit, so a tremor seemed to pass across Jennifer's face when I said this, before defiance made a swift, thin line of her lips. She crossed her arms; overripe fruit bulged. 'I've no plans to go anywhere today, Harry,' she said. 'But you never know. Take your keys.'

★ ★ ★

The part of Freddie's journal that Fira had interrupted me rereading reveals that he didn't fly for eleven days following the raid on the Opel works. Neither did he manage more than two hours' consecutive sleep. 'The tiredness burns,' he notes. 'My eyes smart, my stomach's a furnace, there's a ghastly prickling feeling from my scalp to the soles of my feet.' He decided to consult the base doctor. Yet en route to the medical hut he found himself clinging to a section of perimeter fence in tears over the memory of the recently deceased Fitch – with whom he had often walked the rabbit-bitten airfield – and he turned back to his billet in shame. From there, when summoned, he duly tramped to the crew room for what was to be his last ops briefing of the war.

But not before looking in the mirror. From the scratchings-out in his notebook I'd say he tried conscientiously to describe what he saw. The final version reads, 'It was my face, of course, but not mine at all. The eyes had not seen what I had seen. There was too much light in them. My whole face was too bright, in fact, my cheeks were too pink, my lips too red, my teeth glistened. Altogether too alive! It was a lie of a face, I understood that, a mask, hiding the obvious, which was death. This was my chop look. It was a relief to see it at last. I said "good show" as I turned for the door.'

A northerly wind was blowing outside: the willow's leafless branches were flailing ineffectually at the house. Spongebob lowered his head – as if against admonishment. My hands stiffened with cold the instant I removed my gloves. But I had to: the clasp on his lead is a fiddly thing. I fixed it to Spongebob's collar, not to prevent him from running off, but to give him some help keeping up. We set off slowly towards the paddock. I helped him over the stile. We trudged together along the bridleway. It should have been obvious to me that Spongebob was no more up to this walk than he had been to Jennifer's cold-meat platter, and indeed it *was* obvious, but I couldn't help myself, I just pressed on, talking to him all the while, telling him we'd both feel better for the effort, and for a bit of distance between us and the Tithe Barn. By the time we reached the gap in the hedge through which he had flushed my Korean rabbit, however, I was having to encourage him along with a tug of the lead every few steps, and knew that what I was doing was wrong. The instant I stopped walking Spongebob did, too. He looked up at me. Then he teetered sideways and fell down on the frozen path.

I understood his expression. It wasn't the unblinking stoicism I'd seen in the dog home, though that, too, had been tinged with resignation, but a wider-eyed look, the amazement of defeat. I knelt on the ruts (my knee, my knee!) and lifted his head in my hands. A shiver ran through him, part spasm, part ecstatic shudder. His eyes narrowed.

He's a big, solid-boned dog. I don't remember how I got him home, just that the weight of him set the Audi's alarm off when I laid him on its bonnet to fish for my car keys. The Discovery was still there, meaning Jennifer hadn't gone out, but I didn't knock on the door to ask for her help. As I sped off the drive I caught a glimpse of her face in the kitchen window. A greenish oval. It shrank back as the car passed by.

Freddie's indifference to what he'd seen in the mirror persisted through the briefing, but in the hours that followed, the waiting hours, his misgivings grew. He sat down to a plate of eggs and bacon, saw his chop look swimming in the greasy yolk, walked outside and threw up. Lethargy soaked through him. He took Benzedrine to counter it but instead of waking him it made him feel as if he were watching himself from a distance. Arriving at dispersal, where S-Sword – the crew's new Lancaster – stood monumental on its tarmac pan, he heard himself reassuring the new mid-upper gunner (a nineteen-year-old postman called Michael Holden) that the raid (which, again, they were to lead) would be a piece of cake, but 'in a voice that sounded as if it was coming out of the bomb bay, not from my mouth'. In the cockpit Freddie grew convinced the problem was something to do with the new crate. Yet the checks he and engineer Tom Spears ran through all went without a hitch. The pitter-patter of the booster pumps, the chuffing wheeze before each Merlin caught with a bang and roared to life, it was all normal, and yet, Freddie reports, 'thoroughly u/s too'. 'I can't explain it better than to say the plane looked OK, sounded it, smelt it, but wasn't the real thing at all, and neither were we, the crew. The whole show felt fake, ominously so.' Nobody else seemed to notice. Len Rushworth took his place behind his curtain, whistling as usual. Freddie had no reason not to trundle S-Sword on to the runway and throttle up for take-off. Hoping he'd see things differently from the air, that's what he did.

But of course he felt no better aloft. He felt worse. 'Putting us on to Len's heading took a sickening effort, holding the crate there stretched every fibre – of me and, it felt, S–Sword – to breaking point. It was as if I was trying to propel us against an over-powering magnetic current. Every yard we pressed on increased the likelihood we'd fly apart, atom by atom. The question wasn't whether we'd have to turn back, but when.'

I drove to Fira's again. It was barely three in the afternoon, yet St Clare, as I sped through it (*pop! thank you for . . .*), was already a village of half-tones. When I was a boy it always upset me that my birthday was so close to the year's shortest day, and now, too, I found myself grinding my teeth, angry that the December sun had again given up without a fight. Still, the car's headlamps poured a tunnel of light for Spongebob and me to rush through, and soon we'd made it from the village to the town, and its street lamps, sliding across the bonnet, were waving us in to land.

My throat thickened as Fira opened the door. Expectation stood in her face. Need, even; she stepped close to me, gripped my hands between both of hers and pressed her face into my neck. When she stepped back her eyes were glistening.

'I'm sorry, Fira. I'd have called ahead.' I pointed at the car. 'But I don't have a number, and he's worse again. Much worse. Help me. Tell me what to do.'

Fira stiffened, reached out for the door jamb. 'The dog?' she said.

'Yes, I was out with him, walking, madness, too cold, and he collapsed . . .' I trailed off, daunted by a shift in Fira's expression, cloud over water, a hardening about the eyes. She looked unimpressed. Or perhaps just professional, and in need of a sensible account. I explained myself again, slowly. She crossed her arms as she listened (I thought of Jennifer, and had to stop myself from leaning forward to kiss Fira's beautiful brow) and she kept them crossed as I popped the Audi's tailgate.

She peered into the back at Spongebob. His coat was coppery beneath the street lamps. Fira ran a hand across him (more in sympathy, it seemed to me, than with investigative intent) and said quietly, 'If he is sick you must take him to a proper vet.'

'Yes. Of course. But, Christ, is it bad? Can you tell?'

'No.' She shrugged, stared off down the street. Was she avoiding meeting my eye? My stomach was a knot. It drew tighter as she continued: 'He looks sick to me, lying there. I do not know.'

Convinced he could not go through with the raid, Freddie announced that S-Sword's port-outer engine was overheating, and ordered the flight engineer to shut it down. He told his wireless operator to hand control of the raid over to the deputy master bomber, but Tom Spears interrupted him, insisting the engine, according to his instruments, was running perfectly well. At which point Len Rushworth's voice came over the intercom, calmly pointing out that with three serviceable Merlins they must go on in any event. Freddie heard himself repeat that the engine was duff, but again his words seemed to be coming from elsewhere, and before he knew it that remote voice was telling the crew he was sick, couldn't trust his judgement, wasn't safe to fly.

He dropped S–Sword into a descending turn, beneath the oncoming bomber stream.

Len demanded that he put the plane back on course and let Doug Fisher, the Canadian bomb aimer – a trained reserve pilot – take over the controls. With Freddie's help he could wield S–Sword. But Freddie ordered Fisher – and indeed the entire crew – back to bed. My father was becoming confused. They were over the Channel, at 14,000 feet instead of 22,000, and he'd somehow turned the Lancaster through 360 degrees, heading towards the French coast again. Now Len was growling that Doug had a *duty* to take control if the skipper had gone LMF. Freddie was only partly listening. He'd become transfixed by the feathery columns of the coastal defence searchlights. The newest of these were six feet across and shone with the brightness of 2.7 million candles, propelling a pillar of light some seven miles high. Abhorrent to Freddie until now, tonight the lights seemed welcoming. 'The arms of God,' he calls them, 'heralding a new dawn.'

Still descending, he pointed S–Sword towards the sun.

Fira sat beside me in silence as I drove to the vet. She's not the type to offer hollow reassurances, I know that, but her silence worried me. It had a brooding, stunned edge. School-run traffic waylaid us. I'd chewed a strip of skin from the inside of my bottom lip by the time we pulled on to the clinic's forecourt. This time we were not made to wait our turn: before I knew it Spongebob had been hooked to a drip and admitted for tests. He looked small on the stainless-steel trolley, and he still hadn't woken up when they wheeled him away. Unlike the whistling seamstress in Shepherd's Bush, this vet was a man my age. He had a goatee like Lenin's, which failed to hide the pursed-lip *not good* look he shot his assistant as they whisked my dog backstage.

With the crew a cacophony in his headset, Freddie piloted S-Sword into the searchlights. The main force had passed this coastline already. Here was another Lancaster, alone, low and slow. Easy to spot, with or without radar. It was only a matter of time before one of the beams swept over them. Freddie describes the waiting as 'ecstatic'. When the brightness hit, every rivet in S-Sword's fuselage cast a sudden shadow, every metal edge in the cockpit jumped knife sharp, and then Freddie was engulfed, snow-blind. 'After the darkness, that heavenly light!' He knew what he should do: hit the rudder and side-slip down the beam, let the searchlight overtake him, then corkscrew in search of safety. But he didn't. 'I was staring at the sun through closed eyes. It was warm on my face. I felt safe.' Transported, he held the plane straight and level. A second searchlight caught them up, and another latched on, and then there were more. S-Sword was coned. The flak began bursting around them. Radar-governed, predictive guns, pounding a distinctive rhythmical beat. The Lancaster jumped and plunged as, with a stultifying obviousness, the shock waves drew closer. Then there was a bang, an incomprehensible realignment of forces, and everything went black again.

The rush hour proper swallowed Fira and me as we made our way back from the vet. Again we sat in silence, our faces pink with brake lights, exhaust fumes rising around us, cocooned in Audi-hush. I rested my hand in her lap; her thigh tensed, as if with anger. She was fond of Spongebob, I knew that, but I had not suspected her feelings for him ran so deep.

'I'd invite you back to the house, Fira,' I said, 'but Jennifer's there, no golf today, if you know what I mean, and she and I haven't yet had a chance to discuss the next step, though we will, soon, I swear it, and then–'

'Jennifer,' Fira repeated. 'Your wife.'

'Ye-es.'

'She is an excellent cook.'

'She is.'

'Please stop this car.'

Even as I said 'What?' I did as she asked. We'd only been crawling forward but the brakes bit, throwing us against our seat belts, rocking us back in our seats.

'I will walk home from here.'

'Why on earth?'

Fira ran her fingers over my knuckles, wrapped tight over the leather gear stick. 'I have things to do as well,' she said.

It was out before I knew it: 'Like what?'

She shook her head, breathing out through her nose.

'Well, for a start, I must transmit my findings back to Moscow,' she said.

'Fira?'

'I'm hungry,' she said, opening the car door.

A gap had opened up in front of the Audi, only ten feet or so, but enough to prompt the driver behind me to obliterate what Fira said next by leaning on his horn. She slid through a crack between two parked white vans, giving me a little wave. She is too thin. The nervousness in my stomach — for Spongebob, I thought — twisted tighter as I watched her go. I crept forward, one eye on the road, craning to keep her in view. It might have been wishful thinking, but as I rounded the corner on to the High Street I'm sure I caught a glimpse of a neon Kentucky Fried Chicken sign in my rear-view mirror.

The last third of S-Sword's port wing, from the 'faulty' outer engine (which carried on working even after the explosion) to the wingtip, had been shot away. Flak had also torn holes along the length of the plane's fuselage. Len Rushworth was killed outright. So was the new mid-upper gunner. In the tail Michael Harris was also hit by shrapnel; he said he could cope but stopped groaning within minutes. The hit had thrown the bomber into a deadly — and searchlight-evading — spin. It had also reignited Freddie's sense of where he was and what he was doing. He was fighting the controls, unscathed, holding hard to life. The Lancaster, in a slow spiral now, was losing more and more height, but Freddie, using rudder and throttle alone, managed to wrest the plane straight and level – and on course for England – again. His headphones were full of somebody pleading. It was the nose gunner, Mark Oldfield, begging for permission to jump. Unsure of his height – the altimeter had failed – Freddie ordered him to stay put, but the gunner opened the forward hatch and jumped anyway. There was a clunk as he struck the underside of the fuselage and he was never seen again.

'I'd lost men before,' the journal notes, 'brought dead and wounded home more than once, but this time it was my fault.'

The bomb aimer came on the tannoy with a reminder: S-Sword still had a bellyful of target indicators and HE bombs. Freddie gave the order to jettison immediately, but the bomb bay wouldn't open properly and persevering with the doors destabilised the Lancaster again. What was left of the port wing dipped suddenly and they lost more height. Below the broken cloud now, Freddie caught a glimpse of moonlight on the water ('glimmering obliviously') and estimated they were at about 1,500 feet. Despite the miracle of apparently operational engines, 'S-Sword now had the aerodynamic proficiency of a colander'. Freddie decided to gamble on clearing the coast nevertheless. 'Whatever else happened, I wasn't putting down in the drink a third time,' he wrote. With any luck they'd make Woodbridge, the emergency aerodrome on the south coast.

This was beyond wishful thinking. S-Sword's navigator was dead and the wireless operator had reported the radio unresponsive. Freddie ordered him to keep broadcasting, but they had no means of knowing whether S-Sword's pleas for help were being received. Spears – the flight engineer – couldn't confirm that the plane's undercarriage would lock down, either. The gunmetal seascape beneath them grew a white fringe and turned into land, but as they cleared the Kent coast Freddie saw his chop look reflected back at him in the cockpit side window. They were lost, without confirmed wheels, carrying 2,000 pounds of high explosives and enough target flares to light up Berlin, and – with the hop fields skidding past below – losing what was left of their four or so hundred feet.

He ordered the remains of his crew to prepare for a hard landing. Somebody began wailing over the intercom. Freddie tore off his headset, then realised that the noise was coming out of his own mouth. Ahead, darkness. He stopped shouting and gripped the controls: no matter what lay beneath them this was S-Sword's final approach.

I drifted back to the Tithe Barn in daze. Jennifer was loading Tupperware containers – filled with canapés, no doubt – into the back of the Discovery. Sensible, really: on a night like this the truck would be as good as a fridge. She didn't try to hide what she was doing and I didn't pretend not to have noticed. As well as being indestructible, Tupperware stacks neatly. I stood on the drive watching Jennifer work, my car ticking as it cooled, no Spongebob in the back. If etiquette – or concern for one another's feelings – prevented us from acknowledging the surprise party, something less fathomable stopped my wife from asking after my dog. I drew a heavy breath to tell her the bad news anyway, then held on to it, letting the sharp air soften in my chest. Jennifer slammed the Discovery's back door and I followed her inside.

The Lancaster screamed over the village of Little Woolpit, taking the top off a horse-chestnut tree by the cricket pitch, said to have stood eighty feet tall. It crash-landed in a field. Royal Air Force investigators later said that the undercarriage had collapsed on impact, causing S-Sword's broken wing to dig into the ground. This flicked the aircraft into a cartwheel, which split the fuselage open along its length, much like a pod of peas. Freddie had no recollection of how he scrambled clear of what remained of the cockpit. Despite numbering a broken ankle and a punctured lung among his injuries, he managed to make it a hundred or so yards before stumbling into a ditch filled with silage effluent. It smelt sickly sweet. Freddie lay there looking at stars scudding through gaps in the cloud.

It occurred to him that he should go back and check that the rest of the crew had managed to escape the wreckage.

(They hadn't.)

He raised himself on to his knees and fell back as the remains of S-Sword exploded. The low cloud forced the shock wave to roll laterally, as if beneath a lid, so that the end of Freddie's war was heard in Canterbury, thirty miles away.

★   ★   ★

Cold air makes me need to pee. I went to the downstairs loo and had one of those moments when the utterly familiar takes on an alien cast: the wooden-handled toilet brush, the pottery gondolier we bought home from Venice in '91, the stripy pastel wallpaper I'd hung about the same time − all of it had been invisible to me for years, but now seemed suddenly new. Even the porcelain bowl I was shaking myself into looked unfamiliar, much as it must have seemed − I thought − to Fira, when she first bent down to clean it just a few months ago. I imagined her picking up the little man − cemented into his boat, there on the windowsill − to dust. What did she think of it? I had no idea, but I did understand one thing as I zipped up my fly: Fira's opinion of that figurine mattered more to me now than Jennifer's. I dried my hands, thinking: now, *now*, is the time for me to admit as much.

'Have you got a moment, love?' I asked as I entered the kitchen.

Jennifer shrugged but did not turn from the countertop.

'It's important.'

'Since when did you need an appointment?' she said, wiping vegetable shards from her knife. 'I can listen and make soup at the same time.'

'How long have we been married?'

'You need to ask?'

'No. You're right, I don't. We were married four years before we moved here.'

'Sounds about right.'

'And I've been happy with you here, a long while.'

She turned around now to face me. The halogen spotlight rippled over her glossy hair.

'But,' I began. Then I saw three things. First, that the light had also caught the defenceless down on her cheek. Second, that her eyes were red. And third, that as she pressed the heel of her hand into each eye in turn, the underside of her arm wobbled within its tight cotton sleeve. 'But . . .' I tried again. The words 'Fira' and 'Ryder Evans' were out of the question, as was 'somebody else', it seemed.

Jennifer sniffed and said, 'Yes?'

'But I'm not sure we can go on living here together much longer.'

'Why ever not?'

'Well . . .' Through the utility room door the stepladder winked at me. Winked because my own eyes were stinging now. 'My pension,' I heard myself say. 'It hasn't worked out. The company it's with—'

'Mutual Friends.'

'Yes.' I looked directly at her in time to see her dab at her eyes with a handkerchief. 'Yes, Mutual Friends. They wrote saying the amount we stand to get back is much less than forecast.'

'Is that so?' Jennifer slid the chopping board's contents into a saucepan on the hob. Onions: the pan hissed. When she turned back round there was a stillness to her which made me realise she'd been fidgeting before. The stillness looked like relief. 'How much are we short?' she asked.

I told her.

'Phew,' she said.

She balled her handkerchief and tucked it up her sleeve. The gesture was familiar and homely and it made my throat tighten up. But I pressed on, telling her how it was only a matter of time before we'd have to sell the house. Though I felt for her a part of me wanted to paint the bleakest picture possible. Unable to address the real issue, I might as well make the most of this one.

'Phew,' she said again when I finished, and there was no mistaking the hollowness of her concern this time. The news obviously hadn't sunk in yet.

'The quicker we sell up, the better,' I emphasised. 'The longer we hang on the sooner we'll end up in the poorhouse.'

'Don't be melodramatic, Harry.' Jennifer stirred the onions, which spat. I was about to protest but she cut me off, saying more gently, 'Whatever happens, it won't be as bad as all that.'

I balled my fists.

'A change might even be good for us. We'll cope.'

If she was truly taking this news in her stride I should feel humbled, grateful even, but her spatula, tracing sensible circles through the browning onion shards, was also stirring annoyance in me.

'I paid into that fund for thirty years.'

'Yes, I know you did.' My wife gave me a sympathetic smile.

'And now they've stolen our savings.'

'It's not fair, you're right. But–'

'But what?' Did the golf professional have money, was that it? Though I wanted to ask, I could only repeat, 'But what?' again.

'There's always a measure of risk in such schemes, Harry. It isn't your fault. We're not the first people to have lost out like this. The newspapers have been full of warnings. Investments can go down as well as up.'

Was she on the payroll? My knee throbbed. Outrage, that's what I needed, not platitudes. I ground my fists together, knuckles scrummaging painfully.

'The future,' I said.

Having shrunk the flame under the saucepan, Jennifer stepped towards me and separated my hands. 'I know, I know,' she said. That moisturiser she uses keeps her fingertips wonderfully soft. 'But we really don't have to worry as much as all that, Harry. We're not alone in this. Robert would never let us sell up. He's told me so already. If push comes to shove, he'll step in.'

Freddie's mouth tasted of blood and there was a dead weight across his chest. Guilt, he assumed. In fact, the punctured lung had collapsed, and as well as having snapped his ankle he had bitten off the tip of his tongue. Still, he managed to drag himself along that ditch, one eye on the cloud canopy above, now flickering with the burning Lancaster's Halloween glow. S–Sword hadn't missed the village by much. In no time a crowd would gather around the wreck. He had only one impulse left, not to be found. The ditch provided him with cover. It also pointed in the way. 'Where to?' the journal asks. 'Just away. I had to run away.'

The ditch fed into a trickling stream. At daybreak my father found himself following its current on his hands and knees. The water ran clear over shiny pebbles and red earth. Each hand he put on the stream bed stirred up a puff of sediment, explosions in a city far below. The stream deepening, he dragged himself along its bank through reeds as tall and thin as searchlight beams.

'My memory was the enemy territory, I saw. Pain afforded a no man's land of sorts. But the only real safety lay in oblivion.'

Parting the rushes, Freddie came upon a wooden boat turned turtle in the mud. He thought of crawling underneath it to hide, then had a better idea and pried the thing right side up. There were no oars. He edged the boat into the stream regardless, fell over the gunwale, curled up on the wooden planks and felt them scrape and bounce and float.

When he awoke night had fallen again and the boat was caught among the branches of an overhanging tree. Thirst made him drink from the stream. The water was like a hot knife drawn across his injured tongue. It brought him to his senses.

He had no idea how far he'd drifted, but he did realise this: to the cowardice, LMF and general dereliction of his duties as a skipper the air force brass could add now add a new charge, that of having gone absent without leave.

20

Old floorboards are a natural burglar alarm. At a
quarter to three on the morning of Felix's last
birthday I intercepted him crossing our landing – he
and Pearl were staying over – en route downstairs. His
uncle was a devil for sleepwalking: rouse Jimmy from
his trance and you risked a meltdown. We found steering
him back to bed in silence worked best. But as soon
as I gathered Felix in my arms I saw that he was awake
and shivering with pre-birthday anticipation.

'Bats, barn owls, badgers and boys,' I whispered.
'Which is the odd one out?'

'Boys,' he conceded.

'That's right.' I wrapped his dinosaur duvet around
him. 'Because the others are all . . .'

'Noc-noc-noc . . .'

'You've got it. Nocturnal. Unlike boys – and grandads.'

Yet after I told Jennifer about my pension – on
the eve of my sixtieth birthday – I also found it hard
to sleep. I spent the small hours night-flying, the
digital alarm clock my only instrument. It's a long
while since a birthday of mine has fostered such a
state of nervous excitement. Four o'clock overtook

me before I fell asleep, and I was downstairs making tea by six.

The better you know a person the easier it is to say nothing in their company. Assumed truths make this possible, as do tacitly ignored lies. At breakfast Jennifer chose to avoid topics such as my failed pension, her affair with Ryder Evans, Spongebob's absence and my 'surprise' party, and confined herself to wishing me a happy birthday instead. We could have dinner out that evening to celebrate if I liked. Tenacity is an admirable quality, but there's something heartbreaking about it, too. I buttered her toast the way she likes it – right to the edges – and told her I'd be ready to go out at eight.

The morning ground past. I tried to order Fira some good-luck flowers ahead of her appeal hearing, but my computer crashed as I typed in my credit card details. Robert has an IT helpdesk at work; we self-employed pay our dues on hold. I spent the next four and a half hours resetting my machine on the instructions of a young man from New Delhi whose patience rivalled Gandhi's. Joy Ghosh came to mind. While I waited for the computer to thaw I tried her number again, without success. Neither was I able to speak to the vet. The receptionist at the clinic couldn't tell me what was wrong with Spongebob, said of course I could drop in to spend time with him if I wanted, and assured me I'd hear as soon as they had news. I put the phone down for the first time since breakfast and connected to the Internet, tentatively, much as I'd taken my first step after the cast came off my leg in '79. I needn't have worried. As my knee had held up then, so my inbox began to fill up with emails now.

There, among the diplomas, stock tips and performance-enhancing drugs, sat an email from Wasserreich, my German shower manufacturer friend, containing what appeared to be an order – success! – for a first batch of silicone washers. I was reading it through when Bannerman called with the news that Fira's appeal had failed.

'What?'

'She hasn't told you herself yet?'

'The hearing is tomorrow. Thursday. You've made some sort of mistake.'

'No, it was yesterday morning, at nine o'clock. I thought you knew that. It's been down in the diary for at least a week.'

Merlins were misfiring in my chest. I whispered, 'Sandeep told me just last Friday that Fira's appeal hearing was scheduled for this *Thursday*. That's what he said.'

'Thursday? Maybe you misheard him. Or . . . I don't know. He's a first-class lawyer, but he's not the best with dates.'

I found myself short of breath.

'Look, Mr Brinkman, *Harry*, your being there wouldn't have made any difference. This appeal was always a long shot, as I explained. But worth a serious go. As it was you were spared a very frustrating day out. The Crown was a step ahead of us on the tents point, sadly. Chechen camps are distinguishable from Somali ones on a number of counts just now. The tribunal were with them on that. It's very disappointing. Sandeep did a marvellous job explaining away young Fira's less than prompt attendance at Croydon, but to no avail. As I say, it was certainly worth a try.'

Henry Tan deserved this silicone ring order, I was thinking, as I listened to Bannerman, the phone a hot blade wedged between my collarbone and ear. This verdict wasn't final. I'd find a way of forcing another appeal. Even as the lawyer explained the futility of such hopes I was topping and tailing the damned email and forwarding it to China. The screen before me was a blur. Bannerman, delicate as a surgeon, pared the tissue of my disappointment in search of his bone. He'd give me plenty of time to meet the firm's fee, he said. I mumbled assurances with my eyes shut, but Fira's face came to me, the expectation with which she'd answered the door yesterday, her stunned blankness when I'd showed her Spongebob, comatose in my car.

Bannerman paused, content with his justification. I imagined a bricklayer stepping back to admire a finished course of bricks. My own walls were dust now.

'What happens next?' I asked.

'As in?'

'To Fira. What steps will the Home Office take?'

'Oh. Well, given that the tribunal presented its determination on the day, and that there's no leave to appeal in this instance . . .'

'Just tell me.'

'Under the new regime they've taken to acting – deporting people, that is – pretty swiftly. Within a matter of days.'

I stabbed at *call end*, put the phone down, and stepped back from my desk. Then – as Bannerman's 'Hello?

Harry? Are you there?' chirped through the speaker-phone – I swept the handset on to the floor and kicked it hard. The problem with destructive rage is that the satisfaction to be had from it is so short lived. Relief blipped in my chest as the phone and its battery flew apart and then I was engulfed in dread.

I pocketed my passport and wallet and set off for town again.

When Pearl was thirteen we received a call from a paramedic in North London saying she'd been found unconscious by Camden Lock and was en route to hospital in an ambulance. The paramedic didn't mention that Pearl was covered in Martini-scented vomit at the time, or that the friend who bought the bottle had made the 999 call. I think the hour and a half I spent on the M25 that day amounted to my worst prior experience of dread, that sensation of impending, irrevocable – fatal even – compromise, and even then I remember being aghast at the fact that I was somehow carrying on, that mundanities (I had spent the morning juggling the cash-flow problem at S.P. Components Ltd, and Rentokil were supposed to be turning up at the Tithe Barn that afternoon to deal with a wasps' nest outside Jimmy's bedroom window) still had the power to break in upon my thoughts. The same was true now. It was as if Fira – my inadvertently shocking treatment of her the day before, the incipient catastrophe of what might happen to her next – was too painful a subject to look upon for any length of time, so instead, as I ground the entire eight miles into town behind a tractor and trailer (stacked with what looked like solar panelling – in December),

I let my surprise party – who might show up and how would my acts of resistance turn out? – jostle for attention with my throbbing toe. I'd kicked that phone hard, and trainers are not as tough as rugby boots.

In failing light I faltered around the one-way system. It was only 2.30, but a bank of worsted clouds pressing down on the rooftops had leached all definition from the scene. Grey slate, umber bricks, blank windows: even the painted doors and windowsills were washed out, disappointing, like jaundiced eye-whites or a smile of tea-stained teeth. The red-and-blue pulse of a police car parked somewhere around the corner – perhaps that was why we were waiting? – cut the street with its only colour. In turn we stuttered to the junction. No, it wasn't a police car, but a fire engine, a fire engine trailing a drum of unwound hose and reaching upwards with its extended ladder.

The ladder was pointing to the window of Fira's bedsit.

I bumped the Audi on to the kerb, tight to the wall, so tight in fact that I had to slide over the handbrake and climb out of the passenger door. Horns beeped. I waved them away and put a hand out to stop an advancing 4x4 and sidestepped it as its bull-bars dipped towards me. Something was whining. It was the ladder, withdrawing in jerks from the window. I yelled, 'Fira!' The window was a black hole empty of glass. A tongue of soot reached up out of the hole to where the gutter had been. I ran around the back of the fire engine, treading and sliding on the slick hose, shouting, 'Please, somebody!' Fira's front door was open, or rather it had been knocked off its hinges and dragged out on to the pavement, where it lay like an outsized 'Welcome' mat. Two firemen were standing talking by the fire engine, hats tilted back, drinking from steaming cardboard cups. I ducked past them towards the opening.

One said, '*Skinny* means low-fat milk. *Tall* is small. And always ask for *two shots*.'

The other said, 'Woah, wait, hold on a minute, mate!'

I said, 'You don't understand,' and kept going.

'Hold this,' the first fireman said. And, 'Sir, sir!'

I stepped over the door and into the hall. The carpet squelched underfoot. There was an overpowering burnt-tyre smell and the walls were alive, still running with water. A wing of plaster had fallen and broken on the bottom stairs. I paused and took a step back but before I could leap this obstacle two hands gripped me firmly by the shoulders.

'You can't go inside yet.'

'Fira?'

'Is this your place?'

'Please, let me go. I have to check.'

'There's not much left *to* check, I'm afraid.'

'Where is she?'

'Who?'

'The girl.'

'There were no girls here. Or boys for that matter. The place was empty.'

I took in the fireman's face. He had long sideburns and a tattoo – it looked Maori, but his complexion was Scots white – on the side of his neck. He had guile-less eyes, too, and a reassuring smile. Firemen embody competence: he would not be mistaken, yet I couldn't stop myself asking, 'You're *sure* nobody was in?'

He nodded and steered me back down the corridor, talking all the while in a voice honed, I imagine, on would-be rooftop jumpers and children with their heads stuck in railings. 'A neighbour raised the alarm. Saw the occupant leave around lunchtime and the next time she looked the roof was pouring smoke. Are you saying you know who the place belongs to? Watch your step . . . don't touch anything . . . the walls will still be hot. A girl, you said. Somebody close, a relative? If you know her, perhaps you'd like to break the bad news to her. It didn't look like she had a lot of stuff in there *to* burn, which is something, I suppose, but what she did have is ash and foam now. She's going to find that disappointing.'

'Counterpane.' The fire could not have destroyed Fira's beautiful bedspread. Why? Because she would have had rolled it up to take with her before setting the place alight.

'What's that?'

'Who'd blame her?' I began, then realised what I was saying and changed tack. 'She doesn't have a mobile phone,' I told the fireman. 'At least . . .' My voice was shaky. . . . 'I don't think she does.'

'Know where she might have gone?'

A whisper: 'No.'

'Oh well.' The fireman accepted his coffee cup back from his colleague. *Camaraderie,* I thought with envy. Having taken a sip, he looked up at me to say, 'Don't worry about it. Nobody was hurt. She'll come back eventually.'

★ ★ ★

I skirted the rear of the fire engine (the pumps, the valves!) and swayed to my car. The ground pitched and rolled beneath my feet like a ship's deck. I steadied myself for a moment, both hands hanging on to one of the Audi's roof rails. All estates have them these days but I'd never used mine before. I'd never told Fira that I loved her, either. I just assumed she knew. The look in her eyes after our time on the counterpane: I hadn't imagined she might doubt my intentions. But my only response, when she had told me that we were to be married, had been blithering shock. I'd never told her what I planned to do. I tried now to focus on what she must have assumed the day before, when I'd turned up with Spongebob, and not mentioned her court appeal, just hours after it had failed, but it was as if I were trying to hold my hand over a flame. I couldn't. Some base instinct – for self-preservation – simply refused to let me think the thing through. Fira had reached a conclusion, though, hadn't she? Yes, and she'd spelled it out in fire and smoke.

I climbed back into my car, slid across the passenger seat again (*her* seat), and sat considering the leather steering wheel, the chrome-edged dashboard, the sat-nav's underwater glow. Nothing. The car's ability to reassure me had gone: it was *a car*. My hands upon the wheel looked pale and weak and incapable.

And it was Anthony Woodward's fault.

Dream logic preceded this realisation, a sequence of thoughts as contiguous – and ominous – as a hand of cards turned face up one by one. Mutual Friends had robbed me, so I'd climbed my ladder, and Joy Ghosh had told me to resist. Resistance led me to Fira and Spongebob. Now Spongebob was sick and Fira had gone. I made white dots of my knuckles, tightening my grip on the steering wheel. Why had Bill H. Marshall kicked Spongebob? Because Anthony Woodward stole my pension. A better lawyer than Bannerman would have saved Fira, or at the very least employed an assist-ant capable of telling me the right date for the hearing, but I hadn't been able to afford a better lawyer because Mutual Friends had robbed me, so I'd missed the hearing and we'd lost. Anthony Woodward had as good as deported Fira. Then he'd doused her place in petrol and helped her strike the match.

I had only to type the first three letters of Woodward's village into the sat-nav before it homed in on Waverly Edge. After that it was simply a matter of following orders. Unlike on my previous visits, I nosed my car right up to the wrought-iron gates today. They were dusted with frost: it shimmered in the glow from my headlights, so that the gates appeared almost to move as my car came to a halt. In fact they *were* moving, triggered no doubt by some sort of sensor. I eased the Audi on to the drive and through the colon-nade. Up close the trees brought blast victims to mind; a succession of outraged amputees. I trickled to a halt in front of the triple garage and cut the engine. I climbed out of the car and marched up to the front door and stood on the step.

Deep, deep silence.

I reached out for the doorbell.

Big Ben chimed inside a biscuit tin.

I straightened my cuffs and smoothed down my shirt front and realised that I hadn't brought a coat. It wouldn't do to meet the man trembling. I thrust my hands deep into the pockets of my cords and held myself rigid. They were a well-prepared, festive family, the Woodwards: they'd already hung their beautiful Christmas wreath. It made a porthole of the door's single pane of glass. I'd been fighting the urge to shiver a good while before I saw what the porthole had been trying to show me all along, that there was no light on in the hall. Unsurprisingly, given that it was mid-afternoon on a weekday, nobody was in.

I retreated to the warmth of my car to wait.

Each second that passed made me more impatient, while at the same time adding to my sense of resignation, so that as the prospect of Woodward's return grew more likely it also seemed to recede. About now he had to be behind the wheel of his Range Rover, just turning into his drive. No, no, no, he'd be in a business-class recliner, en route for Tokyo. I should leave, make a proper plan, and come back to execute it. No, no, no, I should wait.

At a quarter to seven a fox – I felt sure it was the one Spongebob had failed to notice, but what do I know? – trotted up the drive and skirted the flagpole with apparent respect. Did it mind the frozen gravel under its paws? I wondered. The fox paused in front of the house, a grey cut-out against a charcoal hulk, and then leapt away as my phone rang. Like all dogs, foxes have phenomenal hearing.

Home, said the screen.

Ahead of thought I punched the answer button and Jennifer's voice came at me from sixteen speakers.

'Darling?'

Darling? She'd last called me that with warmth in her voice when breakfast television was a novelty. 'Yes,' I said slowly. 'I'm here.'

'Where's "here" Harry?'

'Well . . .'

'Never mind. It's just . . . dinner. I've gone ahead and booked us a table for eight o'clock. You haven't forgotten, have you?'

The truth was, I *had*. Confusion — gratitude struck with annoyance — sparked in my chest. 'I'm on my way home now,' I said, and started the engine.

But before I'd made the end of the drive frustration — at having to leave off dealing with Woodward until after my party — had fanned the sparks into an angry flame. My car let out a thin, high engine growl waiting for the man's ridiculous gates to swing inwards, and spat gravel as I surged out into the road. Its rear end snaked entering the first bend, too, but instead of slowing down I floored the accelerator and straddled the white lines into the next glassy sweeping curve. *Thank you for driving carefully.* Speed is its own bliss: the Audi made the corner, so who cared that its back wheels had lost sight of the front end? Not me. In a beautiful rush I realised that there were headlights coming at me through the side window. I let go of the wheel, joyfully. My car spun. Feathery blue haloes rushed at me and shrieked past, chased by slashing shapes of black and white. Searchlights! And screeching shells and the boom of a direct hit. If only a jolt had accompanied the flak-burst. But it hadn't; my car had partnered itself in a lone waltz down the icy lane and was now drifting unscathed to a halt. I was pointing back the way I'd come, with my headlights fixed on the silvery hedgerow. For a second I struggled to make sense of the shapes breaking up that hedge. Then they made themselves clear. The white triangle was the nose of a jet-ski. The tepee frame was an empty trailer. And the shiny green-black rectangle was the side of Anthony Woodward's Range Rover embedded in the ditch.

The hedge was moving. No, the Audi had begun creeping forward of its own accord again. It was as if a magnet were drawing me back to the man: in fact the automatic transmission was still set in 'Drive'. I pulled on to the verge – scored with great black gashes – next to the Range Rover, cut the ignition, and started my hazard lights flashing. They lit up the veined underside of the Range Rover in emphatic yellow bursts.

What had I done?

As if in answer the Range Rover's driver's-side door levered upwards towards the night sky and fell back a with a clunk.

I scrambled around the front of my car. The 4x4 had ploughed a furrow into the ditch and hedge: its radi-ator grille, wing and roof were wedged hard into a bow-wave of broken hawthorn and frozen black earth. I stretched for the driver's-side door handle, then jumped back with a start as the exhaust pipe burnt my stomach through my cotton shirt. Retreating to the rear of the vehicle, I managed to pull myself up on to its side, and was reaching for the handle when the door cracked open of its own accord again, pushed from within – I saw – by a deck-shoe-clad foot. I grabbed the metal edge of the door and helped lever it up. Anthony Woodward was a folk music fan, it seemed: Donovan – or somebody like him – warbled out into the frozen air. The stripe across my stomach began to throb dully.

'Are . . . ? Are you . . . ? *Are you OK?*'

It took me a moment to realise that Woodward was asking this of me.

'Yes, yes. I didn't mean for . . . Christ, please, tell me *you're* all right. I'm so sorry, I . . .'

I leaned into the open door. Woodward was hanging awkwardly, head stretched away, one leg on the dashboard, the other in space, a hand cast up towards the open door. He looked like a man trying to reach something on the bottom of a pond without getting his head wet. Why hadn't he unbuckled himself?

'Here. Let me . . .' I stretched across him and undid his seat belt and he fell in a heap across the passenger seat into the far footwell. For a second he didn't move. I'm ashamed to admit that I became transfixed by the interior of the man's Sports Range Rover. Cream leather in an 'off-roader'! A world away from Jennifer's old Discovery. Woodward slowly began to right himself. The top of his head, bald, framed by that stripe of iron-filing stubble, looked horribly naked. 'I'm so sorry,' I repeated.

Eventually he looked up. 'Six of one, half a . . . of the . . . other. Ice. I'm fine. Is your . . . Did you . . . crash too?' He reached up to me, fingers outstretched. The hazard-light pulse caught his wedding ring. I took hold of his hand and helped him stand up. Only then did I realise that, as well as the music, the Range Rover's engine was still racing. I turned the key and both noises were engulfed in silence.

'Ben's jet-ski.' There was a breathless edge to Woodward's voice. 'He's going to kill me.'

'Are you hurt? Can you get out of there?'

'Yes . . . no . . . I think I can,' he said.

And he could. Although the man moved as if he were underwater, he was indeed able to climb up the seats and steering wheel and on to the Range Rover's side. I, meanwhile, slid gingerly to the rear, trying to protect the heat across my belly from pressing against the metalwork. I was just about to warn him not to touch the exhaust pipe, too, when he put a hand on the truck's running board and vaulted down to the torn verge. The relative ease with which he performed this feat beat back my guilt and remorse, revealing base disappointment. But I needn't have feared he was unscathed: having stepped from the grass to the road his knees crumpled and he sat down abruptly on the verge. His fingers, which had been steady when he reached up to me, were twitching.

I bent down next to the man. Now that he was sitting down here the Audi's headlights painted his face in full. It was the pale grey of driftwood, apart from an odd mark down the right side of his head, just above his dusting of hair, not a cut but a dent, a long red groove. He fingered his ear beneath this mark. It, too, was already swelling with an ugly bruise. He was muttering apologies at me now, confessing all sorts of nonsense about driving too fast with a load. 'But I'm due back in town for a meeting this evening,' he said. 'Swift turnaround. Christ, it's cold. Have you eaten?' He turned towards me, then quickly looked away and shuddered.

'You're in shock,' I told him.

'No, no, no,' he said.

'We have to get you out of this cold.'

'I ran the marathon once,' he said. 'All that way, for a foil blanket.'

'Here.' I helped him up. 'Let's get you into my car.'

A part of me *did* want to help the man – he was shivering harder now – but the rush I found myself in could not be explained by that alone. This was an *opportunity*. I was nervous that another car might come round the bend, stop to help, and undo my advantage.

'I couldn't possibly,' he muttered as I closed the door on him, and, 'At least you kept yours on the road,' as I buckled myself in.

With comical care I rolled the car off the verge and made a three-point turn. We had crawled nearly a mile – away from West End Farm – before he said, 'This *is* good of you, you know. I'm just around the corner. Why don't we sort this mess out over a drink?'

'We need to get you to a doctor first.'

'Nonsense. Trust me, I used to feel worse most Saturdays, after rugby.'

Until Woodward said that I believe I *was* planning on driving him to the hospital in town. But something about his remark, in unknowingly yoking us too obviously as allies, pricked me to feel the opposite. It made me think of weeping bricks and Spongebob and my grandchildren. Ryder Evans and James Lovett and Bill H. Marshall and the Reverend Frayn, they all swarmed to mind. If I drove Woodward to the hospital now I'd be late for my party. I would miss the opportunity to see my resistance bear fruit. I shut my eyes and saw Fira's stunned face. The confused man sitting so meekly in the passenger seat had robbed me of my pension and paid himself a bonus out of the proceeds. He was culpable. I lowered the window, let the stunning cold air rush in, and said, 'I live quite close by, too. Let *me* stand *you* the drink. My GP friend can check you over. We'll let him decide.'

Woodward shrugged and yawned and fingered his ear again. I'd read that about people in shock. They're either talking nineteen to the dozen or apt to fall asleep. To keep his attention I asked him how long he'd lived in the area, which got him started on the subject of barn owls. He's had one living in his garden for four years, apparently. From there he was swiftly bemoaning the impact of the new Channel Tunnel Rail Link. It has made no real difference to us here: the man had definitely lost his sense of proportion. A spiel about wetlands, water tables and crop circles came next. He was one of those people with an opinion about everything. The blow to his head appeared to have jumbled them up. My stomach-stripe was throbbing. I let the man talk, interrupting only with 'This is us', as I pulled on to the Tithe Barn's drive.

I parked next to the office, explained that the doctor's number was on my computer, and showed him inside.

'Nice place,' he said, 'very nice. My study isn't a patch on this, but then I'm not lucky enough to conduct my business from home. What is it that you do here?'

'It was a working garage, once,' I explained.

'Really? Is that right? So it would once have had an–'

'Engine pit.'

'Petrol pump, I was going to say. A petrol pump outside. Not much call for a garage here, now, though, is there? With a ring road full of service stations around town.'

'That's the small businessman's lot now, you're right.'

Woodward nodded in enthusiastic agreement, then gripped his brow. 'I should call a garage myself really, shouldn't I? Organise somebody to retrieve my car, don't you think?'

'This is where the engine pit was,' I said, lifting up the carpet-tiled trapdoor. 'It's a cellar now.'

Woodward blinked from the hole to me. His eyes widened. Piggy in the photograph, up close they were in fact brown and soft and wet, like a calf's.

'Please,' I said. 'Take a look. The steps are steep but they go all the way to the floor. There's plenty of room in there to sit down.'

Woodward's mouth opened and shut. He was looking into the brick-lined space – out of politeness, still shaking slightly, with a new bafflement knitting his brow.

'I don't think–'

'I insist,' I said, steering him down the first step. 'Go on down.'

He stiffened and half turned and reached to grab my wrist, which I withdrew.

'What are you doing?' he asked.

It was a good question. I didn't attempt an answer because I didn't have one. Instead I pushed him squarely between the shoulder blades with my open palm, side-stepped his flailing arm neatly, and watched as he lurched and half fell down the steps on to the cellar floor. For the second time in half an hour he was now sitting in a heap beneath me as I peered at him through an up-flung door. The look on his face this time was different. Still confused, still shaken, but the blanched brow and open mouth were unmistakably filled with fear now. Guilt swept over me like driven rain. I shut it out, closing the trapdoor swiftly, and I rolled my swivel chair across the carpet tiles and sat down.

'Christ!' His voice was thin and high, if muffled. 'I said I was sorry. I'm the one that ended up in the ditch!'

'It's not about that.'

'What? I can't hear you. And I can't . . . see.'

I leaned forward on my chair and told the trapdoor: 'Our crash isn't important.'

'How do you . . . ? What is, then? What do you want from me?'

'My name is Harry Brinkman.'

Silence.

'And I know who you are, too. You're Anthony Woodward. You are my Mutual Friend.'

If he said something intelligible I couldn't make it out. It sounded like a groan to me.

'You stole my pension,' I explained. My voice came out patient, calm almost: in fact my palms were clammy and my heart was jumping in my chest. I was thrilled and aghast at the same time. Why had I put him down there? What could it possibly achieve?

Muffled, plaintive: 'What? Oh, Christ. What?'

'Pension!' I repeated.

Quietly: 'You ran me off the road on purpose?'

I was staring at my gunmetal filing cabinet. It's five feet tall, four wide, three deep, and holds thirty years' worth of paperwork, including a file marked *Pension*. In that moment the cabinet stood as a monument to frustrated endeavour. More importantly, it also stood on wheels. I got up quickly from my chair and kicked the footbrake off and in one burst dragged the cabinet the five or so paces into the middle of my office. Then I stamped on the brake again. My breath was coming in snorts, yet young mothers have performed far more impressive feats of strength, lifting crashed cars off their children and so on.

More muted still: 'Christ. Oh, Christ. What are you doing? Is it money? You want my money?'

'No! I don't want *your* money. Any money owed to me is my *own*.' I sat down on the swivel chair again, unbuttoning my shirt to stare at the angry red stripe across my midriff as I went on. 'But it's not about the money now. You've cost me far more than that. And not just me . . .'

'You're disappointed, about your pension.' Woodward's voice was still quiet, but it sounded as if he was speaking softly deliberately now, pulling himself together, which was a relief and disappointment all over again. He went on: 'But you're right, you're not alone in that. I understand, believe me, I understand. We agonised about the restructuring. Agonised. But our duty is to all our policy-holders, not just those whose pensions are maturing now. We *had* to act on our actuaries' advice. Not to have done so would have been negligent. Our hands were tied. The whole industry has been affected by this downturn. In fact, at Mutual Friends we've managed to cushion the blow better than most. But listen . . . I know that isn't . . . I know hearing that isn't about to make you feel better now. Tell me what I can do . . . what you want from me . . . I'll do my best . . . You have my word.'

The strange thing about this speech was that I half believed it. No wonder Woodward had made it to the board. Tripe sounded like truth coming out of his mouth. In an argument, any argument, he'd outpersuade me every time. He was more convincing than me because he was more convinced by himself.

Still, he was in my engine pit now.

'How does it feel, to lose control?'

'I'm scared, and cold. I want it to stop. I'm at your mercy. Please, let me out.'

'My dog, Spongebob,' I said. 'And my . . . and *Fira*. It's not me you have to make it up to, it's them.'

'Let me out and I'll do what—'

'But you can't. It's too late. No, there's only one person I can think of who you can help. Somebody who saved me from your worst effects in the first place, and who is suffering for it now. Her name's Joy Ghosh. She lives in Calcutta and she works in telesales. At least, she did. Between us you and I lost her her job. Don't ask how.'

A whisper: 'Calcutta?'

'Yes.' I filleted a piece of A4 from the printer tray and, referring to my corkboard, copied down Joy Ghosh's name, address and telephone number. 'Calcutta. Don't act like you've never heard of it. Your own annual report makes it perfectly clear Mutual Friends has an interest in the place. That's where you built your new call centre. Pretty much all the calls your customers – including us *pensioners* – make to you are answered by Joy Ghosh's friends there now.'

'Our new call centre is in the Rohini business park, in north-west New Delhi,' he explained quietly. 'I was there for the opening six weeks ago. But keep talking. How can I help?'

Had I got that wrong? I couldn't believe I had, but . . . the man was more convincing than me again.

'She lost her job. Give her a new one.'

'You . . . you want me to employ a friend of yours . . . in New Delhi? That's what this is about.'

'In a way, yes, it–'

A knock on the office window stopped the words in my mouth. Jennifer's face looked like a waxwork, framed by black window and illuminated as it was by the harsh office light. I motioned to where the phone should have been, made a blah-blah-blah gesture with my hand, then mouthed *one minute*.

Woodward said, 'Harry? Harry?'

Jennifer held her wrist up to the window and tapped accusingly at her watch. Then she drew a finger across her throat. Steam poured from her nostrils. She was squinting past me at my filing cabinet. Any second now she'd walk round to the office door and demand to know why I had moved it. I was almost tempted to let her come. What difference could it make? None. And yet, and yet . . . Something base and shameful and hard-wired into me made me move quickly to cut her off, speaking loudly as I went. 'Listen, Bob. I'm late for an engagement, I'm afraid. We'll pick this up again in due course. In the meantime, just give my suggestion some thought.'

I paused at the door, giving Jennifer a head start back to the house. My fingers hovered over the light switch. He couldn't see down there anyway, so why did it feel cruel turning out the office light?

21

The cold outside made me realise I hadn't done up my shirt. Shuffling to the house, I crossed my arms and pressed them to my stomach, in part to shield the scorched cotton from Jennifer, but also because my exhaust stripe was a source of warmth. I ducked upstairs to the bedroom, calling out, 'Exciting opportunity!' in response to Jennifer's 'How hard can it be, Harry? We're *late.*'

With the door shut safely behind me, I turned and saw that she'd laid out new clothes for me on our bed. I thought of Jennifer choosing this outfit, queuing up with her credit card, hiding it in her cupboard, and I welled up. Then I swallowed: what would Ryder Evans be wearing tonight? In the mirror my red stripe looked like comically localised sunburn; inspecting it more closely under my reading light proved there was little to laugh at: the skin above my right hip, at the reddest end of the stripe, had bubbled into a blister. Jennifer's hand-cream boasts 'aloe extracts'. I clenched my teeth and emptied the remains of the tube across my midriff. Pain is distracting: climbing into the new Italian shirt and lightweight linen jacket wasn't a problem, but my eyes were swimming. Never mind that I couldn't face changing my trousers, much less my trainers, Anthony Woodward hadn't once entered my mind before I stood in front of the mirror again.

'Har-ry!'

'Just . . . coming!'

She has a real knack for picking me out things that fit, but beyond that Jennifer chooses what she likes. This combination, I now noticed, was in two shades of her favourite colour, dark brown. Had I not reclaimed myself with my cords and trainers – orange, and mine now, *mine* – I'd have looked like a TV football pundit.

The Discovery was already belching white clouds on the drive. In I climbed, muttering apologies, braced for further admonishment, which didn't come. Instead Jennifer leaned across and tucked my collar under my lapel and said, 'You look great!' I didn't recognise the plunging neckline of her dress, or, as she leaned forward to clear a hole in the windscreen mist, the shimmering wrap hanging down her back, which meant they were probably new, too, but although I wanted, badly, to return her compliment, I couldn't. I tried, believe me. But the Tithe Barn's security lights came on at the wrong moment, and cut through her new feathered hairdo and softening make-up to the expectant collapse of her face, and although this made me yet more intent upon saying something kind, something loving, I was even less able to, because I knew, just knew, that I was in love with Fira, and that whatever I said to my wife then would come out sounding fake.

'Thank you,' was the best I could manage. 'As ever . . . perfect fit.'

It began to snow as we drove to *the dove ascending*. Powdery little flakes driven in gusts, clouds of ice blown across the hedgerows and through the trees. Jennifer is an excellent driver. Twenty winters of school runs – and trips to the golf course – honed her natural coordination. Perhaps she would have been able to save Woodward's Range Rover from the ditch. Even for her, however, treacherous conditions demand concentration. We made the short trip in silence, and in that silence I realised I was nervous. Never mind my pension angst, or the concerns I had for my family, or even my fear that I had lost the woman I loved; and forget Spongebob's inexplicable illness, and the fact that I'd somehow locked a top executive in my cellar: I was still nervous about my surprise birthday party. My face felt like a rubber mask. How would I recast it in the right shade of pleased astonishment? Jennifer would know I was pretending. That didn't matter much in itself: ours isn't the first marriage held together with white-lie cement. But if I failed to look surprised at all, and if she noticed others noticing, she'd feel humili-ated, I knew she would. She dropped a gear, slowing for the last corner before the village (engine braking is safer when the conditions are icy), and pursed her lips, easing on the power as we swept round the apex. I could spare her that hurt at least.

'Jennifer. I–'

'We're nearly there, Harry.'

'I know, that's why I–'

'Ne-ee-arly there.'

'That's why I must tell you I know–'

'You don't need . . .' – she raised her voice over the Discovery's engine shudder – '. . . to tell me anything at all, Harry. It's your birthday. Let's just do our best to enjoy the evening, shall we? For the sake of . . . Just . . . Look, here we . . . You're not going to believe what Alison has done with this place.'

We crunched across the frozen gravel of the car park, following spidery blue shadows of ourselves cast by sunken swimming-pool-style lights. I practised my pretending by not remarking on the cars we passed, but there stood Pearl's dented Prius, between the Walliams' Renault and Mrs Hendall's Mini Cooper, beyond which sat Robert and Marie's Mercedes saloon. As we reached the galvanised metal awning, which now tops the pub's half-timbered porch, the hubbub inside quietened, betraying itself. When I was a young man I used to try to stop myself from climaxing before Jennifer by thinking inappropriately mundane thoughts at the crucial moment: now, on this threshold, I attempted a similar distraction, pausing to consider whether my having left the lawn long for a winter would help it win out over the weeds come the spring, or whether the opposite would prove true. It didn't work. Jennifer – a magician's assistant, her sparkly wrap billowing – drew open the door. I was already holding my breath.

'Sur-Hap-For-Birth-He's-Happy-Harry!-A-Surp-Jolly-Harry!-Day!-Good-Fellow-Prise!' said the pub.

Coned, blinking blindly, I stepped inside.

On the presentation skills course I attended at Stennen Parkes back in '83 the instructor ('guru', is what it said on his card) suggested that the best way to address an audience confidently is to look out over the top of its heads. I did this now, struggling to bring the tall cement-rendered walls into focus, but of course they weren't blank grey walls now, they were blocks of silver and black and dirt brown, cut with orange and green streaks, full of tracer and tailfins and cloud and smoke and cross-hatched turrets and broken wings, glinting steel and falling bombs and fire, fire, fire. I gripped the gunmetal balustrade, my eyes round, my mouth open. They were stunning paintings. I began to cry. Down the mesh steps I swayed. Somebody thrust a champagne flute at me – it was bulbous-nosed Dave, the publican – and clapped a thick arm across my shoulders, and somebody else – Penny Adcock's mother, Judy – was shaking my free hand and saying 'congratulations' and kissing my wet cheek. Her lips were sticky, warm and bright pink. I half reached up to wipe my face, but was distracted by something clinging to my bad knee. Felix. Though he hung on tightly, I managed to pick him up.

'What is bourgeois?' he asked.

'Never mind that for a moment.' I hugged the breath out of him. 'Just remember that for a proper rugby tackle you must take out both a man's legs.'

Jennifer, pink with pleasure, retreating with Dave to the kitchen, winked at me over the top of our grandson's head. There was a pause. Although the room still spun with people, a gap had opened up around me. The same thing often happens at weddings, I've noticed, to the bride and groom. I clutched Felix tighter to my chest, thinking: what must it be like to be famous, or diseased? Jimmy stepped out of the melee.

'What do you think?' he asked.

'They look fabulous, but I need to take a proper–'

'I'm talking to Felix, Dad.' He peeled the boy from me, asking, 'How old do you think he is?'

'Very old,' said Felix, leaning back to look at me. 'Seventy-seven?'

Jimmy spun Felix away and the next wave came at me. There were names and there were faces but the two weren't necessarily connected: here was a barrel-chested old man on stick legs, there was Sally Thatcher; this woman, whose dress looked like a curtain, was greeting me with a prematurely bald schoolfriend of Robert's. Ben Yates. Raymond and Priscilla Locke. And there was a woman in a hat fit for a wedding, next to somebody else, who was standing beside Jeremy Orton and Gene Simmonds, one of whom had a moustache which had gone yellow. Everyone was smiling. I grinned back in all directions, swamped in goodwill, shrugging my appreciation and shaking hands and repeatedly – the older the woman, the more lipstick they seem to wear these days – turning the other cheek.

I tried to reclaim myself with a sip of champagne. As ever, the stuff didn't go down easily, fizzing uncomfortably in my throat. I managed two conversations despite this. One was about an igloo I helped build for Robert's cub scout group in 1980, the other had to do with an accident on the ring road. The soles of my feet felt unaccountably warm. Flee Vincent, in leopard-print trousers, was telling me I didn't look a day older than fifty, but I was concentrating on the shape over her shoulder. Not the four propeller blades raked across twelve feet of canvas, but a hulking suit-back in front of them, the bald head, the misshapen ear. He'd come!

'Terrific!' I told Flee, and stepped past her.

But before I made it to Bill H. Marshall somebody grabbed my upper arm. It was Marie, with little Flo on her hip. Gone was the wintry, greenish tinge to my daughter-in-law's complexion, and her eyes had darkened to a preoccupied black. She glanced from Flo to me, then prompted her daughter with a squeeze.

'*Bon anniversaire!*' they both said.

'Listen, Harry—' Marie immediately went on.

'Why are your shoes dirty?' asked Flo.

Marie, gravely: 'This is a big day, an occasion.'

'Because I've been on safari,' I explained to my granddaughter.

'Robert has some news.'

'Is it elephant dung?'

'No, giraffe.' I searched Marie's face. Despite the heft of Flo in her arms, she was bouncing from foot to foot. 'What do you mean, news?'

Her eyes flicked to the bar and back. 'You'd better ask him, I think.'

We set off together, but I was again waylaid by a hand on my shoulder. I thought of Freddie in his leaky rowing boat, snagged by overhanging branches on his way downstream. He hid in that boat for nine days, surviving on river water alone, absent without leave. Kim Cartwright was telling me how she'd never have imagined herself condoning a decision to brick up an inglenook fireplace. I agreed, and excused myself, and let Marie, who was brittle now with impatience, steer me to the bar, where Robert stood pouring beer into a tall glass.

Though he knew I was there (his brow stiffened, much as it did when he feigned sleep for Father Christmas), he emptied the bottle of its last drips before looking up.

'Ah. The patriarch.' He raised his glass. 'Happy birthday to you.'

I lifted my champagne but did not drink from it.

Robert was still struggling to keep all expression from his face. He looked around the room with the forced impartiality of a judge. 'Quite a gathering,' he said.

'Yes. It's some surprise.'

'Tell him, *chéri*. You have to tell him.'

Ignoring his wife, Robert took another sip of beer. 'And with Jim's new paintings on show, too. You must be very happy. Quite overwhelmed.'

Following his gaze, I took in another big canvas. This one showed concentric firestorm rings bisected by a ladder of bombs. A new knot of worry tightened in my chest: Robert could not tell me his GCSE results the day they arrived, either. Knowing I would be so thoroughly pleased had left him too proud to speak. It was teatime before he slipped his results under my office door. Geography was the only subject in which he hadn't achieved a starred A grade. My filing cabinet flashed to mind, jutting from the carpet-tile sea like a limestone stack. I took Robert's glass from

318

him and set it on the bar. 'What have you got to tell me, son?'

My elder boy set his jaw.

Little Flo: 'Grandad? Have you seen your surprise cake?'

'Shhh!' Marie clasped her hand over her daughter's mouth.

Robert put his hands behind his back, stiff as a royal. 'I *do* have a bit of news, as it happens. But,' he shook his head, 'it's just work stuff, not really party material. Nothing we need to discuss here.'

Marie: '*Alors!* Robert?'

Stephen and Jackie Cole, whose pony had the run of our paddock for eight years (our attempts to get the two girls together cemented Pearl's antipathy towards their daughter), were standing behind Marie now, beaming self-consciously at me over her shoulder. A dress-code mistake meant the Coles were in black tie. And behind them, with his back to the room still, Bill H. Marshall was crabbing sideways to inspect another of Jimmy's paintings. Somebody else, a woman with a smoker's voice, breathed, 'Well done, old boy!' into my ear and ran a hand across my shoulder, as if testing the quality of my jacket. She'd turned to hail the barman before I could respond.

'Another time. I don't want to spoil things now,' Robert went on, eyeing his beer again.

'What do you mean?' said Marie. 'This is the cake icing! Tell, tell!'

My knot of worry redoubled at this. 'Stop buggering about, Robert,' I agreed.

'Ah, well. I had hoped this news would please you

when it came, but I'm not so sure now.' Despite his best attempts to keep it still, his face now sped up, yet this wasn't the shyness of old, at having exceeded my expectations; no, the light in his eye was triumphant, the twitching brow vindictive even. 'But . . . since you insist. They've made me a partner. Effective immediately. It's still just Madison & Vere on the letterhead, but we Brinkmen have a stake in the firm now.'

The room swam. 'The bucket,' I said. 'The stones.'

'You what?'

Robert was still wavering before me but all of a sudden I could think only of my father curled in the bottom of his boat. Giddy with hunger, delirious with lack of sleep, broken – presumably – by guilt. My poor, poor father. The journal records none of that. It simply notes that the stream was full of bird life, and that the boat had run aground a yard from a mallard's nest. After a week the duck's eggs hatched, and a day later it swam out into the current, ducklings in tow. Shortly after the flotilla had gone Freddie realised he couldn't remember the moment of the crash, and began thinking about the panacea of oblivion. Why not forget the whole raid? He would be free to fall back into line – and upon the old certainties, bravery, loyalty, duty – then.

'I found the ball in the bucket, Robert. With the stones.' *Be careful where you lead your children.* 'It was a good trick. I understood why you did it.' *They will follow.* 'I was wrong to pretend otherwise. I should have let you know.'

Robert's shoulders froze mid-shrug. 'Partner,' he repeated. 'Partner.'

Pulling myself together, I said, 'That's . . . brilliant news. I know it's what you wanted. Congratulations, son.'

He slid woodenly along the bar and hissed: 'If you knew that, then why the hell—'

'Harry! *Harry! Har . . . ry!* So good of you . . .'

Eliot Goldman runs the German car dealership in town. Loyalty is a big thing with him, too. I bought my first Passat from Goldmans in 1985 and he included the Audi's leather seat upgrade for free. At least he said he did. He's a big, unavoidable man, who favours patterned waistcoats. Now he was advancing towards me with his arms spread wide, pink and white stick-of-rock stripes expanding.

'. . . to invite me.'

Blood, overcoming Robert's deadpan defences, had rushed to his puffy face. His mouth was twisting silently.

'No problem,' I told Eliot.

'There we go. I knew it!' the big man boomed at Robert. 'You never want to tell this man a lie!' He prodded my chest. 'He rumbled us! A good actor he may be, but I spotted it. I knew his "what-me?-surprise" was fake!'

Eliot corralled me away from the bar and into a conversation about the Greek island of Santorini with Pam Herron, whose eldest child, Michael, burnt himself badly squirting lighter fuel on to the village's royal wedding barbeque. Volcano, I found myself thinking, staring at another of Jimmy's paintings, a wall full of night and smoke. My feet felt suddenly hot again. There, in front of the painting, was a face that meant something at least. My eyes widened – *help me!* – on catching Pearl's.

Relishing the invitation, she called out loudly, 'Dad! Come here. Those old people can wait.'

Rolling my eyes – *who'd have daughters!* – at the crowd, I ducked out of Goldman's grasp and sidestepped towards my youngest child. She was wearing protest clothes. Skinny black jeans with holes in the knees, silver trainers and a tight T-shirt depicting a stained–glass–window design of two suited men, each of them holding what looked like a cucumber, or phallus. The men were labelled 'Gilbert and George'. The T-shirt meant nothing compared to my daughter's startling insubstantiality when hugged. Her forehead felt papery beneath my chin, her cheeks, cupped in one of my hands, were pale and drawn.

'Dad, Dad!' she protested, but did not pull away.

I said, 'Canapés,' and hailed a passing waiter.

She ignored his outstretched platter of . . . stuffed wraps . . . and asked, 'Do your friends here know about the police caution?' by way of smiling retort.

'Listen, Pearl. You're going to be proud of me. I've sorted things out. For Felix, I mean.'

The notch at the base of her throat deepened. 'In what way does Felix need sorting out?'

'You know, his school, St Silas's.'

'Oh, school.' Her face softened 'Don't worry yourself. Is that Penny Adcock? She was my age once, wasn't she?'

'I'm not worried, Pearl. The Reverend Frayn should be, though. You're not going to believe what she admitted to me, let alone that I recorded her saying it . . .' I fished out the tiny tape from my trouser pocket. '. . . on a Dictaphone, a Dictaphone!'

Pearl, still staring at the new Mrs Adcock: 'Why is she dressed like a Wimbledon umpire?'

'I . . . I . . . I don't know. Listen to me. I've got Felix a place at St Silas's. And no, before you ask, we *don't* have to get him baptised.'

'Hmm?'

'Or go to church.'

'Church? Right.' Pearl smiled at me and took hold of my hand, as if to reassure me. 'He'd still have to go to school there, though, wouldn't he. I'm afraid that's not going to happen.'

'That's my point! He can, now, he *can*! All the vicar wanted was a *donation*. Can you believe it? Cash for places! A bribe! I've got her on tape spelling it out.' Pearl raised an eyebrow and opened her mouth to speak, but I went on before she could. 'Of course, it's up to you. We don't have to use the tape if we don't want to. It's probably best for Felix if we hold the trump card back. All the vicar asked for is a couple of grand. I'll pay it. I'd have paid the school fees proper if I could have afforded them. You know that.'

'School fees?' She gave me fingers a squeeze. 'You're worse than Rees, Dad.'

'Rees?'

She laughed. 'The one with the haircut you so admired.'

'His own son wouldn't recognise him. Aren't you listening? I've done something constructive for Felix, something to help!'

Pearl fixed me with a benign smile, which stung worse than indignation. Had she been drinking? Bill H. Marshall's fleshy face rose like a sun above her head. When I failed to tear myself away from Pearl's non-response, the critic veered away again, on his own orbit. What did my daughter's rat-tailed ex-boyfriend have to do with anything? I repeated myself weakly: 'Forget Rees. I've got Felix in. I've . . . helped!'

'Yes,' Pearl breathed kindly, '*help* is what Rees offered, too. There's this trust fund, set up by his late father, a pot of money put aside for educating the grandchildren, for that alone. Don't look so surprised. Rees's family still owns most of Pembrokeshire, you know. They made a fortune importing slaves to Bristol three-hundred-odd years ago.'

'What? But—'

'Not that the money is the point. It's a kind offer. And . . .' Pearl was stroking the back of my hand now, with fingers as soft as petals. Perhaps, like Tupperware, hand-cream is a mother–daughter trait. '. . . and so is yours. You bugged the vicar? Fantastic! One day I'll tell Felix all about it, the lengths to which you were prepared to go. But although I appreciate what you've done . . . and I really do . . . it wasn't necessary. Felix can go to the local, non-religious primary school. I've been to look around the place. It isn't as bad as all that. Nobody' — she was warming up now, righteous and lovely and infuriating again — 'is going to taint his education with Welsh blood money. I wouldn't have let you pay private school fees, either. And, although I can see where you were coming from, I'm not about to start blackmailing clergymen just to get him a seat next to the offspring of a load of other corrupt, hypocritical, bourgeois separatists. Thanks, but no thanks. That's an end of it. Pawn Felix to the God-squad? No, no, no!'

I withdrew my hand from between Pearl's and passed it across my eyes. Age doesn't alter the map of a person's character, it just makes us better at covering our tracks. Pearl must have sensed that I was falling through the vault of myself as I swayed there before her, and regretted her fervour; next thing I knew she had winnowed under my raised arm and was giving me a hug. Her elbow pressing into the burn on my side, it was all I could do not to gasp. When I opened my eyes again, the room was blurred by more tears. And my feet, my feet! They were burning up.

'You're vibrating,' said Pearl.

'I'm sixty. It's the shakes.'

'No. Your phone.'

Fira! It had to be. I fumbled for my mobile in the wrong pockets before finding it, and was all blinking and thumbs as I flipped open the screen. 'Hello!' I said, and then I shouted 'Hello!' again, loud enough to turn heads from surrounding conversations, as party din echoed back at me through the earpiece.

'Mr Brinkman?'

Despite the hubbub – or perhaps accentuated by it – the man's voice sounded actorly, slow and sure. 'Harry Brinkman,' I replied. 'Yes?'

'A pleasure to speak to you in person, Harry, though I apologise for calling outside office hours. My name is Henry Tan, from Stone River Light Industrial Co., here in Wutan. You have been kind enough to confirm an order for silicone rings with our company, as I'm sure you recall.'

'Yes. Mr Tan . . .' Somebody thrust a tray of glazed prawns into my midriff. '. . . I'm away from my office just now, it's not really the best—'

'I understand,' he cut me off politely. 'Of course. This won't take a second. I just wanted to confirm the numbers in your email. The order is for a first batch of three-quarters of a million units, to repeat monthly until further notice, at a cost of fourteen point five English pence per unit. We can increase capacity to meet such a production run, of course, but before I authorise our foreman to take the necessary steps – with such quantities – well, forgive me for wanting to make sure.'

In forwarding Wasserreich's email I had not checked the final order figures, which at least meant I hadn't transcribed anything incorrectly. This Henry Tan had a voice like Roger Moore's, and the prawns jiggling in front of me were as pink as sucked thumbs, and now Felix, poor Felix, was doomed. Business? Order numbers? Who cared?

'Of course,' I told the phone. 'Seven hundred and fifty thousand units a month. That's what the end user needs.'

And as I spoke I was not thinking that this was a colossal order, placed by the Germans despite my outlandish mark-up on Henry Tan's cost price, which – I did the sum later – would net me a cool sixteen thousand, two hundred and fifty pounds *a month* – obliterating my pension problem in one fell swoop. No, and neither was I considering that even given this brickwork-repointing, SUV-purchasing, school-fee-paying sum, I would nevertheless divorce my wife and give her the house and be refused permission to contribute towards my grandson's education. Those realisations came afterwards. At the time I was simply struck by the idea that washers, although tiny, are *fundamentally important* to pumps. Without them, the things leak.

'Splendid,' purred Henry, whose own mother hadn't apparently baulked at the prospect of sending her son to a British public school. 'In which case it's a good job I'm in early – to start the ball rolling and so forth. This is a promising opportunity, Mr Brinkman, for our companies to form a mutually profitable partnership.'

I snapped the phone shut and brought the flickering room into focus. Somebody was waving a knife in front of my face. It was little Flo. She was on Jennifer's hip and my wife was saying, 'For goodness' sake, Harry, come and cut your cake!'

'Lay down your arms,' I told Flo, unfastening her fingers from the knife-handle, one by one. She grinned and turned and burrowed into her grandmother's neck, and the sight of this unselfconscious affection undid me.

I heard myself speaking.

. . . '*and listen, Jennifer, I invited your friend Ryder Evans here this evening, but I've not seen his face among the guests, and I just wanted to let you know that I asked him here for your sake, because I think he means something to you, and I don't intend to stand between the two of you, and what we have shared we will always have shared, but I think you want to be with him now, and if that is so then I want you to go, and*' . . .

Jennifer's free hand had snaked round little Flo's head to cover her ear, and she was taking steps backwards, which was pointless, because I was moving with her, advancing us both into a scalloped corner of brushed steel and cement.

'Cake!' hissed Jennifer.

'. . . yes, yes, I know, what we've shared we've enjoyed, but it's all eaten up now, we're down to crumbs, and . . .'

'Stop this nonsense,' she pleaded, wide eyed. 'Stop right now and cut the cake!'

When Freddie emerged from his hiding place in the boat he was filthy, emaciated and convincingly confused. His ankle had set badly. He hobbled away from the riverbank and into an allotment, where he disturbed an old man dozing in his deckchair. My father could not have explained himself, even without a wounded tongue. The old man began shouting for help and until Freddie convinced him he meant no harm – by collapsing to the ground – he kept my father at a distance with a hoe he fetched from his shed. It turned out that the gardener's daughter was a WAAF radar reporter. Before the day had finished Freddie was back in the custody of the Royal Air Force, a miraculous crash survivor, a hero all the more tragic for his apparently lost state. He was placed in Princess Mary's Hospital at RAF Halton. Within weeks the doctors there had narrowed his diagnosis down to shock-induced amnesia. They were hopeful that he'd recover his memory in time, and he did not disappoint them: the black hole of that last op aside, everyone was delighted with the progress he made.

'A true hero admits his failings,' I told Jennifer. 'But Freddie lied. To them, to himself, to me.'

'What?' said Jennifer.

'Except that he didn't, not in the end.'

'Stop this,' she hissed.

'I see it now. The indexing. The point was in what he left off the list. He wanted me to find the journal, Jennifer. He didn't destroy it, or try to hide it, he left it somewhere he knew I'd check. In his desk.'

'Silly Grandad,' sang Jennifer, glancing at Flo.

'Who am I to forgive him anyway?' I shuddered. 'Yet it's to me that he confessed.'

'You're frightening her. Just stop talking. I will not have a scene.'

My granddaughter was fitting with giggles, not fear, but in shifting my attention to her I lost my thread. I took her from Jennifer. 'Help me carve this thing up, then,' I said.

The cake in question stood at the far end of the room, on a cloth-draped table pushed against the wall. As I advanced towards it somebody turned up a spotlight, bathing the table in a wash of brightness. An altar: the cake upon which was a bespoke affair, commissioned by Jennifer, I guessed, from her good friend Margaret Eaves, who specialises in scaled reproductions of famous golf holes. This hole was unusually short, with what looked like a fence down one edge, and it had a castle in the middle of it instead of bunkers. The Tithe Barn! There was the willow tree, there the paddock, and that little brown oblong had to be my office, where – right now – Woodward was still imprisoned. Guilt shuddering through me, I shifted my attention to the little iced man pushing an orange Flymo around the word SIXTY carved into the back lawn. We have a sit-on mower, in fact, but this was the model's only inaccuracy. Noticing that Margaret had even aimed our satellite dish in the right direction, I found myself mouthing two words: Google Earth.

Conversations faded behind me with varying degrees of reluctance: although the guests had congregated because of me they were, as ever, there for themselves. Little Flo squirmed against my ribs and once again my smarting side made it impossible for me to do anything but grit my teeth. I lowered her gingerly to the floor. Then I turned around, the heat of the room's collective attention vying with the exhaust burn.

From over by the bar a voice called out, 'Speech, speech!'

I waved the suggestion away with the knife, saying, 'No, no, no, I'm just here to . . . to . . . carve up my estate,' and before anyone could object I drove the knife into the Tithe Barn's gabled end wall. True to form, it crumbled. I kept on slicing anyway, paring the house from its surroundings, and then, as the silence deepened, beginning on the lawn. It was disconcertingly green.

But the voice at the bar, drink-blurred though it was, had undoubtedly belonged to Robert, and as Jennifer came forward (her lips white with uncertainty) to take over the cake-carving, my elder son followed her through the crowd, saying, 'No, no, no, 'fraid not, this won't do at all.'

I smiled and shrugged, unable to think a single constructive thought.

'Dad, Dad, Dad,' Robert began, throwing an arm around my shoulder. 'Sixty years old, eh? What an achievement. That alone deserves a big hand.' One or two people began to clap uncertainly, but the applause soon fizzled out when they realised, with the rest of the audience, that although Robert had finished with his goal-scorer's hug he was not about to pause. 'And what a fine figure you still cut, the very picture of a . . . self-sufficient man. Everyone knows that about you, Dad. You're reliable. You're organised. Your ducks are always . . . so to speak . . . in line. But very few of you good people out there' – he was squinting in the spotlight, sweating at the temples, thick tongued but blithe – 'very few of you friends-of-Dad, can understand exactly how generous this man has been in organising us, his family, in policing our wildfowl, if you will, on his own time.'

At this Pearl laughed and said, 'Hear, hear,' and I looked for her in the crowd, but could see no farther than a painting I hadn't yet noticed hanging high on the wall above the bar. It was long and thin and dark, a streak of grey flame torn vertically from the sky.

'In fact . . .' He took another slug of beer. '. . . it seems Dad has been more than usually generous with his attention of late. Behind the scenes. Now . . .' He waved expansively, and ended up pointing at me. '. . . I'm prepared to give you the benefit of the doubt, and concede that your help is well intentioned. But, I don't know, maybe this turning-sixty malarkey has skewed your sense of proportion. Because, from where I'm standing, it doesn't look much like help at all. With me at least, it's almost as if you've turned from gamekeeping to *poaching*. You know, taking potshots, *setting snares*.'

Beneath the painting, with his arms folded, Bill H. Marshall stood watching me. And moving towards me through the faces to his left came Jimmy, with furrowed brow. 'That's enough,' Jimmy whispered to Robert, but he stopped short of his brother, who ignored him and carried on.

'So I suppose what I want you to agree, Dad, in front of all these good people, is that at sixty it is perhaps time to hang up your gun. A mower's more your style anyway. Yes . . .' He waved at the decimated cake. '. . . get back to tending your garden, to pottering on your lawn.' I think Robert would probably have stopped here had Jimmy not stepped between us to make sure that he did. I felt sorry for Robert then; thirty years of keeping his younger brother at bay were not a precedent he could overturn. He swatted at Jimmy and leaned past him to shout at me, 'I mean it, Dad! Try anything like this last stunt again and I'll . . . I'll . . . I'll . . . disown you! Don't take your *own* failures out on *me*!'

Jimmy grabbed hold of his brother's biceps at this point, with enough ferocity to make Robert drop his glass, which exploded on the metal floor. Although my younger son's face looked more aghast than under strain, he must have been lifting his brother up: looking at the spillage, I saw that Robert was on tiptoes, his brogue heels an inch from the floor.

Into the silence Felix said, 'Uh-oh!'

And Jennifer was immediately bent double (yoga!) with a wad of cake napkins, saying, 'Don't worry, don't worry! It's only beer!' and Pearl's laughter, tinkling over the top of this scene, was overtaken by a woman saying 'Delicious!' loudly and somebody else, Dave, I think, rumbling, 'Plenty more!', and before I let out a full breath more conversations – 'A406' and 'insurance premium' and 'centre stump' – had started up in an advancing, inevitable wave, expertly intent upon smoothing the sand before it, on burying the briny mess at its feet.

I separated my sons. Robert tried to pull away from me but I reeled him back in, a hand around the hot, sticky back of his neck. I wanted to say 'sorry' but it seemed easier to kiss his forehead. Two things happened as I did that. First of all Jimmy gave his brother a no-hard-feelings punch to the upper arm which, in his confused relief, perhaps, he dealt out hard enough to knock Robert sideways. And second, as Robert's head jerked out of my way, the sheet-metal pub door behind him swung inwards, revealing Fira.

She was wearing the waterproofs I'd bought her, and she stopped where the mat should have been to take her cycling helmet off and brush the snow from her shoulders. I could not dwell upon the memory prompted by Fira's glowing cheeks, because her red-rimmed eyes gave away her distress.

'I love you, son,' I told Robert, and I stepped past him in the direction in which many of the guests – feeling the inrush of cold air – were now staring. Their attention had left me crowd-blind a minute earlier, but

I now saw one thing clearly: all else could turn to dust; if Fira was here, I did not care.

'Moss-killer,' she said when I made it to her.

'What?' I reached for the helmet. 'Here, let me take that.'

Fira dismissed the view over my shoulder with a glance, as if, instead of a roomful of faces turned our way, she'd been distracted for a second by the pub's TV.

'I'm sorry,' I said.

Jennifer, a note higher than the hubbub: 'What on earth is she doing here?'

'The appeal,' I said. 'Your flat.'

Jimmy's voice: 'Sit down, Mum. It's a surprise party, after all.'

'Your dog. Spongebob,' Fira muttered, looking at our joined hands.

'Never mind him for now.' I pulled her towards me and held her, reassuring myself with the sharp feel of her elbow in my palm. Her face was cold and her breath hot against my neck. In a rush I told her that I'd thought she'd been so upset by my ignoring her failed asylum bid that she'd burnt down her flat in protest and fled, and that she shouldn't leave my sight now, that I would not let her, and that if she had to go somewhere, anywhere, then wherever that place was I would go there with her too.

'That's not what I'm here for,' she said. 'The dog—'

'You want to see him? Fine. We can go there right now if you want.'

But she resisted my attempt to turn her towards the door, leaning back so that she could see my face as she talked. 'I have been to the hospital already, Harry. Before I returned to my room and found that it was burned, and before the fireman investigating decided this was an electricity fire, and before we worked out that your helpful multiple plug was probably responsible for it. Yes, and before I cycled to your house to find a man I did not know telephoning to India in your office. Before this man suggested I should not take the phone from him and call the police but instead help him push the filing cabinet you tried to kill him with back against the wall. Before he told how he had rolled it off your cellar door without too much difficulty because it seemed you only locked one wheel. And before this kind man had told me that you were at what you told him was a "prior engagement" tonight, which of course made me remember this unsurprising party your wife has been organising with invitations and a cake for weeks. Yes, before all of that. I was waiting at the veterinary hospital this afternoon until they could explain why your fine dog Spongebob had died. He was hurt with poison for your grass, they said. Moss-killer. To eat such a quantity he must either be a dog without the ability to taste or somebody was giving it to him on purpose. In his food. He died from this. I am very sorry he is dead.'

I took in what Fira said. It made the sort of sense a blow to the stomach does, so obvious as to be meaningless. Her eyes weren't red, I saw up close, but tinged blue and pink, and the bloom of heat across her cheeks was fading now that she'd stopped cycling. As ever, news of a death defied its implications. In fact, far from feeling

335

sorrow for Spongebob – though that of course came later – I think I first truly appreciated that my father was gone as I stood with Fira in *the dove ascending*'s entrance.

'I'm in love with you, Fira.'

She squinted at me. 'Bad luck.'

'It's not bad luck, it's the only thing I know.'

'You know Spongebob is dead too, now. And another thing. You know the lawyer lost. So I am going home.'

'I'm coming with you.'

'Pah,' said Fira. 'Don't say things you cannot mean.'

'But I *do* mean it. I will divorce Jennifer and marry you, like you said.'

'I don't think so.'

Dave had set some world music playing in the aftermath of Robert's speech, and now turned it up, so that I misheard Pearl when she arrived beside me and asked, 'Whose is this woman?' over the pan pipes.

I stared straight at Fira and said, 'Mine.'

'*Who*, not whose!' My daughter's smile was determinedly unfazed, much the same as when she told me she would have her fatherless baby.

'Fira. Meet Pearl.'

Pearl shook Fira's hand and asked, 'Drink? Canapé, slice of cake?'

'No, I think we're–' I began.

'Yes. Some of everything.' Fira nodded. 'I have bicycled today seventeen miles and all of the food in my cupboard was burnt.'

Refusing to question this, Pearl steered Fira to the bar. I followed in my separate world, unable to ape their defiance. When I finally summoned the courage to reassemble the room from the blur of shapes and colours before me, however, I discovered that most of my friends' faces had turned to one another – and away from us – out of embarrassment, or obliviousness perhaps. Jimmy had weighted Jennifer down in a seat, using Felix and little Flo as ballast, and Marie was consoling her husband, who had already found himself another glass of beer. Fira piled a plate high with brightly coloured shards of food and asked for a pint of water to go with her champagne. She was trying to protect me by refusing my offer to go with her. That had to be it. Otherwise, why had she come? From the speed with which she got through her drink, it was obvious that she does not struggle with champagne as I do. This thought made a fleeting reality of Spongebob's death. *Poisoned by my wife.* It seemed Pearl had started a conversation about global warming with Fira. I steadied myself on the bar.

'Look. This has been fascinating,' a deep voice, belonging to Bill H. Marshall, said.

I swayed before the critic. 'But you're not about to review Jimmy's paintings favourably in your paper, are you?'

'I doubt it,' he said. 'I can't see the editor giving space to a show this minor.'

He was big, yet out of shape, and he'd kicked Spongebob. My hands balled up into fists at my sides.

'But thanks for inviting me. I'm glad I came.' He patted me on the arm. 'Cheer up. These paintings are certainly more . . . commercially viable . . . than the last lot. Good venue for them, too. I'm sure your son will get lots of commissions from restaurants and bars.'

'Your other column,' I said. 'The human instincts one. You came to get material for that, didn't you?'

Bill H. Marshall laughed and said, 'Interest, human interest.'

I fished the Dictaphone tape out of my pocket. 'Well, here's a corrupt vicar story for you. Cash for state school places.' I pressed the tape into the man's hand. 'If you're interested, give me a call.'

He marvelled at me with the detachment of a visitor to an aquarium and said, 'You'll be asking for a commission next,' as he tucked the tape into his breast pocket.

Velvety drums punched holes in the pan pipes. My hot, hot feet! I thrust an open palm towards the critic's midriff. Why, when I felt sure that his pocket was merely a way station en route to his office bin, did I still feel compelled to shake the man's hand and thank him for coming?

Fira slid her plate on to the bar and tossed back the last of her champagne. It was all an act, of course, but not one that she was about to let slip. She didn't even break from her conversation with Pearl when Eliot Goldman, doubly raucous now with drink, stage-slunk past me booming, 'You sly old dog!' in my ear. But I could take no more, I felt like a nocturnal animal thrust on to a Mediterranean beach.

'You're a good girl,' I told Pearl. And to Fira: 'Let's go.'

'No,' she said. 'You stay here.' She bit her bottom lip, steadying herself. 'I will leave.'

She may have been speaking in little more than a

whisper but it felt to me as if she was shouting, so I raised my voice in return. 'Don't you get it? I'm serious! We're leaving, together, you and me!'

The music seemed to have quietened.

'Tents?' she said.

'Bugger that! *I love you.* I don't give a damn if we have to live in a hole in the ground!'

Drums and pipes swelled as I waited for her response. It's shamelessly emotive stuff, rainforest music.

'I think this beautiful man *is* in fact loving me back,' Fira explained to my daughter, 'but he still prefers your boy, Felix, and the little cousin, Flo. Make sure he sees them still or my future will have problems.'

Pearl stuck her hands in the back pockets of her jeans and shrugged her most nonchalant 'of course'.

'And we,' Fira turned to me, 'must say goodbye to your wife before we leave.'

Proving that the crowd had been aware of us despite their turned backs, the leopard-skin trousers and blazers and chinos and floral-curtain dresses parted as we crossed the room with Pearl resolutely in tow. Jimmy saw us coming and moved into the space between me and Robert, but unnecessarily: I knew from the chastened look in my elder son's eye that his anger was spent now. I kissed Marie on both cheeks wordlessly, congratulated my elder son again, hugged Jimmy and told him that I wanted to buy the bomber paintings – all of them – for his grandfather's sake.

'Find me somewhere to store them, will you, until I have space.'

'Where are you going?' he asked.

'Ultimately? No idea. But I'm going with Fira to the Tithe Barn now,' I told Jennifer. 'In your car. We won't be there long. I just need to pick up a few things.'

My wife, with a grandchild on each knee, appeared to be using them as a last line of defence. She squirmed for her car keys as if giving them up to a mugger. I could not bring myself to mention Spongebob, not in front of Felix and Little Flo, but after I had knelt to kiss them both goodbye Fira took hold of my wrist and twisted something into my hand. I looked at it and studied my wife. It seemed she had reapplied her lipstick; on reflection I think the blood had drained from the rest of her face. I was still kneeling in front of the chair, struggling to say something forgiving. My knee grew warm. Of course: under-floor heating. That was what had been cooking my feet.

I pulled Jennifer's head towards me and whispered, 'Abandon aircraft,' into her ear.

Then I forced Spongebob's collar into her closed fist.

Epilogue

As we drove back to my house Fira explained that she had left Anthony Woodward there, calling for a taxi. I'd hoped to speak with him again, apologise even, but that wasn't to be. He'd scrawled a note on my desk jotter (what is it with people of influence and handwriting?) which read, I think, 'I have done as you asked but don't think it worked. Yours sympathetically.' A magnanimous man is almost as hard to resist as an honest one. I sent my Mutual Friend a postcard from Georgia a week later, with details of my car insurance, but to date he has not contacted me.

There wasn't much I wanted to take from the house. All the information I need to run my business is backed up on a server in Palo Alto anyway. (Oh, technology!) I scribbled down Joy Ghosh's telephone number inside the back cover of Freddie's journal, filled a bag with clothes and my shaving kit, and put it on the Audi's back seat. At the end of the drive I felt a weight lift from my shoulders. Jennifer knows very little about maintaining the physical fabric of a house, but she'll have Ryder Evans's help, and failing that, Robert will step in. From now on, it's rented accommodation for me.

As ever, the Wasserreich deal turned out to be too good to be entirely true. The Germans soon worked out they could source their washers more cheaply elsewhere, but I cut my margin and they have kept with us so far, impressed by the quality of Henry Tan's engineering, his reliability. What's left of my slice is enough for Fira and me.

It took me a few goes to make contact with Joy Ghosh again. She's not often in; by day she works in a supermarket to fund the night-school course she's taking in dental nursing. I offered her money to help with her studies, but she refused to take it. She also told me firmly that although she was grateful, there was no point in me having my friends call her up with job offers in cities thousands of miles away. 'You have enough on your plate as it is,' she went on. 'What results are you having with your own resisting?'

'I wouldn't say I've been entirely successful, not on a case-by-case basis at least.'

'And yet here you are today, talking to me.'

I started telling her about Fira then, but she misunderstood me, and suggested that although my taking up the cudgels on behalf of Third World refugees was laudable, I should really be helping them to defend themselves. 'The first rule of resistance,' she said before hanging up, 'is that it comes from within.'

She's a perceptive, forceful woman, but as with so many survivors – Freddie, for example – I detect in her now that tendency to think her own way is the only way. He insisted on passing down a code that he'd tried and failed to live by himself, in the hope – perhaps –

that the code would better serve me. By the time he died it was obvious that I was no more able to live up to his expectations than he had been, but he could not admit as much face to face. He left the journal for me to find, so that I might strip him of his medals posthumously. Which was wrong headed, because my only regret now is that I never had a chance to tell him I admire him all the more for his fallibility.

The thin patch of hair behind Fira's left ear had nothing to do with the Chechen soldiers, I discovered. When she was a baby her mother left her cot too close to their electric fire, and a melting plastic rattle bonded itself to Fira's head. It seemed only fair to explain my misshapen nose after Fira told me this. Together we have over ninety years of past to catch up on, and a new world to explore.

Read more . . .

Maile Meloy

A FAMILY DAUGHTER

**For everyone who has yet to meet the Santerres, an
unmatched pleasure awaits**

It is 1979, and seven-year-old Abby, the youngest member of the
close-knit Santerre family, is trapped indoors with chickenpox during
a heatwave.

The events set in motion that summer will change her family's lives
for ever. In a story spanning decades and continents, the Santerres
become entangled with an ageing French playboy, a young Eastern
European prostitute, a spoiled heiress and her ailing, jet-set mother.
An engaging and insightful novel about the joys and complications of
modern life, *A Family Daughter* is a delightful read.

'A deliciously duplicitous book, a darkly perceptive examination of
American mores disguised as a light family romance' *Sunday Telegraph*

'Maile Meloy writes wonderfully well, with an efficiency so lithe it's
like watching an athlete' *Guardian*

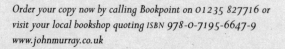

*Order your copy now by calling Bookpoint on 01235 827716 or
visit your local bookshop quoting ISBN 978-0-7195-6647-9
www.johnmurray.co.uk*

Read more . . .

Belinda Seaward

HOTEL JULIET

A love story

Memory Cougan, beautiful, black and in her twenties, has a successful career and a boyfriend who adores her. But on the eve of her engagement party, she panics. Brought to London and adopted at the age of five, she has no recollection of her childhood in Africa or why she left. Leaving her life in London behind, she returns to the country she no longer recognises – and to Max, the reclusive coffee planter who may just have the answers she needs.

Moving from Scotland and London to Africa and back again over twenty years, *Hotel Juliet* tells the poignant story of four people whose lives play out against the endless skies and wild beauty of the African landscape. An exquisitely written novel with at its heart a passionate love triangle that resonates down to the present day, it combines pathos and tragedy with the possibility of glorious redemption.

'A thrillingly observant writer and crafter of highly sensual prose, Seaward employs the language and lore of the skies to considerable metaphorical effect . . . its richly descriptive escapism is seductive'
Daily Mail

Order your copy now by calling Bookpoint on 01235 827716 or visit your local bookshop quoting ISBN 978-0-7195-2450-9
www.johnmurray.co.uk

Read more . . .

Anne Marshall Zwack

THE DIPLOMATIC CORPSE

A roller-coaster ride of revenge through the great capitals of Europe

When Maggie's husband, smooth, silver-haired, patrician Jeremy, the British Ambassador to Vienna, drops dead unexpectedly of a heart attack, she is stunned. But her shock soon turns to fury when she discovers that he died in the arms of a beautiful Viennese hostess. But Mausie turns out to be, as it were, only the tip of the iceberg. As Maggie uncovers a trail of infidelities conducted under her nose in every one of the European cities she had so dutifully made her home, she determines to exact her revenge. With Zoltan, Jeremy's mournful Hungarian driver, she embarks on a Grand Tour of their former postings, wreaking a pleasurable havoc wherever she goes. Along the way, Maggie undergoes her own transformation and learns just who her friends really are.

'Magnificent' *Tablet*

'Revenge is sweet!' *OK!*

Order your copy now by calling Bookpoint on 01235 827716 or visit your local bookshop quoting ISBN 978-0-7195-2320-5 www.johnmurray.co.uk